# CHRISTINA DODD'S

"Scorchingly sexy and superbly
suspenseful."—*Booklist*

"Dodd has earned her place on
the bestseller list."—*Publishers Weekly*

**THE SUPREME BATTLE OF GOOD AGAINST EVIL.**

**THE ULTIMATE ROMANCE.**

**THE STUFF OF LEGEND.**

*continued . . .*

# CHRISTINA DODD

## CHAINS of ICE

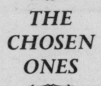

### THE CHOSEN ONES

A SIGNET SELECT BOOK

SIGNET SELECT
Published by New American Library, a division of
Penguin Group (USA) Inc., 375 Hudson Street,
New York, New York 10014, USA
Penguin Group (Canada), 90 Eglinton Avenue East, Suite 700, Toronto,
Ontario M4P 2Y3, Canada (a division of Pearson Penguin Canada Inc.)
Penguin Books Ltd., 80 Strand, London WC2R 0RL, England
Penguin Ireland, 25 St. Stephen's Green, Dublin 2,
Ireland (a division of Penguin Books Ltd.)
Penguin Group (Australia), 250 Camberwell Road, Camberwell, Victoria 3124,
Australia (a division of Pearson Australia Group Pty. Ltd.)
Penguin Books India Pvt. Ltd., 11 Community Centre, Panchsheel Park,
New Delhi - 110 017, India
Penguin Group (NZ), 67 Apollo Drive, Rosedale, North Shore 0632,
New Zealand (a division of Pearson New Zealand Ltd.)
Penguin Books (South Africa) (Pty.) Ltd., 24 Sturdee Avenue,
Rosebank, Johannesburg 2196, South Africa

Penguin Books Ltd., Registered Offices:
80 Strand, London WC2R 0RL, England

First published by Signet, an imprint of New American Library,
a division of Penguin Group (USA) Inc.

First Printing, July 2010
10  9  8  7  6  5  4  3  2  1

Copyright © Christina Dodd, 2010
All rights reserved

SIGNET SELECT and logo are trademarks of Penguin Group (USA) Inc.

Printed in the United States of America

For Kerry Donovan.
Here's to the future!

# ACKNOWLEDGMENTS

Leslie Gelbman, Kara Welsh, and Claire Zion, my appreciation for your constant support, and more appreciation to NAL's brilliant art department led by Anthony Ramondo for the unique covers. As always, I value the work of the publicity department with my special people, Craig Burke and Jodi Rosoff. My thanks to the production department, and, of course, a special thank-you to the spectacular Penguin sales department.

# THE SEVEN CHOSEN

❖ **Jacqueline Vargha:** Gifted with the ability to see the future and an eye on her palm to prove it. With Caleb D'Angelo at her side, Jacqueline must take her adopted mother's place as chief seer to the Chosen Ones.

❖ **Aaron Eagle:** Raised by Native Americans and marked with the wings of an angel, Aaron has a talent for melting into the shadows that surround him. But he can only be truly whole once prim and proper librarian Rosamund Hall enters his life.

❖ **Charisma Fangorn:** A young Goth with tattoos on her wrists and the gift of hearing the earth song in crystals and stones.

❖ **Isabelle Mason:** One of the upper-class Boston Masons, Isabelle is a physical empath with the ability to absorb the pain of others and heal them.

❖ **Samuel Faa:** A lawyer with the ability to control minds; he has a mysterious connection to Isabelle.

❖ **Aleksandr Wilder:** Aleksandr is a college student; he has no mark, no discernible gift, and is blessed with a loving family, yet he is drafted into the Chosen Ones because of his connection to the Wilder family of Washington State (from the *Darkness Chosen* series).

❖ **John Powell:** Former member of Gary White's team, he is famous for the strength and power he wields . . . as well as for the dark and dreadful secret that torments him and has driven him into exile.

# FRIENDS AND ENEMIES OF THE
# CHOSEN ONES

❖ **Irving Shea:** The ninety-plus-year-old retired director of the Gypsy Travel Agency and the owner of the mansion the Chosen Ones now use as headquarters.

❖ **Martha:** Dedicated Gypsy servant of the Chosen Ones.

❖ **McKenna:** Scottish butler, chauffeur, and aide to Mr. Shea.

❖ **Vidar Davidov:** Owner of Davidov's pub located deep in the tunnels under New York City, where the Chosen hang out. Davidov sports an inexplicable knowledge about the Chosen Ones and their descendants.

❖ **Osgood:** The mastermind behind the destruction of the Gypsy Travel Agency and the devilish director of the Others.

❖ **Gary White:** A former team leader and one of the most trusted Chosen Ones, Gary has awoken from a coma that claimed four years of his life . . . and his soul.

# Chapter 1

———✦———

*Five years ago*
*In the Andes*
*Chile, South America*

**"I**'m not the psychic in this group, but this looks like a trap to me." John Powell walked into the cave carved into the base of the retreating glacier. His breath hung white on the frigid air, and he had to duck to avoid the low stone lintel constructed to hold back the ice. He glimpsed the prehistoric paintings on the walls, showing bloodied intruders pierced by spears, crushed by boulders, and swept away by a raging river.

*Not good signs.*

"It smells like a trap to me." Kim Sun Hee walked at his side.

He glanced down at the diminutive Korean. "Is it the Others?"

"What do you think the Others smell like? Fire and brimstone?" she mocked him gently.

"Yes?" He listened to the creaks and moans of the man-made stone cave as the glacier pressed against its walls and ceiling. He flicked glances ahead, behind, and around the group before them, alert for the slightest sign that they needed to escape *now*.

As he always did, Gary White led the way, forging ahead. Amina Berhane walked on his right—she exuded an ambient light that illuminated more of the shadowy passage than their flashlights and headgear. Max Novak walked on his left—get Max close to treasure, and the gold and gems called to him. Sophie Moore and Bataar Lohar walked one step behind them.

Then there were Sun Hee and John, lagging ten feet back from the rest of the Chosen, acting as the rear guard.

"There isn't an *Others* smell. They're people—they smell like people. If I could get close to them, I'd ID them"—she lowered her voice—"but I never get close. It always seems like they're scooping up the Abandoned Ones while we're having grand adventures."

Was that a complaint? John suspected it was. These people, Gary and his six compatriots, were the most powerful group of Chosen in the world today. The Gypsy Travel Agency sent them to carry out feats suited to Spielberg's best action-adventure films. The way they lived was dangerous, exhilarating, and made them the rock stars of the Chosen Ones.

But they never seemed to get to perform their modest and important mission statement: rescuing discarded infants before they could be taken and their special gifts used by the devil's henchmen.

Sun Hee turned her head from side to side, sweeping the area for scents. "Yesterday some *people*, I don't know who, were walking near the entrance and came a little way inside. But last night's wind and snow have confused the smells. Still, I don't think we need to be concerned with an ambush."

John scrutinized the symbols cut into the slabs of stone that made up the wall, the way the ceiling arched overhead, then—like some amusement park optical illusion—curled downward to a vanishing point. "At least not from any living being," he said.

"You're worried." She glanced at his bare right hand, her brown eyes shadowed.

He looked, too. In this dim passage, his fingernails glowed with a faint blue light. He flexed his hands, containing the power inside. "Yeah."

"Hey, back there, don't be such chickens," Gary called. "Max says we're almost there." His voice echoed along the long, dark tunnel and came back amplified, enlarged.

Pebbles fell from the ceiling in showers.

"Shit," John muttered. "Not so loud."

"I'll be as loud as I like," Gary shouted.

Again, the amplified voice. Again, the rain of pebbles, but more this time. Something immense thumped behind them, shaking the floor, rattling John's confidence. He turned. Sun Hee shone her flashlight over the huge stone that now blocked their way out. Not totally; it was possible to climb over it and back to the outside world, but the easy way had vanished.

Gary would be delighted—and that was the trouble with Gary. John respected him; he really did. Because Gary was older, in his early forties, and charismatic as all hell. Gary had joined the Chosen Ones when he had been a brilliant, handsome, fit eighteen-year-old. He'd been elected the leader—of course—and stayed at the top for the required seven years.

Traditionally, after one term, most of the Chosen opted to become part of the real world again—bankers and ranchers and tour guides, people who knew more than they should about the battle between good and evil but who no longer served on the front lines.

Not Gary. He had stayed to command a second team, then a third, and now he directed this group. In the last two years, John had seen Gary fly an airplane, discover a previously unsuspected Mayan ruin in Guatemala, trek across the Sahara Desert, and rescue a kitten for a grateful old lady. The man was impressive.

But no challenge was big enough for Gary, no victory decisive enough. If he thought the mission was too easy, he looked for ways to make it harder.

Before John had joined the Chosen, he'd been part of the military. You didn't go looking for death; that wasn't the way it was done. You prayed it didn't come looking for you.

Oh, he didn't say anything. But lately, he'd been wondering if it was smart to follow an adrenaline junkie. Worse, he suspected Gary knew of his doubts— the man was, after all, a mind reader—and John feared those doubts drove Gary to new heights of daring.

"Aren't your hands cold?" Sun Hee whispered and tucked her gloved hands into her armpits.

"I grew up in the Russian mountains and Siberia." About his origins he was brief. None of the Chosen Ones knew their birth parents, but most of them didn't have a background like his.

Frankly, most children didn't survive a background like his.

"Are you okay back there, Sun Hee?" Gary called.

She smiled, flattered, as they all were, by his attention. "Yes, Gary."

"The big guy's not making you afraid with all his worrying?"

"No. John is cautious, but always for good reason."

John appreciated the sentiment. Yet, at the same time, he almost wished she hadn't said it. Six feet tall, fit, with a head of black hair and compelling hazel eyes, Gary attracted women, all women. Amina was sleeping with him now, but it was John's impression that Gary had gone through every female who worked at the Gypsy Travel Agency, every female Chosen he'd ever had on his team, and had plans for every female not yet screwed.

Sun Hee was one of those still-untouched females. John didn't need to get into a pissing match because Sun Hee had spoken admiringly of him, and he really didn't want Gary to feel pressure to seduce Sun Hee sooner rather than later.

Yet he said nothing when Gary called, "Come on up and join us reckless ones. It's more fun than hanging around with that dour Russian."

John wasn't Russian. He hadn't lived in Russia since he was seventeen, when he walked south through the Ural Mountains, then west to the Black Sea and across to Turkey. He'd paid his way with work. He'd earned his ID, a passport, and an American visa with a service done for the right official—the only time he'd traded his power for a favor. If there was any truth in kismet, he should have suffered a turn of bad luck for misusing his gift. But in fact, he had never regretted what he'd done. He'd wanted out, and he'd gone about it the best way he knew how, and kismet had remained uninterested . . . or perhaps it simply was biding its time.

Now he waited for Sun Hee to skip forward to join Gary. She surprised John, though, with an eye roll and a shrug. Then she walked up to be part of Gary's group.

John watched her. Her exotic features and delicate body gave the impression of fragility. She'd stand back and observe, and she seldom spoke, but faced every challenge boldly—walked and climbed and fought with all her strength, and he had always admired her.

Bataar dropped back and joined John. He was short-legged and stocky, with high cheekbones and straight, dark hair. He heard things: the breathing of a lost child, the whisper of a butterfly's wings. Now, in his quiet voice, Bataar asked, "Can you hear that?"

John stopped and listened. He heard the tap of feet, the slither of ice down a wall, the soft whistle of some unfelt wind. "Hear what exactly?"

"Water," Bataar said.

The hair rose on the back of John's neck. He listened again, but heard nothing. "Where?"

"Ahead of us." Bataar gestured vaguely forward.

John thought back. The helicopter that had flown them in had repeatedly circled the mountain valley.

The long, massively heavy glacier snaked down from the snowy heights, fractured and rugged, moving ponderously toward the lower elevations. The ice dragged sediment off the surrounding rocky mountains and carried it in long, dirty lines that marred the pristine blue ice with gray. The pilot proved that he'd carried tourists there before when he told them how much the ice had retreated in the last year. "Twenty feet." He grinned, showing tobacco-stained teeth. "I saw the cave first, a cave my people built thousands of years ago out of stone and ice, and I called your people. I'm good, huh? You pay me?"

At the time, John had been so amused by the fellow's open greed he hadn't bothered to think that they had landed on bare rock where the glacier terminated—and although the glacier was clearly melting, no stream flowed from its base.

Now Bataar's words made him realize—somewhere, something within the glacier dammed the outflow.

"How much water?" John asked.

"Not much. Not yet. But do you know what will happen when the outflow for this glacier is released?"

Yes, John knew. It would be a flood of devastating proportions. When it broke through, the glacier, lubricated by the water, would rush forward, obliterating the cave and everything—and everyone—inside.

"Should we tell Gary?" Bataar was Mongolian. He'd traveled in the Himalayas. He understood their dire situation, had probably understood even before they entered the cave.

"No. But let's see if we can hurry them along." John glanced forward—and the group in front of them had disappeared. He ran forward, Bataar on his heels. An icy wall, painted to resemble a tunnel, suddenly loomed before them, while the passage abruptly opened to the left. John skidded on the ice, his studded boots barely stopping him.

Bataan slammed into him, and they hit the wall hard.

The stone slab gave, almost as if it rested against a sponge. Ice rained down from the ceiling, breaking on their faces like shards of glass. Suddenly, John could hear the faint, mocking trickle of water.

The two men took the low, left opening. Two steps in, and another wall loomed before them. An abrupt right, and they stood with the Chosen Ones staring into a long, narrow chamber illuminated by a diffused blue, glacial light that leaked between the slabs in the walls and through the cracks in the stone ceiling.

"It looks as if this room was created to collapse like a house of cards," John said.

"I wonder what's holding it together," Amina said.

Sun Hee's dark eyes examined their surroundings. "Superstition."

Gary laughed. "Exactly. Foolish superstition."

John and Sun Hee exchanged troubled glances. He didn't think superstition was foolish. Quite the contrary. In battle, he'd seen far too many examples of superstitions fulfilled.

The floor had been created by stepping-stones separated by ice. At the far end, rough stones had been piled into an altar with a carefully crafted flat stone table. Atop that in a small stone bowl rested a leather bag, stiff and frozen.

In the rough whisper of a dedicated treasure hunter, Gary asked, "Max, is that it?"

"It's not . . ." Max's eyes half closed and fluttered as if he could see the treasure inside the bag. "It's different. Not gold. Not jewels. But it's ancient and it's . . . it's important."

"Great." Gary smiled and started across the floor.

Sophie grabbed him. "No!"

"What?" Gary looked disdainfully at her fingers curled around his arm.

Sophie wasn't an eloquent woman, or even intelligent; she ran on instinct and now she simply repeated, "No."

Sun Hee turned her head from side to side. "There's another way."

"Oh, for God's sake—" Gary started out across the floor again.

John didn't even think. He grabbed Gary's shoulders and yanked him back. "You've got a team. Now listen to us!"

Gary turned blazing eyes toward John.

John protected himself automatically, lifting his hand and holding his power like a shield. He felt the energy of Gary's mind slam into him and bounce off.

John staggered back, his neck whiplashing as if he'd been hit. For a moment, his eyes rolled back in his head.

Amina caught him.

Gary glared at John. "I'm the leader here."

John recovered, and in a low, intense voice, he said, "Yes, and Sophie is the one who knows about traps. If she says no, then you don't go. If Sun Hee can catch the scent of another passage, then you follow her. We are your team. We are your backup. We're in mortal danger. So *listen to us.*"

One by one, the team members looked around. Stone creaked behind them. John glanced up, and as if a giant's fingers pinched the ends of the ceiling slab, the center bulged downward. If it shattered, the glacier would capture them, crush them. Drown them.

Sophie covered her head with her hands and whimpered softly.

"This way," Sun Hee said, her voice strong and sure, and she disappeared through a narrow crack in the wall to the left.

Gary hesitated, still wanting a fight.

John could almost see the realization strike him: if Gary didn't move, Sun Hee might reach the treasure, and the danger, first. His gaze promised retribution, but swiftly he squeezed through the crack after her.

As Gary disappeared, Amina's glow faded, but she demanded, "John, why did you say that? Why did you do that?"

"My God, Amina, have you looked around?" Max answered.

The ice was visibly failing everywhere, slipping down the walls and pooling as water on the floors.

"And listened?" Bataar lifted a single finger.

The melting glacier growled like a hungry beast.

John watched the shifting shadows inside the treasure room. "There they are!" He pointed across the altar room and up.

Somehow, Sun Hee and Gary had worked their way through the tunnel, then crawled up through the rock.

Now they perched on a ledge close to the ceiling and almost directly over the small, frozen, leather bag.

Gary gripped Sun Hee by the waist and held her.

She wiggled, head down, over the treasure.

Gary braced his elbows against the rock to hold himself steady as she stretched, pulling against his grip.

John's heart pounded so loud he feared Bataar could hear it.

All the while, tremors shook the floor and walls and the noise of running water got louder.

Sun Hee's fingers brushed the red cord that held the bag closed. Once. Twice.

Behind the altar, the increasing pressure behind the stone made it appear gelatinous.

John gritted his teeth, held himself back. He wanted to use his power, support the cave with a force field. But not with Sun Hee in the way.

On her third swing, she snagged the cord.

The Chosen held their breaths as she lifted it from the altar.

For a moment, the shaking in the cave eased. The sound of water diminished.

She shot them a triumphant grin. Winked at John. Signaled Gary to pull her back.

The Chosen laughed and clapped.

John raised his hand and prepared to use his power to help Gary lift her—and a violent jolt shook the room.

The glacier roared.

A huge slab of rock tilted back as if some beast was deconstructing the cave.

The ledge that held Gary shook so hard it slowly

separated from the wall, and behind him dust rose from the passage.

Amina screamed.

Sophie backed away.

"Go on." John took Sophie by the shoulders and shoved her toward the passage out. "Bataar, take her. Max, get the hell out of here. Amina, you need to *leave*."

But Amina shook her head, her eyes glued to the drama before her.

In a feat of athleticism that rivaled anything in the Olympics, Gary swung Sun Hee up, flipped her and caught her wrists, then lowered her toward the altar.

John ran forward, across stepping-stones that tilted like ice floes on a rushing river. As he reached the altar, her weight settled on the table—and beneath her, the stone legs cracked. The top collapsed.

John caught her, yanked her away. A large obsidian ax blade dropped from the ceiling, barely missing them. Shards of black stone glass shattered into a thousand pieces.

Red trickled from Sun Hee's cheek.

John's forehead stung, and blood ran into his left eye.

The back wall bulged. Water leaked through the cracks. The roaring grew louder.

"Go on!" John pushed her toward the entrance, then turned in time to see Gary launch himself off the ledge.

The ledge collapsed behind him, dragging a huge chunk of stone off the back wall.

For the first time, John got a clear view of the dam of

glacial ice—blue, clear, cold, and impersonal. The dam held back a raging river of turbulent water—and it was failing. In minutes, seconds, the water would break through and drown them all. "Go!" he yelled at Gary.

But Gary, of course, took his place beside John.

*Ever the hero.*

More stone peeled from the back wall, opening up wider views of the frenetic river rampaging behind the ice dam, demanding to be free.

John didn't want to worry about saving the hero. He'd be damned lucky to save himself. "You have to go," he shouted. "You have to save the women!"

That worked. Of course it did.

Gary clapped his hand on John's shoulder. "Hold it off as long you can." Then he was gone.

"John!" Sun Hee screamed.

John didn't turn. He knew Gary would get her out. All his focus had to be on that thinning wall of ice. He had to stop it long enough to get the team—and possibly even himself—out of the cave.

He needed to save his energy, delay until the last possible second before the collapse. Yet if he waited too long, the water would break through and he'd be lucky to contain it.

This disaster felt unreal, as if John were watching the climax of *Titanic* on his own personal IMAX screen. Every moment, the water and sand ate away at the ice. Once, twice—boulders the size of a refrigerator rose and fell on the mighty, churning current. If one of those hit the ice dam. . . . *Then one did.*

John flung his hands up, slammed his strength into the ice, catching it before it cracked, bracing it with the force of his will. He could see waves of power emanating from his hands, blue as the ice but ephemeral, fleeting. The smallest crackle told him the ice was failing; the water was winning. . . . Then a louder pop. And a crack that echoed like a gunshot in the tiny chamber.

He staggered back.

Water leaked from the fissure that had opened across the length of the ice. Water ran from the ceiling. The chamber looked like a tropical storm had struck . . . a frigid tropical storm.

John didn't feel the cold. Sweat broke out on his forehead, trickled down his spine. The might of the glacier, of one of nature's most commanding forces, clashed with John's subtler, more unfathomable power—and John knew he couldn't hold on forever. But long enough for the Chosen to escape . . .

His arms trembled with the strain.

Where did the power come from? He didn't know. He did know it wasn't his—that he drew energy from the stones, the stars, the universe: he was merely a conduit. But as a conduit, he could only push so much power.

The water's roar deafened him; the whole cave trembled violently, continuously. Around him, he heard the glacier shift forward. The stone slabs wavered.

He hoped to hell the Chosen had escaped, because he had no choice. If he was going to get out, it had to be now.

He retreated. The range of his power retreated with him.

Wall slabs slammed to the floor. Water smashed

through the ice, breaking it into bergs that rampaged through the water.

He held it away, a seething, destructive dome. He backed around the corner and into the main corridor.

Inside the altar room, blocks of rock and ice collided.

He hurried now, concentrating on his footing. The walls narrowed, crushed by the ice. His hands grew numb with the force needed to push against the stone, to keep the way clear.

He breathed hard. His muscles spasmed with the constant outflow of energy. His mind grew foggy, his reflexes slow.

And all the time he could feel the force of the glacial outflow fighting to be free. He could feel it inviting him, luring him—if he would let it through, he and it would become one, a force of nature.

He ran backward, wanting to get away from the voices that babbled in the water. *Let us in. We'll protect you, make you greater than you already are . . .*

He was hallucinating.

Lack of oxygen in the enclosed space . . .

He stumbled backward into the boulder that blocked the corridor. His focus failed. Water rushed forward, slammed him, lifted him toward the ceiling. Trapped in the water with the stone at his back, he couldn't breathe.

Then, swiftly, irresistibly, the water pushed him through the crack, over the boulder—and he swirled out of control in the frigid current.

*If I live through this, I'm going to get a life.*

He snapped back to consciousness, punched out with his power, reaching up to the air, then surrounding himself with a protective bubble.

He didn't kid himself. If the water had been unobstructed, he could have never stopped it. But as the boulder rolled, it slowed the flow, letting him surround himself with space.

He stopped. Fell to the unstable floor.

*Yes. A life . . . A woman . . . Someday, children . . .*

The boulder ground toward him, roaring, crushing the gravel beneath it . . . threatening him with the same fate.

He staggered to his knees, to his feet.

The water around him rushed and buzzed, angry at being thwarted.

He backed away again, reaching behind him with his power to keep the way open.

*Gotta survive. Get a woman. Sun Hee. . . . Yes. Sun Hee.*

The passage went on and on, ever shifting, growing smaller . . . Abruptly, the walls twisted, warped with the weight of the ice.

He hit his head on the collapsing ceiling. His power failed. He toppled backward. The rush of water hit him, clawed at him, holding him under . . .

He had failed. He was going to die.

*No wife. No children. No Sun Hee. Nothing . . .*

The torrent shoved at him, pushing him through a narrowing crack. Then, like a rebirth—sunshine! Air. Sweet, cold air!

He was out! He gulped in a breath, fought to stand.

The water laughed and tossed him over, thrashing him with sand and stones. He caught a glimpse of the helicopter as it lifted off, its struts lifting out of the rising water while the team leaped to catch the struts and climb in.

They were abandoning him.

Something snagged his collar and dragged him toward the shallow edge. He floundered to his feet—and found himself facing a furious-eyed Sun Hee.

*Yes—this was the woman for him!*

She shouted something and pointed toward the cliff that rose above the glacial valley, then up toward the mountain peak.

His ears rang, but he understood. He pulled her through the fast-rising, knee-deep water to dry land. Shoving her ahead, he clambered after her, moving fast, moving up, knowing this gush of water was only the beginning, that the glacier would gobble at the stone walls, launch giant boulders downstream. If he and Sun Hee didn't climb fast, the ground would disappear under their feet and they'd hurtle downstream, never to be found.

They ascended the equivalent of two stories before Sun Hee stopped and looked, and pointed.

In the valley, only Gary and Amina remained on the ground. The helicopter hovered overhead. The glacial outflow rose to their thighs. As they staggered against the strength, Gary lifted Amina above him. Hands reached out of the helicopter and pulled her in. Then, so smoothly it looked easy, Gary jumped, caught the strut, swung, and lifted himself inside.

"You know he's going to take credit for the whole operation, don't you?" Sun Hee's teeth chattered with wet and cold.

"I don't care." John really didn't, because she was pressing herself against him, and when his arms went around her, she burrowed deeper into his embrace.

John watched the helicopter circle them.

Gary leaned out the door. "Heads up!" he shouted.

A survival pack hurtled down right at them.

John and Sun Hee jumped apart.

John caught the pack, slid it onto Sun Hee's shoulders, then caught the second one. Dry clothes, a thin tarp, a bedroll, some rations. . . . They would survive.

"Tomorrow!" Gary shouted and waved a jaunty hand.

"How odd," John murmured, and with a glance at the rising torrent below, he shouldered the pack and started up the mountain once more.

"Not really. It would have been more odd if he sat down and put on his seat belt." Sun Hee followed on his heels.

"Not that." No, what surprised him was that Gary was supposed to be a mind reader. Not a mind controller, not a mind feeder; only a mind reader. Gary had been tested by the Gypsy Travel Agency. They all had. Gary couldn't hide a gift; the Gypsy Travel Agency didn't make mistakes about things like that. Yet that burst of energy he'd flung at John, the one John had blocked—that had been a thought. John was sure of it.

"John?"

"Hm?" What had Gary done to escalate his gift?

"Do you think tonight . . . you and I could share our body warmth?"

John stopped. Turned.

There stood Sun Hee, smiling at him knowingly.

He had made a good choice. They would have a good life together. . . .

A year later, when his carefully constructed life burned in the fires of jealousy, rage and despair, he remembered his misplaced optimism . . . and he escaped to the ends of the earth.

He escaped to the hell that had given him birth.

# Chapter 2

G enesis Valente had always believed in magic.

Her father was one of the dark-business-suited men who ran the Gypsy Travel Agency, and one of her earliest memories was standing in front of him as he sat in his leather chair, reciting the legend in her high, lisping voice. *Long ago, when the world was young . . .*

When she was five, she could rattle it off, and she was excited about it, the way a five-year-old is excited about the pledge of allegiance, mouthing the words without understanding them.

When she was ten, her vivid imagination brought the legend to life.

*Long ago, when the world was young, a beautiful young woman lived in a village on the edge of a vast, dark forest, and she declared she would marry only a man whose magnificence matched her own. She took the eldest son of the local lord, a lazy lad as famed for his dark, wavy hair and deep-set blue eyes as for his vanity, and before the year was out, she grew large with child. But in the spring, when it came time to deliver her child, she gave birth to two scrawny, wailing, red-faced babes. Worse, they were not perfect. The elder looked as if red wine stained him from the tips of his tiny fingertips to his bony shoulder. The younger, a girl, had a dirty smudge in the palm of her hand, which to the mother looked exactly like . . . an eye. Disgusted, she rose from her birthing bed. She took her children, carried them into the deepest part of the forest—where old and hungry gods waited to consume any human who dared venture close. She abandoned the boy, and tossed the girl into a torrent of icy water . . .*

Yes, at ten Genny believed the legend and spent every night cowering beneath her covers, imagining the indifferent eyes of the long-ago mother as she abandoned her children. Those eyes looked so familiar—big and golden brown like Genny's but, unlike Genny's, without an ounce of warmth. Genny had never understood what she did wrong, why her own mother didn't care about her. All too easily she could imagine being left for wolves to eat, or being thrown in a river to drown.

Three years later, Genny was thirteen and mad at the world. She did everything she could to physically discard her bewildered, lonely childhood. She pulled her dark curly hair back from her face, binding it at the back of her neck. She wore bras that flattened her breasts. She painted her fingernails black, used black lipstick, dusted her face with pale powder.

She cut off her eyelashes.

It didn't help. Nothing helped. Her mother never noticed and her father paid her no attention except to demand she recite a stupid old legend.

Sure, she knew it . . . *At the moment when the mother abandoned her children, they were devoid of the gift every child should receive at birth—its parents' love. Their small hearts stopped beating. They died . . . and came back to life changed, gifted; the vacuum in their hearts filled by a new gift, one given in pity and in love. They were the first Abandoned Ones. Wanderers saved the boy, and when he grew up, he could create fire in the palm of his hand. He gathered around him others like him, babes who had been tossed aside like offal and, in amends, had been given a special gift. They were the Chosen, seven men and women who formed a powerful force of light in a dark world.*

When Genny was fifteen, her father got fired for stealing from the Gypsy Travel Agency, from the very people who organized and protected the Chosen Ones.

Helpless, Genny watched as her world was smashed to bits.

Her mother walked out and never looked back.

*The girl baby floated down the cold torrent, bobbing to the surface and screaming when her tiny body caught on a branch. A woman—a witch—heard the shrieks and pulled the baby from the water. Disappointed by the scrawny thing, she intended to toss her back . . . until she saw the eye. She knew then that the child was special, so she took her to her home and raised her, starved her, tormented her, used her as a slave.*

*She taught her how to hate.*

Kevin Valente plea-bargained his way out of a prison sentence, indicting one of the board members, two company librarians, an assessor, four travel agents, and one of the Chosen. He became the most hated squealer in New York City.

At first Genny cried tears of relief that her father merely had to return the money he'd stolen and pay a fine. Yes, she'd lost her mother, but her mother had never cared. Yes, she had to move out of her luxurious home on Long Island and into her grandparents' crowded home in the Bronx, but she still had her father and she didn't have to go into foster care. That was the important thing, right? *Right?*

With a daughter's desperate faith, she told herself that somehow there was a mistake, that her father had been framed, that he hadn't really taken those valuable antiquities.

Then she found out she had to give away her dog and two cats and parrot and mice. Especially her mice. Her grandmother screamed when she saw them.

Worse, Genny discovered that her father, who had been absorbed in work, suddenly turned the blowtorch of his attention to her.

Genny was his second chance, his opportunity to make good; and Kevin Valente intended to create a Mini-Me that would lift him out of the cesspool wherein he'd fallen. Genny would go to NYU, study pre-law, then go on to get a graduate degree in business. When she said she wanted to go to college to become a veterinarian who specialized in wildlife rescue, he looked at her as if she were speaking Martian and continued to make his plans, which were now her plans—whether she liked them or not.

He drilled her in accounting, negotiations, and

business etiquette, right down to how to establish her dominance from the first handshake and how to take command of a room from the moment she walked in. She learned how to dress, how to walk, how to deal with a sexually aggressive boss or an asshole coworker. She was equipped to claw her way up the ladder.

She didn't even want to set foot on the bottom rung.

*On the day the girl became a woman, she looked at the witch and, in a vision, foresaw her future. In a voice warm with delight, she told the witch a horrible death awaited her.*

*The girl was a seer. That was her gift.*

*Determined to evade her fate, the witch set up an altar to her master, the devil, and prepared to sacrifice the girl. But as the girl had grown up, the woman had grown old. The girl took the knife and plunged it into the witch's heart.*

*The devil himself took form.*

*He scrutinized the girl, as beautiful as her mother yet not heartless. No, this girl was steeped in anger; and with her gift, she would be a worthy instrument in his hand. So he showed her his wonders, promised her a place at his right hand, and commissioned her to find others like her, and teach them to do evil in the world. Around her, she gathered six other abandoned children—warped, abused, and special— and they were the Others. The Others used their powers to cut like a scythe through the countryside, bringing famine and fear, anguish and death.*

Genny should have insisted on her right to pick her vocation. But her mother was gone, her father was all she had, and he seemed so sure he knew what was best for her . . . when she wasn't sure of anything anymore.

So she applied to NYU, but told her father there was no way she was going to make the cut.

Her father told her he could still pull strings.

She was accepted.

Then the bills arrived. The bills for tuition, housing, and books.

Father couldn't pay them.

But he negotiated a loan for her, one that guaranteed the money for her education—all the money for her education. All she had to do was sign this contract, one that made her promise to do the lender a simple favor sometime. . . . This time she looked at Father as if *he* were speaking Martian, but he said, "For shit's sake, Genny, the Agency screwed me over. Did you think they don't know that? They owe me. *They owe me.*"

She stared at him, picked up the pen, crossed out the "favor," figured an approximate amount her education would cost, added a fair interest, ordered herself to pay it back within five years of graduation, and signed the amended contract.

*So through ages and eons, through low places and high, in the countryside and in the cities, through prophecies and revelations, the battle was joined between the Chosen and the Others, and that battle was fought for the hearts and souls of the Abandoned Ones.*

*That battle goes on today . . .*

Genny wasn't a complete dummy.

On that summer day six years later, when her life fell apart, that was her only comfort.

# Chapter 3

❖

"Would you take my picture with Father?" Genny handed her camera to Chloe, her roommate for two years, and hurried back to her father's side. He'd bought a new suit for her graduation, a really nice one, and with his gray-streaked hair and distinguished air, none of her friends knew Kevin Valente drove a UPS truck for a living.

Not that it mattered to Genny, but he'd forbidden her to tell them. He was ashamed of being blue collar. He would always be ashamed. She accepted that, dodged the questions, and right now didn't worry about him. Because after six years of hell, four working for her pre-law degree and two in grad school, she'd finished NYU Business School Summa Cum Laude, landed a job at CFG, the preeminent brokerage account management firm . . . and her father was proud of her.

Several cameras flashed as they posed for the

photo—she'd made friends here—and voices called, "We'll forward the shots."

"Thank you!" She waved and grinned. She couldn't stop grinning.

"I've got a reservation for dinner. We're going to have to hurry if we're going to make it." Father smiled charmingly at the group of graduates and their parents. "You'll forgive me if I take Genny away for a private celebration, won't you?"

"Of course!" Brianna's father shook his hand. "But if you get a chance, stop by the house. We're having a party to celebrate the girls' accomplishments."

"We'll be there!" Father promised, taking Genny's hand, swinging it as they walked away. As soon as they were out of earshot, he muttered, "Pompous ass."

"He's not really. He's nice." Genny didn't know why she tried. Brianna's father was a top exec, had used his influence to help Genny land the job; and if he knew about her father's disgrace, he never indicated it by word or deed.

Yet Father didn't care. For him, the humiliation of his disgrace was as fresh as if it had happened yesterday.

So Genny told herself stoutly that she didn't care if she went to the party with her friends. She had her father.

Father always said if he couldn't dine as he chose, he wouldn't dine at all. So they never went out to dinner.

But he must have been saving up for this one grand gesture, because the restaurant was among Manhattan's finest. As they walked behind the maitre d', she prayed they wouldn't be seated by the restrooms or in a corner. She didn't want her father in a bad mood all evening, angry because he'd been slighted.

Luck or providence or Father's expensive suit worked for them, because their table was against the window with a view of Manhattan's lights laid out like jewels tossed on a black velvet cushion. The waiter was attentive, and Genny relaxed into the evening— her pleasure complete as she watched her father transformed from the bitter worker into this cool, elegant gentleman.

She had a bad moment when he ordered for her. Yes, perhaps a gentleman did order for his date, but this was her father. He didn't know her tastes; he only knew what he wanted her tastes to be. But it was a small quibble, not worth fighting about. When the appetizers arrived, she had a nibble of each—she hated caviar, but he insisted—then Father pulled an envelope out of his jacket and pushed it across the gleaming white tablecloth. "Your graduation present."

"What's this?" She picked it up gingerly, half afraid—well, more than half—he was giving her a gift certificate for another course on how to crush your business opponent.

"Open it and see." He leaned back in his chair and watched with a satisfied smile as she broke the seal.

She slid a travel itinerary out of the envelope. She examined it. One round-trip plane ticket in her name, leaving next week, returning in September—New York to Berlin, Berlin to Moscow, Moscow to . . . someplace called Rasputye? Bewildered, she looked up at him. "I don't understand."

"Remember that Russian woman? The one with the cats?"

"Lubochka Koslov?"

"That's her."

What that had to do with this ticket, Genny didn't understand. "They're not just cats, Father. Koslov is the world's leading expert on the rare Ural lynx, one of the big cats believed to be driven to extinction at the start of the twentieth century. She proved a small group had survived in the depths of the northern Ural Mountains in the area spanning the border between Europe and Asia. She spends her summers studying the lynx, and her winters lecturing at universities to raise money to support her research." When Lubochka Koslov had come to NYU, Genny had gone to hear her speak and been enthralled. "Her team is the only one who's ever taken pictures of the big cats in the wild."

"You already filled me in. When you came home from her lecture." He sounded bored, but . . .

"You remembered I went to one of her lectures?" Genny was flabbergasted.

"You carried on about it for hours."

"Maybe ten minutes." If Genny wasn't talking about business, her father always tuned her out. Or so she had thought. Maybe he was listening to her after all?

Her father glowered in disapproval. "You still read *National Geographic* like it's the Bible."

"I read *National Geographic* when I can." A total lie. She read it every month as soon as it arrived in the mailbox. She'd even managed to scrape together enough to get a lifetime subscription.

"Well?" He took a sip of champagne. "Don't you want to go study some endangered wildlife? Rasputye is some tiny-ass hamlet with four hundred people. I thought you'd like it. You always used to babble about forests and observation and preservation and tagging."

Genny gazed again at the itinerary.

*Mountains.*

*Wilderness.*

*A deep, peaceful, soulful quiet.*

*The chill wind in her face . . .*

She didn't dare believe this. That her father had done something so out of character. . . . She swallowed; she looked up. "*You* arranged for me to work with Lubochka Koslov, studying the Ural lynx?"

"You deserve a reward."

She just . . . she couldn't believe this.

Working with wildlife was the dream of her life-time, and for her, the Ural lynx were special—wild, shy, clever. The big, beautiful cats left their marks on the mountain forests that were their homes, providing proof of their existence, yet they were almost impossible to find and photograph. Genny wanted to help them, save them, do something in her life that had value for future generations.

To have her father understand at last . . . that made it all the sweeter.

Reality brought her up short. "B-but the job at CFG?"

Father's mouth grew pinched. "I still have some pull. CFG is holding your position until September."

Still she stared at the itinerary until he said, "Don't you want to do it?"

*Mountains.*

*Wilderness.*

*A deep, peaceful, soulful quiet.*

*The chill wind in her face . . .*

"Don't I want to do it!" For the first time in years, since that day when he'd come home in disgrace, spontaneous pleasure ignited in her and brought her to her feet, moving her around the table to fling her arms around his neck. "Father, you've made me so happy!"

He stiffened, pushed her away. "Remember where we are."

"Right." Kevin Valente was a stickler for proper behavior. Even now, when people were beaming at them, father and daughter celebrating together, he thought about appearances. She straightened, returned to her seat, sat down. But no reprimand could stop her from grinning at him. "Thank you so much. I'll never forget this as long as I live."

"Good." He watched as the waiter brought a clean white linen napkin, flipped it open and placed it in her lap. "There is one condition."

"Anything!" She looked again at the itinerary, then leaned it against the pepper mill where she could gaze at it with wonder.

"There's a man living in the area."

She didn't understand what he meant. But she knew she didn't like his tone. "A man? In what area?"

"In the Ural Mountains." Father pulled a snapshot out of his jacket and pushed it across the table toward her.

She glanced at it. The guy had been caught in profile. He was young, tall, with rugged features, broad shoulders, and a military haircut. He was laughing at someone off camera, and his amusement made her smile. Whoever he was, the man seemed likable—the kind who lived big and embraced life.

"They want you to talk to him," Father said.

Her smile faded. "They?"

"If you can convince him to come to New York City and talk to them about taking a position, they'll forgive your student loans."

The excitement, the joy, the chill wind in her face faded as if they had never been. In a slow, deadly tone, she asked, "Father, is this the favor I crossed off the loan papers?"

"You don't cross anything off their loan papers. It doesn't work that way."

"Legally—"

"*Legally* means nothing to those guys. They use *legally* to get their own way."

"I would never have signed if I had known that!"

He got that look on his face, the one that sneered at her idealism. "For God's sake, Genny. You're not the same girl you were six years ago. You've interned for two summers. You know how business works now. You scratch my back, I'll scratch yours."

"I can pay back the loan."

"Be practical. It'll take you as long to pay it back as it took you to accumulate it."

"The price of doing business," she reminded him, the fire of her elation cooling in the pit of her belly.

He slashed the air with his hand.

She flinched back.

"I promised them you'd handle this," he said.

She gripped the table edge so hard her knuckles

ached. "You shouldn't have promised what you can't deliver."

"Then you don't want to go?" He reached across and took the itinerary.

She grabbed it and held on. "So it's not really a present?"

"It's a present!"

"With strings attached!"

"I'm a goddamn UPS man. How do you think I can pay for a trip like this?"

*Steal the money?* She was breathing hard. *Sell your daughter?*

He'd done it again. Father had disappointed her again. He'd used her . . . Again. "Oh, I don't know. Maybe save up?"

"I'm a goddamn UPS man," he repeated.

Like that made this less of a betrayal.

Still she clutched the corner of the itinerary.

*She wanted this so badly.*

For the last six years of college and business school, she had seen her dreams fade.

No, she had seen herself kill them. She ignored her ideals, her natural talents, her own desires. She had become a business major. She had turned her face away from the wilderness, from mountains and forests.

From freedom.

She had accepted the fact she would spend her life trapped in a steel-and-glass building, doing things she despised, being someone she hated.

With one gesture, her father had ripped away her resignation. In one moment she remembered who she was meant to be, and she couldn't bear to lose the . . .

the mountains, the wildness, the good she could do in the world.

"Well?" Her father raised his thin, dark eyebrows.

She sat, breathing hard, wanting to keep to her principles, but . . . she could almost smell her destiny. "I have to convince him to come to New York City?" she asked slowly.

"To return so they can talk to him." Father carefully didn't show triumph.

"Is he a criminal?"

"Not at all." Father seemed to be choosing his words. "He had a few problems with his gift."

"His gift? Is this about the *legend*?" Her voice rose.

"Sh!" Father looked around.

"Am I still supposed to believe in the *legend*?"

Father leaned forward, and spoke rapidly and softly. "We don't talk about the legend in public. You know that. And what does it matter whether you believe in the legend or not? You can still do this favor."

"This guy is supposed to be *Chosen*?" She was still too loud, and probably she shouldn't be. She didn't want the people from the funny farm to come and take her away.

"He *is* Chosen, and he needs help," Father said persuasively. "You'd be doing him a favor."

In business school, they'd trained the students to be logical, to look at the issues. So which concern should she bring up first?

That on her father's urging, she'd minored in the Russian language in her undergrad studies—so obviously he, or *someone*, had been planning this for a long time?

That he'd promised the Gypsy Travel Agency she would "handle" this matter?

That he believed in the legend he'd taught her so many years ago, and apparently expected her to believe it, too?

But if she pinned him down, wouldn't he grow angry or evasive like he always did when she tried to talk about their relationship?

She was such a coward. Her throat closed up every time she thought about confronting her father, and all because she was haunted by the sight of her mother's back as she walked away.

Genny didn't want to be alone.

So, hoarse with frustration, she said, "This . . . place, Rasputye, is a long way from Moscow. My Russian probably isn't going to be appropriate for the area. He won't understand me."

Father's eyes sparkled the way they did when he knew he was winning. "He's American."

"Is he violent?"

"Of course not. I wouldn't expose you to violence!"

She didn't believe her father. Not anymore. She didn't believe him about a lot of things. She wished she could, but she didn't.

She hated it, but with the past six years of schooling, logic had made her turn a cool eye on her father's legal problems and helped her realize . . . no one prosecuted his kind of white-collar crime unless they were sure of their facts.

He was guilty. He had stolen the artifacts, sold them for an obscene profit, and even now he couldn't admit that justice had been done.

Her father was an unrepentant criminal.

Even now, a few artifacts—the ones that had been appraised for nothing, she supposed—rattled around their house.

"If this Chosen doesn't want to come, what do I do then?" She knew Father would have an answer. He had an answer for everything.

"All they ask is a good try on your part." His dark eyes gleamed. "But, Genny, you aced Negotiations."

"I've got nothing to offer him, nothing to negotiate with."

"You don't know that until you meet him."

Father wasn't suggesting she sleep with this guy, was he? Even *he* wouldn't prostitute his only child.

But he would offer her an irresistible gift to get her to do what he wanted.

He leaned forward, his tense posture matching hers. "If you do this, if they forgive your loan, I can move out of your grandparents' home. With my help, you'll get to the top fast. We could buy a condo in the city, live the way we used to, entertain, be important again."

"You're going to sell Grandma and Grandpa's house?" Her grandparents had lived there as long as she remembered. They had lived there until four years ago when they'd died within six months of each other. The house had been his childhood home.

"It's in the Bronx." The way he said *Bronx*, he made it sound like a leper colony.

Then he saw her revulsion, and changed tack. "If you go to Russia, you'll spend a whole summer with your lynxes. You'll get to observe them in their natural habitat. They're an endangered species, and you'll help save them."

*Mountains.*

*Wilderness.*

*A deep, peaceful, soulful quiet.*

*The chill wind in her face . . .*

She didn't want to do this. It was wrong. She knew it was wrong. But . . .

*Freedom.*

"What else do you know about this gifted guy?" It was a surrender. She knew it. So did Father.

"What do you want to know?"

"Start with his name."

He pushed the itinerary back across the table. "John Powell. His name . . . is John Powell."

# Chapter 4

*Apasnee Airport*
*Ural Mountains, Russia*

"That man will make you believe he's the yeti."

Genny pulled her wheeled travel duffel off the airport luggage cart and wished the guy in the group by the door wasn't so obviously projecting his voice so she could hear.

"He's got hair down to his shoulders and a beard to the middle of his chest, and his clothes look like a sheepskin factory exploded all over him. He's the Abominable Snowman, but not as cute and furry."

The guy sported that short-guy cockiness. Personally, she would bet he whimpered when he got that tattoo around one wrist. He probably went in for both wrists and chickened out before the artist finished.

Or maybe he was marked because he was Chosen.

One corner of her mouth quirked in a smile, then drooped again.

Chosen. She didn't want to think about them, about her father and the deal he'd made, and John Powell. She wanted to—needed to—concentrate on the Ural lynx and what she was doing here.

"The yeti's got nothing on this head case." Mr. Loudmouth was American, obviously; a couple of years older than she, with a G.I.-surplus khaki shirt and reddish sandy hair cut into a long buzz that made his head look like a burr. His beard was exactly the same length and covered his jaw and chin, surrounding his freckled, pale-skinned face to create a monotone of color. In that overblown, dramatic tone, he said, "They say the yeti catches rats with his bare hands and eats them raw. They say he picks out a woman, watches her obsessively, then drags her away and when he's done with her, she's never interested in a man again."

"For God's sake, Brandon, do we have to listen to that claptrap again this year?" There were two women and four men in the group, and the woman who spoke was young, attractive, East Indian, with black hair cut neatly around her shoulders and dark eyes with sweeping eyelashes. Her English was precise, faintly British, with only the faintest Hindi accent—and perhaps, the fact that she towered over Brandon by a good five inches may have had something to do with her open impatience.

"Yes, and telling stories to frighten children is not why we are here." The other woman had a heavy Russian accent and a heavier frown, which she bent on Brandon. "We are here to study the Ural lynx."

"I know, but look. The last member of our group has arrived, and she needs to be warned." Brandon grinned at Genny. "You would hate to be abducted by a big hairy beast, wouldn't you?"

"Better than a short hairy beast," muttered the East Indian woman.

With a pugilist's quick reflexes, Brandon turned on her. "Are you trying to pick a fight, Avni? Already?"

"Shut up, children. I'm not listening to you fight all summer." The Russian woman stuck out her hand. "Genesis Valente?"

"Genny." Genny shook hands. "You're Lubochka Koslov. I'm a big admirer of yours."

Lubochka was middle-aged and attractive with pale skin, short dark hair, and dark eyes; six feet tall and big boned with swimmer's shoulders and man hands. "Genesis, this is Misha Sokolov, my assistant." She indicated a squat, middle-aged man with wire-rimmed glasses and dark, thinning hair. "He'll work out your schedule and give you direction."

"I'm honored to be accepted on your team." Genny shook his hand.

Genny had used Russian language software day and night to prepare for this trip, but she didn't need a translation for Misha's grunt of response. She knew what that meant: *someone paid us well for the privilege.*

Yes, someone had, the Gypsy Travel Agency.

And she . . . she would pay, too, when she found the Chosen and tried to persuade him to return to New York City.

But she shied away from that thought, ashamed that she'd so desperately wanted this adventure she'd been willing to agree to the terms. More than that, she was embarrassed because for those few minutes after her father had presented her with the itinerary, she had believed . . . believed her father wanted her to be happy. Buried so deep, she didn't dare admit she felt the old, familiar hurt of knowing he didn't care at all.

But although she suppressed a jumble of feelings, one floated along the top of her consciousness. No matter why her father had given her this present, no matter why she accepted it—this was three months of freedom before she began work to repair Father's reputation and their finances. And nothing and nobody, not even Brandon the Short, was going to ruin it for her.

Lubochka continued the introductions. "Reggie Caverlock, English, first year here, but he's a respected wildlife expert with many years in the field." Lubochka's brown eyes twinkled with anticipation.

"I'm Scottish, actually. A pleasure to meet you, Miss Valente." Reggie had the accent and voice of Gerard Butler. Unfortunately, the face didn't match up. It was a lived-in face, a face that had seen a lot in his forty years, the face of a sun-worshiper, a drinker, a smoker, and. . . . And then he smiled.

Genny caught her breath.

Oh, yes, he was a womanizer, too. His hazel eyes crinkled in the corners, his generous lips quirked cynically, and his lived-in face reminded her of . . . of George Clooney. Reggie Caverlock was a charmer who had seduced many a girl out of her panties.

"Good to meet you." She tried to shake his hand.

He kissed her knuckles.

Avni bumped her shoulder. "Don't pay attention to Reggie. He's a piece of work." But she sounded affectionate, as if he'd already kissed her knuckles. "I'm

Avni Patel, this is my third year here, and I guess my last. I graduated from Oxford this year and I'm going back to India to work in wildlife studies there."

"We'll miss her. Avni has been the best at catching and photographing lynx in daylight. They are seldom seen then, but she is able to remain so motionless, they don't realize she is around." Lubochka whipped around and glared once more at Brandon. "Unlike some people who fidget so much, we have only photos of the great cats' hindquarters as they run away!"

"I have bad luck," Brandon muttered.

Genny lifted her eyebrows at Avni.

Avni pointed at Brandon and rubbed her fingertips together suggestively.

He'd paid for the right to be here. So Genny wasn't the only one.

Lubochka introduced him abruptly. "Brandon Lam."

As Genny shook his hand, he squeezed it meaningfully. "I've been doing this two years. If you have any problems, you let me know and I'll help you out."

"Thank you." Genny already knew she wouldn't go to him if she was being attacked by ten yetis.

"Thorsen Rasmussen, an amateur observer so talented we invited him to drop in at any time." Lubochka smiled at the tall, pale, thin Dane with obvious affection.

Avni stood behind them and rubbed her fingers together again.

Okay. So Genny needed to get together with Avni, because Avni was the one who had the goods on the team. "I need to use the restroom before we leave," Genny said.

"Me too." Avni picked up her battered suitcase and headed toward the sign.

Genny followed.

"Hurry up. We're late already," Lubochka shouted.

"I've got to go, too," Brandon said.

"No, you don't." Lubochka snapped her fingers at him like he was a dog. "You help Misha carry the bags."

In a loud, sullen voice, Brandon asked, "What is it with women having to go to the bathroom together?"

"It's so I can tell her what a snot you are, you little pipsqueak." Avni projected her voice, too; then she and Genny hustled into the chipped, bare, utilitarian restroom.

Genny looked around and grimaced.

Avni laughed. "Europeans aren't as fussy as Americans about their creature comforts, and the Russians are particularly hearty. Wait until you get to Rasputye. We're at the inn, built before the 1917 Russian Revolution. It makes this look like luxury. Did you bring toilet paper?"

"Camper's TP." Genny took one open stall.

Avni took the other. "Guard it with your life." She lowered her voice and talked fast. "The walls are thin everywhere in Russia, so always figure someone's listening."

Genny looked around uneasily. "Got it."

"Here's the deal. Lubochka will accept anyone on the team if they pay for the privilege. She'd make a pact with the devil himself to save even one of her lynxes. But she is absolutely uninterested in the team except as employees and fact-gatherers. She'll throw your ass out if you don't perform. Brandon had to pay more this year than last to come back because he's such a loser."

"Like how much?" They were both chatting quickly.

"I don't know for sure, but I just finished my degree in wildlife studies, so I'm trained to the job; plus I'm good at what I do, and my father had to pay twenty-five thousand for me."

"Twenty-five thousand dollars?" Genny was horrified. "American dollars?"

"American dollars," Avni confirmed. "How much did it cost to get you here?"

"I don't know. It was a graduation present. But do you think it was more than twenty-five grand?"

"I don't *think*. I *know*. I listened in on a little conversation between Lubochka and Misha and twenty-five is the least they'll take, and for that you have to have training and/or experience." Avni flushed the toilet. "So they may have taken Brandon the first year for twenty-five because he's got the degree and experience in wildlife observation. But the little jerk doesn't need employment—"

"Wealthy family?" Genny had to jiggle the handle to make it work.

"And big trust fund." Avni washed her hands in the rust-colored water. "So he goes from study to study being a pain in the patootie until they decide he's not worth whatever he's paying them. Which is a bundle."

"What about Thorsen? He's an amateur, too." The water was gritty. The bar of soap was yellow, old, and cracked. Genny was glad she didn't bite her nails anymore.

"He's good at observation—plus he writes a big check every year to the cause, so he can do no wrong in Lubochka's eyes. In the last two summers, he came through at least once a month and stayed a few days every time. He usually comes in his helicopter."

"Wow."

"Yeah."

As they headed for the door, they clearly heard footsteps, a zip, and a guy on the other side of the wall using the facilities.

"See? Thin walls." Avni headed into the airport lobby and then out the door into the chilly sunshine. "It's a four-hour drive to the village on lousy roads that just get lousier. Don't drink anything—they won't stop. There aren't any seats in the vehicle, so try to catch some sleep or you'll get carsick."

Genny stared at the faded yellow sixties Volkswagen van parked in front. "I already feel a little sick."

Avni followed her gaze, and laughed.

Lubochka sat in the driver's seat revving the engine. Its muffler was a long-ago memory, and billows of blue smoke belched from the tailpipe. Misha sat beside her, polishing his glasses and looking irritable. The windows in back were held shut with bungee cords, and inside, they could see the men moving bags around.

"Look at it this way. Once you get to Rasputye, nothing else can be as horrible."

"Not even the yeti?" Genny waited for Avni to laugh again.

Instead, she shrugged uncomfortably. "I'm not going to admit it to Brandon, but the guy is scary."

Taken aback, Genny said, "You mean there *is* a yeti?"

"Oh, yeah. I've seen him come into the inn for his mail. The villagers are all scared of him. He's a hermit, and he's got, I don't know, PTSD or combat fatigue. Or he's just plain crazy. The guy is *feral*."

"Feral? What's he done?"

"He was in some kind of Special Forces unit, and he went nuts and killed his whole group. They say he's violent. I know for a fact that thing about the women is true."

"What thing about the women?"

"He gets in the mood where he wants a woman. He picks one out. And he watches her, stalks her, takes her to his cabin and he . . ." Avni waved a helpless hand.

"He *rapes* her?" Genny was more and more horrified.

"No! No. Wow. No. Apparently not." Avni's eyes gleamed. "No, he seduces her. Gives her the best sex in the history of the world. When he's done with her, other men just don't measure up."

"Pull the other one!" Genny laughed.

"I'm not kidding you." Avni tried to grin, but it looked wilted and lopsided. "Last year, I met one of the women. Halinka was on her way out of town because she couldn't stand it anymore. She said she wanted to see the world and forget about John."

"John?" For the first time, the ridiculous tale had a face, and it was the face of the photo in Genny's backpack. "John *Powell*?"

Lubochka honked the horn, loud and blaring.

Misha opened the door and in his heavy Russian accent, shouted, "Get in! We've got to get there before dark!"

"We gotta go!" Avni was all too eager to abandon the subject.

Genny caught her arm and held her in place. "Is his name John Powell?"

Misha yelled again.

Avni broke away. As she headed toward the van, she called back, "How did you know?"

# Chapter 5

———◆———

"Another flat tire? Why does this happen every year?" Lubochka slapped the side of the aged Volkswagen van.

The bumper flapped.

"Because the tires are so thin, you can see the air through them," Thorsen said in his distinctively Danish voice.

Misha knelt in the dirt, examined the rusty rim and ragged tire, and muttered Russian swear words.

"I thought I gave money for four new tires?" Thorsen asked.

Lubochka stood watching, her large hands planted on her hips. "I bought two. But we needed a new low-light Flip Video camera to set up at last year's lynx trail."

"Of course, foolish of me to think the money would be spent as I directed." Thorsen knelt in the dirt beside Misha.

"I make the decisions," Lubochka said stolidly.

Reggie gave a shout of triumph as he located the tire iron under the driver's seat.

"Hey, how come the men have to do the work?" Brandon groused loudly.

During the four-hour drive up into the mountains, Genny had come to realize he did everything loudly, and every sound exacerbated the pounding of her headache.

"It's not like *you're* doing anything." Avni cast Brandon a dark look as she helped Misha place the aged and feeble jack under the fender.

Genny didn't even think Lubochka knew she was standing behind her, gulping fresh air, until she said, "Genesis, sit down. You're green."

Great. Lubochka had eyes in the back of her head.

"Really, Miss Valente, go for a walk." Reggie handed the iron to Thorsen. "We have enough hands. You'll feel better with some fresh air."

Thorsen grunted as he loosened the lug nuts.

"I can go with you." Brandon looked her up and down. "In case you faint or something, I could give you mouth-to-mouth."

"No. Brandon, you stay here," Lubochka commanded.

"I'll be fine." Genny gave an embarrassed smile and fled up the narrow, winding mountain road.

"She'll get lost—wait and see," she heard Brandon say.

"Don't go too far!" Lubochka shouted.

Genny waved a hand and walked around the curve.

They were three-quarters of the way to Rasputye. Twilight turned the light a grayish blue, and it would be dark when they got there. But as far as Genny was concerned, the flat had been a godsend.

She had, disgracefully, been the one who got car-sick on the trip. She hadn't tossed her cookies, but the dust of the road and the smell of the exhaust combined with the bumpy ride had nauseated her. Brandon had mocked her, of course. Avni had patted her hand. The men had offered encouragement. Lubochka had tersely told her not to vomit on the equipment.

Now Genny made her way to a fallen log a few feet into the woods, sank down, and wrapped her arms around her knees.

All about her, tall trees lifted their branches to the sky. The forest was tall, deep, and dark—and somehow Genny thought it smelled old . . . so old. Something drifted down to the ground, and Genny half expected to see some of Hansel and Gretel's bread crumbs. But it was a pine needle . . . no, two . . . no, three . . . shaken from the trees by the barest wisp of wind. Then the breeze died, and the silence was profound; the soil and trees swallowed every sound.

*And someone was watching her.*

The hair at the base of her skull lifted. She froze. Warily she looked around.

She saw nothing. Nothing in any direction. This feeling was her imagination . . . It had to be her imagination . . . The stuff that Avni had told her had clearly been working on her mind.

She did a double take.

Eyes. Pale blue eyes staring at her from the under-brush.

She rose, her gaze fixed on those eyes in the distance, a man's eyes . . .

"John?" she breathed. As she did, the face that went with those eyes . . . faded into the twilight.

She was alone. She could barely breathe, and all she could hear was her pounding heart.

Around the bend, the Volkswagen roared to life.

Genny backed up, her gaze flicking from tree to tree, trying to see where the man—it had been a man; she was sure—had gone.

She reached the road as the van drove up.

Behind her, someone opened the door.

"Get in, Genny! We're late already." It was Avni.

Genny pointed a shaking finger into the woods. "Eyes. Watching me . . ."

"Oo, the yeti's been watching her," Brandon mocked. "Oo, she's scared of the yeti."

"No," she said, "it's not a yeti. It's—"

And a forty-pound female cat with red fur and distinctive black markings strolled out of the brush, posed for a moment, its eyes fixed on Genny, then turned its back on the astonished group and slid back into the forest.

"My God, Genesis, my dear"—Lubochka's voice shook with awe and reverence—"you spotted our first lynx of the season."

John Powell rose from his blind in the underbrush, stepped out on the road, and watched the Volkswagen van chug away, spewing blue smoke out its rusted tailpipe.

The girl had seen through his cover-up, and that surprised him. He had been in Special Forces. He was so adept at camouflage that wild animals had bounded over the top of him in the underbrush.

But then, the girl herself surprised him.

Every year he came out to look over Lubochka's new team. He didn't fool himself about his motivations. He came to make sure none of the Chosen Ones sneaked in to spy on him.

He wasn't paranoid; he was realistic. He had signed a seven-year contract to work on a team of Chosen. He had left before his term was completed. There was no-where on this earth he could run where they couldn't find him. So sooner or later, they would come and demand his services. Because the Gypsy Travel Agency might serve a higher cause, but its board of directors were ruthless in its pursuit.

Without modesty, John knew he was one of the most gifted and useful Chosen in recent memory. The power he commanded could lift a huge stone, bring a speeding car to a stop, hold back a glacier . . . when he was in full possession of his faculties.

It was what happened when his concentration failed that had sent him into exile. He no longer used those powers, holding them back like the ice dam held back the water. Someday the dam would explode. Someday the power would blast him apart. When that happened. . . . Better for him, and the world, that he be here near the *rasputye*.

Oh, he was weak.

Every once in a while, his needs overwhelmed his resolution. Every once in a while, he took a woman and showed her what he could do for her. The tiniest pulses of power, imbued with his passion, could in an instant move a woman from fear to pleasure.

Did he seduce those women merely as a release of lust and energy building within him? Or was he proving something to himself? He didn't care to examine his motives too closely.

He didn't dare look into his own soul.

Sooner or later the Gypsy Travel Agency would do what they could to force him to return. But first they would artfully scope out the territory. He figured Lubochka's team was the Agency's best chance for sneaking up on him, so with a handful of metal debris on the road and the bald tires on Lubochka's van, he guaranteed they would break down.

For the third summer in a row, it worked.

In past summers, all unknowing, they had talked to each other and he had listened.

So far no one, by word or deed, was suspicious of him. So far, he'd been lucky and the Gypsy Travel Agency had left him alone.

Seeing Genesis had been a shock for which he'd been totally unprepared. For the first time since he'd started observing Lubochka's female Americans, he'd been attracted.

No, worse. He'd been enthralled—and he didn't know why. Usually his women were beautiful, seductive, knowing. They might not choose him to begin with, but once they realized the pleasure he could give them, they flirted, tempted, laughed, met him halfway and more.

Nothing about Genesis's appearance gave him reason to believe she was that kind of woman.

She was pretty. Not beautiful, but with the kind of face that caught and held his attention. A head full of dark curly hair pulled back into a careless ponytail. A beautiful olive complexion, a cleft in her chin, and the most exotic golden brown eyes he'd ever seen in his life. They glowed in her face like coals burning with the kind of rosy hope and enthusiasm he only dimly remembered.

She couldn't be for real. She just couldn't be. Because simply seeing her made him *feel*.

Those events two years ago had cured him of emotions. He was hollow, empty inside; and if he started feeling sorrow or amusement or loneliness or joy, it would mean life was returning to his soul, like blood to a limb that had been frozen.

If there was one thing he understood, it was how painful that could be.

He didn't want it. *He didn't want it.* His power had been contained for so long. Better that it stay contained forever. He couldn't trust it.

He couldn't trust himself.

Like a bear fleeing a swarm of mosquitoes, he shook his head and fled into the woods. But for the first time he couldn't escape his thoughts.

What was he going to do when the Gypsy Travel Agency sent a representative to demand his return?

What was he going to do if Genny's golden eyes

mirrored her soul; if she was truly a dreamer, bright and idealistic?

He didn't know either answer.

He wanted her. He wanted to slide his hands through her dark hair, kiss her warm, tanned skin, ravish her, worship her, teach her how a man who had abandoned civilization made love.

Yet if she was real, if the warmth in her eyes thawed the ice in his veins . . . then he would have to leave her alone.

Because he would destroy her . . . just like he'd destroyed all the rest.

# Chapter 6

Someone shook Genny's shoulder. "We're here."

She opened her eyes, took a long breath of the cold, fresh air pouring through the van's open side access panel, and sighed. "Thank God." She'd managed to live through the ride to Rasputye.

She waited while everyone removed their bags and the equipment; then she dragged out her duffel. The team was traipsing into the only two-story building on the town square, and she lagged behind, peering around.

She couldn't see much. There were no streetlights. But the quarter moon showed a tiny hamlet, a throwback to the nineteenth century. Squat stone buildings with tin roofs were built around a village square. In the middle, a woodstove glowed dimly red. Dirty patches of snow hugged the houses and ice crunched underfoot.

In the daylight, she suspected this place would be

quaint. Now, with the forest looming close and darkness crouching beneath its boughs, the village felt foreign. Not Russian-foreign. Not I've-never-been-here-before foreign. *Foreign* as if . . . as if at any moment, the twins from that long-ago legend of the Chosen Ones could stroll out and carry Genny away, too.

*Because someone was watching.*

Again the hair on her neck lifted.

What had been spooky in the daylight was terrifying now. With a gasp, she hurried toward the inn, from which light, warmth, and voices spilled forth.

She descended six steps—the bottom floor was half dug into the ground—and stepped into a large taproom filled with the team, their baggage, and two dozen strangers. Lubochka stood between two long, laden tables directing traffic. "The girls get the attic. You men—you can fight for the regular rooms."

Brandon groaned.

Obviously, he was low man on the totem pole. Genny hoped he had to sleep hanging on a hook.

"Misha and I will take the front bedroom," Lubochka finished matter-of-factly.

Lubochka and Misha? In the same bedroom? Genny had the impression that Lubochka, big and deep voiced, played for the other team.

Surprise made her careless; she tripped on the uneven wood floor and stumbled.

Every person sitting along the length of the two oak tables turned to stare, and every voice hushed.

Genny froze in embarrassment, and stared back.

The big room was longer than it was wide, with stone walls covered by rough plaster. A huge stone fireplace yawned in one wall. Bottles and kegs lined another. The lighting was dim; nothing more than a few naked bulbs hung from the ceiling with pull chains dangling beneath them. Mismatched mugs and glasses studded the bar, and a huge polished brass samovar bubbled on one end.

A female stood next to Lubochka, and it struck Genny the two women were photographic negatives of each other. Both exuded strength of will. Both were the same height, the same age. But this new female had a tanned face, pale blond hair, and blue eyes. Where Lubochka was strong boned and strong featured, this woman was delicate, with the shape of a supermodel.

In fact—Genny looked around—none of the locals in the inn looked like Genny's idea of a stereotypical Russian. They were all tall, thin and tanned, with blond hair and blue eyes. They gawked at Genny without an ounce of delicacy; gawked as if incredulous about something.

Genny looked down at herself. Was her zipper open? She touched her upper lip. While she was asleep, had Brandon used a black felt-tipped marker to draw on a mustache?

But no. No one was smiling. Slowly, one by one, the villagers stood and retreated from the benches around the table.

Lubochka looked around at the locals and scowled. "What's wrong, Mariana?"

The supermodel lifted a pitcher off the table with the kind of competence that marked her as someone who knew her way around the barroom. With a nod

toward Genny, Mariana said, "That one will bring . . ."
She hesitated.

"Trouble . . ." The faintest whisper floated from the
back of the room.

"No!" Mariana shook her head. "Not trouble. But
change."

Genny didn't like this attention, didn't like the signs
of wide-eyed recognition from people she'd never met
before. "I, uh, am not here to change anything."

"She saw the first lynx of the year," Lubochka said.

*And the first yeti.* Genny bit her lip on the comment.

Mariana smiled, her eyes looking deeply into Genny's eyes, sending a message Genny didn't understand. "Then she has already brought luck. More is
sure to follow."

Dropping her bag on the floor, Lubochka gave
Genny a shove toward the stairs. "Go to bed."

"But I . . ." She thought she should remain down
here with the others, bond with the rest of the team.

"Are you hungry?" Lubochka asked. "No? I thought
not. So go to bed. You have first shift. Tomorrow at six,
I will take you to your observation post and you will
watch for the Ural lynx."

"Okay." Genny smiled, so exhausted and excited
her eyes filled with tremulous tears. "I can't wait."
Turning, she fled up the shadowy steps, then paused
on the landing.

A man spoke in Russian, quickly and with a local
accent that was hard for Genny to follow, but she understood one word, repeated over and over. *Trouble.*

During the ominous silence that followed, Genny

sat and, keeping to the shadows, slid down the steps far enough to see Lubochka dominating the room with her strength of will.

"You listen to me. All of you." Lubochka's voice was low and intense. "Up here, the flowers die too soon. The snow stays too late. The soldiers come and stomp around in their big boots. The big cats barely cling to existence. I bring my team to you while we track the Ural lynx. We pay you for our lodging, our food. We bring you prosperity, money until the crops come in, until you can mine the gold. I don't care what you think, what your superstitions say. Do you hear me?" She pointed, marking the villagers and the team with her attention. "You all heard what Mariana said. That girl brought us luck. Up here, we need all the luck we can get. So hear me. I want no bad blood. No strife. No unpleasantness at all."

Genny knew she was talking about her.

She just didn't understand why.

# Chapter 7

———— ❦ ————

*L*ost. In the forest. A dozen pairs of indifferent eyes watch her strive to save the world's last lynx. Darkness falls, and one pair of eyes begins to glow red . . .

The door slammed open. The light flashed on.

Sweaty and frightened, Genny jumped out of her nightmare.

"Sorry," Avni mumbled. "Dark in here."

"Not anymore." Genny pulled the thin pillow over her head.

"Sorry," Avni said again, and dragged her bag to her cot. "No head for liquor, and that vodka. . . . I'm going to be so sorry in the morning. So sorry . . ."

The attic was a whitewashed space with a single lightbulb in the middle of the low ceiling, with two narrow iron beds tucked in among boxes and trunks. Genny's lumpy mattress rested atop rusty springs— but for her tense and travel-knotted muscles, it was heaven; she'd settled in and listened and smiled as the party downstairs had grown louder and more raucous. Yet when she fell asleep, she had fallen right into that nightmare.

Avni flopped on the bed. Said, "Crap. I forgot to turn off the light."

Genny knew why she'd been dreaming about those eyes. What she'd seen today had creeped her out. Those eyes . . . were they John's eyes? And if they were, did that mean he had known she was coming?

Genny sat up on one elbow. "Listen, Avni."

Avni moaned in response.

"I want to know more about the yeti." Genny figured she could ask anything she wanted. There was a pretty good chance Avni wouldn't remember talking to her tonight.

"Can you imagine?" Avni sounded dreamy. "Days and days of such great sex that you never want another man?"

"No, I can't imagine." Genny had been busy graduating at the top of her class. She hadn't had time for sex. "Listen, I want to know—"

"How he does it. I know. Me too. I know it's weird, but Halinka said he does things with his mind." Avni gave a high-pitched giggle that sounded incongruous coming from such a tall woman.

"'He does things with his mind,'" Genny repeated, and her heart sank. She might not believe in the Chosen Ones, but evidence was building that John was extraordinary . . . in more ways than one. "What do you mean?"

"That he can move things and. . . . Listen, it's silly, really. But the people in Rasputye are so superstitious, you have no idea. It's all hooey." Avni struggled her way up onto her elbow, too, and looked drunkenly solemn and sincere. "I mean, what idiot believes in magic?"

"*You* believe that John is so good in bed, a woman never wants to sleep with another man."

Avni snorted and giggled again. "That's why Brandon hates him so much. Brandon knows no woman is ever going to moan for him. Not with that little, teeny weenie."

Genny did not want to know that—or how Avni knew. "TMI, Avni. TMI!"

Avni giggled uncontrollably, and finally managed, "You're kind of a prude, aren't you? Listen, that John . . . he's good in bed. He gives a girl what she wants. That woman I met . . . Halinka. She said there was something about him. . . . He smelled so good, she wanted to lick him all over. She said he cooked for her, massaged her, kissed her, told her she was pretty, that her body excited him. He did everything for her pleasure: spent hours touching her, going down on her, worshiping her." Avni's eyes got dreamy. "At the same time, she said, he was a *man*. You know—a *big* man." Avni gestured.

"I get it."

"She said when he was inside her, there were, like, these pulses of power . . ."

"It sounds like she was screwing a light socket."

"You're a *sarcastic* prude." Avni squinted at Genny. "Doesn't the idea of a big, hot man do anything for you?"

"A big, hot, hairy yeti?"

"Apparently he's not hairy *there*."

"How would you know that?"

"I asked!"

"Was there anything you didn't ask?"

"Hey, Halinka was more than willing to talk about it. She was telling anyone who would listen." Avni fell backward on the cot. "Which is probably why none of the men in Rasputye like John Powell. Because according to her, when her time was over, she was exhausted from coming so much. But she would do it again in a minute."

"So John Powell is crazy, and he's good in bed."

"That about sums it up." The springs squeaked noisily as Avni turned her back to the room. "Now, if you don't mind, I'm going to go to sleep and dream about . . ." Her words slurred. She snored.

Genny got up, turned off the light, then groped her way back to the bed. She knew she'd found it when she banged her toe on the steel frame.

No wonder Avni had "forgotten" the light. The moon had set, and Genny stared into a night so dark it pressed like a weight on her eyes. In the city, there was always ambient light. Here . . . everything was foreign, and she wondered what she'd done, taking this job in this strange place . . .

Why didn't the people of Rasputye like her? Why did Lubochka feel as if she had to threaten the townspeople to make them behave? How could Genny's hope of saving the world become so twisted and tangled with whispers of danger, a pagan promise of sexual ecstasy, and a pact to reason with a madman?

*Lost in the forest in the darkness, sprinting away from*

*an unseen menace only to encounter a pair of glowing red eyes. Screaming for help. Screaming for John Powell to save her. He stepped out of the woods. She ran to him. He kissed her on the mouth, on the throat . . . His hands around her waist, he lifted her, nuzzled her shirt aside . . . She closed her eyes as his mouth covered her nipple. She wrapped her legs around his waist. She held his head to her chest and whimpered in need, and whimpered as he suckled at her, then bit hard enough to make her jump. She looked down in protest . . . and screamed.*

*Because he looked up at her, and it was his eyes that glowed with that peculiar, disturbing light.*

# Chapter 8

<hr/>

*J*ohn tilted Genny backward onto the bed, reached between her legs, and slid his big hand under the waistband of her jeans. And at his touch, she came. And came. Hard. Fast. Over and over, while she whimpered and tossed, torn between fear and pleasure.

*And all the while, John watched with those glowing eyes, and he smiled . . .*

Genny's alarm went off. She grabbed it, muffled it under the covers, turned it off, lay breathing hard. She felt as if she'd been running all night.

*And coming.*

Across the low attic room, Avni scowled in her sleep.

Genny sat up quietly. She reached for her clothes, her camera, and her backpack.

*Man, that dream: equal parts terror and sex.* That stuff Avni had told her about John Powell and his carnal prowess had worked on her subconscious and . . . well, what did Genny expect?

She crept down the stairs to the bathroom. She splashed her face with the frigid water from the yellow porcelain basin, washed away memories of her nightmare. Brushed her teeth. But it wasn't as easy to wash away the taste of unwilling arousal.

She unzipped the thin outer pocket of her backpack and pulled out the photo of John Powell. She studied him—the way he stood, hands on hips, shoulders square, chin back as he laughed.

He didn't look like a yeti or a lunatic or even one of the Chosen. He looked like a nice, solid guy; the kind of guy she'd like to ask her out. In profile, she couldn't see his eyes, but someone or something had been looking at her from those bushes yesterday. Was it him?

Was he watching her with the intention of carrying her into the woods . . . ?

*Okay. Enough of that.*

She slid the photo back into the pocket and zipped it shut.

Night was over. The dreams were gone. Sunlight was turning the sky a thin, clear blue, and she let loose her slow rise of exultation.

Lubochka was taking her out to show her the ropes, and she would soon see a Ural lynx. In the wild!

She would seize every day of this trip—and would make such memories that when she sat in an office or a boardroom, she could pull them out, polish them off, and remember each gleaming moment.

She hurried down another flight of stairs to the taproom.

Lubochka and Mariana were already there, sitting at the end of the long table in front of Lubochka's computer, speaking in low voices about . . . about Genny, if the way they broke off meant anything.

She pretended not to notice.

Lubochka looked her over and nodded. "Good."

Genny felt as if she'd passed a test. Lubochka's instructions had been to wear military-style clothes— heavy cloth khakis, camouflage patterns, and boots over the ankle.

Mariana rose. "Feeling better this morning? Ready for breakfast?"

"I'm starving." Because she'd spent half the night fleeing John Powell with the glowing red eyes, and the other half the night having the best orgasms in the world. She smiled. And blushed.

Mariana's eyes narrowed as if she knew, but she said nothing more than, "Have a seat." She went into the other room and came back with a mug of black coffee and a bowl of oatmeal topped with two eggs and a thin slice of bread.

Genny pulled up the bench, looked at the food, then at Mariana. "That's a lot more than I usually eat."

"Eat it all," she advised. "Every observation point is straight up the mountain and Lubochka will work you relentlessly until someone sees the first sign of the big cats."

Lubochka grunted and typed on the keyboard in front of her. "That's what they're here for. To work."

Genny dipped her spoon into the oatmeal and found it wasn't oatmeal, but buckwheat porridge—very different, very distinctive. The eggs added a familiar flavor; the toast was rough and yeasty.

"You like it?" Mariana asked.

"It's good."

"Some . . . They complain because it's not American." Mariana indicated her opinion with a wrinkled nose.

"I've been waiting my whole life to eat different foods in a different place," Genny assured her. "This looks remarkably like my favorite English pub in SoHo."

"No. Not a pub. A *traktir*," Lubochka corrected her.

"Right." With the morning, the faded brocade curtains were pulled back from the long narrow windows to let in the light. The view looked out at street level, and now and then a pair of leather-laced boots tromped past.

With a well-honed knife, Mariana cut a loaf of the dark bread into hearty slabs. "In Rasputye, we are still mostly farmers. We found it was not good to depend on the state for support. We are very far from Moscow. We are not ethnic Russians. And in times of trouble, we are easy to forget."

"Is that why . . . ?" Genny waved at the corner where Orthodox icons—traditional paintings of saints done on wood and canvas—hung on the wall over a table draped in a red cloth where white candles burned.

Genny knew the *krasnyi ugol*, the beautiful corner, held the place of honor in every Russian home. There families kept all that was holy to them, placed on a table covered with a red cloth or on walls painted with red paint. Genny's studies had told her that the Soviets had replaced those gilded icons with newspapers and portraits of war heroes, yet in Rasputye the *krasnyi ugol* looked as it had for a millennium.

Mariana followed Genny's gaze. "Here, we have kept to the old beliefs. No one from the government has ever had the strength to live through our winters long enough to enforce the party's orders."

"Saints. Icons. Superstitious nonsense," Lubochka grumbled.

"It is not superstition to seek protection from those who would harm us." Mariana's voice was soft but firm.

"There's nothing out there but some hungry animals and Mother Nature, and a few paintings of saints won't save you from those," Lubochka retorted.

"It is not nature which we fear." As if she feared she had revealed too much, Mariana glanced uneasily at Genny.

"As I said—superstitious nonsense," Lubochka repeated.

Genny looked between them. This sounded like an old argument with no heat behind it, yet clearly the weirdness of last night lingered.

Mariana poured Lubochka more coffee, and Genny nodded when Mariana offered her another cup.

"No!" Lubochka pulled the cup away. "Don't drink. I want you watching for lynx, not hanging your rear end over a log."

Genny thought about pointing out the perils of dehydration, or explaining that caffeine was her addiction and her golden door to consciousness, or that her personal habits were not Lubochka's concern. Instead, mildly, she said, "Actually, I have the bladder of a camel."

"I know camels drink and hold water, but do they

also retain that water? I suppose they must." Lubochka did not crack a smile.

Mariana and Genny both muffled theirs.

"Very good." Lubochka nodded and shut down the computer. "You may take fluid with you." She covered the monitor with a cloth, then told Mariana, "Let no one touch this except Misha."

"I know." Clearly Mariana had heard it before.

"Genesis, are you ready?" Lubochka asked.

Genny was not, but she took the none-too-subtle hint and polished off her porridge.

As soon as she put down her spoon, Lubochka stood. "Let's go."

Mariana stuffed bread and cheese and a battered canteen of tea into Genny's backpack. "If you don't mind, Lubochka, I'll walk with you this morning."

Clearly, Lubochka did mind. She frowned. "I thought you had an inn to run."

"After last night, no one will be awake for hours."

"These foreigners cannot hold their vodka," Lubochka said.

Genny grinned.

"Yes, Genesis, you smile." Lubochka stalked toward the stairs that led up to the door; impatience showed clear in every line of her big-boned figure. "You're the smart one. You abstained. When I come back, I will kick their feeble *zhopayee* out of bed and they'll vomit all day, and my big cats will laugh at the foolish humans."

# Chapter 9

———◆———

It was spring, but here in the north of Russia, the air outside was bright and cold; Genny could see her breath. The morning sun shone on the treetops but had not yet reached the hamlet square. As Genny donned her ankle-length quilted down parka, Lubochka and Mariana, in shorts and long-sleeved canvas shirts, shook their heads as if she were odd.

They left the inn. With Genny and Mariana on her heels, Lubochka headed toward the narrow road that led out of the hamlet.

Rasputye was stirring. A few men stood on their doorsteps, scratching themselves and staring.

Genny stared back.

Her first impression was correct. They were tanned and blond, beautiful people with blue eyes and sturdy frames. They weren't Komi, the native people who inhabited the area. Perhaps the Vikings had raided this part of Russia and sown some wild oats?

She nodded to one of the men.

He stared hard, and then, as if he were daring, nodded back.

His wife stepped out of the house, placed herself between her husband and Genny, shoved him into the house, and without turning her back, sidled in and shut the door.

They left the last houses behind. The road rose steeply beneath their feet.

"Wow. Friendly people you've got here." But Genny remembered the noise of the party downstairs last night. They had seemed friendly enough after she'd gone upstairs. After Lubochka had threatened them, and told them she didn't want to hear any more whispers of . . . *trouble*.

"Don't pay any attention to them," Mariana said. "They're afraid."

"Of what? Me?" Genny tried to laugh, then choked it back. "Of *me*? Why?"

"You have a look about you that we're all too familiar with here. You look . . . gifted."

Genny almost wrenched her neck turning to stare at Mariana. "What do you mean, *gifted*?"

"There's an old legend . . ." Mariana rubbed her arms as if cold had suddenly gripped her.

"You are foolish, Mariana," Lubochka called back, and sternly. "Don't encourage her, Genesis."

But Genny had to know. "A legend? *The* legend? About the Abandoned Ones?"

"You know it?" Now Mariana looked surprised.

"I do. But why do *you*?"

Lubochka turned off the road. Genny and Mariana followed. The coniferous forest closed in around them.

Mariana gestured widely. "It happened here."

"The legend happened here? No." Perhaps Genny shouldn't so openly scoff. But . . . "It's a *legend*."

"All legends contain a grain of truth. All myths have their beginnings somewhere." Mariana stated a truth she obviously believed with all her heart. "Look around."

Genny did. The forest was cool and smelled spicy with pine. The mossy ground sprang softly beneath their feet. The air grew warmer and, here and there, sunlight glowed like a benediction through the branches.

Peeling off her coat, she stuffed it in the outer pocket of her backpack, then kept trekking. "Yeah. So?"

"This forest was old when the Egyptians built the pyramids," Mariana said.

Genny remembered her feeling yesterday—that the forest was ancient, a living, breathing entity. And it seemed to watch insignificant humans come and go while it waited for a time when the trees would once more cover the earth . . .

"Men come to harvest the trees. They bring their machines. They go into the woods . . . and they don't come back. Or if they do, they've got the wind singing in the empty spaces of their heads." Mariana tapped her forehead.

*They're not the only ones.* This woman was one taco short of a combo plate.

Mariana continued so solemnly, she should be making sense. "Gods walk in these woods, and devils.

Good and bad, all manner of creatures came into the world through this portal."

"Portal?"

"The crossroads is here."

Lubochka marched farther and farther ahead, fallen branches cracking beneath her hiking boots, leaving Genny alone with Mariana and a bunch of trees that listened and nodded.

Genny sped up. "I don't know what any of this has got to do with me."

Mariana's long strides easily kept up the pace. "You had dreams last night, didn't you? Nightmares."

Mariana's certainty set Genny's teeth on edge. "Nothing special, just the usual. Going to the new high school and taking a test I didn't know about. Going to a law conference, getting up to speak and realizing I forgot my speech. Seeing my mother on the street and . . ." She reined herself in. *Seeing my mother on the street and knowing that she would, once again, look right through me as if she didn't know me.*

She didn't mention the nightmare with the eyes that watched her from the depths of the dark forest, or the fantasy—so erotic that again she blushed and hoped that Mariana attributed the color to the exercise in the cool air.

"In the legend," Mariana said, "the mother abandoned the girl baby because she had marks in her palms . . ."

"They looked like eyes." That part of the story always sent a shiver up Genny's spine.

"Yes. Eyes. And when the girl grew up, she looked witchy."

"Witchy. Are you saying I look like the girl? That I look witchy?" Genny was feeling exasperated. Frazzled.

"She was beautiful—"

"Men manage to resist me pretty easily."

"—with an oval face and a dimple just there—" Mariana pointed.

Genny put her finger to the cleft in her chin.

"Exactly." Mariana nodded. "She had an abundance of dark brown curly hair, like yours, and eyes that looked brown. And when she grew angry or excited, gleamed like gold. Beautiful skin. Strong body. And a malevolence that went right to the bone."

Genny stopped walking. "I am not malevolent." She pulled her hands from her pockets and showed Mariana her palms. "I am not marked. I'm certainly not gifted."

"Yes, I see." Mariana stopped, too, and observed her. "Your parents are alive."

"Very much so."

"But I wonder . . . if your mother properly cherished you."

Genny's throat didn't close. Not quite. But she coughed slightly before she could speak, then waved her hand around at the cool, dimly lit trees. "She didn't take me into the woods and throw me into a stream."

No. Instead, when Genny was in college, she worked up her nerve and went to visit her mother. Mother had remarried a wealthy man, of course, but she was still remote, still beautiful; and when her new husband came in, she told him, "Genny's applying for a job as my social secretary." Then to Genny, "I'll let you know my decision in about a week."

No, her mother hadn't tried to kill her. She didn't care enough to bother.

"Look." Genny's voice rose. "Is this some kind of initiation ritual? Because I'm not buying it. Somehow you found out who my father is, right? You made up all this stuff about the legend and now you're ... you're trying to scare the newbie for some weird reason."

The bushes crackled as Lubochka came stomping back, scowling heavily.

Genny turned on her. "Maybe you're in on the joke. Maybe this is how you get rid of unwanted, untrained assistants. But it's too late for that. The fee has been paid, and I promised my *soul* for a chance to observe the lynx in the wild. So I don't want to hear anything else about this legend and the forest and the ... the crossroads"—she turned back to Mariana—"whatever you mean by that."

Lubochka dismissed Genny's tantrum with a characteristic snort. "Girl, if I wanted you gone, you would go with my teeth snapping at your heels."

Genny almost collapsed in relief. She should have known. Lubochka was too straightforward for such a ruse.

Lubochka fixed her attention on Mariana. "Why are you doing this? Trying to frighten the girl? Was the winter too long? Have you lost your mind?"

"I am fine, thank you." Mariana looked earnest and normal. "I'm trying to warn her."

"Warn her of *what*?"

"We have a long memory here." Mariana looked between Genny and Lubochka. "We know she's ... bait."

# Chapter 10

—◆❖◆—

"**W**hat?" Genny couldn't believe what she was hearing.

"She is bait?" Lubochka sounded just as incredulous.

"My English fails me sometimes. Maybe *bait* is too strong a word. But women like you"—Mariana gestured at Genny—"you bring them."

Lubochka leaned forward, eye to eye with Mariana. "*Who* does she bring?"

"The ones who seek evil. The ones who seek innocence, who would corrupt you." Mariana pushed her hair off her forehead. "Of course you had to come here. The crossroads draws you. But I wish you would go home."

"Well, I'm not going to!" The big cats were waiting.

"Did you not hear me last night?" Lubochka demanded. "I said *no trouble!*"

Back at the inn, Genny had liked Mariana. Now she

just thought she was insane. "I mean, if we're going to be superstitious . . . you did say I would bring luck!"

"I said you would bring change," Mariana corrected.

"And luck!" Genny reminded her.

"Rasputye could use some change," Lubochka said.

"The earth shakes when Rasputye changes!" Mariana spread her hands, palms up. "All the elements have lined up!"

"What elements?" Lubochka asked.

"The gifted one has returned. He is angry, like a wounded bear."

That face in the woods . . . it haunted Genny. The man, whoever he was, had looked at her as if she was a vision . . . or a curse.

"He finds the lonely women, the ones dissatisfied with their lives, and he shows them a new world. And now *you*"—Mariana pointed accusingly at Genny— "you come along. You're trapped by life."

"What?" Genny vibrated with outrage.

Mariana continued. "You're lonely. You seek something new, and he'll know. You're *bait*."

"*I am not bait.*"

"Go home, Mariana." Lubochka drew herself up to her full height. "Go home and cook, and from now on, listen to me. *No trouble.*"

Mariana strode down the hill, then turned one last time and said, "I suppose it is your fate, Genesis Valente, to be here now, but you have been warned. Don't weep when the whole world catches fire and you're swept up in the blaze!" Before Lubochka or Genny could respond, Mariana leaped like a mountain goat down the hill.

Lubochka shook her head. "Of course she had to have the last word."

"Is she crazy?" Genny thought she had to be.

"No. Well." Lubochka waggled her hand back and forth. "Not crazy, for one of her people. They aren't Russians. Not ethnically. They're backward. Gullible. They believe in *myths*."

"Legends," Genny corrected.

"In English you would call that splitting hairs."

The rocky trail grew narrower, curved back and forth like a snake, and climbed at such a pitch that Genny puffed with exertion.

Lubochka, of course, did not puff, and she frowned at Genny. "Your application said you were in prime condition."

"I didn't practice walking uphill with weight on my back."

"You'll know better next time." Lubochka continued up the mountain. "Mariana is fancied to be the wise woman in her village, blessed with the gift of foresight. For that reason, she was sent away to Moscow and educated. I thought that would connect her to the real world, but apparently such a hope was futile."

"Apparently." Genny took care to keep her gasping to a minimum.

"Usually it suits me to use their beliefs. They tell me the Ural lynx has been hiding in the *rasputye* all these years."

Confused, Genny asked, "In Rasputye? In the town?"

"In *the rasputye*. The crossroads. Don't you know? That's what *rasputye* means."

"I didn't realize." No matter how Genny turned the words around in her mind, they didn't make sense. "Why is that important?"

"Ah. Here we are." Lubochka stopped abruptly. Waved an arm.

Genny pulled herself up the last few steps, then gaped in awe. She stood beside Lubochka at the top of a cliff, a hundred feet over a broad, snaking riverbed. A sparkling green river wound its way through the sand. Beyond that, the mountains built again, the forest grew green all the way to the Arctic Circle, and in the distance, a series of mighty, jagged rocks protruded from among some of the oldest trees in the world.

"The Ural Mountains. The Great Stone Belt. The spine, and the division, of Mother Russia." Lubochka's voice became more accented, more Russian, more proud. "In the streams and in the mines, miners find topaz and beryl. They strip gold from the soil. Here live the reindeer, the sable, the mink, and the hare. And my cats."

The vista held Genny enthralled. Those jagged rocks were so . . . weird. So out of place "What are those?" She waved a hand.

"The Seven Devils—seven stones that rise out of the ground like huge male erections."

Genny chuckled. "Yeah, most men would like to think that."

Lubochka boomed out a laugh; then her face soured. "Mariana would tell you they're the doorway to the *rasputye*. Which is one more proof that everyone in this region are fools."

Remembering Mariana and her weird warning, Genny said, "I can't argue with that." The rock oddities fascinated her, drew her gaze like magnets. "The Seven Devils are some kind of igneous intrusions?"

"I don't know." Lubochka shrugged. "I'm a wildlife biologist, not a geologist." She looked impatient and irritated. "Genesis."

"What?"

"Okay, listen. Really, I think it's all nonsense. But that man that's out there, the yeti Brandon worked so hard to frighten you about—" Lubochka stopped.

"What is it?" Genny had not thought this woman could ever be indecisive, but she was dithering now.

"Everyone in Rasputye keeps saying this yeti is one of the Chosen Ones."

Genny nodded encouragingly.

"Mariana tells me the Chosen Ones bring danger to everyone around them. She's constantly harping at me, at the rest of the village, that wherever the Chosen are, trouble follows. It's silliness, but in Rasputye, they *believe*—and she's a powerful woman. For some reason, she's decided you're some kind of Chosen magnet."

"Because I have a cleft in my chin," Genny told her helpfully.

Lubochka said something in Russian that sounded incredibly profane.

Genny grinned.

Lubochka did not. "For the sake of this study, for the sake of the cats, don't give her any reason to think that you are extraordinary in any way."

"I won't," Genny assured her.

"It goes without saying—have nothing to do with the yeti. But I don't have to say that. You're a sensible girl. You'll stay away from that murdering, lustful goat."

It was Genny's turn to say nothing. Well, what could she say? That she was only here *because* she'd promised she would talk to the murdering, lustful goat?

"I'm glad we've had this talk." Lubochka pointed down the cliff. "There's your station."

Genny looked.

Ten feet down, a gaggle of warped and twisted pines clung to the sheer rock wall. They grew sideways into the air, their branches intertwined; they swayed softly to the unheard music of the breeze rushing up from the riverbed below.

Someone had constructed a ladder, short lengths of heavy board fastened into the stone leading down to the largest trunk. From there, a person—if she was limber, blessed with great balance, and had absolutely no common sense—could crawl out on the tree trunk to a small wooden platform built among the branches. And that person would have an unsurpassed view of the forest floor and the stream that trickled along the flat, winding riverbed below.

"The lynx are nocturnal animals, but right now the females are nursing and caring for their babies and will sometimes, in the early morning or at twilight, bring the kittens out. This is a wonderful chance for you, Genesis, to see the great cats in the wild. Watch for movement. Then take pictures. Lots of pictures."

Genny lifted her camera from the padded pocket of

her backpack. It had been frighteningly expensive, the thing she had splurged on for the trip. "It also takes video."

"Good!" Lubochka clapped her on the shoulder. "Go on, then. You aren't afraid of heights, are you?"

"No." Not on a normal basis. But this . . . the platform was perhaps four by four and had no rail.

"Good. Brandon will relieve you in ten hours. Until then, watch carefully." Lubochka clomped off into the forest.

Genny started the precarious climb down to her station.

# *Chapter 11*

———◆◇◆———

*Someone was watching her. Again.*

She had spent a week on this platform in this tree hanging over the edge of the cliff. She had seen seven glorious dawns break over the horizon. She had observed foxes scampering cautiously, elk strolling majestically, brown bears standing in the icy river to fish. She'd thrilled to the drama of a snowy owl capturing its last meal, of the waning night, and felt her heart lift as she viewed two eagles swoop and tumble across the clear morning sky. Once a light snow had fallen on her. More than once, the wind had shaken the tree so hard, she'd worried for her life.

But she still hadn't seen a Ural lynx. She had watched until her eyes were dry, with no luck.

Whoever was watching *her* had given her no sign. She knew he stalked her, just as she knew that, in the depths of the forest, the lynx hunted in their established territories. She didn't have to see to believe.

She trusted her instincts. Yet nothing could make her give up.

Although someone manned this site and three others, the big cats had been elusive. Every night, Misha and Lubochka assured the team they had found signs—fresh dung, tufts of hair stuck to a bush. Reggie watched every moment of video taken on the paths where the lynx roamed. Thorsen reminisced about the first year he'd come along on Lubochka's study, when they went a month without a sighting.

But everyone was edgy. Only Brandon openly grumbled about Genny—as if she herself had promised to bring them luck.

Mariana was right about one thing. Rasputye's atmosphere worked on a person because someone had been watching Genny. *Was watching right now.*

The early-morning breeze ruffled her hair and dove down her neck.

She ducked her head, wrapped her arms around her knees, huddled into her coat, and wished she could relax her tense muscles.

The unexpected, shrill ring of a phone made her jump.

Her phone. In the side pocket of her backpack. It hadn't rung all week. She had sort of thought she couldn't get service out here. Sort of *hoped* she couldn't get service out here. Now the sound was loud, shrill, out of place in this wilderness.

She scrambled for it, silenced the ring, glanced at caller ID and tensed.

Closing her eyes, she braced herself, then answered

with modulated serenity. "Hi, how are things in New York?"

"Have you found him yet?" Her father's voice came through clear, cold, and direct.

"Hello to you, too, Father."

"Hello. Hello! Is there a problem with the connection?" His voice cut out on the last word.

"Apparently a little problem." But not enough to break the call. "No, I haven't found him yet. I've only been here a week."

"These people aren't going to wait forever."

"These people? The Gypsy Travel Agency, you mean?"

A pause.

*Had* they lost the connection?

Then his voice came through too loud. "Yeah, yeah."

She held the phone away from her ear, then cautiously brought it back. "You worked for them, and you've said a lot of nasty things about them, but you never told me they were tyrants. Surely they understand that I need time to adjust to a new country and a new job—"

"For God's sake, Genny, would you just go out and find him? How many times have I told you that if you want to get ahead in this world, you need to seize the initiative, go beyond what's expected, and make them—"

"Sit up and take notice. I know." She took a breath. "But I don't care whether they sit up and take notice. I don't even really care whether they forgive the school loan. I told you. I can pay it back."

"And I told you I promised you'd do this small favor for them. How hard can it be? How many John Powells can there be in Russia?"

She decided to give him something to settle him down. "I confirmed it. John Powell is in the area."

"What are you—" The connection dropped.

For a moment, she heard only crackling and she hoped—

But no. Father was back, still talking. "Go get him!"

"I'm *working* here."

"You have time off, don't you?"

"When I'm not observing, I'm studying."

"Studying what?" He sounded incredulous.

"Lubochka has collected a lot of fascinating material on the Ural lynx for analyzing their movements, their social and feeding habits . . ." Genny's enthusiasm began to rise. "In the evening, I—"

"What good does it do you to study the Ural lynx?" Through the crackling on the line, Father's cold tenacity sounded loud and clear. "You're only there for the summer."

"I enjoy it." She clipped off the words.

He must have heard her irritation, for he changed his tactics, became the negotiator, concerned and persuasive. "You just graduated with a business degree. I'd think you would be tired of studying."

"Of studying business, yes."

"Look. Finding Powell is not a big deal. It's merely a favor."

"It seems to be a very big deal." *Such a big deal you can't even ask me how I am.* "I intend to take care of the matter. Trust me, Father, I don't lie or make deals I don't intend to keep." *Nor do I steal.*

Perhaps he heard her unspoken thought. More likely he decided he had made his point. Or maybe he had somewhere to go, because he said, "Okay, let me know when you make contact and how negotiations go. I'd like to give them good news as soon as possible."

"I know."

"Enjoy your graduation present!"

"I will. I am."

But the connection was dead.

How like him to make sure he reminded her that he had given her this trip, and cut her off before she could remind him in turn that she was paying for it by doing this "favor" for him.

Her father wasn't worth all the angst and anguish. She knew it. But her mother had never cared about her. Her grandparents were dead. He was her father, and she wanted one person to care about her, if only he knew how . . .

According to her college roommate, it wasn't Genny's fault her family was a failure. According to Chloe, parents were the grown-ups, and they were supposed to act responsibly. A mother wasn't supposed to give birth to a child and wander away when that child got inconvenient. A father wasn't supposed to use his child to repair his financial fortunes.

Genny knew all that was true, too.

Chloe said it was a tribute to Genny's strength of character that she had turned out to be a well-adjusted human. Chloe said Genny should talk to a therapist, move beyond the childhood fear of being alone, and stop letting her father use her.

Sitting here, miserable in the Russian wilderness, with nothing to distract her . . . well, she had to face the fact Kevin Valente seemed incapable of loving her. Incapable of maturity, for that matter.

Genny wondered what Chloe would say about this creepy sensation of being watched. Probably that the eyes she'd seen beside the road hadn't been real and that the long hours alone or Mariana's dire warnings were preying on her nerves. Certainly no one would tell her that her dreams were coming true and John Powell was watching her with the intention of dragging her to his hut for days and nights of sex.

She shrugged her shoulders, trying to rid herself of the sense of being observed—and a movement far below caught her attention. Some creature prowled low to the ground, its hind end lifted and its gaze intent.

Probably a sable. Every time Genny had seen movement down there and thought she had spotted the lynx, she'd always been disappointed . . .

But no matter how discouraging she tried to be, her heart thumped with anticipation.

*Maybe this was it.*

She got up on her knees. Groped for the camera. Hung the strap around her neck. Lifted it to her eyes. She adjusted the lens, zooming in on the animal that slipped from tree stump to rock.

This creature looked large and moved like a . . . like a cat.

She focused, and there it was—a Ural lynx stalking its prey along the riverbed.

She had it. *She had it!*

The creature slipped from rock to fallen log—beautiful, sleek, brown and black and gold.

Genny shot photos in a frenzy, video first, then stills.

The lynx moved in and out of sight under the cover of brush.

Genny crawled back and forth on her platform, straining to keep the animal in sight.

The cat pounced on some small creature, looking so much like a house cat that Genny's eyes filled with pleasurable tears. Sliding face-first out along the heaviest branch, she extended one leg onto the branch on the next tree, and snapped the best photos of her life. When the cat continued down the riverbed, prey in her mouth, and vanished beneath the cover of the brush, Genny adjusted herself in small increments to hang over the clear space. She held the camera in one hand and waited for the lynx to reappear.

It did. She madly clicked the shutter.

And while she exulted in the beauty of the elusive animal, a gust of wind caught her, yanking the tree away from under her extended leg—and she dangled a hundred feet in the air, one elbow curled over one branch and a knee hooked over another branch.

The camera fell from her hand, catching at the end of the strap and jerking her neck, making the whole tree dip.

She froze, her muscles rigid; the trees swayed in the breeze.

Pine needles dropped in a shower into her hair, onto her face, and she watched in horror as they twirled down, landed on hard gray rocks that protruded from the cliff thirty feet down, then tumbled all the way to the ground.

"Oh, God." She prayed automatically, fervently, fearing death for so many reasons. "Oh, God. Please, God." She swung her free hand onto the branch. The ridged bark dug into her palm.

The wind blew harder, whipping the trees from side to side.

She swayed like a fragile, out-of-season Christmas ornament ready to fall. She hitched herself up. Paused and tightened her grip. Hitched herself up again.

The breeze rippled through the treetops below. The forest bent like dancers, dipping and swaying to a deadly rhythm.

Always before, she had loved the music of the wind in the branches, but now the notes grew louder, more threatening.

Would they be the last thing she ever heard?

A deep male voice said, "Give me your hand."

She started, glanced up to the platform, and there he was, the yeti, the madman, the lover, the bearded beast of Brandon's warnings—and her savior.

Then the wind slammed into the trees, shaking her loose.

And she fell.

# Chapter 12

———◆❖◆———

G enny screamed.

Something caught her around the waist, the chest, the legs. Lifted her and slammed her onto her stomach on the viewing platform. She gasped, the breath driven out of her by the impact . . . and by shock and terror.

The man leaned over her. "Are you all right?"

"Yes!" Frantic, she tried to lift herself on her hands.

He pressed her back down. "Take it easy."

She couldn't take it easy. If he hadn't been there . . . if he hadn't acted . . . She rolled over, struggled to sit up. "How did you do that? How did you . . . ? I was *falling*. And you caught me!"

He stood over her, his boots planted firmly on the swaying platform. "I'm a big man."

She looked up. And up.

He *was* a big man, probably six four or five and over two hundred pounds, bulky across the shoulders, slender at the waist, with long legs and massive hands clad in leather gloves. A black, unkempt beard covered his chin and cheeks and grew down to his chest, and lank dreadlocks hung from beneath the worn cowboy hat he pulled low over his eyes.

She had the snapshot Father had given her, but this wasn't John Powell. This wasn't the assured, laughing military man of his picture. This guy couldn't look her in the eyes. Instead, he stared out at the horizon as if fascinated by the view.

As she watched, his fingers flexed slowly.

Brandon said their yeti was insane, suffering from PTSD or worse.

*Yeah. Maybe.*

Avni said he was a sexual being of unparalleled passion.

And Genny's subconscious had built on that claim.

If he truly had a gift, she hoped it wasn't mind reading, because her thoughts had taken the terror of falling, combined it with her rescue by a big, muscled beast, and she was breathing hard for all the wrong reasons.

"Are you all right?" he asked again. He sounded perfectly normal; American with the slightest hint of a Russian accent.

"Yes. Of course." She swallowed and tried to calm her unruly heartbeat. "Why wouldn't I be?"

"You landed hard."

"The coat is well padded."

"How about your face?"

She explored with her fingers. Her cheek throbbed,

right over the bone. "Well. Compared to what might have happened . . ." She rubbed her bruised chest, then realized . . . she'd landed on her camera.

With a gasp of horror, she grabbed it, looked at the view screen, and flipped through the pictures.

They were fine. Better than fine. They were fabulous. The great cat moved through the photos with beauty and grace.

With a sigh of relief, she took the strap off her neck and tenderly stowed the camera in her case in the backpack.

John stood unmoving, paying her no apparent attention, yet she thought he was aware of her every movement. And he had saved her, saved her camera, saved the photos . . .

She placed the flat of her palm on his calf right above his boot.

He looked down as if her touch startled him.

She jumped, as startled as he, for his eyes were the bleak pale blue of glacial ice. She'd never seen eyes of such a color, frozen and still, without emotion or feeling.

Her fingers tightened on the tanned leather of his pants.

This man had a reputation as a lover?

*No. Impossible.*

She had dreamed about him?

*Foolish.*

A man with eyes like that could kill her with efficiency and indifference.

Instead, he had saved her life. If not for him, she'd

be shattered on the rocks below, swept away by the river; and before her body was discovered, she would be food for the carrion birds.

He was frightening. But she owed him.

"Well?" he asked harshly.

"Thank you," she whispered, still held in place by the chill of those eyes.

"What?"

More loudly, she said, "Thank you for rescuing me."

He stared at her, those peculiar eyes growing a deeper blue—and more wary. "Fine."

"If there's ever anything I can do for you . . ." Her voice trailed off, and once again she was aware of him, of the warmth of his leg beneath her palm, of the compelling masculinity that drew her against her will.

She'd never thought she was dumb enough to be attracted to a dangerous man.

Obviously, she'd simply never met one before.

One thing Brandon had gotten right. This guy really did look as if a sheepskin factory had exploded all over him. Or maybe goat, or rabbit, or deer—she was a city girl. She didn't know. She only knew he wore skins sewn with primitive leather cords like some kind of Russian Daniel Boone.

"Are you sure you're not hurt?"

"Quite sure."

"In the future, be more careful." He turned, pulling out of her grip, walked with perfect balance across the tree trunk and climbed the ladder toward the top of the cliff.

She gaped at his retreating back, then realized—that

was it. He was leaving. Just like that. She hadn't confirmed his identity, whether he was John Powell.

And she sure couldn't ask anyone in Rasputye where he lived so she could go talk to him. She could only imagine what Brandon would say if she asked, or how Mariana would react.

In return for this opportunity to live her dream, she had promised to talk to John, to convince him to return to New York, and this was her break—if that bearded monstrosity was truly him.

Using her backpack as support, she got up on one knee, then the other, then one foot, then the other. Bruises made themselves felt, and as her ribs complained, she groaned softly.

But she hadn't much time. Mr. Yeti had dragged himself over the edge of the cliff, and with his long strides, he would be quickly out of sight.

The wind dragged at the platform, tilting the corner toward the ground.

She panicked, leaping toward the ladder, catching one of the steps in a death grip. She steadied herself, struggled into the backpack, and then climbed as fast as she could up the cliff and onto solid ground.

He was gone.

# Chapter 13

———⟨※⟩———

Genny ran down the path, looking from side to side, and when it took the kink toward the village, she ran the other way. The path here was narrower, the brush closer and less disturbed, and it cut level across the mountain. When she saw the branches swinging back and forth, she knew she was on the right track. She caught sight of John striding ahead of her. He heard her coming; she knew he did, because he picked up speed.

Like that was going to discourage her? He didn't know her at all.

She scampered around a tree and leaped in front of him. "We didn't have a chance to introduce ourselves. I'm Genny Valente." She stuck out her hand.

He ignored it, ignored *her*, and walked around her and kept going. Fast.

She had to skip to keep up. "You're John Powell, aren't you?"

That made him glance at her, those odd blue eyes hard and cool. "How do you know that?"

*It was him.* She had been pretty sure, but to have him confirm it . . . what a relief.

"They talk down there." She gestured toward Rasputye and comforted herself it wasn't a lie. They *did* talk down there. "Thank you, John. You saved my life."

"You already said that."

"I think it's a big deal."

"You would."

"I was wondering how you knew I was in trouble."

He didn't increase his speed, but he didn't answer, either.

"Because since I've been here, I've had this weird feeling someone was watching me."

"Do you always tag along like a yellow Lab?" Which was an answer in itself.

"I'd prefer to walk, but you won't slow down." She didn't wait for the next crushing reply, but plowed on. "Where are you from? You speak English like an American, but I hear a little accent."

"What kind of accent?"

"You sound like the people around here. The people in Rasputye."

His facial expression didn't change. "I've been here two years."

That wasn't an answer, and they both knew it.

So they were both being evasive. And they were both good at it.

"I'm from New York City." She sort of enjoyed the repartee.

The path narrowed.

He strode on.

She fell behind and spoke to his broad back. "Have you been to New York City?"

"I lived there once."

"I'm from the Bronx."

He pushed a branch out of his way, then let it flip back at her.

She ducked, said, "If you're trying to get rid of me, *that* kind of rudeness will never work."

"Why not?"

"I already told you. I'm from New York." She heard a deep strangling noise from him, and smirked at the back of his head. So he had a sense of humor, or at least he had had once. "Which part of the city did you live in?"

"SoHo. Why are you here?"

"Because I've always wanted to be a wildlife observer and my father gave me this trip as a graduation gift."

"That's not true."

Her heart leaped to her throat. He knew why she was following him. He knew the promise she'd made to her father. *How* did he know? "What do you mean?"

"No one comes to Rasputye for so pure a reason."

The best defense was a good attack. "Then why are *you* here?"

He plunged ahead. "I lived here. When I was a boy."

"You grew up here?"

"Sometimes."

That did it. She grabbed at the hem of his leather shirt and held on, and skied along behind him through the pine needles.

He turned on her so suddenly, she staggered.

He caught her arm.

Although his grip wasn't painful, in their joined flesh she felt a pulse of . . . of emotion. Not lust. He didn't feel lust for her. Or if he did, it was muted by grief, pain, loneliness.

The shared feeling was so great tears welled in her eyes. She put her hand over his. "What is it? Why are you so sad?"

"I'm not sad." He released her, and the sensation was gone. "Look. I'm the yeti everyone warned you about. I live alone. I eat rats raw. I capture innocent women and use them for my own pleasure. I'm crazy."

"Are you trying to scare me?"

His eyes narrowed on her as if trying to comprehend the incomprehensible. "Apparently not." He walked on.

She followed. "Because if you are, you shouldn't have saved my life."

"That makes no sense. If I hadn't saved your life, you'd be dead. I couldn't scare you."

"It seems like a lot of effort to scare someone."

He grunted.

She felt more cheerful. If she had driven him back to speechlessness, then she'd won that round. Now to win another. "You're an orphan." Or he was if the legend was true, for Father said John was Chosen, and the legend had been quite specific—the Chosen Ones were abandoned as infants.

She didn't believe in the legend, in any legend. *Lord of the Rings* was a great book, but it was only a book. The sensations which John had passed to her were figments of her imagination. Yet she held her breath, waiting for his answer.

"A boat on its last trip before the Kara Sea froze found a newborn floating on an ice floe. The ice formed my shroud; the fishermen thought I was dead."

"I don't believe it!"

He misunderstood, of course. He didn't realize that the story he was telling paralleled the legend she so longed to discount.

He stopped, and turned to face her. "Such circumstances aren't unique to me."

"No kidding."

"There are other instances of an infant surviving a drowning in cold water, unharmed."

"All right. That's true." She had heard of babies shutting down and living through such trauma. But that didn't disprove the legend of the Chosen Ones. Quite the opposite. "What happened next?"

"The crew put me in the captain's quarters. They intended to bury me when they got to land. But the ice melted. I woke and squalled. They fed me milk and fish they chewed for me. I lived." John spoke in short bursts, as if the effort of so much speech exhausted him. "One of the fishermen lived in Rasputye. Olik brought me back to his wife."

"So you *did* grow up here!"

"In the winters. In the summers . . . no." He started walking again.

Now she understood why he knew the area so well. But did she believe he was one of the Chosen? Did she believe in the legend?

To do so would be ridiculous. And yet . . . surely

what he had said and what she had felt bore testament to the myth?

"In the summers, did you work on the fishing vessel?" Her eyes grew round as she tried to imagine him as a little boy on a boat in the frigid Kara Sea.

"No. What was so important that you had to risk your life to take those pictures?" Subtle he was not. He wanted to change the subject, and he had.

A small, resilient bubble of excitement worked its way up through her residual fear, her anxiety of tracking John Powell, and the exertion of keeping up with him. "I've been watching for the Ural lynx, and it was my first sighting. Or rather, almost my first sighting."

He grunted.

"I know!" She laughed a little. "There was a lynx on the road, and that was beyond cool. But nothing since. Nothing. Not for the whole team. So far, this year hasn't been nearly as successful as anyone was hoping."

Certainly not as successful as her father had hoped.

Her mouth drooped. If she let him, her father's rancor would ruin this summer for her.

The path split and John swerved away, taking the narrower trail, down the hill, leaving her headed in the wrong direction.

Not for long. She jumped a fallen log, slipped on the pine needles, and sprawled across the trail in front of him.

He stopped. Sighed. Grabbed her arm, lifted her and set her on her feet.

He was right. He was a big man, strong and hearty. And she'd followed him into the woods. They were alone. From her father, she'd learned John had a problem with his gift. Since she'd arrived here, she'd learned he had a reputation as a soldier who suffered PTSD, that he captured women to use them for sexual purposes.

True, to her he seemed normal, if normal included wearing skins and dreadlocks and having extremely pale blue eyes. But really, how many times had she heard the neighbors say to the press, *I had no idea he was a serial killer. He seemed so ordinary!*

Maybe she should rethink this.

Then he spoke the magic words. "You want to see the Ural lynx."

She nodded.

"Then come on." He let her go. He started off down the path again.

She stood in place. "What do you mean, *come on*?"

"I mean—I know where Mama Cat has hidden her kittens."

# Chapter 14

❦

John didn't know why he was bothering to lead Genesis to the big cats.

He didn't know why he let her follow him.

He didn't know why he watched her every day . . . except that he couldn't seem to stop. He couldn't believe she was for real. He scrutinized her, waiting for her to yell, to swear, to complain about the rough conditions or the boredom so much a part of a wildlife observer's job.

Instead, when she thought no one was watching, she skipped through the forest. She sang songs from movies like *The Sound of Music* and *Annie*, and she sang like she believed them. She watched an eagle fly, spread her arms and pretended to soar on the breeze. When the wind blew, she closed her eyes, lifted her face to the sun—and he would have sworn she was silently worshiping the day, the place, the joy.

She seemed almost frantic to absorb the essence of the mountains and the woods.

He hated that.

Because he wanted her, and everything she did made him want her more. He craved her the way a drowning man craved oxygen.

He couldn't have her. Because what he felt when he looked at her was a passionate fascination, a longing and a need.

He didn't dare yield to that depth of feeling.

He didn't dare lose control. The last time he'd lost control, death had followed.

Today, he'd been ready to turn away from her forever.

Then she'd crawled off her platform and hung out over that hundred-foot drop to take pictures.

My God. He hadn't felt that desperation since . . . well, just since. He'd jumped off the boulder at the top of the cliff and made it down to her almost in time to catch her as she fell. Almost. Using his power had been instinctive, a brief burst that caught and deposited her without thought or finesse.

*Stupid woman.* She didn't even realize what she'd done to him.

She'd made him use a power he had barely acknowledged for the last two years. Then she'd thanked him. She'd *touched* him. She'd followed him being perky and grateful and cheerful, like a creature who believed in the goodness of mankind. In *his* goodness.

So that was why he was taking the girl to Mama Cat's den. He wanted her to have what she wanted, to take her pictures and see her glimpse of the wildness . . . and then go away. That way, he would never have to see her again.

But . . . what the hell? The girl wasn't behind him.

He knew she wasn't, because when she was close, she was talking.

He stopped, turned.

She stood where he had left her, staring at him, her golden brown eyes wide and heartbreakingly innocent.

Ah, to be so young again . . .

"How old are you?" he asked.

"Twenty-four."

"You look younger."

"How old are you?"

"Thirty."

She said nothing.

"Aren't you going to tell me I look older?" he asked.

"I can't tell. You're so hairy I can barely see your face."

He gave a bark of laughter. "You sound like my drill sergeant." He laughed again, then stopped, surprised at himself. Where had that brief spark of humor come from? "Are you coming with me?" he asked.

She blinked, and her long lashes fanned the air.

He half expected to feel a breeze.

"I don't know," she said. "Is there really a lynx, or are you really crazy?"

So it had finally sunk in for her. She had realized she was alone with the yeti. "I'm definitely crazy. But yes, there's a lynx." He waited, sure she would turn back now.

Instead, she said, "Okay, as long as I know the score," and started toward him.

He didn't really believe he was crazy.

But she sure as hell was.

He didn't wait. He strode off toward the riverbank.

Before he knew it, she was on his heels. "Brandon would laugh if he knew how thoroughly he had scared me with his stories of the yeti."

"Sure." John remembered Brandon from last year. Short, loud, obnoxious, without interest in the animals unless he could torment them.

John had not been happy to see Brandon return.

Genny was still chatting. "About the lynx—there are babies, too, right?"

"Yes. Two."

"That is just too cool." She sounded like an eighties teenager at a Michael Jackson concert. "I would do anything to see those kittens."

*Anything?* He clamped down on the thought before he could take it any further.

"Probably I shouldn't be doing this," she said conversationally. "Maybe you're taking me into the woods to slaughter me."

"Maybe." He fought the urge to grin.

"On the other hand, if you were going to kill me, why not simply let me fall?"

Remembering the things he'd seen during his missions at war and with the Chosen, his face settled into its normal, grim cast. "You really are a babe in arms, aren't you?"

She answered too quickly. "You mean a fool."

Her small, acrid bitterness caught him by surprise. So this seemingly sunny girl had suffered at least a few disappointments. "Who calls you a fool?"

"My father. He doesn't admire my constant chirping about saving the world one creature at a time."

"Is that what he calls it? Chirping?" Clearly, her father was an asshole.

"Dad's not so bad." She defended him in a knee-jerk reaction. "He's had disappointments in his life."

"Who hasn't?"

"At least *he* isn't a hermit."

John's mouth twitched again. Another grin at her lively spirit—a grin that faded as he remembered. "It's safer this way."

"Why is it safer?"

"It just is."

John's cabin had been an abandoned building when he arrived in Rasputye.

For years, a hermit had lived there. The villagers had called the old guy the Mad German, because he was foreign and possessed a gift like John's—odd, otherworldly, and destructive.

The German had built his cabin with his own hands, and John knew why he had chosen that site.

All the hut's windows faced north. Every day, when the sun rose, it first touched the glistening rock towers of the Seven Devils. The Mad German's daughter told John they didn't know what had happened to the hermit.

John knew. The German had finally surrendered to the crossroads' beckoning. He'd gone to the Seven

Devils, to the middle Devil, and done what the gifted had done for centuries. John only hoped the hermit had lived through the transition from this world to that.

John had bought the cabin from the daughter. He cleaned out the one-room hut, fixed the thatching, put new glass in the windows, filled the cracks with mud, and packed straw weighted with stones around the base of the walls. He had moved in, and every day that first winter, John stared at the Seven Devils, studied them, wondered if the stories were true—if somewhere in there was the gate to the *rasputye*.

No one in Rasputye had expected him to survive, because at first they didn't recognize the gaunt, stern-faced, shaggy American. But he *had* survived the winter. He had survived the spring. He had walked into town in the summer, and by then, they had all known who he was—because the first of the letters had arrived.

The people of Rasputye had been afraid, and they were feeling guilty . . . as they should have been. Never during his lousy childhood had any of them interceded on his behalf.

Now they hated him for merely being there, the living proof of their failure, their fears and their greed.

If he tried to explain that, Genny would never understand.

# Chapter 15

The trail turned suddenly downward, plunging off the mountain toward the river, and John let the work of descent finish the conversation. As it was, he'd just spoken more words in fifteen minutes than he'd used in two years. And told Genesis Valente far too much about himself.

With any luck at all, once he was done today, it would be another two years before he repeated the experience.

How odd that she had known he was watching her. Did she possess that small, extrasensory knowledge some ordinary humans enjoyed, or was she gifted, too?

John would have protested that God could not be so cruel.

But he already knew that wasn't true. God was cruel beyond all conception. God tormented a man, broke his heart and his will, and then sent someone like Genny to dangle hope like a diamond on a platinum chain.

No. No, John refused to hope.

Yet Genny said she felt his sorrow.

What did she mean? He didn't feel sorrow, and even if he did . . .

"Are you an empath?" he asked.

"What?" She sounded sincerely confused.

He stopped in the path in front of her, two steps farther down. That put them eye to eye, and he stared at her, compelling her to tell him the truth. "I asked if you were an empath. Do you routinely feel what other people feel?"

Her gaze fell away from his. "I try to be empathetic, if that's what you mean."

Was she being evasive? He couldn't tell.

Perhaps it wasn't she who should be cautious here. Perhaps she presented more danger to him than he to her.

"John . . ." She put her hands on his shoulders.

He stiffened, so sensitive and so unaccustomed to the touch of another human that her touch was almost painful.

"Listen," she said, "I need to tell you something."

Maybe it wasn't his own pain he felt. Maybe it was hers. Or maybe he saw it—those big golden brown eyes were filled with the weariness of a woman who had seen far too much anguish in her life.

He cupped her chin in his hand, smoothed his thumb across her lips.

Her face was innocent. Her mouth was not. It was made for kissing . . . and more carnal pleasures.

Her lips parted. Her breath swirled in his palm. He leaned close, closed his eyes and inhaled her scent:

harsh soap, orange lotion, the fresh scent of loam and crushed pine needles—and beneath it all, the scent of a woman at the peak of her glory.

Did this woman even realize the power she held? What heights of foolishness to which she could drive him?

"John?" Her lips moved against his thumb. Her voice was cautious. "Are you okay?"

He opened his eyes.

She looked apprehensive.

Perhaps in his time alone, he had lost the finer points of polite behavior. As he recalled, a man didn't sniff a woman within an hour of meeting her.

He dropped his hand.

"John, listen, I wanted to tell you—"

He didn't want to listen. He wanted to lay her down in the forest and taste her mouth, her breasts, the sweet cleft between her legs, until she was wet with climax, until he was so deep inside her he would die of bliss.

He turned on his heel. He adjusted himself—his stupid fantasies were causing him pain and havoc—and started down the hill.

"Wait!" Gravel showered down on the path like a dirt waterfall.

Yeah, she was following.

They reached the last drop before the river and the view opened up. Genny slipped. She skidded as she tried to stop herself from going over the edge. She grabbed at branches, then slammed into his back hard enough to make both of them go, "Oof!"

She wrapped her arms around him, pressed herself against him, and everywhere her body rested, he would swear the leather melted under the heat of their bodies.

*Damn it to hell.* He'd just gotten his erection under control and now it was back, bigger and better than ever.

Silly woman—she was oblivious.

She held him in her arms long enough to catch her breath, then peeled herself away and stepped out from behind him. She looked down at the river rushing past the rocks five feet below them, then out at the wide channel it had made during its years of wandering along the flat at the edge of the cliff. "Wow."

She looked up and over at the trees that grew like a fringe of bangs on the tall, rocky face, and located the platform that she had used for observation every day since she'd arrived. "My God." She clutched his arm. "That would have been a long way to fall. I could have . . . have . . . died . . ." Her voice wobbled on the last two words, and she sat down hard, as if she'd suddenly realized how close she'd come to a bloody, painful demise.

Ducking her head, she sniffled.

Suddenly, he remembered one reason why he had become a hermit.

Because he sucked at personal relationships.

"Are you crying?" He sounded horrified. Was horrified.

"No . . ." Out of her coat pocket, she retrieved one of those little flowered packs of tissues, pulled one tissue out and used it.

"Because I don't know what you do back in the U.S., but out here in the Ural Mountains, we don't cry."

"I hold a business degree."

"*You* do?" What moron career guidance counselor had suggested this softhearted, outdoorsy girl go to business school?

"Graduated from NYU. That's why I don't cry." She sobbed, then held her breath as if she had the hiccups instead of a legitimate reason to cry. "In business, that's a weakness I can't afford to show."

"Who the hell told you that?" Like he didn't know.

She sobbed harder—a summer storm that struck out of the blue and left him feeling weak, alarmed, and helpless. At the same time, she held her hand over her mouth, struggling to stop.

"Business school. What kind of business?" He wasn't just asking to distract her. He was curious.

She took a long breath. "Br-brokerage account man-management." She hiccupped, took her hands away from her face, and took another long breath. "When I get back to New York, I've got to start my job with CFG. B-but to tell you the truth"—her voice was wavering again—"I'm not very good at the k-kind of business that makes a profit regardless . . . regardless of the consequences."

"No. Really?"

She didn't seem to sense the sarcasm, just looked down at her hands, loose and upturned in her lap. In a cold, steady voice, she said, "On the other hand, I succeeded in killing most of my ideals in graduate school. I suppose I can kill the rest of them in pursuit of wealth." Then her hands came up to her face again, and she cried so pitifully she sounded as if she'd never cried before.

How the hell did Genesis Valente manage to turn him on one minute and break his heart the next? He didn't need this kind of crap.

"Son. Of. A. Bitch." Which was about as polite a curse as he could think of right now. "Look. I lied. Lots of people cry up here."

She raised her face from her hands. Her nose was red, her skin blotchy, and she looked like a kid who had dropped her ice cream in the sand. "Do y-*you*?"

"Do I what? Cry? *No*." He didn't care enough about anything to cry. "But I'm crazy, remember?"

"Yeah. I know." She nodded emphatically. Tears flew. "I really do."

He paced away, wanted to run.

He hated this whole scene; hated himself for getting involved, hated that he couldn't stand to leave her like this.

Not that John liked it when a girl cried, but with Genny he quickly discovered he hated more that she was stifling her sobs as if she was embarrassed by her emotions. Or maybe she struggled because she didn't want to make him uncomfortable. In his experience— not that he'd had a lot of experience with crying women—it was better if they let it all out.

He came back to her.

She had pulled her knees up to her chest and put her head on them, hiding herself away.

Someone had really done a number on her.

"Shit." In the bravest gesture of a roughneck life, John sat down beside Genny and put his arm around her.

# Chapter 16

In a life filled with few moments of hope and much duty and wretchedness, this was the worst.

Because in addition to Genny's unexpected breakdown caused by a brush with death, she was being comforted by the man she'd been sent to betray.

A guy so crazy he dressed in skins and avoided human contact.

A guy who promised to fulfill her dream, make her a hero to her group, and show her a female lynx and her two kittens.

Genny was a living, breathing, traitorous creep.

Which just made her cry harder.

When was the last time she'd cried? Had it been when she'd been forced to give up her pets? When her mother left?

No. She knew exactly the last time she'd cried: when she had given up on living her own life, given in to her father's wishes and applied to business school.

After that, nothing was worth crying about.

Except now, when for three months she could make a difference in the world. For that, she'd given up everything . . . including her integrity. Especially her integrity, crumpled and compromised as it was.

"Jes . . . geeze." John's voice rumbled in his chest. Under her ear. "Nothing is this bad."

"Y-you're ri-right." She huddled into his arms, trying hard not to sob and failing miserably.

He waited, stock-still and stiff, like a rock on which her stormy emotions broke. "You're reacting to the shock of your fall."

"I know. You're right."

"Soldiers do that. Take a fit after they face off with death."

She peeked up at him. He wasn't drooling or twitching. He didn't look so much mad as just . . . weird. Gifted. Traumatized, maybe, by something in his past.

She half laughed in the midst of her crying. "Imagine that."

"Soldiers babble about what they almost missed. About the dreams they didn't follow. About the loves they left behind."

"At least I have no loves to regret." Remembering the guys in business school, and how carefully she had ignored them in the pursuit of grades and success, she had to bite her tongue to avoid whimpering.

"You're lucky," John said.

He spoke so stoically, she knew he had suffered a love lost. She wanted to ask, but if he told her a sad story, she'd probably puddle up again. And not for his pain, either. She'd cry because if she *had* taken that fall and her life flashed before her eyes, it wouldn't have occupied the whole trip down to the ground. She'd have to ask for a rerun. She'd been seriously dedicated to studying and nothing else.

She had no life. Oh, a few friends, some casual dates, but nothing that occupied her mind and her heart. When she returned to New York City, she was facing more *no life*.

She'd been the fool her father called her.

"You were a soldier?" She felt her anguish easing, used another tissue, and waited for his answer.

"Yes. In the wars in Afghanistan."

*And in the war between the Chosen Ones and the Others?*

He didn't mention that, though, and nothing about him encouraged her to think he would.

Her tears dried on her cheeks.

This mission she'd taken on . . . how could she accomplish it without hurting someone? Without hurting him, a soul already so wounded he avoided human company?

"Are you better?" He didn't wait for her answer, just took his arm from around her shoulders and stood. "If you want to see Mama Cat and her babies, we'd better go."

"Yes. Thank you." She stood, dusted off her rear, and dusted off her enthusiasm. "Yes, let's go." After all, she hadn't really done anything to harm him. And didn't intend to. The people in New York only wanted to talk to him. She was merely going to steer him their way. There was no harm in that. If he didn't want to leave his ways as a hermit, they couldn't force him, but perhaps they could entice him to return to a life filled with good people and good deeds.

And if the legend was to be believed, good deeds were what the Gypsy Travel Agency was all about.

"Come on." He started down the path that paralleled the river, continuing around a bend away from the cliff and the observation platform.

She hurried after him.

The river curved away from the bank, leaving a broad swath of sand below.

He jumped, then offered his hand to her.

She leaped, too, and landed on him, making him stagger. "Sorry!"

"We have to cross the river, but it's shallow. Mama Cat is on the other side." He indicated the stones scattered across the surface of the cold, green water. "Can you make your way across?"

"Of course."

"Let's go." He leaped the rocks to the opposite bank, then called, "Are you coming?"

Like a goat, she sprang over the stones and followed him to the line where the sand ended and the forest began.

With a hand on her arm, he stopped her. "Wait," he said softly. Then in the lilting tone of a lover, he called, "Mama Cat, we've come to admire your kittens."

Morning had fully blossomed. Sunshine dappled the water. Genny had been assured time and again that the Ural lynx was a nocturnal animal, yet the cat responded to his voice, poking her head out of a narrow grotto in the pile of stones set five feet above the river.

The cat looked at him, then at Genny.

They were almost at eye level, she and the cat, and mere feet apart.

Genny shed her backpack and coat and sank to her knees in the sun-warmed sand. She marveled at the creature's sleek coat, its neat mouth with its handsome side whiskers, its golden brown eyes that weighed her so intelligently.

She marveled more that John Powell, a man with a reputation for being violent, insane, and a killer, could charm a wild cat out of her den in broad daylight.

Every moment of this encounter made her wonder if the legend was true. If the real world she had occupied all her life was the only world, or if special gifts and superpowers existed side by side with flow charts and stock reports.

"May we see your babies?" John crooned to the lynx. "I promise we'll treat them like the treasures they are."

The great cat gazed at him, then pulled its head in.

John knelt beside Genny. "Now we wait and see what she decides."

Genny couldn't stop smiling, at the den where the cats resided and at him. "No matter what, I'll never forget being so close to such a beautiful beast."

His lips twitched as if he wanted to smile back—and she thought that if only she could see more of his face, he might be a handsome man. Certainly in this moment, his eyes no longer were the chill ice of a glacier. Instead, they reflected the blue of the river and the sky.

He looked back at the den as a bundle of fur tumbled out and fell down the rocks to the sandy riverbed. Another followed, propelled by Mama Cat's nose.

Genny barely contained a gasp of delight.

The two kittens blinked in the sunshine, and mewed piteously. Mama Cat slipped out of the den and followed them, nosed them, licked them, nudged them to let them know she was nearby. They were the size of small house cats, fluffy and soft; their coloring blurred and pale, an indistinct brown and gold.

"How old are they?" Genny whispered.

"They're seven, almost eight weeks old, a boy and a girl."

Genny trembled with the desire to touch, but she knew better. Mama Cat was wild with forty pounds of muscle and a predator's instinct. These were her offspring, and if Genny made the mistake of alarming her, she would attack with tooth and claw—and they were very impressive teeth and even more impressive claws.

But if Mama Cat had doubts, the kittens did not. They had met John before, felt his touch, and when he made a deep, rumbling sound in his chest, they scampered to him and into his lap.

Mama Cat seated herself and watched, on guard but at ease.

Genny watched as he picked up first one, then the other, and lifted them to his face. They sniffed noses, the three of them, and something about that gesture of trust made her heart catch.

Was she supposed to be scared of this guy? Really? The guy who rescued her, who showed her the great cats, who held her when she cried?

No. She couldn't do it. Like the kittens, she wanted to touch her nose to his, her lips to his, her body to his. Like the kittens, she trusted him.

Slowly, she sat up straight, forcing her mind back to reality.

She'd heard way too much about John Powell and his sexual prowess, and dreamed far too often, and now her mind had skipped merrily along to daytime fantasies. Great.

Greetings over, he placed them back in his lap. There they bit at his fingers and scratched at his leg, and when Genny chuckled, they turned their attention to her.

Mama Cat sat straighter, at attention, her eyes narrowed as if to warn Genny that she, like Lubochka, did not want any trouble.

But the kittens saw in Genny a potential new playmate, and pounced. One kitten grabbed her hand and gnawed.

"That is the boy," John said.

One kitten dashed up the bank and down again, skidded to a halt at the edge of the river, then ran back to John. She jumped into his lap, and he absentmindedly gathered her close to his chest.

Genny carefully did not smile.

"This is the girl," he said. "She frequently imagines she's missed an important appointment and races to keep it."

"They're so alive." Genny marveled as her fingers sank into the kitten's soft fur and felt his wiry muscles contract and stretch. "You should name them."

"No. They're wild cats. They're not my pets."

Rebuffed, Genny sat back on her heels. *Yes, John Powell, if you name them and some harm comes to them, you can't pretend you don't care.* But so small a distancing wouldn't protect the man who now cuddled a kitten under his chin.

He sounded deliberately casual as he said, "Tell me about Brandon."

"Brandon." What had she said to him about Brandon? "Why?"

"I deserve to know about some guy who is calling me a yeti."

"Ohh." Now she remembered. "Brandon is this little creep on the team. One of those guys who has to pick on somebody, and I'm the one." She shrugged. "It's not important."

"What does he do?"

"Not a whole lot. Lubochka is exasperated. She suspects he's going out into the woods to sleep rather than looking for signs left by the lynx." Genny thought Lubochka was right.

In a patient tone, John said, "No. I mean—what does he do to you?"

"Oh. That. It really isn't important. He makes fun of me. Blames me for the lack of lynx sightings." She smiled at her lap full of kitten. "No one pays attention to him, and I feel sorry for him. He's such a loser."

"He's in love with you."

She chortled. "Hardly."

"Some men never grow up. When they like a girl, they pinch her. This Brandon is still on the playground." John sounded sure of himself.

And his talk of Brandon reminded her of what she should do next. "I'll tell you what." She grabbed her camera. "This will fix Brandon. I can take him down a few notches tonight with the pictures I take of these cats!" She pointed the camera toward John, toward the kitten sleeping against his chest.

He moved so swiftly, she saw only a blur.

Catching her wrist in a strong grip, he turned the camera away. His voice sounded low, rough, like the warning a lynx would give before it attacked. "Genesis . . . do not betray me."

# *Chapter 17*

———⟡———

John's grip on her wrist made Genny wince. He showed his teeth like a threatened wildcat, and his eyes glinted icily.

"Don't take pictures of me. Don't tell them that you saw me."

"Them?" He knew. *John knew about the deal Genny had made to talk him into going back to New York.* "I didn't mean . . ." Fear made her tremble. Guilt gnawed at her nerves. "I shouldn't have, but I was desperate . . ."

Through their joined flesh, she felt his rising emotion. Not anger at her, but rather an old, curbed anguish. "Do you know where I lived . . . in the summers of my childhood?"

That was not what she expected him to say. "In Rasputye? No, wait. You said you lived there in the winters."

"But not the summers." As she watched, his eyes bleached to a pale blue.

Yes, she was right to be afraid. He was a former soldier. He knew how to fight. He knew how to kill. And he had run away from the world because . . . because he had suffered too much? Or because he'd done something heinous?

He could hurt her; she knew that for sure. Yet still she believed . . . that he would not hurt her, not as long as she kept faith in him. She kept her voice hushed and calm, the way she spoke to the lynx. "What happened in the summers?"

"Every year, Olik and his wife sold me to the circus."

"The . . . circus." If this was anyone else, she'd say he was pulling her leg. "Like . . . under the big top? Tents and trained seals and acrobats?"

"No. Like fortune-tellers and puppet shows and . . . freaks."

A picture formed in her mind of broken-down vans, of tents covered with grimy stars, of a large, bearded, heavy-handed master named Stromboli—she had tapped into her childhood memory of Pinocchio. "You're kidding." A burning started in her gut. "What kind of people would sell a child?"

"People who seize the opportunities presented to them."

"What idiot told you that?" Her voice rose in indignation.

"Olik's wife. Tanja is not an idiot. She is shrewd. They had no children, so Olik brought me home to work. She heard the story of my return to life, remembered the legend, and saw a greater prospect. The circus paid them very well for the chance to showcase me."

Genny cupped her hand over the kitten in her lap as if to protect it from harm. "She's a horrible woman!"

"Don't you know? There are many horrible people in this world."

"I do know. But I don't have to like it!" The boy kitten dug his claws into her sweatshirt, walked his way up to her shoulder, then rubbed his chin against her ear. "John, what did you do in the circus?" She tried to imagine the worst job. "Clean the elephant cage?"

"It was a small, run-down circus, a Russian circus run by people who had no place in the world. They certainly had no elephants." He held her wrist in an unbreakable grip, frozen in midair as if he'd forgotten he even touched her. "Gaspard was old and cruel, and he owned the act. Owned his wives. Owned his children. Everyone was afraid of him. We traveled from town to town. You can imagine. A dancing bear. Cockfights. A few freaks."

"Freaks." John's story sounded like some horrid retelling of the *Hunchback of Notre-Dame.* "What do you mean, *freaks*?"

"Freaks like me." John released her wrist, but not before she felt a surge of desolation.

She rubbed her skin and knew she ought to scoff at his contention he was a freak. But his hair was wild around his face and his eyes glinted hard as ice, and she was afraid—of him, and for him. "How did you . . . ? What did you . . . do . . . in their act?"

"There's a legend that says when a baby is abandoned by its parents and dies, then returns to life, that child has special powers." He spoke intensely, yet so quietly the lynx kitten snuggled into the wilderness of his beard and purred.

But Mama Cat read his mood, reflected his torment. She began to pace. Back and forth. Back and forth.

Genny lifted the boy kitten off her shoulder. She set him down, found a long, spindly twig, dragged it across the sand, back and forth, while he pounced and played. "I've heard that legend," she admitted.

"I was their circus freak with special powers."

"What special powers?" She stilled, held her breath.

"I can . . . move things. Push things. Hold things. With my mind."

What an absurd story. She didn't trust it for a minute. Yet . . . on the platform, he had caught her, when she would have sworn he hadn't been physically close enough. Nevertheless, she had been saved.

He was obviously waiting for her to demand proof.

She didn't have the guts. She didn't want to know. Not here. Not now.

She resumed playing with the kitten. "What did they have you do?"

He laughed softly at her cowardice, then picked up his story. "When I was very young, I had no control over my . . . gift. So to make me perform, Gaspard locked me in a cage, put a rug over it—I was always in the dark—then when the crowds gathered, he offered me food . . . from outside the bars. I could only have it if I brought it to myself. It was particularly entertaining if it was a bowl of soup too wide to pass through the bars, and I spilled it and cried."

"Okay." Genny felt like Mama Cat facing a threat to her babies. "This guy locked a little kid in a cage and starved him. He shouldn't have been allowed to keep you. Where were the authorities?"

John's mouth twisted with scorn. "This was Russia in the eighties. The authorities were lucky to be paid. They weren't even in authority. The circus moved all the time, from here all the way across Siberia to the far sea, then south, then west to the Crimea . . . and no one with any sense challenged Gaspard. No one."

She flicked the twig back and forth, quicker and quicker. "And no one had any compassion for a child?"

The kitten leaped and attacked, wild with the joy of play.

"I was different. A freak! Everyone was afraid of me. Especially when I got older and refused to do what Gaspard wanted. Then he poked me with a pole until I got mad. I shouted. I rattled the lock, made the straw inside fly around. I wanted to break the bars, but I wasn't strong enough. My powers weren't strong enough." John gazed into the forest, but he was here only in body. His mind dwelled far away and long ago. "The summer I was eleven, my voice changed, I grew tall . . . and I came into the fullness of my powers."

She moved the twig more and more slowly. "Did you realize it?"

"No. No one did. I only knew that Gaspard had trained me well. Every time I saw him, I grew angry; and one day, he poked me with his pole . . . and without actually touching it, I pulled it out of his hands and beat him with it. Beat him until the blood ran. Beat him unconscious."

She forgot the twig, forgot the kitten, forgot to play. "Did you kill him?"

"No. I wanted to, but the audience ran and screamed.

The circus workers cowered. One of his daughters, the one who slipped me food on the sly, begged me to stop."

"You stopped because she asked you?"

"Yes. I would have done whatever she told me."

"Was she beautiful?" Genny imagined a sloe-eyed, dusky-skinned woman whose every movement was seduction.

"She was so beautiful." He spoke worshipfully. "She was a tiny thing, only seven—"

Genny felt stupid.

"—and I all of a sudden realized that she was watching me beat her father to death."

"And a father, any father, was something you envied."

That brought John back from the past. "That's true. Gaspard was a pitiless bastard. He treated everyone brutally. But his family never went hungry, and the only violence they feared was his."

"Praise indeed."

"Russia is a vast country filled with unbending rules and petty dictators. It's tough to be different in Russia. It's tough to be independent. They were, and no one who challenged Gaspard ever won."

"Except you."

"Except me." John sat there, cuddling a baby lynx in his two broad palms, looking as wild as the cat he held. "The little girl unlocked the cage, gave me a little food and a little money—to this day, I don't know whether her mother gave it to her or she stole it—and told me to get away before the police arrived. So I ran. Stowed away on trains. Hitchhiked the trucks. Made it all the

way across Siberia, thirty-eight hundred miles, back to
Rasputye. It took two months. I ate raw fish. I ate mag-
gots from the garbage."

Mama Cat paced harder, faster, casting more hard
glances their way.

The boy cat pounced on the twig, over and over, trying to make it move.

"I ate snow, because in some places it never melts.
I got back to Rasputye about the same time as the circus," he said. "I went to Olik and Tanja and begged for
sanctuary."

"What happened?" Genny's heart beat as if she'd
been racing the whole length of Siberia . . . with him.

"They tried to sell me back to Gaspard."

She felt as if she'd slammed down hard on her face.
"What did Gaspard do? Did he take his revenge?"

"He would not have me. He was still limping from
my attack."

"Good for you! I wish you had—" She stopped herself.

"Don't worry. I've killed enough evil men since
then." John wasn't bragging. He wasn't proud. He was
merely telling the truth.

"Then what? When you weren't profitable for those
people, the ones who . . . raised you, owned you?"

"They took me to the station in Apasnee, bought me
a train ticket, and told me never to come back."

"And?"

"And I took the train. I found an orphanage. By the
time I was seventeen, I was headed to the U.S."

Troubled, she had to point out the one salient fact.

"Yet here you are now. When you were hurt, you ran away and came back to Rasputye again."

Gently he put the kitten on the ground, watched her ambush her brother. "If you ask the people of Rasputye, they say the crossroads draws people like me."

"If you ask the people of Rasputye, they say everything we do is controlled by an ancient legend and such silliness." Genny would not admit to him that Mariana believed fate had drawn Genny here. It made her seem bound to John in some mystical way.

The kittens rolled over and over, wrestling with youthful enthusiasm.

"Those people who raised you. Olik and Tanja. Are they still here?"

"Olik died at sea."

"Good." Genny hoped it was a cold, wet, miserable death.

"Tanja lives and thrives in Rasputye. She is respected for her business acumen." With fine-tuned irony, John said, "Selling me was, after all, merely a business decision."

Genny opened her mouth to reply hotly, then remembered—she had made a similar decision when she agreed to the deal her father offered. But surely she wasn't as bad as a woman who sold a child to the circus . . . although perhaps that was only a matter of degree. "I haven't met her in the *traktir*."

"She seldom visits the *traktir*. She is far too respectable for that."

"Oh, John." Genny had never seen a man look so alone. She ached for the lonely, abused little boy he had been, and for the desolate, remote man he had become. She was angry at the couple who should have been his parents, at the circus people who so brutally mistreated a child. She wanted to do something for him, melt the anguish behind those cold blue eyes.

She knelt beside him, put her hands on his shoulders, and looked into his eyes.

He stared back at her, motionless, waiting, a man whose shoulders were warm beneath her palms, who smelled like clean air, like evergreen trees, like leather, and, incongruously, like lavender shampoo.

"John." She needed to say . . . something. Something wise and comforting about how everything would get better soon.

But that was such a lie. How did one recover from a childhood such as his? What events drove him back here to the place of his torment? And what could she say, or do, to ease his suffering?

Her heart beat hard. She swallowed to ease her dry throat.

And she leaned into him and kissed him.

# Chapter 18

※—⟫⟪—※

It was nothing, really. A brush of her mouth against his.

But John's lips were cool and firm, his beard unexpectedly soft, and his eyes fluttered closed as if Genny's touch gave him pleasure. Beneath her hands, his shoulders flexed and settled, and he gave off a gentle heat.

She drew back slightly.

He sighed as if her retreat disappointed him, but did nothing to stop her.

So she kissed him again. This time when his eyes closed, her eyes closed, too. That changed the kiss, made it more intimate, less comfort and more sex. It was man and woman now, lonely adults who explored cautiously, afraid of revealing too much of themselves.

He opened his lips and touched his tongue to her lower lip, the flavor of inquiry.

Would she allow him more freedom?

She would . . . she offered him a shy sample of herself, and the pleasure he gave her in return was warm and profound, primitive and sensual. As each moment passed, as he led her deeper into passion, it became increasingly clear that the time he'd spent in the wilderness had stripped away any semblance of civilization. Until this moment, she had never tasted pure, unadulterated masculinity.

*No wonder women lusted after him.*

He allowed her to take the lead, yet she sensed intensity, need . . . passion. Power, his power, hummed beneath her fingertips, feeding the small, shy, hidden bit of wildness within her.

He went to her head like a shot of distilled virility, and she kissed him more deeply, sinking onto his knee and against his chest. He seemed to be allowing her all the choices, but the way he kissed, as if she were the first, the best, the most important . . . the only. It was flattery and ardor and, oh, the way her body felt against his! The slow thrum of passion moved from his skin to hers, from his heart to hers, from his loins to . . .

Deliberately, leisurely, allowing her time to protest, he tilted her to lie in his lap.

Dimly she realized that he was drawing her in, a hypnotism of her body by his, but she didn't protest.

Why should she? He held her with one arm beneath her head, the other embracing her waist, and she felt, not threatened, but safe as she had never felt before. And cherished. And worshiped. A firestorm ignited in her, burning away any wariness, taking her out of herself and into him.

With him, she was whole.

Giving a small moan, she wrapped herself around him, drew him down to her, opened her lips, and breathed in his soul.

This wasn't the John Powell of her dreams. He was not forceful, not arrogant, not relentless. Avni's friend Halinka had claimed he did everything according to the *woman's* desire.

Right now, Genny believed it. Every movement, every touch was designed for *her*.

On the periphery of consciousness, she knew the sand was warm beneath them. She heard the river rippling across rocks, the kittens riotously gamboling. She smelled the sun-warmed pines, and felt the brush of the wind. She was alive as she had never been before . . . and when he lessened the kiss, loosened his embrace, she said, "No," and tried to bring him back.

But he took a long breath, and lifted her to sit straight.

"Genny." He brushed his lips across her cheek, pushed the tousled strands of her hair behind her ear. "Genny."

She opened her eyes and stared at him, dazzled by the sunlight and dazed by . . . by the lack of oxygen to her brain. Because that was the only explanation she could give for her reaction to what she had intended to be a comforting kiss.

And while she still teetered on the edge of sensual oblivion, he looked serious and concerned. "You need to take your pictures," he said in his deep, calm voice.

"Right. Sure." With a bump, she slid off his knee and groped for her camera. Retrieving it, she focused randomly and shot photos of Mama Cat, who posed at the lip of rock overlooking the river. As Genny's hand steadied, she used more deliberation to capture the kittens as they leaped around. In a voice that sounded as if it came from a great hollow within, she asked, "Would you move the twig and see if you can get them to play with it? It would direct their attention . . . and I promise not to get you in the photo."

Picking up the twig, he knelt beside her and thrashed it across the sand, and when the babies dashed over, intent on beating it into oblivion, John asked, "Do you know why I told you the story of my youth?"

*To tear my heart out.* "You needed someone to talk to, and I'm a good listener." Every guy in college had told her exactly that.

"No. I wanted you to understand, really understand, why you can never take photographs of me. Why you can never tell them in Rasputye that you've met me." He put the twig down. "That's enough. The kittens are tired."

As if he had read her mind, Mama Cat came to get them. She interrupted their play with a paw on the back of the boy kitten. As he lay sprawled on the sand, she picked him up by the scruff of his neck and carried him toward the den, the girl kitten dragging behind them and yawning.

Genny switched to video mode, catching the maternal concern of the lynx as she fed the boy cat into the den, then nudged the girl cat inside. Mama Cat followed her babies, slipping through the crack in the stone and leaving no trace behind.

The pictures were going to be beyond anything ever

seen before, and Genny was going to win every acco-
lade for her success. Yet it didn't seem fair. "John, it's
you who knows the forest so well!"

"I will not be betrayed again." Gone was the lover
with power in his body and passion in his taste. This
man was grimly serious.

Really, what did she expect? That he would have
been as overwhelmed as she had been by one little kiss?
"No one's going to believe that I found those kittens."

"Make them believe, Genesis. Make them believe."

That was the second time he had called her
Genesis—and most people, unless they knew differently, assumed her name was Jennifer.

She put the lens cap on her camera and tucked it
away, shouldered her backpack and picked up her
coat. "How did you know my name was Genesis?"

"Genesis. Lubochka's voice carries well into the forest." His voice faded as he spoke.

She turned to him . . . but he was gone.

# Chapter 19

———◆———

"**I** did it!" Genny burst into the *traktir*, heart pounding with excitement.

The team was there, all except Brandon, taking an afternoon break.

Everyone stopped eating and writing and talking to stare.

"I got pictures!" Genny held up the camera as if it held treasure.

From the expression on Lubochka's face, it did. The big woman rose slowly from her place at the head of the table and extended her arm. "Show me."

Genny rushed to her side. They performed a silly tug-of-war as Lubochka tried to take the camera and Genny fought to get the strap over her head. Then everyone gathered around as Genny clicked to the first photo.

Lubochka took a long breath. Groped for her reading glasses. Looked hard at the small, backlit screen. And

said, "Kittens? You got pictures of"—she squinted—
"of Nadja with her kittens? Outside in the *daylight*?"

"Yes! Yes! It was the most exciting thing I've ever
done in my life!" Genny's heart was pounding as hard
as it had when she had almost taken a plunge off the
cliff.

A babble broke out among the team.

Thorsen Rasmussen had not said two words to her
all week. Now he slapped her on the back with such
hearty goodwill she stumbled forward. "Brilliant," he
said. "You'll be written up in the journals for this!"
Turning to Mariana, he grabbed her and whirled her
across the *traktir*.

Avni hugged Genny, then shook her, then hugged
her again. "You did it. You did it!"

Reggie lifted her hand, kissed it, and in that fabulous Scottish accent, said, "Congratulations, my dear."

"You are our heroine." Misha grabbed her shoulders
and kissed first one cheek, then the other. Leaning over
Lubochka, he kissed her in a totally different way, on
the mouth.

Reggie laughed aloud at Genny's expression. "They
are an odd couple, aren't they?"

"I didn't realize that Lubochka and Misha . . ."
Genny wished she'd never started her comment. "That
is, Lubochka doesn't seem to be the type to . . ."

"I of course cannot speak with any amount of
authority on the matter." Reggie looked wickedly
amused. "But the rumor is that she puts him on and
spins him."

Genny laughed aloud at the mental picture, then
laughed again as Misha and Lubochka pulled the

memory card from the camera, fed it into the computer, and brought the pictures up in brilliant color on the nineteen-inch monitor.

The team gathered around and watched the video of the kittens playing, then ran through the stills Genny had taken.

"You must have been startled to see the cats." Lubochka pointed at the first pictures Genny had taken and laughed exuberantly. "These are tilted sideways."

"Yes . . ." Genny had been shaken, but not by the appearance of the cats. She'd been shaken by the kiss she'd shared with John and his unremitting insistence that she tell no one she knew him.

"Easily fixed. We have Photoshop! We will tilt them the other way. And crop. We can crop." Misha pointed at the fourth picture, the one of Mama Cat posed on the rocks. "Look. Look at this one! Nadja came through the winter in prime shape."

"She is a beautiful cat." Lubochka worshiped with her tone. "Genesis, you must tell me where you saw Nadja and her children."

Genny had been thinking about how to answer. She didn't want everyone to know the den's location. Not everyone respected an endangered species. There were people who would pay to have a coat made from lynx fur, and people who imagined owning a wildcat would be fun. And maybe no one on the team was one of those people, but the villagers of Rasputye were for the most part poor, and Genny didn't believe in testing their integrity. So she told the truth—but not all the truth. "On the riverbed around the bend from our observation station."

"Good." Lubochka rubbed her palms together. "Later, when we're alone, we'll get out the map."

Genny guessed Lubochka didn't trust everyone, either.

Laughing like maniacs, Reggie and Avni grabbed Genny and danced her across the room—right into Brandon's path as he swaggered through the door.

Genny halted in front of him and, still over the moon with delight, offered her hand for him to shake.

Brandon viewed it suspiciously. "What's up?"

She grinned at him. "I found them!"

"She's our new wildlife observer champion!" Reggie announced.

Brandon caught sight of a picture on the monitor, the one of Mama Cat carrying the boy cat back to the den. "Who took that?"

"Genny did!" Avni triumphantly punched her in the arm.

"Come on." Brandon sauntered over for a closer look. "She got those photos off the Internet."

Just like that, the celebration withered and died.

Everyone stared at the monitor, then back at Genny.

"I-it's not true," she stammered. Behind her, the door stood open, but not even the breeze could cool her hot cheeks. "I . . . I didn't . . ."

"Of course it's not true," Lubochka said scornfully. "I know every picture of every Ural lynx there is. I took most of them. These are original. Genesis took them, and she took them today!"

"Damn you, Brandon, can't you be human for once in your life?" If Avni stood closer, she would have punched Brandon.

If Genny stood closer, she would have *killed* him.

"He's human, all right." Reggie used an upper-class, derogatory tone that brought an ugly flush to Brandon's face. "He's jealous because he isn't getting all the attention. He's a lousy excuse for a human."

"Is it the fact you sleep in the storage closet? Or the fact you forgot to bring toilet paper and you're getting slivers from the Russian kind?" Thorsen's laugh was a jeer.

Genny advanced on Brandon. "What is wrong with you? Why would you say such a mean thing? There's no reason for that kind of accusation!"

"Speaking of mean things"—Brandon flicked the bruise on her cheek—"who hit you, babe?"

She flinched back. "I fell." Then she was angry again. Angry that he'd noticed what no one else had. Angry that she had allowed him to distract her. "That's not the point. The point is, you can't stand it when someone else gets attention—"

"Got issues, honey?" Brandon used his most patronizing tone.

"—which I deserve for taking those pictures today!" Genny couldn't believe she needed to rescue her reputation after a morning spent holding a lynx kitten.

"Brandon is a pimple on the face of humanity," Avni said.

"You placed the pimple a little high and on the wrong side," Genny snapped.

Lubochka slapped her knee and laughed with hearty enjoyment.

Brandon flung himself around to face them, and glowered at Genny. "Look, you. You don't know who you're trashing here. I'm Brandon Lam, and my family is worth a lot of money. I don't have to put up with a woman like you mocking me."

Genny grew cold. "What do you mean, *a woman like me*?"

"Let's face it, Genesis, the thought of you stealing pictures off the Internet shouldn't surprise anyone." He leaned forward, his eyes narrowed with satisfaction as he took his shot. "I know about your dad. I know about his arrest. And now everybody knows that larceny is the Valente family business."

# Chapter 20

The next morning, Genny came out of a dead sleep thirty seconds before her three a.m. alarm went off. She smothered the sound before it happened, grabbed her clothes and slipped downstairs to the bathroom, dressed and brushed her teeth.

And all the time, a low-level humiliation buzzed in her veins.

Good ol' Brandon. He had been doing his research. He'd found out about her father, and in a masterful stroke, he had used the information to undermine her.

He'd done a good job of it, too.

Everyone on the team had said the right things—that she wasn't her father and they trusted her. But they didn't meet her eyes. And when Lubochka took her aside, asked for the directions to the lynx den, and assured her she had thoroughly examined the photos and certified they hadn't been Photoshopped, Genny's mortification was complete.

Now she couldn't wait to escape into the forest.

She groped her way through the dark *traktir,* slipped out the door, and stood staring upward at the stars. When her eyes had adjusted, she moved toward the edge of the village and into the forest. Shadows blanketed the ground, and she saw nothing, heard nothing, not a footstep or a breath, yet she sensed John's approach.

He stopped a few feet away, a darker spot in the forest.

"John?" She reached out her hand.

He gripped it. "What's wrong?"

She tensed. "Nothing. Why?"

"The earth, the trees, the animals are at peace, yet there is dissonance in the woods, and it emanates from you. What is it?" He squeezed her hand and repeated, "Genesis, what's wrong?"

In the dark, in that moment, when she could see nothing, her senses expanded, entwined with his—and through him she absorbed the scent and atmosphere, felt the growing trees and the living creatures.

As she did, the turmoil inside her calmed.

Since her father's downfall, she had faced worse slander and more dire situations than this. Out here, the ghost of her father's disgrace wasn't important. All that mattered was learning to know the forest as John knew it. All that mattered was the lynx and the owl, the elk and the bear. In a tone as dismissive as she could make it, she said, "Yesterday I had some trouble with Brandon. Don't worry. I can handle this. I always do."

He slid an arm around her waist, pulled her close.

Was he absorbing her emotions as she had absorbed

his? Did he feel the increased beat of her heart, the way her temperature rose with his closeness?

His breath brushed her face, and his scent filled her head; she closed her eyes and wished for his kiss.

"Are you ready?" John whispered.

"Ready?" She was so ready.

Last night she had tossed and turned, suffering teenage-like angst, and once she did sleep, she had dreamed not about Brandon and his nasty little revelation, but about John. The dream had been lusty, illicit, politically incorrect—calibrated by her subconscious to keep her balanced on the edge of desire.

She cleared her throat, lowered her voice. "Yes. Yes, I am ready."

"Tonight's the night," he said. "We will find our male lynx."

Her heartbeat went into a skid.

Of course. What else would he mean? Among the other humiliations she had revisited last night was the knowledge that she had initiated that kiss yesterday.

He had embraced her, but he hadn't touched her as if he felt any lust at all.

He had kissed her so thoroughly, she had been shaken to the core. But he had called the halt.

He had probably slept perfectly well.

She had not.

When he was close, she breathed in sexual tension. She fought the urge to pose, chest thrust forward, or put on makeup, or sew ruffles onto her down vest. It was embarrassing and humiliating to react with such primitive instincts to such a primitive man.

She had to get over this. Starting up the trail, she

said, "You're right. I feel it in my bones. Tonight we'll find our male lynx."

"I had trouble with the exposure. When I spotted him, it was completely dark. I was terrified my flash would go off. Then he moved so quickly I could only snap photos. Video was impossible." Genny sat beside Lubochka in front of the computer, still so excited by the encounter she was talking too much, too fast.

*No one cared.*

Avni, Reggie, and Thorsen hovered behind, staring in rapt attention as the pictures came up on the monitor.

Misha was out on observation duty.

Every few minutes, Mariana wandered in from the kitchen, looked at the photos, looked at Genny, muttered some dark imprecations, and left again.

Two villagers sat in the corner, drinking vodka.

Brandon was hunched over a cup of coffee, back turned, pretending he didn't care.

And nobody believed she had stolen *these* photos.

"Where did you spot him?" Reggie asked.

"His territory is outside the boundary of Nadja's, and all around it, so I think we can safely say he's her mate." Genny pointed to the beautiful, isolated beast on the monitor. "Look at his coloring!"

"This is the first time we've observed this cat." Lubochka zoomed in on the male lynx.

The big cat stared right into the camera—its white teeth bared, its whiskers flared, its eyes wide and menacing. Where Nadja's face had been softened by motherhood, this animal's expression, the epitome of danger and beauty mixed, clearly warned off trespassers.

"He reminds me of something." Genny cocked her head, trying to place it.

"In India, in Madhya Pradesh, we had a tiger preying on a village." Right now, Avni sounded very Indian. "He was lame, so he was coming in, dragging away women and children and eating them. Easy prey. I was there when he was trapped. We had to put him down or he would have gone back for more, but I tell you, he had exactly that expression in his eyes. He wasn't afraid. He was angry."

"Why would that lynx be angry?" Brandon turned on the bench. "He's got a good life, roaming the forest, screwing all the female cats he can find." He laughed, and looked meaningfully at Genny.

So she answered him, telling him things he already knew. "There are so few, we thought they were extinct. People who should be protecting them would do anything to hunt them down, kill them, skin them and sell their skins. Or capture them and sell them as pets to rich assholes."

"Yeah." Brandon's eyes gleamed brightly.

And she realized—*he was the guy the poachers would sell to.*

She really didn't like him.

Her pity for him had vanished, chipped away by the day-to-day exposure to his smarmy remarks and lazy attitude. He was a little rich boy, a bully, with no morals and no strengths. Maybe he had had a rough life. Maybe his family was unfeeling or abusive. But like everyone else in the world, he had had choices. He didn't have to be an uncaring jerk. That was the choice he made.

The door opened.

Brandon glanced, did a double take, and gaped toward the entry.

Lubochka did the same, and Avni.

The Russians stared and muttered.

John was here. He stood in the door of the *traktir*, his face in shadow. He blocked the afternoon light, a broad man with a football player's silhouette and beefy hands that clenched and unclenched in a slow, hypnotic rhythm.

Genny's heart took a leap of joy. And then wariness.

Because . . . what had he come for? To see that she'd gotten back safely? To make sure she kept her promise not to speak of him? Or to claim her as only a wild man could, lifting her into his arms and carrying her away so that once more they could kiss and do all the things she'd dreamed about . . . ?

Hurriedly she turned her back.

Nope. She had to remember. He wasn't interested in her.

So she could be casual.

Yet right now she strained to hear his almost noiseless footsteps as they moved into the room.

Mariana walked out of the kitchen, stared inquisitively. "May I help you, sir?" Then she did the same double take the others had.

Genny meant to keep her back to him. She really did. But everyone was acting so oddly . . .

Genny turned to face the room—and stood, riveted . . . by this guy who *wasn't* John.

He wore jeans and a faded denim shirt and, most important, close-cropped hair and clean-shaven face.

Then he looked at her, and she couldn't turn away from those clear blue eyes.

# Chapter 21

———— ❧ ————

"John," Genny whispered.

"Wow." Avni whispered, too. "I had no idea that was under all that hair. He looks like Matt Damon. In *Bourne Identity*."

"Paul Newman in *The Long, Hot Summer*." Lubochka kept her usual boisterous voice to a murmur.

"Brad Pitt in *Troy*," Thorsen said softly.

Okay. So Lubochka was definitely not gay, and Thorsen definitely was. And everyone was speaking so quietly, they might have been in a place of worship, and standing so still, they might have been saluting the flag.

The yeti was gone, replaced with this guy who looked splendidly normal and American and . . . my God. Hot. John looked at home in a military haircut, and without that mass of hair clogging his face, Genny could gaze at his fine-crafted bone structure: the hawkish nose, the broad forehead, the olive skin molded over the strong jaw and cheekbones.

Actually, the truth was—Genny couldn't look away.

This was the man in the photo she kept in her backpack. He wore his experience like a dark cloak. He paced across the floor, all his attention apparently on Mariana, but Genny thought he was aware of every detail in the *traktir*: who was there, what they were doing, how they stared . . .

"John, we haven't seen you since early spring." Mariana hurried toward him like a hostess anxious to deal with a surly guest.

"I had to come into Rasputye for supplies." His voice was deep. He spoke slowly. He walked in, and he dominated the atmosphere in a way he hadn't out-of-doors.

Genny thought perhaps it was because the room couldn't constrain his size. Or perhaps he deliberately stalked rather than walked, glared rather than stared. He pinned the gaze of each person, one at a time, as he walked past.

But not Genny's. His gaze slid past her, and she realized . . . she had been waiting for him to nod to her, speak to her, acknowledge her.

But no. He pretended he had never met her.

She deflated like a three-day-old balloon.

No one noticed, thank God. Everyone's attention was fixed—on John.

Gathering her dignity, she turned back to the monitor.

Fat lot of good it did her. Lubochka was still watching John. Everyone in there was watching John. And his image was burned on Genny's brain.

As a yeti, John had looked powerful, but the furs

and leather had masked the details of muscle and bone that formed his body. He was built like a swimmer: massive shoulders and ripped arms tapering down to a slender waist. Then long legs with thighs as ripped as his arms. His body transformed denim into Armani.

"John, you look—" Mariana hesitated.

"Yes?" His voice was absolutely without inflection.

She changed her tone to match his. "You look well. Do you want your mail?"

"Yes."

Curiosity tugged at Genny, pulling her half around in her seat.

Mariana dug underneath the bar, and came up with three envelopes of assorted sizes, all battered and with American postage.

John sorted through them, his expression brooding.

Mariana placed her hand on his arm. "They are still writing you."

"Yes."

"They don't give up," Mariana said.

"No."

As he turned away, Mariana's hand slid away from him.

"I'll bet you could bounce a quarter off those abs," Lubochka murmured.

"I'll up your bid and bounce a silver dollar," Avni answered.

"Really." Reggie's accent sounded quite stuffy and disdainful. "All this staring and muttering isn't good form."

"*He's* got good form," Thorsen said.

Lubochka pushed him and grinned.

"Only Genny's had the taste and moderation to re-member the elementary rules of civilization," Reggie said. "She's managed to handle any feminine reaction to Powell with complete restraint."

If only Reggie realized his praise was unwarranted. Genny knew from personal experience that John's lips were soft and full—but before the shaggy beard and mustache had covered their contours. Now she could see his mouth; and something about the color, the shape, the texture made her want to test him once more, to see if he really was as good at kissing as she remembered.

She was pretty sure if she took a vote, the women in this room—and Thorsen—would be willing to bet he was.

Walking over to the table, John dropped his mail. He sat down opposite Brandon. He pulled some crumpled rubles out of his pocket and put them down, looked at Mariana and raised his eyebrows.

Her surprise made her slow to respond. Then she hurriedly said, "I made *zharkoye* and bread. Do you want some?"

He nodded, picked up his mail, opened it, and read as if no one else was in the room.

Mariana rushed into the kitchen.

Genny refused to stare. Resuming her seat beside Lubochka, she said, "I figure he's fifty pounds of solid muscle."

Lubochka looked at her in a daze. "Fifty pounds? More like two hundred, two ten . . . Oh! The lynx. Right." She examined the photo on the monitor. "Fifty pounds, maybe more."

"I thought so." Behind her, Genny could hear Mariana's footsteps, the clink of the bowl and silverware as she set them in front of John.

"The cat," Reggie said, "is in prime condition. I think the reason we've never seen him before is that he's a young male just come to adulthood. He probably had to beat another male for his position of dominance and right to breed."

"That's very likely," Lubochka agreed. But she kept glancing back at John.

Avni said, "When a handsome new male comes onto the scene, there's a pretty good chance there'll be a fight between that male and any ugly, undersized specimen lurking in the forest, and the handsome new male is going to win."

Avni wasn't talking about the cats.

Careful not to make a sound, Genny scooted her stool around so she could observe the room from the corner of her eye.

John ate the Russian stew with a hearty appetite, smeared the dark bread with butter, drank from his mug of beer, and sneered at the contents of his letters. At least, that's what she thought he was doing. Certainly one corner of his mouth curled up and his eyes were narrowed on the page.

Across the table, Brandon watched him warily; and when John paid him no heed, Brandon smirked, then made faces, then scratched himself like a baboon.

Reggie shook his head in disgust.

Avni leaned against the wall and grinned.

Genny waited.

John caught sight of Brandon, and scrutinized him for a long, cool moment.

When Brandon realized he'd been caught scratching his crotch, the way he flinched almost started Genny laughing . . . except she wasn't sure John wasn't going to flatten him.

"You're Brandon Lam," John said. "The one who calls me a yeti."

Avni let out an explosive laugh that changed to a fit of coughing.

Brandon blanched. He glanced around accusingly, or maybe he was merely looking for escape. He looked back at John. "How do you know that?"

"You haven't been quiet about it."

Brandon clearly couldn't decide what to answer . . . and keep his life.

Lubochka covered her mouth with her hand to hide her grin, and leaned back in her chair to enjoy the show.

"Brandon. Do I look like an abominable snowman?" John asked.

Mesmerized, Brandon shook his head.

"No. I don't. So I could be unhappy about that kind of slander from a sawed-off shrimp of a guy like you. Couldn't I?"

"Yes," Brandon breathed.

"Yes. But I won't take my revenge. At least—not right away . . ." John's attention shifted back to his bowl.

Apparently that gave Brandon the courage he needed. "You look different. Did you get a deal on that haircut?"

John lifted his gaze again and observed Brandon with all the fondness of a cowboy boot for a cockroach.

Emboldened, Brandon asked, "Why did you do it? You got a girlfriend? Some hairy, yeti girlfriend you want to impress?"

Genny ducked her head and realized . . . her hands had involuntarily curled, and she held them protectively close to her belly.

What had made John shave his face? Had he picked out his new four-day playmate? Was he stalking a female with the intention of taking her to his cabin and using her to . . . to relieve his masculine desires?

Was that female Genny?

John put down his spoon. "Never doubt the yeti still lurks within, waiting to tear you limb from limb."

Brandon's oily amusement vanished.

The Russians in the corner guffawed.

Genny glanced up.

She wanted John to want her. She wanted to kiss him again, to take off her clothes, to press herself against his sculpted body and feel his pecs, his belly, his thighs. She wanted to hold his erection in her hands, measure its length and breadth, put it between her legs and accept him into her body. She wanted to do all those things, and at the same time . . . he was the perfect gentleman, nice and kind, helping her search out the lynx in the area so she could take photos.

*Nice*. A blah word for what was obviously a blah sentiment . . . for her.

She cringed a little. Was he teaching her, showing her, because he felt *sorry* for her?

Reggie caught her eye and shook his head in disgust.

Genny blushed. How had he realized what she was thinking?

Then she blushed more. He hadn't. He was disgusted about Brandon. Of course.

John picked up his spoon again.

Brandon rushed into speech. "These villagers say you're here because of the crossroads."

The two Russian men cast evil glances at Brandon.

He continued. "Because you're some kind of freak that's attracted to a mystical place that exists somewhere around here."

John lifted his cold blue eyes to Brandon. He scanned the room, stared hard at the two villagers, who pretended to be blind and deaf to the scene. His gaze drifted over Genny without a sign of recognition. "What's your question, Brandon? Are you asking if I'm a freak? Or are you asking if I'm here because of a mystical connection to the *rasputye*?"

John's mild reaction lent Brandon courage. "I *know* you're a freak. I just don't understand why a decorated American would run away to this particular Russian piss-hole. I mean, if you need some woo-woo to cure whatever's wrong with you—your PTSD or your crazy fits—Sedona, Arizona, is supposed to be the bellybutton of the world, and it's one hell of a lot closer to home."

Unhurriedly John reached out. He gathered a handful of Brandon's shirt in his fist. He stood, and as he did, he lifted Brandon up and dragged him across the table.

Brandon kicked wildly.

The stew and beer went flying.

John brought him close, so they were face-to-face, eye-to-eye. "I don't want to cure my crazy fits," John said with precision. "I feed on them." Opening his fingers, he dropped Brandon.

Brandon smacked the table, fell off onto the stool, waved his arms to get his balance and lost the battle. The stool skidded out from under him, shot into the air, and he sprawled on his back.

The Russians chortled and slapped their knees.

So did Avni.

John kicked his stool aside, put more money on the table—"For the mess," he said to Mariana—and walked out the door.

Brandon scrambled to his feet. He glanced toward Genny.

She pretended like she hadn't noticed any of it.

No one else bothered to pretend, and Genny felt almost, *almost*, sorry for Brandon again—until he stomped up the stairs, kicking each tread like a boy sent for a time-out.

Genny felt as if she were suffering from a fever.

The other members of the team were wrong. John wasn't like any modern movie star. The gaunt face, the dark tan, the light blue eyes surrounded by dark lashes: they belonged on a castle wall, a mural full of knights and armored horses, of battle depicted so realistically one could hear the clash of swords and smell the blood spilled on the ground. And the heart of the battle would beat around this man, swinging his flaming sword or a mace with menacing accuracy.

No, there was nothing fake about this man, nothing modern, nothing weak.

He was the real thing, and only Genny was acute enough to see the truth. Only Genny was smart enough to be afraid.

Genny glanced back at the monitor where the splendid lynx still forbiddingly glared, and now she knew why the snarling cat seemed familiar.

He reminded Genny of John.

# Chapter 22

———◆———

The next morning, when Genny's phone rang, she was so deeply asleep she tried to turn off the alarm. Only Avni's indignant, "Come *on*, Genny," snapped her out of it.

Genny answered and mumbled, "What?"

"Have you talked to him yet?" It was her father. Of course.

"Wait a minute." Using her cell as a flashlight, she fumbled her way into her parka and stumbled down the stairs.

Where to go?

The bathroom had a door. She could go inside and shut it. So she did. Putting her spine against the wall, she sank down on the floor. "Okay, Father. I talked to him."

"And?"

"He's different."

"What did he say about coming to New York?"

"I haven't asked him."

"What is to be gained by delay?" Father snapped.

"His trust," Genny snapped back.

Father said nothing. Perhaps he was taken aback by her attitude. Perhaps he wanted to make her break and ask pardon.

She didn't know. She didn't care.

Finally, grudgingly, he said, "All right. I'll give you that."

"Thanks. Now I have a question of my own. Where did the legend originate?" Genny listened while her father tried to decide why she wanted to know, how much truth to tell, what could be gained from a lie.

"What legend?" he asked cautiously.

She didn't snort. She didn't dare, or he'd pretend their connection was bad and cut her off and not pick up when she called back. And she needed this information. "*The* legend. You know, the one you had me reciting before I was in kindergarten. The legend of the Chosen Ones."

"Why do you want to know?"

"I think it might be important." God, if he would only just for once answer a freaking question. "Did it originate here? Around Rasputye?"

"No one knows for sure."

"But the Gypsy Travel Agency has done studies and . . . ?" She patiently drew him out.

"There's no telling what those bastards are saying now." He sounded more than bitter. He was bone-spewing vengeful.

"What was the Gypsy Travel Agency saying when you were there? Where did the legend originate?"

"They believed it originated in central or eastern Europe." Reluctantly he added, "Perhaps on the Russian steppes."

Exactly as she had suspected. "So if you looked at a map of the border between Asia and Europe, there's sort of a bull's-eye and I'm in the center of the target."

"Not a bull's-eye. More of a long crack in the earth where things . . . happen. There used to be this theory . . ." He was getting more eccentric every day.

She no longer worried about John being mad. But should she perhaps worry about her father? "Tell me."

"They think there's something there, all along the crossroads."

"Something? What something?"

"If you look at the old stories, the fairy tales, the ones that have come down through eons and ages, there's a belief that the crossroads is where the new rules don't apply."

"The new rules?" What was he talking about? "Are you talking about the rules that have come into being with the advent of civilization?"

"Exactly. The old rules say that the fairies, the demons, the devil himself wait at the crossroads to trick an unwary traveler, to send them off into the woods where they'll never be seen again. The crossroads is the place where people fight and people die, and their blood soaks into the earth and the earth laps it up as a sacrifice and the old gods are satisfied." Her father's voice became dreamy. "People who believe, go to the crossroads to make deals for beauty or love or talent, and come back changed."

"So deals made at the crossroads are like the deal

Faust made with the devil. Sooner or later, their souls are forfeit."

"I suppose," he snapped.

"Did you go to the crossroads? Is your soul forfeit?" She didn't know what made her blurt forth the question except that . . . except he sounded so odd, as if he had visited those crossroads. Clutching the phone hard, she willed him not to hang up.

He didn't. Instead, he snapped back, "No. Not *my* soul. Do you want to hear this or not?"

"Sorry, Father. Please, tell me."

"So basically Eurasia should be one continent— geographically, it *is* one continent—but because of the huge cultural divide between Europe and Asia, it's not. The ancients drew an arbitrary line and said, *This is Europe* and *This is Asia*."

"I thought mountains and rivers made up the division."

"There are mountains and rivers all over Europe and Asia. Why that line? And why, along that line, did the old, dark legends take form? Vampires, werewolves, Baba Yaga flying on her broomstick, evil mothers who take children into the woods and leave them . . ."

In business school she'd been trained to think that the way of numbers and facts was the only way. She had deplored their rigidity, but right now, as she faced believing the unbelievable, she realized . . . there was comfort in a closed mind. If she were truly unreceptive, she wouldn't believe any of it.

But now she was awash in myth, and her mind was opened . . . and she didn't like it one bit. "So the legend of the Chosen Ones is based on reality and the reality happened here, and the Chosen Ones are drawn back here because of . . . the crossroads? There's something mystical that draws them? That's why John is here? Because his misfortune made him feel there was nowhere else in the world he could live?"

"You tell me. You've talked to him!" Her father's voice rose in excitement.

"He's been very kind."

"He's interested in you!"

"Not interested. Not like that." She was the one interested. She was obsessed. "I'll let you know when I've talked to him about New York. Until then, Father, don't call me. I'll call you." And she hung up.

She looked at the phone.

Never in her life had she imagined she'd have the guts to hang up on her father. Ever since Kevin Valente had lost his job, he'd dominated her life, her thoughts, her ambitions. She'd been afraid of him, afraid he'd walk away as her mother had walked away.

But since she'd arrived in Russia, her soul had blossomed. She sensed the forest; she became a part of its darkness. She had seen the eagles and flown on the wings of wind. She had been sister to the father and mother lynx, guardian to the babies. She had found John; she'd tasted his torment, his desire, his being.

She thought—she hoped—she could make a difference to him. With him.

Maybe this place was magic. Maybe the crossroads did exist here.

A duct connected the bathroom to the closet where Brandon slept, and there he grimaced in agony.

Genny hadn't been out hunting lynx every night. She hadn't been taking wildlife photos because she cared. She'd been out there because she had the hots for the yeti. While Brandon slept, she'd been sneaking out to screw the stupid, hairy, muscle-bound yeti.

She had been lying to Brandon. Every minute of every day, she had been lying to him.

Oh, sure, he hadn't *told* her how much he loved her. But he'd made it clear. She had known what he meant. Hadn't he been the one to warn her about the yeti? Hadn't he been the one who noticed that bruise on her cheek? The bruise the yeti had given her! Yet still she sneaked around at night like a slut.

What was it with girls? He had money. He had education. He had family. Not that his father ever thought anything Brandon did was worth a damn, but that didn't matter. When Brandon said he was one of the Lams of San Francisco, he got respect.

He had a great body. He knew that, because he worked it with weights and trainers until he was toned as any of the giants that towered over him at the gym.

Yet whenever he got involved, the girl always betrayed him. And this thing with Genny . . . this was worse than any other time before.

Because he loved Genny. He would always love her. Genny was the light in his dark, miserable, loser of a life.

He would make her pay—

A hand fell on his shoulder.

He jumped, turned, stared.

"What a disappointment Genny has turned out to be. Hasn't she?" His friend stood there, understanding his pain as no one else could.

"She's a thief. She stole my glory. She's a whore. She ignored my love."

"Yes, but there are ways to deal with thieves and whores." His friend put an arm around his shoulders and drew him close. "Would you like me to tell you how?"

# Chapter 23

As he had done every night for the past week, John walked through the dark woods to Genny's side.

Wherever she was, he knew the way that led to her. She pulled him like a magnet. She changed the texture of the forest. She gave new air for him to breathe.

She had kissed him. Without urging, without a sign of revulsion, she had kissed him.

She didn't realize what she'd done.

For two years, no human had initiated contact with him. Not to shake his hand, not to slap his back, not to slap his face.

The women he had collected had wanted him for only one thing—for the pleasure he could give them. They had been greedy, and that was fine with him. Because he hadn't been interested in tenderness. He hadn't been interested in love. He hadn't been interested in communication. Lust had been enough. Except for his occasional forays into Rasputye for supplies and to pick up his mail, he had been completely isolated. He had been satisfied to be a wild man. A yeti. He'd worn skins of animals he had killed, eaten berries and nuts, lived in a hut dug into the hill, and figured this was his penance.

Then . . . without any provocation, Genny had touched him.

He hadn't misread her intention. It hadn't been a particularly sexual kiss—at least not on her part.

But for him it had been a miracle.

He touched his naked chin.

Now look at him. He'd cleaned himself up and come courting like a boy.

Genny had lured him back to civilization.

It was odd to be so intent on gently wooing this woman. Although she was twenty-four years old with a graduate degree and, apparently, a prick for a father, she seemed innocent and untouched. She wasn't stupid about people—she seemed to have a good grip on reality—yet she believed in the intrinsic goodness of mankind. In all of his life, he had never believed in goodness, yet everything about her seemed genuine. It was as if she'd been sent for him, to break him of the morass of agony that had trapped his soul.

For the first time since he'd lost Sun Hee, he believed he could survive the agony of living alone in a world that considered him . . . what was it Brandon Lam called him? A freak.

John laughed softly.

Ah, what Brandon didn't realize was that there were freaks everywhere he looked. This was the *rasputye*, and not just any *rasputye*. This was *the rasputye*, and *the rasputye* attracted freaks. John didn't always recognize them, but they were here. People like—

Something cold brushed his mind. Something evil slithered through his consciousness.

Lifting his nose, he sniffed the air. Turned his head back and forth. Listened to the trees talk.

Danger stalked the woods.

Brandon was in the woods.

*Genny was in danger.*

John ran, trusting to his senses to guide him.

He'd provoked the stupid young man, taunting him, then humiliating him.

Would Brandon take his revenge on Genny?

As John got to the edge of the forest outside of the village, he was panting, gasping with effort and anxiety.

Then Genny's presence reached out and enveloped him.

She was alive. She was unhurt.

She grabbed his arm as if she could see him in the dark. "What's wrong?"

He embraced her, closed his eyes, and held on to her, gasping with relief.

"I can feel the forest. It's worried . . ." she said.

Unseen, John nodded. He could feel it, too.

Brandon was out there, doing . . . something . . . wicked.

"Come on." John followed his senses, and led the way toward the river.

When they were halfway there, he knew where they were going.

The truth hit Genny at the same time, because she

whimpered and tried to move more quickly through the darkness under the trees.

But her instincts weren't as finely honed as his. The brush and roots tripped her.

He caught her once. Twice.

They broke out of the forest above the river and below the observation post on the cliff. The moon glimmered on the water, the sandy bed was pristine white—and across the way, the trees leaned inward almost as if they were racked with the same anxiety that brought John to an abrupt halt. He held Genny back, looked up and down the river, and *listened*.

"This way." She pulled him back into the trees and along the path that led to the den where Mama Cat lived with her kittens.

"Quietly," he said on a breath. "Be silent as a bat on the wing."

"Yes." Here, close to the river, the quarter moon provided enough light to see. Barely enough, but she no longer stumbled.

They went around the bend, came to the place where the path slid steeply down to the river. The trees parted; John saw Brandon standing across the river by the lynx den, a kitten in one hand, a blue plastic crate tilted up and open beside him.

The kitten cried pitifully.

Genny dropped her backpack and exploded into action.

John tried to stop her, but she jumped six feet onto the riverbed, ran across the stones that spanned the water, as silent as a bat on the wing . . . but in the open, she had no chance.

For Brandon saw her—and pulled a revolver. "Forget it, Genny. You can't keep these for yourself. I'm going to make a little money, too."

Genny skidded to a stop, slipped off the stones, splashed ankle-deep into the chilly water. "What money? I haven't made any money."

"Then you're a fool," Brandon said viciously.

"So I've been told," she said with awful irony.

Behind her, unseen, John smeared dirt on his face.

"Brandon, are you going to shoot me?" she asked.

John noted with approval that she managed to sound hurt and slightly pathetic . . . and he began the methodical process of moving into position.

"I won't shoot *you* as long as you don't try and stop *me*." Brandon sounded tritely pleased, as if he were reading a script. "These kittens are going out on a plane tonight."

"No!" Genny darted forward out of the water.

John froze, lifted his hands, prepared to willfully use the power that two years ago had broken his will . . . and his heart.

But when Brandon clicked the safety off, Genny paused again. "Those kittens are tiny babies. If they're taken from their mother, they'll die."

"They're weaned." Brandon was callous and triumphant, and he focused intently on Genny.

Keeping low, John crossed the river upstream, in plain sight—camouflaged by movements that so closely resembled a stalking cat, and by dirt on his skin and clothes.

What was happening here was John's mistake. John's fault. He had humiliated Brandon, and when he did, he underestimated the depths of the boy's wounded pride and malice. John had to make this right.

The second kitten climbed out of the den and yowled as if defending its sibling.

Brandon dropped the baby cat he held into the crate.

"Oh, Brandon. Be careful!" Genny's anxiety was not feigned. "These are rare creatures and—"

"I know. You love these pussies, don't you? Love them more than anything in the whole world." He reached greedily for the second kitten.

Out of the corners of his eyes, John saw a movement, the slow, slinking motion of a lynx. Mama Cat blended with the night. Her eyes gleamed as she stalked Brandon.

Brandon didn't even realize he was in trouble. He picked up the other kitten, holding it loosely in one hand, the way a drunk would hold a snifter of brandy.

John moved on him from one direction.

Mama Cat moved on him from the other.

By his foot, the crate rattled as the ten-pound kitten fought its captivity.

Genny moved forward by inches, her gaze fixed on Brandon's face. "I do love them. Don't you? You came here to find them, to protect them."

"No, I *didn't*." He sounded absolutely scornful. "I came because my father insists I do something useful; and if I had found a lynx, I would have gotten credit. But as it is, I'll still get attention."

The crate beside his foot rattled.

"It's the wrong kind of attention," Genny said urgently. "There's no honor in this."

"Oh, right. You get all the honor, all the glory, because you managed to find the lynx. Gee, Genny, how did you do it?"

John heard the mockery in his voice.

Genny was too focused, too worried for the subtleties. "I was lucky."

"Lucky?" Brandon's laughter put John's teeth on edge, made Mama Cat move a little more quickly. "You weren't lucky. You were a ringer. You're a cheat!"

"I didn't cheat. What do you mean?" Genny was obviously bewildered. "How could I cheat?"

*Because he knows about me.* John now realized the source of the trouble that swirled through the forest; somehow Brandon had discovered the truth about the photos, about John, and . . . and he knew how John felt about her. Because John had visited the *traktir* to see her. Because John had cut his hair, changed his clothes, subdued his wild self for her. Because he had courted her without saying a word. Most of all, to protect her, John had carefully, so carefully, ignored her in public.

"You pretended you didn't know about that creep. That yeti. And all the time you were *sleeping* with him."

Genny halted. She put out her hands, palms up. "I'm not sleeping with anyone."

"You lie. John Powell. John Powell!" Brandon's voice rose, echoing up and down the riverbed. "You know him! You used him to find the cats. You used him like you used me."

"I never used you."

"You've known him all along!"

The lynx was moving into position, her gaze fixed on Brandon and the kitten he held.

"I have never lied to you." Genny's voice sharpened. "But, Brandon, I'm not required to tell you the truth. I owe you nothing."

John wanted to shout at her. *Error. Genny! Error.*

Brandon's face worked; then he smiled a crooked, maniacal smile. "I don't owe you anything, either, but I'll give you something."

In a careless, graceless motion, he tossed the kitten toward Genny.

# Chapter 24

Everything happened at once, and in the feeble light of the moon, Genny saw, heard, felt it all.

The kitten soared through the air, spitting and clawing. Desperate, she leaped to catch it.

Brandon fell backward so hard, he might have been hit by a freight train, and the pistol flew out of his grip.

The kitten froze in midflight.

Genny stood underneath it, her hands up, her jaw dropped.

The mother lynx leaped out of the darkness, claws extended, intent on taking Genny out.

And something heavy hit Genny from the side.

She flew through the air, hit the sand and skidded, the breath knocked out of her by the impact.

A muscled mass—John—landed on her.

In a daze, Genny heard Mama Cat snarl, felt her weight drop on top of John.

Something tore. *John* tore. Genny felt John convulse, heard him gasp in pain.

Then Mama Cat sprang away . . . and Brandon shrieked in terror.

In a tiny corner of her mind, Genny experienced a savage satisfaction.

Some fluid dripped off John and landed beside Genny's ear.

She opened her eyes, breathless under the burden of his body.

A dark liquid pooled beside her and sank into the sand, the coppery smell of blood all too evident.

Mama Cat stalked toward Brandon, eyes fixed on him, teeth bared.

And although Genny knew it was impossible, the kitten still hung in midair, curled up as if held by an invisible palm.

Then she knew the truth she had so carefully ignored.

*John was truly Chosen.*

For one incredulous moment, she rubbed her forehead on the cool, packed sand. She couldn't believe it. She didn't want to believe it. But to deny what was before her eyes was ridiculous and futile.

And someone needed to handle this situation before it got any worse.

She pushed at John. "John? John? Can you hear me? Let the kitten down."

John gathered himself, an obviously painful process, and rolled off her. By slow inches, he lifted his hand.

Like a feather on the wind, the kitten descended to the sand and ran toward its mother.

Genny was reminded she wasn't the only one who had seen the miracle, for Brandon was breathing in loud, irregular moans.

To break through his terror, Genny sharpened her tone. "Brandon. Let the kitten out of the crate. Let it out *now*."

Gibbering like a monkey, Brandon pushed over the crate with his foot.

The second kitten sprang free.

Mama Cat paused, distracted by the return of her babies.

"Brandon," Genny said softly. "Run."

He did, and his flight excited Mama Cat's predatory instinct.

The lynx sprang after him.

He screamed and disappeared into the forest, the big cat on his heels.

"I hope he gets lost." Genny turned to John.

"I hope she eats him alive." John lay sprawled on the sand, eyes closed, breathing deeply. The denim shirt was shredded at the shoulder; blood oozed from the wounds.

In pursuit of her kitten, the lynx had attacked Genny, and John had put himself between them.

Mama Cat had clawed him, sliced his muscles into ground beef.

"Stay here." Genny ran back across the river and up the path, grabbed her backpack, then pelted back down again. She had water in her shoes and sand up her nose, and her ribs hurt when she breathed. But compared to John . . . She knelt beside him, pulled out her first-aid kit, opened it.

She had one roll of gauze. That wasn't going to do it.

She dug deeper in the backpack. Her hand touched her sweatshirt. She pulled it out and pressed it against his shoulder. "Hold it on there," she told him.

He did as he was told but otherwise wasn't moving, and that told her all too clearly how much he suffered.

She got the scissors, the small pack of sterile wipes. She lifted the sweatshirt, cut away the shreds of his denim shirt, saw three slashes across his pectorals. The longest cut was the length of her hand and had laid back skin, showed muscle and sinew. She dabbed at it with the shirt, and worried about the fecal matter and bacteria that the lynx collected on her feet. The wound should be cleaned, and the first-aid kit wasn't equipped to handle something so serious. "How polluted is the river?"

"Gold mines above. Best not to take a chance."

The lynx returned, her pace measured.

She was clean, with no blood on her fur, but she fixed her cruel gaze on Genny and stalked toward her.

Then her kittens ran to her, crying their distress. She halted in her tracks and nuzzled them, licked the Brandon scent off their fur, picked up the boy in her mouth, and started up the river. The girl cat scampered behind them.

"She's moving them to a different den," John said. "We'll never see them again."

"I think that's the least of our problems." Already, his body was giving off waves of heat. It wasn't possible for a normal man to sicken so quickly, but this man wasn't . . . normal . . . "John, why didn't you use your . . . your . . ."

"Power?" he supplied softly.

"Power," she agreed. "To block the lynx's attack?"

"I needed to knock Brandon and that damned pistol out of the picture. I needed to protect the kitten. When I'm on the run, I can only project in so many directions at once. Since I knew I could reach you in time, and an attack by the cat was probably not fatal . . ." He shrugged, and winced.

"We have to get you into town to a doctor."

His laughter held a raw sound. "After what happened here? No. If Brandon lives—Mama Cat wasn't bloodied, so I assume she let him go so she could return to her kittens—he'll be back at the inn, babbling his version of events. We'll be lucky if the villagers don't lift their torches and come to hunt me down."

"You're not Frankenstein," she snapped.

"I'm a freak."

"You are not a freak, you're . . ." She paused, struggled.

"You can't even say it."

"You're Chosen." There. She did say it.

"I warned you that's what I was, didn't I?" He sounded affronted and bitter. "The first time I met you, I told you the truth. I didn't let you walk into this situation blindly."

"I always knew what I was getting into." Before this went any further, she had to explain who she was, who her father was, what she had promised to do. "John, I have something to tell you."

"Whatever it is, I don't want to know right now."

"You really should let me talk."

"I can't. I haven't got a lot of time." He struggled to sit up.

She helped, and tears filled her eyes as blood sprang anew from the marks on his shoulder. "If you don't want to, we don't have to go into Rasputye, but you *do* need a doctor."

"No, I don't. I'm Chosen. This is going to be a serious infection—"

"How can you sound so certain?"

"I can tell." He challenged her with his gaze. "But I heal quickly. A few bad days, and I'll be all right. Help me up and I'll be on my way."

All right. She would tell him later about her father and the notorious deal she'd made. It was probably better that way. John needed to recover without fretting about her motivations.

As she slid her arm around his uninjured shoulder, got her feet under her and lifted him, she shivered in shame. Because she wasn't keeping the truth from John merely for his good health. She was quiet because she was afraid—afraid he wouldn't understand, afraid of his anger, afraid that when he knew the truth, he would turn away and she'd never see him again.

He fascinated her. He challenged her.

She'd witnessed the truth about him. He'd proven his gift.

And now . . . she wanted him more.

He was heavy, but stronger than she realized; and when he was on his feet, he tried to disentangle himself. She looked up at him, into his bare face that still looked so alien, into the eyes that were so familiar. "Where are we going?"

"*I'm* going home."

"Then I'm going with you." She felt his body tense against her. "There's no use arguing."

"What are you going to do? Chase me through the forest?"

"What are you going to do?" she mocked him back. "Run away when you're in pain? Leave a trail of blood like bread crumbs for me to follow?"

He opened his mouth to retort, then closed his eyes and swayed.

He was fevered. He was weak. He was in shock.

She picked up her backpack and, using the same cheery, ruthless tone as the nurse who had helped her prep for her tonsillectomy, said, "You know me. I'm not letting an injured man go off to take care of himself. I've never done stitches before, but if you won't go to Rasputye, I guess I can learn."

"No stitches." He shook his head in heavy amazement, and started walking down the sandy riverbank. "Do you know that some of the Chosen Ones are marked at birth, and some must earn their mark?"

"No, I didn't."

"I've never had a mark. I've been shot at, stabbed, burned, but I've never had any scars or permanent marks that would prove I was Chosen." He staggered slightly. "I believe an enraged mother protecting her babies finally gave them to me—and perhaps there is justice in that."

# Chapter 25

John didn't admit it, but if Genny hadn't helped him, he wouldn't have made it back home. The infection swept through him, stealing his strength; and when she asked how the illness could come on so quickly, he mumbled about being Chosen.

He sickened quickly. He healed quickly.

It was what happened in between that he worried about.

He barely made it up the last steep, rocky climb to his home.

He had oh-so-carefully made his cabin secure, using the subtle tricks he'd learned in the military, and now he leaned against the doorframe and ran his fingers over the latch. The narrow pine needle he had placed there last night remained, assuring him no one had come through the door. So he opened it and stumbled in.

He dragged Genny after him. Or rather—she refused to let go, to allow him to fall to his face on the dirt floor.

She used his weight to propel him facedown onto the primitive wood bed. The feather mattress was barely wide enough for his shoulders and long enough for his legs, but flat enough that he felt every rope stretched across the frame beneath the mattress. It wasn't comfortable. It wasn't large. But it had been here when he moved in and he hadn't cared enough to improve it.

"Roll over," she said.

"Right." He gathered himself, pushed away the pain, and rolled over.

She shed her coat and backpack, carefully climbed on him and unbuttoned his shirt.

The heat of her soaked into his flesh. The scent of her filled his head like potent perfume.

He groaned in exquisite agony.

She paused. "I'm sorry. I didn't mean to hurt you, but I don't know how else to get you out of these clothes."

"No. You didn't hurt me. No, it's not that." She didn't mean anything sexual. Even in his fever-racked state, he was sure of that. She was only interested in his wounds, and making wincing sounds as she peeled shreds of cloth and blood clots away from his oozing flesh.

But she *was* sitting on top of him, looking down at him, her fingers touching him lightly. He had dreamed of this. His imagination filled in details that he knew weren't real—her hand sliding down his belly, beneath his waistband, to caress his cock. He could almost feel her fingers curling around—

"John, can you hear me?"

He blinked at her.

She cupped his chin with her hand, looked into his eyes. "John, do you have any clean rags?"

Had he been raging in delirium? Had he been saying things about her? About *them*?

"John." She enunciated clearly. "Do you have any clean rags?"

"I heard you. The bottom drawer . . . by the woodstove." He watched as she went to the chest, bent over, and . . . she had a bottom shaped like a kiss.

She straightened, her arm full of linens, and looked at him.

"What did I say?"

"Nothing." She frowned as she gazed at him, looking like a mother with a sick child. "Can you hang on a little longer? Stay conscious a little longer?"

"Sure."

She went to his sink. "How's your water?"

"Well water. Good. No contaminants, not much sediment, recently washed the filters." He was making sense, he noted with gratification. Really good sense.

But the next time she spoke, she was standing next to the bed and he could smell wood smoke. She had managed to start a fire in the woodstove. "John, I'm going to put a damp cloth on your forehead. All right?"

He opened his eyes. When had he closed them?

She was holding a white cloth . . . and some scissors. "Then I'm going to cut off your shirt."

"My only denim shirt."

She stroked his forehead with the cool cloth, then covered his forehead and eyes. "Mama Cat shredded it."

"That's right." He heard her clipping the material, felt the tug as she pulled it out from underneath him.

"Now I'm going to clean these scratches. It's going to hurt." She climbed on top of him again, sat on his stomach.

He wanted to tell her to sit a little lower.

"Can you hold still?" she asked.

"Yes." Because if he got restless, she'd get off him, and he didn't want that. "Are you going to take off my pants?"

"After I clean your wounds . . . My God, John, she really dug her claws in."

"Females always do."

Genny rubbed his shoulder, wiping away more blood. "Do you have any antibiotics?"

He snorted. "They don't work on me."

"Aspirin? Anything to bring down the fever?"

"Only time works." He heard water splashing nearby. Somehow, she'd placed a basin beside the bed.

"How do you feel?"

"Good." Every place she touched him felt good.

His mind and body knew what they wanted, and with his control growing more and more precarious every minute, he worried that—

"Good?" she scoffed. "Sure. I think you're miserable, and likely to get worse."

"You don't even know what's happening to you, do you?"

"Know what, John?" She was indulging him.

He didn't care. "You don't know that the *rasputye* is affecting you."

She froze in the act of wringing out her rag.

"More and more, you feel my emotions." He pushed the cloth off his eyes and looked at her. "Don't you?"

She placed the clean, damp rag on his wounds and let the warm water ease the stiffness forming in the joints. Picking her words with care, she said, "That's part of the process of getting to know you. I'm starting to understand how you think."

"Darling, you absorb my emotions. You reflect them back at me. They echo back and forth, transforming, growing, linking us." Dimly, he was aware he had to stop talking before he spoke of his desire for her.

"John." She lifted the cloth, wet it again, and placed it back on his forehead. "You're babbling."

"Am I?" Beneath the cover of the cloth, he closed his eyes and released the smallest, the very tiniest, pulse of power.

God. It felt so good to deliberately release that power that had been pent up in him for so long. It was like an orgasm long desired and long delayed.

She gasped and scrambled off the bed.

He moved the cloth quickly and looked at her, and realized it had been, not pure power but pure desire, for she stood shocked, flushed, and embarrassed.

How could he not want her? He'd asked if she knew about the Chosen Ones, and she did. He'd told her about himself—not everything, but enough—and she hadn't run away.

But now she would. Now she knew.

He closed his eyes. He turned his head away. "Just go. I'll be all right."

"John." She put her hand on his chest. "You're not getting rid of me that easily."

# Chapter 26

G enny lifted John's head, held him against her chest, and put the glass to his lips. "John, drink some water. Please, John, you need water."

Because he was burning up, his fever so high she feared for his life.

He took a sip, then another. Then for the first time since he'd been wounded last night, he greedily drained the glass.

"Good," she whispered, and filled the glass from the pitcher beside the bed. "John, that's good for you."

Seeing this man, usually so vital, stretched out flat on his back unable to move . . . it tore her heart out.

He turned his head to look up at her, and his eyes sparkled a deep, rich blue, as if his soul had filled with sapphires. "Genesis, listen to me. You have to leave."

"I'm not leaving a man in your state alone." She urged him to drink again.

"I can't control it much longer. It's been so long

since I released it . . . last night I had a taste, and it felt so good . . ."

"I know," she said in a soothing tone. "It's okay. I can handle it."

"But should you?" He kissed the hand that held the glass. "Is it the right thing for me to do?"

"When you're feeling better, we'll talk about it." She laid his head back on the miserably flat pillow and stood.

He'd been sick all night and all day with no end to his fever.

She had slept on and off for the remainder of last night and in two-hour stints during the day, rousing when he called out to someone called Sun Hee in tones of such desperation, Genny's eyes prickled with tears.

He sternly ordered Gary to remain where he was, then groaned as if in pain and clasped his head as if dizzy.

Exactly at noon, he had ranted about the Seven Devils, sat up in bed and pointed, told Genny to go look to see if the door to the crossroads was open. He'd been so insistent. When she looked out the front windows, she realized the tall stone formations towered close, rising out of the forest to glisten as if they'd been polished.

At one point, he had been so feverish she stripped him down to his shorts, wiped him down with cool water, and fervently wished she was seeing him under different circumstances. As it was, he was lifeless and unresponsive, the scratches on his shoulder oozed and his muscled frame looked almost gaunt from dehydration and infection.

As the sun began to set, she picked up her cell phone

to call for a physician, but she had no signal. No signal of any kind. It was as if those huge stone formations cast a damper over their surroundings.

It was now past midnight. When she tried to return to the woodstove to stir the soup she'd made with his store of root vegetables and cans of beef broth, he caught her arm. "Don't leave me. I see the faces of all the people I killed, all the friends that are gone, and I can't bear to be alone."

"I'm not leaving," she repeated. Her heart ached for him, for the torments he suffered in his delirium.

He twined his fingers in hers. "But you should go. I'm not safe to be with."

"No, you're not." Because even hurt and torn, he was attractive to her. She felt a different kind of fever, and it wasn't pretty. It wasn't romantic. What kind of woman lusted after a sick man?

Yesterday, when they arrived here at his cabin, she had sat on him because she needed to remove his shirt and have free access to his wound. She would have sworn that's why she did it. Then something crossed between his body and hers, a pulse, a surge of such heat that she had instantaneously trembled on the edge of orgasm.

He had used his power on her.

She didn't blame him. He had been sick; she'd been stupidly provocative. And since then, he had held himself in check. He didn't want to embarrass her. He didn't want to drive her away.

All too obviously, he feared what he would do next.

Going to the fireplace, she stirred the soup. It was

taking longer to cook than she had imagined. Who knew? She had never been a Girl Scout. She was more of a microwave girl.

She glanced at John.

That pulse of sexual power . . . was that why the women he had carried away wanted him still? Because he provided sexual ecstasy far beyond any normal man's skill?

"Genesis. Genny . . ." His voice was hoarse. "You have to go. You have to go *now* . . ." He threw off the blankets, twisted on the bed, in thrall to some great pain.

And a glowing blue wave of power arced off him, knocked her backward into the wall, shook the walls, and cracked the logs stacked beside the fire.

She shook her head, trying to clear it. Got her balance and straightened. Staggered from the shock. Then hurried to his side, and caught his shoulders in her hands. "John, are you okay?"

He opened his blue, blue eyes, so full of torment. Through fever-cracked lips, he told her, "It's too late to run." His eyes closed again. Again he arched on the bed, and then a red wave of power blew off him.

This time, she was touching him—and the power didn't push her; it blasted through her—her skin, her blood, her brain, every nerve, every cell glowed red with power. Another wave, and behind her eyes, she saw violet. Another wave, aqua this time. She staggered, alive as she had ever been in her life. Afraid and exhilarated and amazed. "John!"

He put his hands over hers. "Hang on," he said.

The next blast was bigger than the others, shimmer-

ing with heat and so yellow she felt as if she was looking directly at the sun.

After that, she lost track of time as pulse after pulse
of power arced off his body, out of his mind, through
hers, and away. Dimly she heard the cabin walls creak-
ing, felt the dirt floor shifting beneath her feet. She saw
all the colors of the rainbow growing and crashing on
the beach of her mind, then receding to be replaced by
another wave, bigger, brighter, more powerful.

She didn't know how long she stood leaning over
him, her hands wrapped around his shoulders, before
the biggest wave swept her off her feet. She lost her
grip on his shoulders. She crumpled onto his chest,
and cried out at the contact, sensitized in every nerve,
every inch of skin.

Beneath her, he gasped.

Dimly she realized she had hurt him, and tried to
lift herself away.

But his arms came around her, held her tightly, and
his voice rumbled under her ear. "Stay with me. Genesis, stay here."

She collapsed back down on him and huddled there,
breathless, exhausted, amazed.

For the first time since the barrage had started, he
lay quiet, breathing deeply. But he still burned with
fever.

Yes, John was Chosen. More than that, he was a man
of great power, greater than she had ever imagined.

No wonder the people who had lent her money for
college wanted John to return.

It was only a matter of time before she felt the energy build up in him again, an energy so demanding it almost raised her off his body.

This time, the waves blew directly from him through her. Everywhere they touched, every cell lit with red and blue, burned with fire and froze with ice, sparkled with rubies and diamonds. Tears leaked out of her eyes; not tears of pain, but tears of sorrow and joy. She felt as if she was being born again, torn from the world where she had lived all her life and thrust into another world.

*What had he said? That the* rasputye *was changing her?* She hadn't believed him . . . but now she knew it was true. Because he was here, and he was changing her.

The waves died away again, leaving her exhausted and exhilarated.

His fever cooled, burned away by the release.

When she could speak, she asked, "Does it hurt you?"

"Choking it back hurts me. Releasing it frees me." He half smiled, an edge of wildness in his eyes. "And you help me stay in control. Will you stay with me tonight?"

"Yes, John. I'll stay with you tonight."

When Genny woke up, the fire had died down, liquid dawn was slipping down the glass of the windows . . . and she lay beneath John on his narrow bed.

His fever was gone. The scratches on his shoulder were deep, red scars. He smelled fresh and damp; he had washed, and his skin had resumed its supple sheen.

More important, he had been watching her sleep.

He supported himself on his elbows. His legs wrapped around her legs.

He was naked.

She was dressed.

His belly rested on hers, his erection hard and hot, and his blue eyes glinted with desire.

Her intimate position beneath him, the intensity with which he watched her—they shocked her awake, made her shrink away from him. "We can't."

"Why not? Because I was ill?"

"Yes."

"I'm one of the Chosen, and I am healed."

She believed he was. "But you're exhausted."

"I feel better than I have for two years."

"All right, then. The truth is—I'm not certain I want to do this."

He didn't like that. That sensuous mouth that could make her feel so much tightened, and his deep voice rumbled in his chest. "I can make you certain."

She stilled. "Make me?"

He lightly touched her lower lip with one finger, a simple gesture that roused her. "Are you afraid?" he asked. "I won't hurt you."

"I know that." But he would wrest her control away, make her weak and clinging, bring her to unwilling peaks of ecstasy . . . make her one of his women.

She didn't want to be one of his women. She didn't want to be one of many.

Then he spoke, and a chill swept through her.

For he answered her as if he had plucked the thought from her mind. "I want you to be my woman . . . my only woman."

# Chapter 27

**"I** searched for those other women, carefully picked each one out to serve a purpose. I always wanted a woman who was dissatisfied with her life, who would take the worship I gave her body and use it to go on to a better life." Looking stricken, John turned his head away. "Except for the first one. I chose badly with the first one."

Genny shouldn't care, but a thought niggled at her. . . . "Who?"

He shook his head.

Of course. He would never tell.

"So you want me because I'm dissatisfied with my life?"

John kissed her, his lips chapped by fever. So sure in his touch, he might never have been sick.

"Everything about you is different," he said. "*I* didn't find *you. You* found *me.* You found me when I was about to give up, to go into the crossroads and never come out, to die there like all the old experiments gone wrong . . ."

His words chilled her. "You could die there?"

"Time runs differently in the crossroads. Sometimes you can waste your whole life dreaming the dreams you can find there."

"So you truly believe that the crossroads are . . . are a special place out of time?"

"I've seen the crossroads, not in reality but in my past." He slid his fingers into her hair, looked into her eyes. "Let me show you. Watch . . ."

His power opened her mind, and opened his mind to her.

The cabin faded away . . .

*In its place, Genny saw a strange countryside. The air was bright, but there was no sun. The sky was blue, but it sparkled preternaturally. Spring-bright grass spread like a carpet over the ground. Flowers grew in profusion around the misshapen oaks and yews. A wide waterfall spilled ten feet into a large, tranquil pool.*

*And on the east and the west, the horizon slanted toward the ground. Even in this hallucination, Genny knew that wasn't right.*

*Into this landscape strode a beautiful woman, tall and blond like the women of Rasputye. As she walked, the grass sprang up from beneath her feet as if she weighed nothing.*

*Yet that was an illusion, too; her weight was more than usual, for she was heavily pregnant. Her belly pressed into her pelvis, and once she stopped and bore down with her hands to her stomach as if trying to push the baby out.*

*She was in labor.*

*Yet she strode determinedly, her gaze fixed north.*

*Genny followed, not really there yet held in thrall by the
drama unfolding before her eyes.*

*The landscape rolled past faster than it should, and as
they approached a bleaker land, the woman fell to her knees.
She groaned in the agony of birth, then held her screaming
son in her bloody hands. She cut the cord, staggered to her
feet, and carried the child at arm's length toward the steel
blue sky ahead.*

*Genny heard the waves crashing on the rocks, saw the salt
spray, felt the bone-chilling cold. Miniature icebergs rested
on the rocky shore and bobbed in an ocean that stretched as
far as the eye could see. The female walked into the water
up to her waist—Genny shivered—held the baby up to her
face, and spoke as if the infant could understand her. "If you
survive, you can have your gift, whatever that will be, and
mine, too. And if all that comes to pass, you'll be the one they
fight over." Throwing back her head, she gave a wild burst of
laughter. She placed the infant on an iceberg, listened to its
shriek as if the sound gave her pleasure, then turned . . . to
look directly into Genny's eyes.*

*Her eyes were the same pale, cold blue as John's when
rage held him in its grasp.*

With a gasp, Genny came out of the trance. She was
sitting up, her back against the headboard, stiff with
horror. "John. John, that was your mother!"

"Yes." He slid his hands through her hair, touched
her rigid shoulders, then wrapped the blanket around
his waist and sat facing her.

"She was going to drown herself."

"Yes. She did." His eyes were the color of the steel
blue sky, of the steel blue sea.

"But . . . how do you know what happened that

day?" She lifted a hand, needing an explanation. "Did someone tell you?"

"There is no one alive who knows. That day, there was only my mother and me . . . and her despair and fury."

"Why? Why would she do such a thing? To herself, to her baby?" Why would she look at Genny as if she knew she was there? Who had this woman *been*?

"Genny, listen! People like me, like my mother, like all of the abandoned children . . . we're given a gift, a special talent, but that's weak compensation for coming into this world without the support of a mother, a father, a family. Sometimes we're lucky and adopted by people who love unstintingly, and those children grow up normally, a part of the real world." He reached for her hand as if needing the contact. "But sometimes the babies are taken by those who want to use them and their gifts."

She twined her fingers in his, unable to deny his unspoken appeal for comfort. "Like your adopted parents? Like Olik and Tanja?"

"It can be so much worse than that. The Others seek out the infants. They weigh their gifts; and if the gift has potential, they keep them, abuse them, raise them to be steeped in evil. Very few ever escape that influence." He clenched his jaw. "My mother never escaped that influence."

"Your mother . . . was one of the Others?" Of all the things Genny had imagined about John, she never thought this. That he was a son of a gifted mother; that his tragic birth was part of a chain that extended back at least one generation.

"When the man who fathered me discovered who she was, what she was, he ran like a coward, taking the last of her hope and leaving her alone . . . as she had been her whole life."

Through their clasped hands, Genny experienced a buzz, as if tapping into his mother's memories created a low level of electric current that ran through John's body and his mind.

He continued. "She put me on that ice floe not out of malice. For her, life was nothing but misery, cruelty, and evil—and killing me before I could suffer was a kindness."

"Yet she didn't drown you. She didn't hurt you. She gave you a feeble chance to live and let fate make the decision."

He nodded. "And she gave me her gift should I somehow remain in this world."

"What is it? What is her gift?"

"Sometimes I can see things about the people who are truly connected to me. As in . . . I've always known why she did what she did. And I've always known her fate." He gazed at Genny's face, but his mind was far away. "I've been able to look back and see, like gazing into a flame in the heart of a lamp. The story's there, told with every flicker. I don't know how I hear it, but I comprehend the words. I see the scenes. I know them in my heart."

Something else occurred to Genny, something not so easily explained. "B-but how did you *show* me the story?"

At once John focused on her face, his eyes intent. "When you absorbed my power, you absorbed a part of me."

# Chapter 28

"What? No!" Genny patted her chest, trying to feel the difference.

John's mouth quirked. "It's not fatal."

"Is it permanent?" She didn't want to have absorbed a part of John.

"I don't know. It's never happened before."

A battle raged in Genny's mind and heart . . . and lower.

She was flattered to be the only one.

She was terrified to be the only one.

And as much as she had lusted over John's body, she didn't know if she wanted to be joined with him so intimately, so exclusively, and possibly . . . forever.

John seemed not at all fazed by the doubts that consumed her. He cupped her chin, trailed his fingers down her throat, opened the buttons of her shirt. "You know so much about me, yet you've only seen the sadness, heard my childhood terrors. You cared for me in my illness, helped me control the un-controllable."

"You don't have to worry about that. Nothing about you has ever given me the impression of weakness." She meant to sound brisk and no-nonsense, but as he used his fingers to push her shirt apart, her voice grew husky.

"No. I'm not weak. Yet I suspect I'm not worthy of you, when everything I've seen of you has proved you are the best of women."

She pushed his hand away. "No, I'm not." She didn't even want him to think such a thing, not with the com-mitment to the Gypsy Travel Agency hanging over her head.

Yet his hand returned to her throat, stroking again, using his thumb to test the pulse that beat so strongly and ever more swiftly. He leaned close to her ear, his breath brushing her skin, bringing chills to play along her nerves. "Let me show you the best part of me."

"Oh, I've seen it," she assured him.

He looked startled, then laughed softly. "What did you think?"

"It looked nice."

He pulled back, gazed into her eyes. *"Nice?"*

"You were sick. I wasn't paying attention."

Still he watched her, compelling her to tell the truth.

"I haven't got much to compare it to," she con-fessed.

"How many *best things* have you seen?"

"Pictures of naked guys out there," she mumbled.

Catching her waist, he pulled her flat on the bed.

Leaning over her, he asked, "How does a twenty-four-year-old business college graduate manage not to get any practical experience with *best things*?"

"I was busy."

"You were wary of involvement." He was still smiling, but something about his gaze made her think he was angry. "You're still wary. I'm not the expert, but I think sometimes no parents is better than bad parents."

"I'm all right." But she didn't think he believed her protestation. "And probably a little wariness has saved me a lot of heartache."

"Certainly, and a lot of living, too. But who am I to complain?" As he spoke, he was wrapping her ever closer in his arms. "I'm a yeti, remember? I'm a primitive, chest-thumping beast. The idea of being first is a politically incorrect delight."

"I said I wasn't certain." She was less certain now that he'd told her she had absorbed a part of him.

"Yet you feel my wanting, don't you?" he murmured, his lips barely touching the sensitive skin behind her ear. "As I feel yours."

She turned her head away, denying him although she knew it would do no good.

Placing his mouth over the pulse at her throat, he caressed her with his lips and tongue and teeth. From this one touch, he spread a riot of pleasure through her veins. Pleasure rushed to her belly, her thighs, her toes . . . her arms, her fingers . . . her mind, her heart. . . . Every inch of her body was infused with desire, a desire that quickly became . . . not enough.

When he lifted his head, she was holding him by the

shoulders, fighting against the moan that threatened to break from her, for a moan would tell him too much.

Then she realized her shirt was open, her bra unsnapped, her pants unzipped, and he had done it while she thrilled to his mouth on her throat.

A *moan* would tell him too much? What could he learn from her intense focus on such a simple caress? "How did you do that?" Her voice was husky. "Make me desire you so much that you can do whatever you want?"

"Do you want me that much?" He smiled at her whimsically.

That whimsy coming from him, from this strong, gorgeous man, made her melt like a teenager, and feel silly for doing it. "You're using your gift on me."

"While I kissed your neck?"

"Yes. Not like you did the night I undressed you." Because that had been a pure, unadulterated straight shot of sex. "But a sort of low-level buzz."

"No. I was not. Here, let me show you the difference." He lowered his full weight onto her, pressing his bare chest to her bare chest, opening her legs with his knee and making a place for himself, wrapping his arms around her.

Sensuality shot through her.

"*This* is what my gift feels like," he said, and fed her another warm, slow, persistent shot of sex. "Like a slow slide into crimson passion. Like the first candle lit in the scented darkness. Like the first blush of a spring flower as it opens its petals. . . ."

She knew which petals he was talking about, because while he was talking, his energy was pulsing in her body—a slow, steady assault of heat and light and arousal. Her objection that he would make her one of his women, one like all the rest, was splintering and falling to dust while she was still mostly clothed, while his essence sank deep into her body. Her breasts ached; she bit her lips to control the lush desire for his kiss and the feeling between her legs—supple, damp, desperate.

She caught his face between her hands and kissed him on the mouth, and told herself it was to shut him up. And for curiosity, really. She wanted to know if his kiss was worth all those nights of erotic dreams.

But she couldn't tell, because his response to her kiss was so completely different.

Before, he had been gentle and undemanding. Now . . . he wanted her, and wanted her to want him. So he slanted his lips to hers, thrust his tongue into her mouth, and a slow pulse of desire blossomed inside her. It was a demonstration of the pleasure he could provide.

She kissed him back, putting her tongue in his mouth, curling it against his, tasting and challenging him.

When he pulled back, she was pleased to see he was panting, too.

By golly, she might not have much experience, but she made up for it with enthusiasm.

He sat up, straddled her as she had done to him that first night when he was so sick, and stripped off her shirt and bra. He loomed—a big man intent on getting his own way, but she wasn't afraid. Quite the contrary.

Yes, while he was ill, she'd seen him nude. But this

was different. Now his muscles were full, rippling with life and movement; his chest and belly strong and taut. His hands were huge, yet his fingers moved quickly, nimbly. His erection was . . .

Well, he was right. His erection wasn't *nice*. It was proportionate to his body, large enough to be worrisome, and for that reason she was cautious . . . and thrilled.

The collision of their two bodies seemed to be rushing at her at the speed of light, and at the same time, John moved so slowly she felt she could have stopped him at any minute.

He admired her breasts as if they were twin goddesses, and when he used a single fingertip to stroke the soft, full skin . . . her breath released in a soft sigh and her eyes half closed as desire tapped at her consciousness.

He used his thumbs to circle her nipples, his face intent and unsmiling; and when he had coaxed them into small, puckered roses, he leaned forward, took one into his mouth—and his power rushed through her, bringing her twisting off the mattress.

He held her down, used more pressure, his teeth, and all the while he fed her his passion.

She wrapped one leg around his thigh, pulled him close, wrapped her arms around his back and clutched him, frantic for more, yet breathless.

He moved to the other breast and suckled again, and again he aroused her in a way that made her realize how sterile her life had been.

When he lifted his head, he hushed her—had she been crying out?—and wiped the tears off her cheeks, smiled into her eyes.

She ran her palm over the shadow of a beard on his chin, lifted her head to his and kissed him, and fell into enchantment once more.

It wasn't until he started the slow slide down, kissing her shoulders, her ribs, her belly, that she came to herself long enough to realize . . . she had never traveled this road before. "Stop!"

His hand flattened on her stomach, and he looked up inquiringly.

Once she had his attention, she didn't quite know what to say. "Listen, John. I'm not doing the usual female *I worry that my body isn't good enough.*"

His mouth quirked. "Your body is exactly the one I want."

The way he said it, in those deep, resonant tones, made her think he meant it. Made her want to sigh and swoon.

But when he started down again, she rushed back into speech.

"Wait. Listen. I know you think you need to remove my pants."

He looked up again, now openly laughing. "That's true."

"Then I suspect, you'll want to . . ."

He raised his eyebrows inquiringly, not helping her a bit.

She squirmed, sorry she'd started the one-sided conversation. "Well, the truth is, no one has ever tasted any of these parts"—she waved a hand down her body—"so intimately."

He slid up, rested his elbow on the pillow, looked into her eyes. "I'll keep that in mind."

"Yes, but I don't know what to do."

"You don't have to know what to do. In fact, you don't have to *do* anything except lie there while I show you"—he brushed his mouth over her eyelids, closing them—"what love is."

# Chapter 29

What did John mean when he said he would *show her what love is?* This wasn't love. This was sex. Wasn't it?

Genny's eyes popped open again. "But—"

He turned her onto her stomach. "Relax."

Relax? While he was kissing the back of her neck? While chills followed his mouth down her spine to her bottom? While he reached beneath her, slid his flattened hand across her stomach and beneath the waistband of her pants, into her panties?

While she wondered what he meant by *love*?

She clutched the pillow between her fists, trying to control her reactions—the shuddering thrill that came with his mouth against the rounded cheek of her bottom, the need to press herself into his fingers in front, that sense of having every fiber of her body illuminated by fire and light and desire.

She had worried about whether she should let him

remove her pants and panties, how they would go about it, whether the whole process would be awkward and embarrassing. Now she barely noticed as he slid them down her legs and off, and returned to kiss the tender skin behind her knees, her thighs, and . . . Oh, God.

When he turned her over, she was no longer aware of the openness of her nudity. Rather, she was consumed with need, a need that grew with every caress.

"So beautiful," he whispered, and gazed at her as if she were perfect, his ideal.

The way he cupped her face and looked into her eyes made her believe it was true. He was a man who was used to getting his way through charm, strength, magic . . . and his pure, unalloyed worship of a woman's form. Of *her* form.

As if they had never touched, he started again. As if he had never kissed her, he kissed her once more: her lips, her throat, her breasts, her inner thighs . . . He took his time, savoring each inch of her skin, pressing his lips into the palms of her hands, into the indent of her navel.

From each place, a sensuous buzz spread along her nerves to the tips of her fingers, the ends of her toes, the lobes of her ears. As the enchantment grew, her body felt as if it was weightless, rising on a billow of pure pleasure.

Holding her knees in his hands, he leaned between her legs and delicately, oh so delicately, touched her with his mouth. Once. Twice. This was no clumsy lunge of overwhelming lust, but the slow savoring of a connoisseur. As he used his tongue more deeply, separating her inner lips, caressing her clit, her heart beat slow and hard. She fought the urge to *move*, to bodily demand more and more.

Because at the same time, she urgently wanted him to continue this unhurried, deliberate symphony of sensation.

Perhaps he read her mind, or perhaps an instinct as old as time guided him; his tongue probed and retreated, probed and retreated, sending tremblers of passion deep inside her.

She was starting to feel empty, desperate. . . . She twisted and fought, trying to get away, then trying to remain still. She didn't know what she wanted; she only knew she wanted *more*.

Finally she surrendered and begged, "John, please. Please. I want you."

He wasn't listening, or maybe he had his own time-table, for instead he placed his mouth over her clit and suckled.

Pleasure burned like a coal, drenching her body with heat. Climax came hard and fast, sweet and intense, and when she tried to pull away to ease the shock, John held her tighter, used his lips and tongue to push her bliss to new levels, to extend the glory and ready her body . . . for him. For as soon as the first, fabulous orgasm faded, he lifted himself onto his knees, elevated her hips to match his, and seated himself at the entrance of her body.

She opened her eyes to see him above her, his face serious and intent, his chest and arms rippling with muscle as he adjusted her, then pressed himself into her damp opening, so carefully prepared. The first inch was tight, slick—and then . . . then he was too big. He hurt her; it burned, brought her out of her pleasurable haze and into the real world.

She knew this was inevitable; she'd talked to her friends, and she'd read the books. No one ever said losing your virginity was easy. So she clutched his wrists, closed her eyes, and bit her lip hard, trying to absorb the impact.

After a second, he stopped and held himself in place.

She looked up at him.

His amazing blue eyes were fixed on her face— she could only imagine her expression—and his chest heaved as if under a great strain. Then he smiled at her, a crooked, comforting smile. "I'm not going to mess this up now," he said, and he eased himself down on top of her.

Everywhere their bodies touched, she felt his desire. He pressed her into the mattress, crushing her breasts, her belly, his weight a pleasure against her clit. There was something comforting about having his arms support her, having his breath against her head.

Inside her, his penis seemed to warm and throb, sharing with her his exultation in this joining. Pleasure came in waves, gently lapping at the shore of her consciousness, easing the pain and painting her mind in subdued shades of violet, jade, and rose.

As she relaxed, he nudged closer, opening her more.

She felt the hurt, she truly did, but she was awash with a desire that grew more demanding as his joy increased, as the colors grew stronger, more pure . . .

Then he was all the way inside, and she was so full of John Powell she couldn't imagine living without him. He began to move, in and out, a large, vital, forceful man. Her man . . .

She wrapped her legs and arms around him, caught up in the primitive glory. She was seeing, smelling, hearing, feeling John inside and out, accepting his passion and radiating it back at him. She knew—she *knew*—he was losing his discipline, driving into her faster and longer; felt his balls tightening, preparing for orgasm, while his mind grappled for mastery.

She didn't want him to regain control. She wanted to know they had made the leap together.

Gathering the fragile shreds of her restraint, she tilted her hips—and deep inside, she stroked him with her inner muscles.

For a split second he paused, shaking.

Then his control splintered. He gathered her close, thrust hard and fast, driving inside with desperate need.

As his powerful desire surged through her, climax flared in her veins and, behind her eyelids, colors burst into fireworks that lit the darkness of her lonely soul.

Tears slid out of her eyes—tears of pleasure and of pain, tears for her lost innocence, and tears of joy because, for the first time in her life, someone was a part of her.

Slowly the tide of pleasure receded. Slowly, she came back to the bed and the cabin and John.

"Are you all right?" He remained on top of her, dominating her, but he brushed her hair off her forehead and the tears off her cheeks. "I was rough. I didn't mean to be. I just . . . I always thought I could stay in control, but you . . . I just wanted you too much. No excuse, of course. I shouldn't have . . . are you all right?"

She repressed a smile at this man who so rigidly took responsibility for his actions, and gave himself no leeway. "I'm fine. More than fine. I wish I'd met you a hundred years ago and we had spent all that time in bed."

He grinned, quick and brash. "So I've got permission to love you for a hundred years?"

Again, he'd said, *Love*. Worse, this time, he'd added something that sounded like *Forever*.

"Sure. A hundred years sounds about right, although sooner or later, I'm going to need some serious sustenance."

"Are you hungry?" With the sensitivity of a man who didn't fault her for her trepidation or dismiss the newness of her experience, he gradually moved out of her, slid to the edge of the bed, and stood. "Let me feed you. It's the least I can do."

"Not the soup on the fire," she joked. "It's got commando carrots and pissy potatoes, and it'll never actually finish cooking."

"We'll eat it later. In the meantime, how about some stew?" He stood, glorious in his nakedness, and walked to the locker at the foot of the bed.

She watched him as he opened the locker and brought out a bulky, crinkled envelope.

"What's that?" she asked.

"An MRE. Army rations."

"Oh." She watched as he poured water into the packet and placed it on the woodstove to warm. "You'd think I could have found that in the first place."

"You were busy . . . taking care of me."

As he dressed, she wrapped her arms behind her head and scrutinized him.

Before she knew John, she had dreamed of a man like him. As she got to know him, her admiration for him had grown—and so had her desire for him. When he sickened and lost control of his power, she hadn't been afraid; she had been compassionate.

Never had she been afraid of him. Not until tonight, when he said she had absorbed a part of him, and again when he mentioned *love*.

Then she'd been torn—she wanted to back off, to run away, to think before she leaped. But he had teased her, tempted her, used every weapon at his disposal to make her yield.

She had more than yielded. He had taught her the depths of her own passion, and showed her the depths of his. Now she was afraid, more afraid than she had been before.

She flung her forearm over her eyes.

What had changed? What had happened during their lovemaking to rock her to the core?

Nothing at all, except . . . except now she couldn't deny the truth.

For the first time in her life, she loved someone with all her mind and soul.

She loved John Powell.

# *Chapter 30*

---◆---

On the table by John's bed, Genny placed a bowl of soup wrapped in a towel, a cup of water, and a note. The note read,

*Am going into town to shower and change. Be back as soon as I can.*

Her hand hovered over his head, wanting to give him one farewell caress.

But she loved him. And she didn't want to feel this way about him or any man. She pulled her hand back, and wished this love she felt could be as easily withdrawn. Trouble loomed between them, and it was a trouble of her own making.

Going to the cabinet, she looked again at the pile of letters sitting on top. They were from New York City, and the postmarks stretched back almost two years. The first ones, from the Gypsy Travel Agency, had been read, then stuffed back into their envelopes. Then came a series of unopened letters from the Gypsy

Travel Agency. Finally, the latest envelope, still sealed, was from a name she recognized—Irving Shea, former CEO of the Agency and one of the men who had been adamant about removing her father from his position in the company.

Ever since, her father had cursed his name.

Yet he'd been willing to sell her services to Irving and the Gypsy Travel Agency. She had to wonder at his change of heart.

With her father, she always had to wonder at his motivations.

What had changed that now Irving himself approached John Powell? Was this because she hadn't produced results in the time he had allotted?

Again she glanced at John, asleep on the bed.

He had an obligation to the Chosen Ones to finish his contract.

She had an obligation to the Gypsy Travel Agency to try to convince him it was the right thing to do.

Yet the unopened letters were a testament to how deeply he resented the commitment. And she had never seen reason to believe that love could overcome any difficulty. If anything, her parents had taught her that love could be withheld. Love could be wielded like a weapon. If Genny wasn't careful, John Powell could hurt her as she had never been hurt before.

Opening the front door, she strode out into the crisp morning air—and stopped.

Under the tree, the lynx Lubochka called Nadja and John called Mama Cat sat waiting, her gaze fixed on the hut. Her eyes narrowed on Genny, demanding an accounting.

Genny sat down on the step.

The great cat strolled forward, smooth and graceful. Reaching Genny, she turned and sat beside her, and together they gazed across the panorama of forest and hills toward the Seven Devils.

"He's okay," Genny told her. "He was pretty sick. I guess you know that. But once he started releasing all that energy, he got better." Once he'd started making love to her, he'd gotten magnificent . . . but Genny suspected the lynx knew that, too. "The scratches you gave him are almost healed"—Genny had never seen a recovery so miraculous—"although the scars will never disappear. No harm done, and John and I are both very sorry Brandon found your den. I swear, I don't know how he did it. But I pray the kittens are safe, and when I return to civilization . . ." She was pierced by the knowledge that all too soon she would have to leave this wilderness, this forest, this man, this cat . . . these feelings, this freedom. Anguish made it hard to breathe.

But she had to leave. She had earned a degree and managed to earn a job offer. She had a father who depended on her. Duty inevitably summoned.

So she cleared her throat and continued to talk to the lynx as if the cat could comprehend every word. "When I return to civilization, I will do everything I can to protect you and your habitat. Eventually, in my own way I'll be powerful. Just survive until I can come back. Promise me you'll survive."

The lynx leaned against Genny's shoulder, leaned *hard*.

"Okay. Good." Genny leaned back, giving support

and getting it. "Do you know what he said to me? He said, *You don't have to do anything except lie there while I show you what love is.*" It made her throat scratchy to repeat it. "That makes me really uncomfortable. He didn't really mean love, did he? Because if I love him, well, that's my problem."

The lynx turned her head and looked at Genny as if she were spouting nonsense.

"I know it's stupid to fall in love with a guy who spent two years dressed in furs and covered with hair, but I can't do anything about it. They're my emotions and I have the right to feel them. What I want to know is—was he saying that he loved me? Because if he does . . . I'm simply not used to that. I wouldn't know what to do. I think I'd be afraid, especially because he's so big and so smart and so . . . much." Genny used her hands to indicate a man and a presence that overwhelmed her. "I do value myself. I do. But I've got issues. If John loves me and I love him, as long as I tell him I came to talk to him, I suspect we could work out the breach of integrity. But what do I do about my father? What do I do about the fact that I . . . since I've been here in the Ural Mountains, I feel as if I've found myself. I should be a forest ranger or at least a veterinarian. Can I force myself to go back to New York? Can I be my father's savior *and* the woman John loves? I don't know who I am!"

The lynx stood and brushed against Genny like a giant house cat.

Genny ran a hand over her fur, not so much giving comfort as seeking it.

Mama Cat looked into Genny's eyes, placed her

paw lightly on Genny's knee, then strolled away, her tail moving in a hypnotic rhythm—and she disappeared into the forest's shadows.

Genny pressed the heels of her hands to her eyes, pushing back yet more tears, and wondered why everything felt so new, so raw, why the world looked fresh. . . . Determinedly, she ignored what she had already realized.

The world looked new because *she* was new. Inside and out, she'd been swept clean by John's energy, pouring through her, reforming her, making her part of him.

He had used the word *love*, the one word she had longed all her life to hear, yet now she was torn by the weight of the expectations on her shoulders, and she almost wished he had never spoken.

She didn't know what she should do. She only knew . . . she loved John, and the emotion was too raw to contain.

With a quick, longing glance at the hut, she started toward Rasputye. She wanted to get there and back before he woke up.

She knew exactly how to find the town, her newfound confidence in the woods likely a result of John's teachings. She couldn't have suddenly developed an inner compass, yet she moved swiftly, tirelessly. Her vigor was probably a result of the energy that had poured through her the night before. . . .

But she didn't want to think about that.

She should discover whether Brandon had returned from their confrontation, whether Lubochka's team was searching for him . . . or for her.

Possibly—in fact, probably—Lubochka didn't care if Brandon had returned safely. Lubochka despised Brandon, and for good reason. For that matter, so did Genny . . . although she supposed she shouldn't *hope* that Mama Cat ate him. The truth was, Genny knew Mama Cat had let him go, and she also knew he had made up some story about her and the lynx and told it to anyone who would listen.

Lubochka wouldn't believe him . . . but would she worry when *Genny* didn't arrive back at the inn?

Perhaps. But Lubochka was dedicated to the science of the lynx. Genny didn't fool herself; Lubochka might be very pleased with Genny's lynx sightings, but she would be just as displeased that Genny had taken time off, and wouldn't give a damn that she had only done it to aid a sick man.

Although not sick at all now. As he had said, he sickened quickly and now he slept deeply, without fever or restlessness.

So if Genny's timing was good, she could sneak into the inn without Lubochka seeing her.

She fervently hoped her timing was good.

As she approached Rasputye, she noted changes in the forest: dead branches broken out of the trees, flowers flattened by some unseen force. She reached the first house, and walked across a sheen of straw spread across the track like a golden carpet. When she entered the village, it seemed oddly empty, as if everyone had evacuated. One of the homes had had shingles from its roof peeled off. On another, the shutters dangled. She stepped on something that crunched under her foot, and realized it was a pane of glass, broken out of a window.

Later, Genny wondered how she could have let her happiness blind her to truth, but as she walked toward the inn, she thought only that a great wind had blown through Rasputye.

In a way, it had.

But really, who would have thought that John could project his power from so many miles away?

Genny slipped into the inn as quietly as she could; she didn't want to meet anyone, to explain where she'd been.

No one was in the *traktir*, although she could hear voices in the kitchen, and she met no one as she climbed the stairs to the attic. There she gathered clean clothes and made her way back down to the bathroom.

As usual, the shower changed temperature constantly, the soap was harsh, and the towel was thin and rough, but after the events of the past thirty hours, being clean was glorious. Or perhaps she didn't mind because last night had been awful and frightening, awesome and splendid, and now she was going back to John.

Despite her misgivings, she wanted nothing so much as to return to his side.

She dressed as quickly as she could in the military-type khakis with her ankle-height boots. She headed toward the stairway. If she could collect that meal from Mariana . . .

But a rumble rose from the *traktir*, voices speaking angrily, one over another, and Genny slowed, wondering what was going on. It didn't sound like one of Rasputye's nightly drinking parties.

And, anyway, it was morning.

But she'd found Rasputye to be an odd little village, a place out of time where housewives worked beside their thin farmer husbands, then cooked their dinners and at night told stories about monsters in the woods. Nothing they did should surprise her.

Mariana called out, bringing them to order, so it was a meeting of some kind.

Genny waited at the top of the stairs, thinking that once the meeting was in session, she could slip through the crowd and out the door.

Then Mariana said, "What are we going to do about John Powell?"

# Chapter 31

G enny froze.
  Mariana continued. "We all felt those waves of power last night."

Genny swallowed her gasp of dismay.

"We all know what that kind of disturbance means. He's out of control. He's targeting us. His presence is creating havoc, destruction!"

Genny had never heard Mariana sound like that— hard and cold, angry and vindictive.

"So I ask again," Mariana said, "what are we going to do about John Powell?"

Grumbling rose into the stairway like oily smoke up a chimney.

Genny leaned against the wall and slid halfway down the stairs. There she could huddle and peer into the *traktir*. The village was there en masse—farmers, hunters, the baker, the grocer, the husbands and wives, the beggars and thieves. Genny's team stood at the back of the room. Misha, Lubochka, Reggie, Thorsen, Avni, and Brandon. Every one of them stood with their arms crossed over their chests. All of them looked grim and concerned—except Brandon.

Brandon looked triumphant.

One of the farmers lifted his pitchfork. "John Powell blew over my haystack. He spread it everywhere. It's ruined, no good to anyone!"

An elderly woman spoke, her voice quavering. "The window in my living room shattered, and the handles on my china cups popped off."

An angry murmur rose, and Mariana said, "Of course he would target you, Tanja. John Powell was never grateful that you saved him from the orphanage and raised him."

Tanja? Genny scooted farther down, far enough to view the front of the *traktir*.

There sat a woman who looked like Jabba the Hutt.

She was the one who had sold John to the circus, and these people of Rasputye believed—or pretended to believe—that she was the heroine of this incident. Because the handles on her china cups popped off.

Genny was sickened.

Tanja hefted herself to her feet. "I'm old enough to remember what it was like when John Powell's mother thought she had been betrayed by her lover. She wreaked havoc in Rasputye before she went off and killed herself, and tried to kill her baby. Do we want those horrors to happen again?"

"No!" the villagers howled like a single hungry beast.

In this hamlet of tall, slender, hardworking people,

Tanja was rolling with fat. She lived richly off the moneys she had made exploiting John and other people, other children.

These people of Rasputye gave their allegiance to her. They should be ashamed. They probably were ashamed. Yet they would go to hell for her rather than face a new day with John.

"My wife left me today." The baker stood there, his ham-sized fists clenching and unclenching. "When Powell was . . . was rutting like an animal, she started wanting things. Lewd things. When I hit her like she deserved, she walked out. Took the train to Moscow." He looked around at the other men and roared, "John Powell is ruining our women for work!"

Genny put her hand over her mouth.

Because of the energy pulses, everyone had known what they were doing. She wanted to die of embarrassment and horror and . . . fear.

Mariana stood up on a stool. Like some popular televangelist, she raised her hands over the *traktir*. "We all felt that horrible disturbance in the air. We all know what he was doing last night."

An older women put one hand to her heart and with the other fanned herself.

"We know who he was doing it with. That girl. That Genesis Valente." Mariana sounded coldly vindictive. "We saw her. We recognized her. We knew she was one of *them*. We knew she would bring trouble."

Genny made herself as small as possible.

Lubochka left her team and pushed her way toward the front of the room. "*You're* making trouble, Mariana. Why are you doing this? It's not necessary. I can send

Genesis away. You'll have no further problems, and we can get back to business."

"No!" Brandon bounded past her, took his place beside Mariana and faced the crowd. "Sending the Valente girl away won't remove John Powell from your homes. He'll stay in his cabin and if you make him angry, any time of the day or night, he will send those waves of destruction to Rasputye, and you'll die." He pointed his finger around the room. "Or maybe you won't die. Instead, he'll arouse all your women to a frenzy, then come and pick out the ones he wants— your wives or your daughters—and take them away to screw them. When they come back, they'll be good for nothing. They'll run away and you'll be ashamed to call yourselves men."

"That's stupid," Genny heard one of the women say, but she said it quietly, and the sound was quickly overwhelmed by the babble from the men.

Never in her life had Genny seen a mob, but she recognized one when she saw it.

Lubochka knew it, too. Genny saw her fighting her way back to Misha.

Thorsen sneaked out the door, calling on his cell phone as he went. He'd be meeting his helicopter nearby.

Avni had her hands over her face, and Reggie had his arm around her.

If Genny didn't get out of here and warn John, he would be trapped, beaten, killed. Keeping low, she slipped down the rest of the way to the floor. With her head down and her back against the wall, she headed toward the door.

She was almost there . . . almost there . . .

A hand shot out of the crowd. It grabbed her arm, and pushed her against the wall.

Genny looked up into her captor's face. Into Lubochka's face. The Russian woman looked both furious and anxious. "I can't save you."

"I know."

Lubochka kept her body between Genny and the mob, pushed her the rest of the way to the door, and followed her up the stairs into the sunshine. "Run the straightest way you can and don't look back. Then disappear and never come back here—or you will die."

Genny ran.

Lubochka watched her go, shaking her head.

Misha joined her. "I'll bring the van. You get the computer."

Lubochka glanced at the team gathering around. "Yes. We've got to get out of here."

In a panic, John came out of a dead sleep and sat straight up.

She was gone. Genny was gone.

Why had she left him? The night before he had done everything in his not-inconsiderable power to serve her the kind of bliss she deserved.

Then his gaze fell on the little table she'd dragged to the side of the bed.

A note. She'd left a note. Not good.

But there was also a bowl of soup . . .

He relaxed back onto the pillows. When a woman leaves a man forever, she doesn't leave him nourishment.

Picking up the note, he read it—and sat up again.

*Rasputye?* She'd gone into Rasputye? Alone?

Leaping out of bed, he flung on his jeans, a T-shirt, a long-sleeved khaki fatigue shirt. He pulled on his wool socks, laced his boots.

He was under no misapprehensions about the village where he had grown up. During his boyhood, he had seen how its proximity to the crossroads brought the gifted, while at the same time, jealousy turned the villagers sour. Rasputye had risen before, taken up arms, chased the gifted and sometimes killed them. When he had left as a boy, he'd sworn never to come back . . . and then, when his life had been destroyed, he'd been drawn back, as so many had before him.

Although delirious when he released his energy, he knew very well where his mind had directed it.

The people in Rasputye would be angry—and afraid.

He strode to the door . . . and staggered.

The energy he'd expended during his illness—and during their lovemaking—had left him weak. He cursed the delay, but he wasn't going to make it to Rasputye without fuel; feared that, once there, he would need power.

So he gobbled the soup—it was dreadful and clear proof Genny was no cook—and prepared to follow her.

His gaze fell on her backpack, open and propped against the table.

Should he take it in case they had to flee? Was there anything in it she desperately needed? He did a quick search of the interior, found her camera, unzipped the side pocket, pulled out a photo . . . of him.

He recognized it. Sun Hee had taken it in happier times, between one mission and the next. He stood laughing at the silly antics of Amina and Bataar as they chased each other through the woods, and after he'd heard the camera click, he had turned and chased Sun Hee, too.

Right away, he knew what this photo meant, held as it was in Genny's possession.

Genny knew who he was. She had always known who he was. She was working for someone who wanted him and his power.

But more than that . . . he'd been a fool. Again. He'd believed Genny's sweet, open facade. He'd thought she was genuinely caring. He had begun to imagine he would be able to return to civilization, to live a normal life, to control his power. . . . with her help.

Instead, she was a fake.

# Chapter 32

———⋄———

Genny ran into John's hut, gasping, panting, desperate to warn him of the mob that would follow on her heels.

He was awake and dressed, standing in the middle of the floor.

"John, thank God." She leaned against the doorframe, glad because he looked so healthy and vital—and that meant he could run. More glad because, in her eyes, he was the most handsome man in the world. "We've got trouble. We've got to get out of here."

He didn't seem to hear her. Instead, he stared at the photo he held between his fingers. "What is this?" His voice sounded curiously neutral.

"I don't know. But really, it doesn't matter. The people of Rasputye . . ." It occurred to her that his complexion looked a little gray. "Are you sick? John, you can't be sick. The people of Rasputye have gone nuts!"

John looked up at her, and his eyes were that pale, ice blue of anger.

"John? What is it?" Troubled, she started toward him.

Then it hit her.

Her backpack was open beside him.

He held the photo her father had given her.

John was looking at the picture of himself.

She forgot about the mob. She forgot about the danger. She lunged toward him, knowing she was being stupid, was admitting guilt. She was too late.

He stepped back and held the photo out of reach. Still in that cool, neutral tone, he said, "You knew who I was when you got here. They sent you. You came here to talk me into going back."

"No. That's not true. I came here to observe the lynx. But they asked me . . . that is, my father gave me this trip, but in return he promised them that I would do a favor. I didn't want to, but I . . . I didn't want to go into business so when he gave me the ticket, I just . . ." She knew how she sounded. She was trying to justify what she'd done, how she'd behaved, to whitewash her own role in a nasty plot.

She needed to take responsibility for what she had done. "John, I'm sorry."

He stared at her, breathing hard, still with that gray cast to his complexion. "So you admit it." His lips barely moved.

"Yes." She reached out to him. "But let me explain how it came about."

"You could have merely asked me to go back with you."

"I meant to. I tried!"

He looked at the photo again, and looked at her.

"I did try," she mumbled.

In that cool, neutral voice, he continued. "You didn't have to sleep with me for leverage."

She felt as if he'd body-slammed her. When she caught her breath, that frantic feeling had evaporated, replaced by the chill recognition of a hurt that would not easily be healed. "I didn't sleep with you for any reason other than I wanted to."

"Ah." He nodded. "I was a curiosity. *I wonder what it's like to sleep with a Chosen.* You're one of the groupies."

"One of the . . ." She wasn't one of anything. So she blurted out the stupidest thing she'd ever said in her life. "How can you say that to me? I love you!"

"What a convenient time to tell me."

With those precise, carefully chosen words, he ripped her heart out and tossed it away as if it were garbage.

In all of her life, she had been so prudent, so meticulous, so fastidious about men. And now, the one man she'd trusted, the one to whom she'd given herself, called her a liar and a fraud. He cheapened the gift she had given him: the gift of herself.

He walked over to the cabinet, picked up the envelopes, the ones from the Gypsy Travel Agency and from Irving Shea, ruffled them like a deck of cards. "You saw these, I think."

"Yes, I saw them."

"Did you write any of them?"

"No. I've never lied to you."

He looked at her and lifted his eyebrows.

She said, "I just didn't tell you the whole truth."

"You slept with me with the intent of influencing me to return."

In the face of his studied disbelief, her guilt and despair began to change. "No. I. didn't."

"Perhaps that wasn't the only reason. You slept with me because you knew I could give you pleasure, too."

What was she supposed to say to that?

Still using that remote tone, he continued. "In fact, I promise I will give you ever more pleasure."

She flushed at his casual assumption. "If you think I'm going to sleep with you again when you think so badly of me—"

Moving so swiftly she never suspected his intention, he wrapped his arms around her and with his hand on the back of her head, kissed her. He took her mouth, controlling her; his glorious savagery tearing aside her defenses.

She found herself clinging to him, not caring about his abysmal opinion of her, not caring about her doubts. All she knew was the taste of his passion, the thrum of his power, the way her heartbeat matched his, the way her skin heated as he melded her to his body.

When he let her go, she stood blurry eyed and swaying, needy and lustful.

Until he said, "You'll sleep with me. It's inevitable. Just as inevitable as your betrayal."

She turned her back to him, put a shaking hand to her lips.

He still wanted her, wanted her enough to use his power to overcome her reservations.

But he didn't respect her. She knew it, yet she had given in to him without a struggle. Shame and desire thundered through her veins, reverberated in her ears. . . . "You cheated."

"You should recognize a cheat when you see one."

She swung on him. "You listen to me. *I* am not a cheat. *I* am not a liar. If you would think back, you'll know I tried to tell you the truth—"

"You didn't try very hard."

"No. You're right. I didn't. I liked you and I didn't want to mess that up."

He wasn't listening to her. No—he wasn't *believing* her. "Did you tell them that you'd talked to me?"

"I told my father I had met you. But I didn't betray you! I never said we'd discussed your return to New York City. *I didn't betray you.*"

He crossed his arms and stared at her, those pale blue eyes so hard she felt as if she were beating herself against an iceberg.

"Look, you have to believe me. Basing all your relationships on lousy foster parents is the road paved with self-destruction. Yes, they were awful. Yes, they deserve to burn in hell. But—"

"My wife slept with my boss."

The abrupt change of subject stopped Genny in midtirade.

Then she realized he hadn't changed the subject. Not really. "Your wife? You had a wife?"

"Her name was Sun Hee, a beautiful, smart, gifted woman . . ." He stared at Genny, but he wasn't seeing her. "Gary was her boss, too. He was the kind of guy who had to make it with every woman he met. But she was different. She never slept with him. He could have let things slide if she had. Instead, she chose me, not him. And I thought she chose me forever."

Genny wanted to plug her ears, turn away, not witness his pain and humiliation. But she couldn't turn away because this explained so much. . . .

"Gary never could resist a challenge and I guess he . . . he was irresistible so finally she . . . gave in." His focus returned to Genny. "The funny thing was, I never saw it coming."

"Oh, John." She put her hand on his arm.

His biceps clenched beneath her touch, rejecting her.

She tried to think of the right thing to say when words were inadequate. "Lots of people are betrayed in that way. Lots of people have to divorce."

"Divorce?" He gave a harsh laugh.

"You didn't divorce her?" Genny knew she was afraid, but she had to ask. "What did you do?"

"I let her burn to death."

# *Chapter 33*

———◆———

*I let her burn to death.*
 Genny stood transfixed by John's confession . . .
*Burn to death.*
 . . . and by the emotions that visibly held him captive:
pain, fury, and—oh God—guilt. He had guilt written
on his face and in the lines of his body, and that, more
than anything, convinced her he told the truth.
 *I let her burn to death.*
 He was crazy. Everyone said he was crazy. Crazy be-
cause he'd killed his wife? Or crazy because he could
do the deed?
 She didn't know. Genny only knew he believed she
had betrayed him . . . as his wife had betrayed him.
 She took a step back.
 John watched cynically. "Are you frightened now,
Genesis? Do you understand now what events you've
set in motion by coming here?"
 "That's what Mariana said all those weeks ago.

That I was setting events in motion . . ." The memory of Mariana's prescient warning frightened her almost more than John's ferocity. In an intuitive leap, Genny realized what had driven Mariana to warn her . . . and to hate John. "You slept with her, didn't you?"

For the first time since she'd walked into the cabin and caught him with the photo in his hands, he looked almost normal: confused and wary. "Who?"

"Mariana. You slept with her."

He hesitated, then shrugged as if it no longer mattered. "She was the first. She was the one who suggested I use her. Why?"

"That's why she's so angry. After you'd taught her the meaning of pleasure, you left her alone. And no one knows what you two did. And you don't care enough to even remember."

He nodded as if the idea made sense. "That could be true, although why she would be angry, I don't know. When I dropped her at the inn, she told me she cared nothing about me."

"You believed her?" Genny laughed scornfully. "John, you're a fool."

"I know." He stared at Genny. "Oh, I know." He turned his head in an attitude of listening. "What's that noise?"

At first Genny heard nothing. Then she recognized the distant, threatening rumble, and almost wept with frustration at her own thoughtlessness. "That's what I was trying to tell you. It's a mob. From Rasputye. They're coming for you!"

"Right." He seemed unsurprised. He caught her wrist. "Come on."

"What do you mean, *come on*? I'm not going with

you. Not after what you said, what you believe!" She twisted her arm in his grip.

"You are going with me, I assure you. I would not dream of leaving you behind to face that mob." He observed her fright with a distant gratification. "Not even if you deserve that."

She fought him. "I won't go!"

"They'll run you through with their pitchforks, pierce your organs, watch you die." John pulled her behind him. "Then like a pack of coyotes they'll tear you apart, limb from limb."

She stumbled after him, out the front door and into the forest.

"No one would ever find your body. The people of Rasputye know how to make a person disappear."

He no longer had to pull her. She was convinced. She followed feverishly, down a narrow path and through the trees.

He kept her behind him, protecting her from the branches and the brush, yet maintaining a fast, steady pace. They ran across an open meadow. They dodged through an area that had been clear-cut. They moved so quickly, Genny could barely breathe.

Yet still she heard the mob behind them. Once John led her up a rise. Stopping, he looked back.

She stood, hands on her knees, gasping for air.

His mouth grew tight and grim.

Turning, she saw a curl of gray smoke rising into the air, and at first she didn't understand.

Then she did. "Your cabin." And, "My camera!"

"That's what you're worried about? Your camera?" He snorted.

"You're right." She relaxed. "Lubochka has the photos of the lynx, and I know she'll protect them with her life."

John viewed Genny the way he might view a zoo exhibit. "You are a very odd woman. Come on." Taking her arm again, he started down the trail.

"No." She set her heels. "Is there somewhere I can hide? I'm slowing you down; I can't go any farther. . . . And listen! They're gaining on us."

He didn't argue. Leaning over, he picked her up in a fireman's hold and ran.

He ran smoothly, a man trained to use as little energy as possible for physical endeavors.

Still, the bouncing made her sick, and she cried out, "John, this is foolish. Where are we going?"

"We're going into the *rasputye*," he said.

"What do you mean?" She lifted her head, got her elbows under her on his back. "How do we get into the *rasputye*?"

He stopped abruptly, leaned down, put her on her feet, and pointed up. "There. The doorway is up there."

They were standing at the foot of the fourth of the Seven Devils, the immense stone formations that lifted themselves out of the forest to tower hundreds of feet in the air. Genny remembered what Lubochka had said about the legend surrounding these formations, but at the time Genny hadn't understood. Now she looked straight up at the black-hued, shiny, jagged stone structures and said, "You're kidding."

"Climb." John pushed her up to the rock and put her hands on the holds. "Climb!"

She'd never done any rock climbing at the gym. But she'd watched. There had always been ropes and safety harnesses involved. If she fell here . . . "Do you even know if this will work?"

"You mean, have I been into the *rasputye* before?"

"Yes!"

"No." He lifted a finger. "But listen."

She did. She heard shouting, dogs barking, and close at hand, someone thrashing through the brush.

"You can stay if you want. But the villagers are not going to spare you. If anything, they hate you more than they fear me." His eyes were that bleached blue of anger. "But if you go up, I can follow you, catch you if you slip."

*I let my wife burn to death.*

"Yes, but *will* you catch me?"

"You'll have to find out." He pushed her up toward the first handhold. "Now climb."

She did.

As long as Genny lived, she would remember the look of the granite under her hands, streaked by nature and smoothed by time. Embedded in the black monolith were glittering vertical lines of gray, gold and brown crystal.

When they passed out of the forest, climbing above the trees, she was panting from exertion. Another ten minutes, and she couldn't stand it anymore. She stopped, took a fortifying breath, and looked down. She could no longer see the ground—only the canopy of the forest waving at her as the wind passed over the treetops.

The higher they climbed, the more the wind blew, whistling eerily.

She looked up. This was the core of some long-vanished mountain, the tallest of them all—a monolith of mythic proportions that pierced the sky and sliced the clouds to shreds.

"Go on." John showed his military training with his calm voice and steady hand on her back. "It's not much farther."

"Much farther where?" She looked up again. They were headed nowhere but *up*.

"You'll see when we get there."

They'd told her he was crazy, and had she believed them? *Nooo.* Now she had let him push her up a rock in the middle of the Ural Mountains toward some otherworldly place that didn't exist.

What would happen when they got to the top? Would he want them to jump like star-crossed lovers to their deaths? Or would he simply kill her as he had killed his wife?

She stopped. Closed her eyes.

He hadn't done it, had he? He'd been trying to frighten her . . .

And done a good job of it. Fear welled up in her. "I don't want to go any farther."

"You've got no choice. Look down."

She heard a shout from below, and opened her eyes and saw Brandon climbing up out of the forest, his gaze fixed on them.

She had feared, suspected, denied that John was crazy.

Now, seeing Brandon's wild eyes and the way he waved a pistol, she knew what real madness looked like.

With a gasp of terror, she started climbing as fast as she could.

But they had no cover here. He could kill them if he chose.

"It's all right." John climbed with her, slightly below and to the left. "He'd have to be a crack shot to hit us at this distance with that pistol."

True to his prediction, the sound of a shot rang out. Genny ducked as rock chips showered onto them. Another shot. Another. She didn't understand where they were going; she only knew every upward effort depleted her energy while each bullet increased her need to *hurry*. One shot hit to the right of them. One hit below. The others landed somewhere, she didn't know where. She only knew she flinched with each report. But she and John were untouched.

Brandon shouted, infuriated by his failure and by their lead, and he climbed faster, better than she could.

Genny tried to speed up. But her palms were sweating, and when she hurried, her foot slipped; her heart stopped.

John sounded so composed. "Don't rush. We're going to make it."

She didn't dare not believe him.

Yet every time she glanced up, the rock structure seemed to grow taller—and nowhere did she see a way to escape. The slow, steady conviction that she was facing death grew in her.

She didn't want to die. And she couldn't stand knowing John believed the worst of her. "You have to listen to me."

"No, I don't." His voice cooled.

"Please, John, I didn't do anything so terribly wrong." She jumped when he put his hand on her bottom.

He steadied her. "Do you see that shelf off to the right?"

She did. Cut into the rock, or maybe part of the natural formation, was a five-foot-wide, twenty-foot-long space with a flat floor, three open sides, and the thrust of rock up on one side.

"Get up on it," John instructed. "Quickly. Brandon has almost caught us."

She scooted to the side until she could pull herself up onto her stomach. "You're bigger than he is."

"Are you sure he used all his bullets?"

Of course she wasn't sure.

"You have to remember to count," John said. "Our biggest problem is that one of the Others got to him. He's on drugs. Or demon possessed. Or both." He shoved her hard.

She crawled all the way onto the splintered, glassy surface, scooted out of the way, and offered her hand to him.

He reached for it.

Below them, Brandon shouted in triumph.

John jerked, then suddenly slid down and out of sight.

Genny screamed. She heard a smack that sounded like John's foot against a soft surface.

Brandon groaned.

John appeared again, his face grim. "Back up. Against the rock." This time he was halfway onto the shelf when Brandon again grabbed his foot and yanked.

John kicked.

Genny sprang forward, caught John's arm, and helped drag him onto the flat surface.

"Get back!" John shouted at her. Then Brandon proved John's intuition was right.

Brandon leaped so lightly onto the rock, his eyes glittering with malice and fearless disregard for danger. He was clearly drugged. Bending his head down, he shrieked with fury and charged at John.

With the grace of a bullfighter, John stepped aside and let him pass, then ran after him and shoved.

Like a loose-limbed clown, Brandon tumbled over the edge.

Genny gasped and listened, expecting to hear the yell of a dead man. Instead, she heard an oomph, as if Brandon had had the breath knocked out of him, and silence.

She stared at John, eyes wide.

John glanced over the edge. Shook his head. "He fell about two stories. Didn't even knock him out. He's on his way back up. Genny, darling, come here. We've only got a couple of minutes alone." He held out his arms.

Like an idiot, she sighed in relief.

He had forgiven her, maybe even believed her.

She rushed to him, prepared for his embrace.

He took her by the shoulders, whirled her in a smooth dance step toward the side where the rock dropped straight down. Down, all the way to the ground.

"John, what are you doing?" She glanced over

John's shoulder, saw Brandon climbing onto the shelf, red eyed and furious, his gaze fixed on John's back. "Look out!"

"I can take care of Brandon," John assured her. "And don't worry—I'm not going to kill you. But I'm not finished with you yet."

Picking her up, he dropped her over the edge.

# Chapter 34

With a thump, Genny landed on the soft, thick grass and lay there, mouth agape, trying to contain the scream she hadn't had the chance to release.

*Am I dead?*

She had to be. She didn't recall falling, but she certainly recalled John dropping her off the edge of the tallest Devil. She recalled the look on his face, angry and vengeful. She recalled the terror . . . but she couldn't remember the sensation of falling.

She should have hit branches on her way down. She looked around. She was on the ground. Where was the forest? Where were the farmers with pitchforks and that one vengeful innkeeper rallying the villagers to murder?

The sky sparkled blue and iridescent. The trees were old and warped, with flowers growing in glorious profusion around their roots. Here all was peaceful . . . but it didn't look like anyone's version of heaven or hell.

*My God. Where am I?*

Close at hand, she heard water trickling. She turned her head to see a small, brilliantly clear brook burbling over smooth, crystalline rocks . . . rocks that looked like they had fallen off the Seven Devils.

The middle Devil. The doorway—to the *rasputye.*

Sitting up, she looked toward the horizons. To the east and west, the horizon looked as if it had been tucked into the earth. To the north and south, the sky went on forever.

The truth hit her.

She'd seen this place before, in the vision John had shared with her of his mother.

Genny was in the *rasputye,* in the crossroads.

John had thrown her off that rock.

Did he truly hate her?

*Yes.*

Yet fool that she was, she couldn't believe he had let his wife burn to death.

She tried to, but she didn't.

She had to believe in the John Powell he had shown her, a man so dedicated to the life of the forest that the rare Ural lynx allowed him to know the location of her den and gave him permission to hold her kittens. Genny had to believe the big cat instinctively knew what kind of man John was . . . and she had to believe in her own instincts, too.

She loved the man.

She covered her face with her hands.

Why had she fallen in love with a man whose life had been so stained with pain and betrayals?

She could have loved any number of civilized,

driven businessmen, but for her, it had to be John. Right from the moment she had seen his photo, she'd been interested. Then the time they'd spent together, the conversations they had shared—that had been a seduction all of its own. And the sex!

She flopped back on the grass.

The sex had been pure fantasy.

What had come after, when he discovered that picture, was more nightmare.

So Genny loved the man.

But he had the right to his rage.

She sat up again.

She had to get out of here. She had to get away *now*, before he made the jump into the crossroads and came searching for her.

Because he would. John and Brandon were probably fighting right now, but Brandon didn't stand a chance against John.

All too soon, John would appear in the *rasputye*. And he'd be after her.

Getting to her feet, she tested her shaky knees, then started running south.

John landed on his feet like a cat. A single glance proved what he already knew. The grass was soft, thick, and an impossibly bright spring green. The sky was sparkling blue, and shaped like an arch that reached the ground to the east and west, then went on forever to the north and south.

He had always known the *rasputye* was here. He had seen it in his vision. He could feel it, a magnet to his soul.

But now he knew the ancients were telling the truth. The doorway was off the edge of the middle Devil.

He was in the *rasputye*; and for at least a little while, it would provide a refuge from his wreck of a life.

He studied the faint footprints in the grass.

More important, Genny was in the *rasputye*. Genny, who had convinced him that she was all that was good and decent. That he was wrong to live alone in despair.

He should have known she was a liar.

Bending to study her footprints, he knew she had taken off in a panicked run.

Yes. Smart girl. She had been afraid of him.

Genny had gone south.

He followed.

He had revenge to exact.

# Chapter 35

The landscape looked almost normal. A little too bright, too colorful, too pristine, yet there were forests, and rivers, rocks and plants—all parts of the real world.

But as Genny ran and gasped and panted, then finally slowed to walk, the landscape still rolled by too quickly, almost as if she were on a Disney ride. That bothered her . . . but not as much as the vast emptiness of the land.

The wind blew, the water ran, but there were no animals, no birds, no people. No sign of any living being.

Had she hit her head when she landed? Was she hallucinating? Again she wondered if she was dead.

Then as she climbed a hill for a look around, she heard a sound behind her. She turned to look.

One living being stalked across the landscape—John.

He was big. He was handsome. He was angry. His gaze was fixed on her.

Her heart leaped into her throat. Blood thundered in her veins.

Oh, she was very much alive, because irrepressible fear sent her into a sprint down the hill toward the gloriously clear pool and the wide, thundering waterfall that filled it. As she ran, she unlaced her leather boots, pulled them off, stashed them behind a pile of boulders. Her clothes had to go, too—the material was sturdy, heavy, made not to swim in but to protect her skin from bugs and thorns. She stripped off her shirt and pants, flung them into the oozing warm mud at the side of the pool, and stomped them in. They were hidden. Thank God, they were invisible. And if she could get in that water and behind that waterfall, she would also be hidden.

She glanced behind her.

John hadn't yet appeared over the crest of the hill.

Dashing to the rocky lip beside the waterfall, she dove in.

The water enveloped her, balmy and clear. So very clear. She could see everything: the sandy bottom bubbling with warm springs that fed the pool; the plants waving among the rocks that rimmed the pool. She swam beneath the splash and boil of the falls, desperately seeking its concealment, and surfaced in the shallow rock grotto.

Pushing her sopping hair out of her eyes, she looked around. She stood on a gravelly shelf, waist deep in the warm water. Smooth black boulders protruded from the water. A pale blue light flickered on her and on the stones. Tiny springs dribbled off the rock, and when Genny tested them with her hand, they were comfortably, marvelously warm. The falls rumbled in front of her, providing a curtain that divided her from the world. From John.

He couldn't see her here. She was safe.

Yet her racing heart didn't believe it.

If he topped the hill at the right moment, he could have seen her swimming in that pristine water.

She inhaled in short, frightened breaths, and kept her gaze fixed on the falls, expecting at any second to see him part the water like Poseidon and tower over her—which was why, when his hands grabbed her ankles and pulled her under, she went without a fight.

He dragged her under the waterfall, out from beneath its roiling din, then let her go.

She fought her way to the surface. As she gasped a breath, she glanced around for him.

He swam on the bottom of the pool, circling beneath her; his expression feral, primal, furious.

She dove away with a silent scream of fear.

He followed, naked, strong, efficient in the water. He grabbed her hips.

She shoved against him, frantic to get away.

He easily let her go. *Too easily.*

As she broke the surface, she realized why. He'd used her momentum to strip off her panties. She was naked, almost, except for her bra and whatever she could cover with her hands.

Looking down into the clear water, she saw him swim to the bottom of the pool . . . and drop her panties on one of the waving fronds.

Like an evil-tempered shark, he looked up at her, savagely satisfied with his actions—and his view.

She shouldn't swim. She shouldn't kick. She shouldn't show him more of herself than he could already see, which from that angle was . . . everything.

She knew, logically, she had no chance of escape. She knew, by looking at him, at the way his body clenched, at the erection forming, that her flight would only trigger his need to pursue.

But when he started toward her, logic counted for nothing.

Panic drove her, and she dashed toward shore. He swam behind her—she knew he did. She was almost there . . . her feet touched the sand . . .

He grabbed her, dragged her under the surface, walked his hands up her calves, up her thighs, up her bottom, up her back.

She kicked back at him. She slammed one foot into his thigh, one into his shin, tried to kick higher, to do real damage.

He paid no attention, handling her as if she were a play toy. He unsnapped her bra. Twirled her in the water. Grabbed her sensible white C-cups, pulled them off her arms . . . slowly, willfully dropped the bra to the bottom of the pool to join her panties.

She hated him. She hated that deliberate demonstration of superior strength, hated the ice blue of his eyes, the heated sleekness of his body. She hated that he taunted her with her helplessness, hated that he wouldn't believe her when she explained.

She hated that he made her want him so badly, she ached like she had the flu.

They came up face-to-face, body-to-body, treading water on the other side of the falls.

He was wet and seething and . . . hard. *Very hard*.

She was scared and outraged and . . . aroused. Mostly aroused.

He bared his teeth. "You shouldn't have run."

"You shouldn't have chased me."

But he didn't care what she said, what she thought. He only cared about one thing.

Catching her hips in one arm, he spread her legs around him and, using his other hand, thrust his fingers inside her.

She arched backward in shock, in injudicious passion. Then, when he pressed his thumb against her clit, she writhed in an orgasm that displayed every emotion, every desire. Wildfire burned her so fast and hot, she had no control. She screamed in pleasure and in a fury of her own.

*How dare he . . . ?*

Then he did it again, forcing her from one orgasmic peak to another, showing her how easily he ruled her body.

"Damn you!" She strained to escape, so mad with rapture she could barely speak.

"Too late. I was damned years ago." He let her go.

Again she tried to swim for shore.

But he was there at every turn, and finally she realized—he was herding her, directing her under the waterfall and into the grotto. And so she went.

She was so angry, she wanted to slap him in the face. She was so aroused, she wanted to pull him inside her and make him sorry he had ever doubted her.

Getting her feet under her, she turned on him, not sure what she was going to do, what she was going to say—and he used her momentum to pick her up and place her on a smooth black granite boulder. The cool stone had been sliced by some great force, and slanted toward him. A hollow formed by long years beneath the waterfall cradled her back, and the spray acted as a lubricant that moved her down to him . . . whether she liked it or not.

She didn't like it. He might already know he was going to win, but she wanted him to have to fight for this victory.

John caught her knees in his big palms. He stood in the water; it foamed up to his thighs. He pulled her onto him and, without a single sign of the gentle care he had shown before, thrust inside her.

He was large, strong, invasive.

Her traitorous body welcomed him, softening around him, easing him inside with a moisture that betrayed her.

He grinned, a triumphant Viking slash of a smile that mocked her and her irate reluctance. Still grinning, he leaned into her—and ruthlessly detonated a power pulse into her. Sexual arousal blasted her: every nerve, every organ, every inch of skin. This was no gentle release of power but a commanding stab, a movement to ruthlessly dominate her.

He succeeded.

She clutched him between her thighs, came so hard and fast it was as if she had waited for this all her life. The convulsion brought her spine off the rock. She clasped his shoulders and dug her nails into his skin. As revenge, perhaps. Or to hang on in a fantasy gone mad.

He groaned, thrust uncontrollably, then caught his

breath. Sliding his hands to her wrists, he pulled free of her grip. Twining his fingers with hers, he pressed them to the stone and held them there He locked gazes with her . . . and drove into her, over and over. The heat of his lust, his temper, his determination, his powers sent her hurtling from peak to peak, scorching her world.

She wanted. She needed.

He gave. And gave. Relentlessly, constantly, until she cried from a devastation of pleasure.

Did he hate her?

Yes, but he couldn't resist her, either—for as her passion grew, so did his. The power he used on her reflected back at him, and he plunged harder, faster—his eyes glittering wildly as his climax seized him. He was out of control.

She exulted in that, in knowing she had undone his revered discipline.

The grotto glowed with a pale blue light. The waterfall roared. The rock was slick on her back.

They moved together into a final, glorious climax, coming and coming until the very ground beneath them trembled with pleasure.

They were one, once more.

# Chapter 36

**B**randon came to consciousness, shook his head blearily, sat up, and looked around.

The grass was deep and soft. The sky was blue. The flowers were purple and red and pink. He blinked as the scene swam before his eyes. The colors were so vividly, brutally bright, he expected those high-voiced freaks from the *Wizard of Oz* to hop out of the bushes and start singing about the lollypop guild.

At the thought, Brandon rolled onto his hands and knees and barfed in the spring green grass. He retched, and retched, until all the stuff in his stomach was in a gross puddle and the spinning in his head had slowed. He fell over again, groaning, holding his stomach, wanting to die . . . needing a drink.

It was the sound of water trickling nearby that roused him, got him to his feet, and sent him staggering to the stream. He dunked his head into the water, drank and washed, stood and tried to figure out where he was. The last thing he remembered was fighting with that freakish giant, John Powell—and winning. He gave the guy a push, and Powell toppled off the edge. Brandon remembered eagerly running to the brink for a bird's-eye view, looking down and being surprised that Powell had already fallen out of sight.

Then something—a brisk wind that felt like a hand on his back—sent him over the edge, too. He screamed and passed out.

Now here he was . . . somewhere on the yellow brick road.

To the east and west, the sky looked as if it was stapled to the ground. To the north and south, it went on forever.

So if he went west, there had to be a way out.

He started walking.


Warm water trickled between Genny's breasts. She opened her eyes and discovered John had redirected one of the springs easing from the rocks behind them, and now he watched, seemingly fascinated, as the water flowed down to the place where they were still joined.

Inside her, his penis stirred. Already, he was getting aroused . . . again.

*He had some nerve.*

She twisted, quick and furious, put her foot on his chest, and pushed—and he was caught off guard. He stumbled backward into the falls, toppled off the shelf and into the pool.

"Note to self: he's easy to overcome when sufficiently distracted," Genny muttered—not that she thought he would go very far.

She slid off the rock and stood, arms outstretched into the falls, then dove into the water and swam to the bottom.

If not for John, she would have been in heaven here. For the first time in years, she wanted to frolic, to play, as the clear water caressed her and warm springs bubbled up from the bottom.

But out of the corners of her eyes, she could see John doing laps across the pool.

She collected her bra off a rock where he had tossed it, brought it to the surface, and threw it on the grassy part of the shore.

She was, right now, sick and tired of putting up with men. They were exploitive bastards, every one of them, and sick with testosterone poisoning to boot.

Taking a big breath, she dove to the bottom again and picked her panties off a waving frond. She started toward the surface, then frowned and dove back down. The rock beside that plant didn't look quite like a rock. In fact, toward the top, the round brown object had a blue string tied around it. Tentatively, she poked at it.

It was a leather bag, like an old-fashioned money sack, small enough to carry in one hand. She picked it up; it didn't weigh much.

Then it occurred to her—it was probably John's, lost during his mad dash to rip off his clothes so he could screw her senseless.

She ought to leave the little bag right here.

But that was the trouble with being upright and honorable. Even if he was a calculating jerk, she held herself to higher standards. She brought it up with her panties and tossed them both on the grass beside her bra. Then she waded out of the water to excavate her clothes from the mud.

Tiny springs bubbled up here, too, turning the smooth, brown clay squishy and wet, warm between her toes. If she hadn't been so aggravated, she would have been having a good time digging around with her feet then, when she had no luck that way, with her hands.

But she *was* aggravated.

John had refused to listen to her explanation about why she'd come looking for him. At the same time, though, he was perfectly willing to hump as if they were rabbits.

*Yes, yes.* She'd been aroused before he touched her. He had that effect on her.

But that didn't mean it was *right*; didn't mean he had to take advantage of her. And she was pretty darned sure that even if she hadn't been interested, he would have used his gift to get her interested. Which, as far as she was concerned, was nothing but cheating.

She must have been muttering pretty loudly, because behind her John said, "You always used your gift to make me horny."

She flung herself around and glared at the naked, dripping man standing waist deep in the water. "What gift?"

"You look and smell and taste like a beautiful woman, and that gift works every time on me."

His expression was so solemn, it caught her attention. *Was he serious?*

Then she realized she was mistaking detachment for solemnity.

"What bullshit." She found her shirt, wadded up in the mud, and threw it at him hard.

It landed with a splatter on his chest.

She continued. "You don't listen to me, but you want to do it with me."

He caught the shirt, glanced at it, then tossed it in the water. "I'm listening now."

"Are you really? Really?" Sarcasm had never tripped off her tongue so easily. She straightened, stared him right in the face, and said, "Well, here you go. I agreed to talk to you, to try to negotiate your return to New York City because it was the only way I could get to have the one thing I wanted most in the world—the wilderness and the lynx. And, yes, I didn't tell you when I should have because I was afraid you'd be so mad I'd never see you again. I liked you. I liked the cats. I liked how you were teaching me to listen to the forest and how to survive in the world. And I didn't want to lose that."

"Yes." He nodded. "That is a motivation I can comprehend."

She was fed up.

He was doing his inscrutable judgment routine.

*Infuriating!*

She continued. "So I'm a big coward, but at the same time—give me *some* credit for bravery. I thought you were probably crazy or violent or both, and I was willing to take that chance to work on Lubochka's team. I was afraid my father expected me to sleep with you to convince you . . ." Horrified, she realized what she had admitted.

John's extraordinary blue eyes sharpened. "*Did* you sleep with me to convince me to go back?"

"No!" she shouted. "No. I already told you, no!" She wanted to slap him across the face for suggesting such a thing. "You can't talk to me that way. You're not my father. You can't abuse me like that."

"Abuse you?" John's fists flexed. "He abused you?"

"He never hit me. Never touched me at all, if he could help it. It was like I was a tool he picked up only when he needed to use me . . ." She lifted her chin. "But he was always pushing me to do what he thought was right . . . for him. If I didn't do it, he said things. Like you just said. Insulting, belittling . . . I'm not putting up with that from you."

"But you'll put up with it from him?"

"No. *No!*" She took a long breath, and realized . . . "No, not anymore. I've been through too much to take that from . . . from anyone."

It was true. She had traveled to Russia, held a baby lynx, been chased by a violent mob, climbed a tall rock and dropped, she had thought, to her death. She had met the man she'd been sent to recruit.

She looked at John, standing two feet away, smeared with mud and watching her far too intelligently.

She'd been frightened by him, cared for him, fallen in love with him, mated with him, had him discover her duplicity. She'd had him accuse her, hate her, save her and take his revenge on her.

She wasn't the same woman who had come to Russia.

She was not even the same woman she was this morning. So she made her declaration of independence. "I'm not afraid of anything anymore. I'm for sure not afraid of you, John Powell." She found her pants and threw them at him just as hard as she had the shirt.

He was closer this time, and when the pants hit him, the splatter of mud reached her, too.

"You should be," he said. "A day after I discovered my wife's infidelity, I let her burn to death."

"Okay." Genny sat down and crossed her hands over her chest. "Convince me."

# Chapter 37

———◆◆◆———

As if he were unsure, John glanced around at the pool, the falls, the perfect, beautiful land empty of people and animals. He looked at Genny, naked and defiant, sitting in the warm mud.

"Go on. Let's hear it." She didn't know for a minute whether he was going to take her up on her challenge or stalk away and protect his dignity and secret. She was pretty much betting on the latter, and told herself she didn't care.

Because after all, *he* didn't care about *her* or he wouldn't believe so badly of her.

"I can't talk while you're naked," he said.

He was stalling. "Okay. I can fix that." Getting up, she searched in the water until she found her shirt. She pulled it on, buttoned it up, and sat down again.

"That's better," he said, although he sounded skeptical.

"You can resist my charms for a half hour," she said.

He mumbled, "I wouldn't be so sure of that."

"Try." Her voice was tart.

He looked at the buttons on her shirt, or maybe the breasts underneath her shirt, as if trying to decide between sex and confession. Then to her surprise, he seated himself beside her—and talked. "I was one of the Chosen Ones, the power member in my team—"

"Hm, yes. I suspected that." Still that easy sarcasm.

"—and I worked with those six people for three years. We were close. We lived together, fought together, ate together, and saved people . . . sometimes. Got our hands on a lot of artifacts and almost got killed . . . too often. Slept together, or rather, Gary slept with all the women except Sun Hee until . . ."

"Until you found them together."

"Gary set that up, I'm sure." John wiped his hand across his forehead, leaving a streak of mud behind. "I think I could have forgiven him, them, if there had been any real emotion behind it, but for him, it wasn't about making love to Sun Hee. It was about being the dominant male. About kicking sand in my face."

"What was it about with Sun Hee?"

"It was about being weak." He sounded indifferent, as if he were looking at events that had happened to another man. "She was a very talented Chosen, but her character wasn't strong. When our marriage settled down into the day-to-day boredoms and frustrations of real life, Gary and his flashy, clandestine courtship looked exciting to her."

"That's all?"

"What did you expect?"

"From you? Some pain, some indignation, some scorn. Something!" Genny hadn't thought that John could startle her, but he did. "You sound like you didn't love her!"

John blankly looked at her.

"You didn't love her!" Genny realized.

"I did, as much as a man like me can love."

Was it true? Was John incapable of real love? If that was the truth, Genny's disdain for Sun Hee changed to something quite different—she felt sorry for her.

"I found them the day before we left on our mission." John started out steadily enough, but now his voice and body tensed. "So then . . ."

"Then you killed them all?" Genny poked at him the same way the circus man had poked at him—to get him to perform.

But she had a different reason to want this performance. John needed to tell the truth. For once, he needed to tell the whole truth.

Genny needed to hear it.

"Five of them. That day, five died." John picked up a handful of mud and squished it between his fingers, and gazed at his own hand as if it was a crystal to see into the past. "Max was our treasure finder. A good, solid man with a real gift for finding gold. Sophie wasn't an eloquent woman. She wasn't even bright, but she could always sense a trap. Amina . . . glowed."

"Like a flashlight?"

John got an affectionate smirk on his face. "Like our own personal Energizer bunny. Bataar could hear anything, even the flutter of butterfly wings; and Sun

Hee was the human equivalent of a bloodhound. Our leader was Gary—Gary White, a guy with this need to be the best, the biggest, the most acclaimed. The Chosen teams are seven men and women who work together for seven years. That's what we signed on for. Gary had led three groups before ours."

"So he wasn't young." Genny could already see where this was going.

"No, but he wasn't old."

"But he wasn't the youngest, the brightest, the strongest. Not anymore."

John looked at her, almost annoyed. "How did you *know* that?"

"I suppose this is going to come as a shock to you, Powell, but men aren't difficult creatures to figure out. First they're young and brash and think they'll live forever. Then when they get a little older, they realize other men are coming up who are younger and brasher, so they buy fast cars, take scuba lessons, get hair transplants. . . . In graduate school, I had two different professors who ended up paying through the nose for their divorces because, to prove their virility, they had to sleep with one of their students." Remembering back, Genny shook her head. "Men are idiots."

"Yes," John said meekly.

*Yeah.* Genny was really terrified of this mad killer. "Back to your story. What did Gary do to prove his virility—besides sleep with your wife, I mean?" Her questioning was callous and indifferent, without an ounce of compassion, but somehow it seemed the right way to approach John.

For he relaxed a little and told the story stoically.

"When it came to our missions, Gary wasn't good at calculating the odds against us. The trouble was, he got away with the impossible time and again. His team kept pulling one miracle after another out of the bag. Finally . . ."

"The miracles ran out?"

"And the bag collapsed." John paused for such a long time, she thought she was going to have to prod him again. Then he flopped back in the mud, tucked his arms under his head, looked up at the sky, and started into the meat of the story. "There was a volcano on one of the Indonesian islands, dormant for years, and it started rumbling. That kind of event always attracted the attention of the Gypsy Travel Agency, because the native peoples had their rituals and sometimes those rituals included some pretty impressive artifacts that never at any other time saw the light of day."

"The native peoples hid their valuables until they needed them?" Genny asked.

"Exactly. A rumor said the native people would place a solid gold goddess statue in the way of the possible lava flow. My team was"—John swallowed—"we were supposed to retrieve it."

"That's unethical."

"The Gypsy Travel Agency doesn't view it that way. They have a very strong capitalistic bent."

"I know." She didn't approve, but she knew. She'd seen that bent in her father.

"Of course they sent us with the usual stern warning not to endanger ourselves, knowing perfectly well that we lived to endanger ourselves." His eyes were clear, without emotion, reflecting the blue of the sky. "I'll never forget seeing that statue. She was about twenty inches high, and she had been polished smooth by generations of her people stroking her. Her body was the traditional goddess body with large breasts and broad hips. She was seated on a throne, and I calculated the base was eight by eight. Not too big, right?"

"No, not too big, but if it was pure gold, it was heavy."

"It was pure gold." He looked at her. "Do you know how much a cubic foot of gold weighs?"

Genny shook her head.

"Twelve hundred and six pounds."

"You couldn't pick her up."

"She was slick and she was heavy, and she had been placed up against a tall rock wall, frozen lava created in a previous eruption. Heavy or not, we might have been able to grab her, but the mountain was shaking under our feet. The fumaroles were venting pure sulfur. We couldn't breathe. I was dizzy. As Bataar tried to lift the statue, lava flow started to the left of us. A huge earthquake struck. Sophie was knocked off her feet and into the flow. She screamed." John's sentences came in staccato bursts, a soldier giving his report. "I'll never forget that scream as long as I live. Then she burned, writhing as she was swept downstream."

"My God. John." Genny placed her hand on his chest.

He didn't even seem to feel it. "We were horrified. Gary was yelling at us to get the statue. Then he started tugging at it. Sun Hee shrieked, *Watch out!* A crack opened up in the wall behind the goddess. Lava poured down on us, fast and hot. I used my power. I created a circle of safety around the six of us who were left. But the gases . . . they were toxic. I kept losing consciousness for a millisecond, and every time I did, the lava crept closer. Then Max fell down, just fell down onto the ground, and the ground was so hot it was burning the soles of my feet through my boots."

"Was he unconscious?"

"I hope he was dead," John said bitterly. "I hope he never woke to that hell."

Genny hoped so, too.

"Gary stayed awake and aware, God rot him, shouting about the statue. *Save the statue, John!* By then, I knew better. I was fighting to save Amina, my wife, and my friend Bataar. And Gary. I wasn't about to lose any more of them. But the mountain . . . the mountain was bigger than I was. It was the force of the whole earth pushing against me. I couldn't control that weight, and when I pressed in one direction, lava spouted up a different way. When I knew I couldn't hold it, I told them all to get up on a rocky slope. I thought it looked as if it might survive the eruption." John stopped, took a breath, then gathered himself and continued. "Gary started climbing. The mountain shook. Gary fell."

"Into the eruption?"

"Sun Hee and Bataar caught him—they weren't about to let him die—and pushed him onto the rock, but he had lost consciousness at last. The lava was rising all around us, but I was holding it back. I *was* holding it back. Amina started to pass out. Bataar caught her. Then a lava bomb blew out of the eruption and hit them both."

Genny bit back a horror-struck exclamation.

"I had been concentrating all my energy on the area around us, trying to keep the lava from burning us."

John waved a hand at the ground, then up. "I never saw that rock coming through the air. One minute Bataar and Amina were there; the next minute they were flattened. Sun Hee was screaming and screaming. I knew she was, I could see her, but the volcano was so loud it was like some ghastly pantomime."

The picture he painted was all too clear in Genny's mind, and she knew what was coming. She feared what was coming.

He continued. "I was afraid I was going to pass out. I told her to hold on to my arm. She grabbed me. I had a clear circle and I thought I could get her up on that rock with Gary. Then . . . there was a big burst of gases. I remember the smell, like rotten eggs. I couldn't get my breath, and I remember consciousness coming down to the size of a pin." John was gasping as if he was living the memory. "When I came back—Sun Hee was gone, burning in the lava flow."

*I let her burn to death.*

Yes, he had. But although she knew he doubted himself and his intention that day, she also knew the truth—he had done the best he could. "The lava must have been right at your feet."

"It was. I thought it had me, and I turned to look at the golden goddess. I swear, she was smiling at me, mocking me. Then the lava swept around the gold and melted it, and swept the goddess away."

Genny's heart wept for him. "How did you get out?"

"When the mountain swallowed the goddess, the eruption stopped. Just like that"—he snapped his fingers—"it stopped."

"The sacrifice had been given."

"Yes. Yes, I think that was it." John stared up at the clouds, and slowly his breathing calmed. "I jumped onto the ridge with Gary and waited. When the lava formed a crust, I picked Gary up and carried him to safety. He never regained consciousness."

"He's dead, too?"

"He's in a coma in a New York facility."

"You weren't hurt at all?"

With obvious self-disdain, he admitted, "I burned the bottoms of my feet."

Genny studied John and tried to think of the right words to reply. But she wasn't a psychology major, and, anyway—*was* there a right thing to say to circumstances like this? Nothing could ever erase his memories. Nothing would ever completely give him peace of mind.

In the end, all she could say was what her heart told her. "John, that is truly an awful story. I don't know how you have carried the burden of guilt for so long. But you did everything you could. People died. I'm sorry, but you're a military man. You know a soldier can't be blamed for a general's incompetence."

"I didn't have enough power. I knew I didn't, but I didn't say anything because I was angry and hurt. And Gary would have mocked me. They would have gone up, anyway, and I didn't want to miss the adventure. I wasn't a man. I was an adolescent bending to peer pressure." A single tear welled up in his eye and ran down his cheek.

# Chapter 38

John was crying. Damn it, he was crying for the first time since he escaped from that cage in the circus, and he was doing it in front of a woman. In front of the first woman with whom he'd connected since Sun Hee . . . died.

He didn't wipe the tear away; didn't acknowledge it at all. It was only one tear, after all. Probably Genny wouldn't notice it. If she did, she'd probably think his eyes hurt from staring at the bright sky . . .

She stood and splashed her way into the pool.

So she did see the tear, knew it for what it was, a dumb-ass weakness, and she had left in disgust.

He was disgusted, too. When had he started caring enough about *anything* to cry? Especially about something that happened years ago? After that disastrous mission, when he got back to New York City, the Gypsy Travel Agency had forced him to go to a shrink. Because of the "trauma."

He didn't suffer from trauma. He suffered from the truth, from knowing it was his fault five people had died.

So after the shrink had told him he would need years of therapy, he had done what any man would do in the circumstances—he'd taken himself off to where he could do no harm.

*Wow, Powell. Look how well that had worked out.*

When his powers had busted loose, he'd managed to bring a mob down on their heads. He'd almost gotten Genny killed, too, and . . . *Oh, God* . . .

His throat closed. His chest hurt.

If Genny had died, he didn't think he could bear the burden of responsibility. If Genny had died . . . he would have died with her.

He felt the pressure of tears, which made him want to rub at his eyes like a three-year-old kid.

He heard Genny swim close to shore, close to him.

Her quiet voice said, "John."

She said his name so patiently, and her voice was so husky, he almost smiled. He would have if this pain hadn't been tearing at his throat.

But he did lift his head, prepared to look casually at her and deny every emotion.

She was standing hip deep in the water. She was cleaned up, no mud anywhere. Her skin was damp and glowing. Her shirt was wet, plastered to her body, its long hem barely reaching her thighs.

His mouth grew parched, but he stoutly told himself that she didn't realize how provocative she looked.

Then she unfastened the buttons, top to bottom, very consciously, and opened the shirt.

Everything—pain, memories, embarrassment—was wiped out of his mind. His brain was empty of activity, because all his blood had moved to a different organ.

*Guilt*, he tried to remind himself. . . . Shouldn't she be reproaching him for the atrocities to which he'd been a party? Despising him for failing to rescue his team? Reproaching him for putting her into danger?

It seemed not.

She fixed her eyes on his and started to peel out of her shirt. First one shoulder—moving with a delibera- tion that made him flounder in a sea of stunned and heated red lust. She struggled to get one long wet sleeve off, then the other.

All the time, her breasts moved with her; her belly rippled. He caught glimpses of her cleft through the thin strip of brown hair that grew over her pubes. Her skin was lightly tanned; her nipples were brown and puckered . . .

This spirited woman was stripping for . . . him.

If she despised him, she had a funny way of show- ing it.

She splashed out of the pool, stepped over him and straddled him, one foot on each side of his chest.

Water sluiced down her legs, her inner thighs.

"Do you have any thoughts in your mind?" she asked.

He shook his head. Although it wasn't true. He did have *one* thought.

"Good. I want this to be written on a clean slate." She leaned over him and spoke slowly and clearly. "You're a man who holds responsibility dear, so you believe that you're to blame for the deaths of your team members."

"Yes. I am." Between her legs, water droplets clung to the inner lips, open for him to gaze upon.

"I think you know logically it's not your fault, but for all of your life, you're going to want to do what you can to pay for what you consider your crime."

"Yes. I will." Her clitoris was tiny, rosy, tucked tight against her body.

"John, if this is the truth, then what are you doing hiding away in a remote corner of Russia? Why aren't you out there in the world, using your special gifts to destroy the bad guys and make life better for the Abandoned Ones?"

"That would make sense." The entrance to her body was a darker rose, warm and inviting.

Still in that calm, slow, sensible voice, she asked, "Isn't that why you signed that contract with the Gypsy Travel Agency in the first place? So you could help children not be exploited the way you were?"

He nodded.

But he must have worn a dazed expression, for she laughed and said, "I know that right now, you can't comprehend the words, but you can hear me. Promise that, later, you'll think about what I said."

"I will. I promise."

Lifting her muddy foot, she placed it on his chest. "What are you thinking about *now*?"

With blunt honesty, he said, "I was thinking that before I met you, I was dead inside."

Her gaze swept down him and lingered on his

straining erection. A smile crooked her mouth. "We seemed to have cured that."

His hard-on, already at full capacity, doubled in size.

Well, it felt like it doubled in size, although he supposed it wasn't true, because Genny hadn't run away yet. "The cure may kill me."

She rubbed her sole back and forth over his breastbone. "One question. Why, if you believe I betrayed you, did you tell me your story?"

His thoughts were a tangle of new doubts and past nightmares, and he couldn't say he believed in her. He didn't know if that was true. But he could admit, "I do understand that sometimes the only thing to do is the wrong thing."

Head cocked, she considered him, then nodded. "All right. That's good enough. For now." Putting her foot back on the ground, she sank down on top of him, onto his erection. She fit them together perfectly, her pubic area to his, and she was damp where her body rested on him.

His cock surged with excitement, a creature intelligent enough to know heaven was close.

She kept her feet on the ground, her knees tucked up beside him, and asked, "Tell me, John . . . how does it feel to lie stretched out in the mud, the springs bubbling against your back, the heat warming your skin?"

He thought about it, *felt* the sensations, said, "Now that you mention it . . . it's good."

"You're so eloquent, John." She was laughing at him.

He didn't care, because she leaned forward and

kissed his nipple, sucked it, kissed it again. Picking up a handful of mud, she smoothed it down his breastbone.

"Earth and water," she said. "So primal, so perfect. Isn't it satiny? Don't you want me to . . . ?" Leaning down, she rubbed her nipples against his.

Her chest was soft, her breasts were glorious, and to have her move like this on him created a havoc he could resolve only one way.

He grabbed for her, ready to turn her over, take her. She caught his arms. "Not yet."

"I can't wait." The pressure of his despair, his painful return to life, her blatant kick-start to his libido—it was too much. He needed satisfaction *now*. "I can't wait," he repeated, and again tried to wrap her in his arms, to turn her, enter her hard and fast—revel in her dark passage and heal himself there.

"Not yet," she repeated forcefully. "You owe me. You know you do."

He froze. He did owe her.

That second time, under the waterfall, had been glorious for him—and her. Yes, he knew that for sure; he had made sure of it—but he couldn't lie to himself. That wasn't the way to make love to a woman who had been a virgin only the day before. He recognized his outburst for what it was—the rampage of a man returning to life, and hating the pain that accompanied the resurrection.

He owed her . . . to control himself. So he surrendered to her demand. He lowered his arms, closed his eyes, and braced himself. "Okay. But tell me when you're ready to . . ."

"You'll be the first to know." Man, that girl managed to inject irony into her tone.

Closing his eyes proved a mistake. He didn't see what she was about to do.

So when she spread handfuls of mud over the top of his shoulders and massaged the muscles of his arms and whispered for him to relax . . . it was a surprise.

When she spread mud across his belly, frosting his skin in small circles . . . it was a surprise.

When she took his cock in her mouth . . . he thought he was going to come right then.

He groaned, twisted, fought—but not too tenaciously. He didn't want her to stop. He wanted that warm, wet, clinging mouth to explore him, suck on him, give him the kind of pleasure he hadn't experienced . . . ever.

Yesterday, today, the sex had been fabulous, a release such as he'd never experienced.

But yesterday and today, and all his life before, he had held a wall between himself and real emotions—a wall he had built to keep out the guilt, the anguish, the memories of a day so horrible no living man could bear to keep it in his mind.

So he blocked it.

Then Genny had forced him to confess his crimes and he felt . . . he felt free. Light. The recollection was still there, waiting for him to deal with it, but now he knew that someday he *could*. And that certainty allowed him to *feel* as he never had before.

As Genny used her mouth on him, her hands caressed his thighs, and again the silky mud created whorls of sensation under his skin. "Genny?" His voice came from deep, deep within. "I can't hold back much longer."

She lifted her head.

He lifted his, opened his eyes, and begged her like a puppy dog with his eyes.

"What?" she snipped. "You're not going to inject me with power love?"

"If you want me to." *Ask me. Ask me.*

"I think it's time you learned to be more subtle with your power. It's not just about how grand a gesture you can make, but also about what small things you can do to make lives better."

"I totally agree." He didn't even know what she was talking about. He only knew she was settling onto him, taking him inside her body, making him feel like the shah being serviced by a slave girl—a slave girl who gave lectures about how he should manage his future. And as long as he kept nodding his head, she kept sliding down on his cock, rising again, sliding down again, until he was buried so deep he trembled, desperately waiting to see what she would do now.

She picked up handfuls of the warm, soft mud, and smeared his chest again, then leaned down. As she moved on his cock, she rubbed her chest to his—and laughed when he groaned.

She was riding him, traveling at her own pace, and he gave up all power to her. He gripped her butt with his hands, strained and wanted to come, agonized as he held back.

He didn't want this to end . . .

He was enveloped in sensuality: the warm mud cradling him, her hands and chest stroking him. She held him tightly, the slow slide of slick heat on his cock an aphrodisiac so compelling he knew he would never forget this day, this moment.

*This was going to end too soon.*

His urgency spiraled out of control.

He drove up and into her and, without his volition, his power surged and sparked. Driven by the motion, the energy, the freedom, she sat up and pressed herself on him, up and down, up and down.

She was glorious, wild and free, a primitive idol with mud smeared across her skin. Her hair flew in the breeze and her breasts bounced, her golden eyes glowed with joy. As climax swept her, she looked into his eyes and smiled, alive with bliss.

He watched her, held her hips in her hands. The muscles of her thighs shifted and strove. Inside, her body rippled and clutched.

And when he came, he plunged into a satisfaction so deep and so distinctly Genny, he knew nothing in his life would ever be the same.

# Chapter 39

———◆◆◆———

Genny rested on top of John's chest, breathing heavily, alight with the joy of their joining. Nothing she had done in her whole life had been as fulfilling, as freeing. She had assumed control, used her powers as a woman to tame the savage beast, and now he rested, sated, beneath her.

At some point, he might even remember the advice she had given him.

She laughed softly, sat up, and looked at his face, replete with glory.

He looked as if he couldn't remember his own name.

"Oh, John." She smoothed her hand across his cheek. "I can't believe you don't trust me now."

His eyes popped open. He stared at her without a trace of confusion, stared at her as he would gaze at a shattered dream.

*And he didn't answer.*

Shock brought her to her feet.

*He still didn't trust her.*

Her legs wobbled. But she smiled. Damn it, she smiled. "Forget I said that." Then she had to get away from him, from that stare that stripped away her pride and turned her joy to dust.

With a jaunty wave—she was very proud of that wave—she waded into the water and swam, fast, from one end of the pool to the other.

Why did she think that just because he had trusted her to make love to him, he would believe in her? That was stupid. Illogical. Womanish.

She had to leave here, leave him.

She needed to spend time alone, with herself, without anyone pushing her, wanting her to be someone she wasn't—or accusing her, imagining her to be a villain when she was just . . . a dupe.

Never again would she be somebody's tool.

Picking up her shirt, she waded out of the water.

He stood on the edge, clean and stern.

The passionate episode in the mud might never have happened.

"What are you doing?" he asked.

"Getting dressed." She spread out her shirt on the grass, then pulled on the panties and bra, already dry. She shook out her pants. Dry and remarkably clean. "The springs in the pool must act like a cleanser. The mud is completely gone."

He ignored her conversation, watching her as he would a stranger. "What are you planning?"

All right. He could be blunt. He could be detached. So could she. "I'm leaving here. I'm leaving this place."

She pulled on the pants. Gestured around. "The *rasputye*."

"That's not possible."

She wanted to snap at him, but she calmed herself. She didn't want to fight. She needed to imitate John, and betray as little emotion as possible. "Of course it is."

"You don't understand." One by one, he shook out the pile of his precisely folded clothes resting on a rock beside the pool. "The *rasputye* doesn't run on the same timetable as the rest of the world. We have no idea how long we've been here."

"A day!"

"Perhaps. Or a month. Or a year." He dressed himself quickly, efficiently, like a military man on a mission. "Time passes differently here. The relationship to the continents it divides isn't the same, either. When we leave, we could come out anywhere along the Asian/European split. We could come out in Afghanistan in the middle of a battle. We could come out on the steppes in the middle of winter. I can't let you go on your own."

"And yet I am going . . . by myself." Catching sight of the leather bag resting in the grass, she picked it up, relieved to have a change of topic. "John, I forgot. This is yours."

He wavered, obviously trying to decide whether to argue or let the subject drop. Being John, he let the subject drop. Being John, he undoubtedly figured he would get his way in the end. "What is it?"

"I don't know. A purse of some kind. Don't you know?"

"No, it's not mine." He walked over, stood close, smelled like sunshine and fresh air.

And she wanted him.

That was so not fair.

"What's in it?" he asked.

She untied the string and spread the stiff leather open.

Together, they stared at the collection of small petrified bones, smooth and yellow with age.

"What in heaven's name . . . ?" Genny picked up one and held it in her palm. "This looks like a finger bone."

"I would say that's exactly what it is."

"Human?"

"Yes. Female. In my time with the Chosen Ones, I have seen enough skeletons to identify the shape and size."

*Everybody had to have his or her area of expertise.*

But she held her tongue. "Two of them have marks on them. Black marks." She stirred the bones with her finger. "It almost looks like a puzzle you could put together, but some of the pieces are missing." A memory stirred in her brain . . . something seen years ago at home. . . a leather bag tied with a string, tossed carelessly in a drawer . . .

"That's not a whole hand there."

"If this purse isn't yours, then whose . . . ?" She looked around at the empty lands.

John took the leather pouch from her, put the bones inside, tied it tightly. He placed it in her palm and closed her fingers around it. "It's a gift from the *rasputye* to you."

Just when she had convinced herself he wasn't crazy, he said something like that. "From the *rasputye*?"

"It's an empty land. A lifeless land. A supernatural place where the devil can walk abroad and creatures that are not human emerge. But nothing can live here for any amount of time. You brought passion and vitality." He viewed her gravely. "You sacrificed your virginity nearby."

She looked around in alarm, then felt stupid. "The *rasputye* doesn't know that!"

"This isn't reality here. The place knows what a virginal sacrifice, freely given, is worth."

"It's worth a bag of bones?" She didn't know whether to laugh or be insulted.

He didn't smile, didn't laugh. "Keep them. We might not know what they're for, but the *rasputye* doesn't give worthless gifts."

"All right." She tucked the purse into her pants pocket. Picking up her shirt—it was *not* dry; apparently the supernatural clothesline was slow—she slid it on and buttoned it up.

He observed impassively.

She didn't know whether to offer her hand to be shaken; it seemed like the mature way to act, so she did. In a voice she kept firm and pleasant, she said, "Okay, I'm off. I've enjoyed our time together, most of it, and—"

"If you must go now, I'll go with you."

She put her hands behind her back, braced her feet. "No."

"You're not leaving without me."

She had tried to be stoic and uncommunicative, like him. She truly had.

But that wasn't who she was. Seeing him hurt, making love with him, being chased by the mob, climbing the Devil, these outrageous sex acts . . . the emotional upheaval of the past few days had brought every long-repressed emotion to the surface, and the truth came out in a rush. "I really don't know why you're so willing to believe the worst of me. I suppose it's easier than facing real life again. You're a man of passion, yet you're so afraid of who you are and what you can do, you've never allowed yourself to feel deeply."

He looked as astonished as if she had slapped him. "Afraid? Me?"

Finally, she had his attention . . . but it was too late. She wasn't waiting for him anymore. "Yes, you. I love you, John Powell, but what good are you to me? I don't want a man who's a coward."

"A coward?" Now he was outraged.

"Think about it." Turning, she walked away, but she wanted to run so he wouldn't see the tears brimming in her eyes.

He caught her arm. "No. I won't have you leave like this."

"John—" She tugged at him.

She heard the sound of running feet.

John half turned.

Suddenly she was free.

John sprawled flat on his face with Brandon pounding his head. "Run! Genny, run!" Brandon looked up, his brown eyes fierce. "I'll defend you."

His inattention was his downfall.

John flipped Brandon off, grabbed him by the shirt, lifted him to his feet and shoved him hard.

Her paralysis broke. This was her chance. "Thank you, Brandon."

"I love you!" he yelled, then charged John.

She had only a few minutes to escape. She ran.

As she approached the sky that touched the ground, somehow, she knew what to do. She sped up, flung out her arms, and jumped.

The sky split around her in flashes of black and red, gold and purple. She heard the scream of a thousand voices; felt the weight of the old legends land on her shoulders, then drop away.

And she fell into the real world—a frigid world, filled with wind blasting down a mountain pass, snow falling, accumulating as high as her waist, and not a sign of human habitation anywhere.

She started walking, struggling against the snow. Flakes accumulated on her eyelashes. Her hair, still damp, froze as she walked, and ice shuffled down into her boots. Her nose grew numb.

John was right.

She was going to die alone with a bag of bones in her pocket.

John ran through the *rasputye*, his face low to the ground, following Genny's footprints. He could only see out of one eye—who knew little Brandon could pack such a punch?

Of course, John had left him stretched out cold on the ground. When John hit him, the kid had gone down for the count. The drug the Others had fed him must have given him strength, then faded. John would bet Brandon was going to have one hell of a headache when he came to.

Then . . . he would seek out the Others for more.

Genny's footprints led toward the edge of the *rasputye*, the sky showed a crumpled patch surrounded by creases of brilliant light. She had exited here, breaking into . . .

John advanced steadily. He had been born in the *rasputye*. It would release him once again into the world.

He was right. As he walked, the air got thin. The sky surrounded him, flashing in protest. He parted the way . . . and he was out. Out in a land of towering mountains, of ice so thick his soles skidded across the slick surface. Massive icicles hung twenty feet or more off a towering rock cliff. The sky was high and blue, the land bleak and wild, and his breath showed in white puffs on the still air.

Where the hell was he? For sure somewhere high and isolated. Kazakhstan? Uzbekistan?

Dismay struck at his heart.

Had Genny come out of the *rasputye* here? *Here*, in this frigid desolation? There was nothing here. Nothing of human habitation as far as the eye could see. He wore jeans, a T-shirt, a heavy shirt, boots. He was tough, and knew how to survive in a frozen wasteland.

But Genny would have been ill-prepared, shivering with cold . . . and in the *rasputye*, time didn't march along at the same speed as in the real world. To him, it seemed Genny had exited less than an hour ago. But he might be standing here a week later, a month later. What if she'd come out in the middle of a storm? Or at night when the temperature was subzero?

He spied a movement across the valley and far below, a dark speck that moved horizontally across the plain. He stood watching, straining his eyes to make out the shape and realized . . . a man led a yak pulling a wooden cart. John gave a shout and started running, waving his arms, slipping on the treacherous ice, trying to get the guy's attention before he disappeared into some cave or up some narrow vale.

Finally the guy stopped and stared up at John. Then as if the sight of a tall, broad, pale-skinned man dressed in jeans and a fatigue shirt scared him, he tugged at the golden-haired yak and moved more quickly across the landscape.

"Hey, hey!" John shouted louder, his voice rumbling up the rocky walls. "I need help. Help me!" So many people across the world spoke some English, and John spoke a smattering of a lot of languages from across Asia—he could thank his time in the circus for that—surely they could somehow communicate.

As John neared, the guy seemed to realize the futility of escape. He stopped and faced John.

The guy wasn't a guy. It was an old woman shaped like a dumpling, five feet tall with a square ruddy face and a body covered with yak fur. She was trembling, probably with fear.

So John dropped to his knees. He tried the Kazakh language. "Mother, I won't hurt you."

She stared at him stonily.

He tried Uzbek.

She still stared.

He started to speak in Russian.

She waved him to silence, grabbed a skin off the cart and threw it at him, then gestured for him to follow her.

Slowly, he stood, his knees already frozen and stiff. Wrapping the fur around his shoulders, he trudged behind her as she crossed the valley and took an abrupt turn into a notch in the mountain. There, protected from the wind, stood a round hut made of sticks and skins. Thin smoke rose from the hole in the middle of the roof, and when she called out, the flap flew back and a squat, barrel-chested man stepped out. The female joined her husband. They were almost identical in height and looks, and they stared at John from eyes so dark they were almost black.

The man pointed west. "*Rasputye*?"

"Yes." John nodded, and in halting Kazakh, he said, "I'm looking for a woman. Dark hair." He made ripples with his hands. "Gold eyes." He pointed at the yak's fur. "This tall." He held his hand at the right level. "Wearing these kinds of clothes." He fingered the material of his shirt and jeans.

They stared again, their dark eyes unblinking.

When the man spoke, John only understood every third word. "The woman. Genny?"

John took an excited step forward.

They stepped back.

He stopped. "You saw her? You met her? Where is she?"

"She came from the *rasputye*. Storm. Wind, snow."

The man wiggled his fingers, then shook his head sadly. "Not good."

John wanted to grab him by the throat and wring the facts from him. "What happened to her?"

The man started to speak, but the woman caught his arm. She glared at him. She glared at John. And she said, "She froze. Genny dead."

# Chapter 40

———◆———

"**H**ow'd it go? Did you break your engagement?" Samuel Faa stood and held the empty chair beside him at the round table in Davidov's brewhouse.

"No." Isabelle Mason tucked her skirt tightly around her legs, and seated herself on the opposite side of the table.

Samuel still held the chair. "What do you mean, no?"

She looked up at him, nostrils flared, eyes narrowed. "I mean no. He broke the engagement, not me."

Grinning was out. Punching the air with his fist was out. Leaping around the room and crowing like a rooster was out.

Gentlemanly calm reaction was in. "Well, good. I imagine that will make it a little easier to visit your parents' home in Boston. Not so many expectations." He congratulated himself on sounding disinterested.

"Yeah, like we all give a crap about expectations."

The vulgarity, combined with the prissy gentility of Isabelle's voice, made him flinch.

Vidar Davidov came out from behind the bar and placed a cold glass of what looked like pink beer in front of her. "Here. A pint of your favorite."

She looked up at him with a grateful smile. "Thank you, Vidar. You always know exactly what I need."

Meaning Samuel didn't.

He felt bad for her. He really did. No one liked to be dumped, especially when you intended to do it first.

*But oh!* That big-ass diamond was off her hand and that jerk from the U.S. Congress was out of the picture. Finally, she was available for Samuel to pursue with all the intensity of his Gypsy soul.

Beside him, Aaron Eagle jammed his elbow into Samuel's thigh. "Sit down," he said out of the corner of his mouth. "You look like the freaking Statue of Liberty up there."

"Right." Samuel reseated himself and pretended not to see the smirk Davidov sent in his direction.

Samuel didn't like Vidar Davidov, hadn't since the first time they'd come through the New York tunnels to his underground brewpub. For one thing, the guy was too good-looking. Six and a half feet tall, probably thirty years old, electric blue eyes, tough, chiseled face. His wavy, white blond hair brushed his wide shoulders. Muscled chest, muscled arms, muscled wrists, long legs. Even Samuel, a dedicated heterosexual, knew the guy was built like a brick shithouse. Worse, Davidov had this arrogant, kingly attitude that set Samuel's teeth on edge and made the women get all soft and gushy.

Added to that, Davidov had created this pub where the Chosen gathered.

The guys felt at home amid the oak-paneled walls and huge, round tapped kegs set into the wall behind the granite bar. There were worn wood tables with deep, cushioned chairs gathered around them. And the smell of yeast and fermentation permeated the big room.

But the women loved it, too, because Davidov had commissioned one of those artsy decorations with a fifteen-foot ceiling covered with leaves and branches to resemble a forest canopy, and the lighting was just right: not too bright, not too dark, and dappled like a sunny day beneath an oak tree in the European woods a thousand years ago.

Samuel didn't know if Davidov made sure the pub was available to them when they needed to be alone, or he just didn't have any other customers—because when they met here, the Chosen Ones were always alone.

Good thing, because this meeting was due to be a stinker.

The problem wasn't between the Chosen. The circumstances surrounding their initiation into the group had been so dark, so horrendous, so dangerous, they'd formed bonds that could never be severed.

Every single one of them was normally pretty pleasant to be around. If Samuel had to point out one asshole in the group, he guessed it would have to be . . . himself. He wasn't proud of it. When a guy like him is told from the time he was born that he was an orphan, that he ought to be grateful for a roof over his head, that he ought to be pleased to be able to settle for becoming a servant . . . well, that gave him an attitude.

So, instead, he became a lawyer—the kind who won every case, the kind who collected enemies. The kind who, if he deemed it necessary, used his gift to influence the judge and the jury.

Hey, he wasn't proud of it, but he wasn't ashamed of it, either.

Now he was paying. He'd been caught, and if he hadn't signed up for the Chosen Ones team, he'd be in prison right now.

At least if he were in prison he'd be safe.

But he would also be scared to death for Isabelle, so he guessed everything had worked out for the best.

Charisma and Jacqueline moved their chairs so close to Isabelle, their shoulders were touching. Rosamund took Isabelle's hand and held it.

Samuel was glad the women on this team were so empathetic. They supported and talked to each other, helped each other pick out clothes and put on cosmetics. They watched chick flicks together. And it was weird, because other than the fact that they had the same kinds of sexual organs, they had nothing in common.

Isabelle was twenty-six, a woman with a proper Boston accent, a classic Chanel watch, and the most beautiful face Samuel had ever seen . . . although as the son of her family's butler, he might be slightly prejudiced. She didn't look at all like her family—of course not, she was adopted—but it was certain that somewhere in her unknown bloodlines, she boasted an Asian ancestor, for her bones were as delicate as porcelain and her dark blue eyes were almond shaped. It was that indefatigable air of always knowing the right thing to wear and the right thing to do that made her a leader. And in recognition of her skill with people and her dedication to the cause, the Chosen Ones had voted her in as their director.

On the other end of the spectrum, there was Charisma Fangorn, flake extraordinaire. He'd known her—what? Seven months? And in that time her hair had changed color four times, not always colors found in nature, either. His least favorite had been the screaming orange with streaks of pomegranate red, but there had been black and purple, black and blue, and now platinum blond. Her makeup was a disaster—charcoal black outlining vivid green eyes and, all the time, red-red lips.

But then, her gift was weird, too. She said she heard the earth song in stones, and so she wore jingling bracelets all the time. She'd convinced the other women to wear them, too, for protection, although she'd redesigned Isabelle's so it didn't jingle. Thank God. He could only imagine what Isabelle's mother would say about *that* fashion faux pas.

Rosamund was a fairly new addition to the team, and the mate of Aaron Eagle, their gifted cat burglar. She had calico cat–colored hair, all natural; big glasses that slipped down her nose, and appalling fashion sense. She was also an antiquities librarian. If there was a piece of information in a library that they needed, she could find it. Well, except for the damned prophecy that had so far escaped her search. But Samuel had seen her work, and he had faith she would somehow discover the truth.

Jacqueline Vargha D'Angelo was their seer, a tall

blonde with her own personal bodyguard whom she just happened to have as a husband. Caleb D'Angelo watched over her like a hawk—and made their expeditions out to save the world a lot safer.

Caleb was the one who had called the meeting. He stood now, slowly, painfully. "I don't need to tell you, we've got problems. Gary White has assumed his return means he's in charge. And I admit—sorry, Isabelle—at first I thought it was a good idea to have an experienced Chosen leading our team."

She waved a forgiving hand. "I can study the past case histories all I want, but I can't be prepared for everything. I looked at Gary's credentials. I thought . . . well, I thought the same thing you did, Caleb. He was the one."

"I don't know what the hell kept us from actually crowning the son-of-a-bitch king, but thank God we never made it official," Aleksandr said.

"Don't swear," Isabelle, Jacqueline, and Rosamund said in unison.

Aleksandr thumped his forehead on the table.

Charisma laughed. "You can't win, Aleksandr."

He really couldn't. Aleksandr Wilder was the youngest member of their team, a college student, big and gangly. He'd been brought in because he was one of the famous Wilder shape-shifters who had eighteen years ago broken their family's thousand-year-old pact with the devil. Breaking a pact with the devil was no small accomplishment, but the kid . . . he had no gift. How could he? He'd been born into a loving family; gifts such as the Chosen Ones possessed weren't given to infants who were welcomed and loved.

Yet for all his lack of woo-woo, he had proved a valuable member of the team. He majored in mathematics and knew his way around a computer. He could find anything on the Internet, hack into any system, and beat the snot out of Samuel playing Dead Zone.

Caleb didn't allow this exchange to distract him from the subject at hand. "We can't continue with this situation. Gary's got a god complex a mile wide, and he's almost gotten Jacqueline killed twice." He looked them over. "And you guys with her."

"Yeah, thanks for noticing, Caleb." But Samuel was actually joking this time.

Caleb had been badly hurt on the last mission. The guy wasn't Chosen. He didn't have any supernatural healing abilities. And although Isabelle had done her best to help him, his battered face bore testament to the recent troubles.

"Gary came out of that coma and came straight to us, right?" Caleb looked around the table. "We're sure he's not a ringer for the other side?"

"He's always been this way. *Mission Impossible* is just a movie to me, but to Gary, it's a way of life." Jacqueline would know. Until she was killed, Jacqueline's foster mother, Zusane, had been the seer for the Gypsy Travel Agency. Jacqueline had known Gary for years before the last mission with his last team had gone sour. If she said he had always been a glory seeker, no one was likely to dispute it with her.

"Every time I see him, I can almost hear the theme music playing." Charisma did not seem amused.

"These missions he brings to our attention—they're not to protect or rescue the children. They're flashy.

They're to rescue jewelry and artifacts. Don't get me wrong. They're good jewelry and artifacts"—Aaron knew his way around such things—"but right now, with the Others holding all the advantages, we can't afford to lose those children!"

"Let's be blunt with him. Tell him we're not going on these missions anymore." Aleksandr had a young man's tact.

"And lose the information he picks up from his mind reading? Most of the time, the missions he suggests are valuable for us and each child we save." Isabelle twirled the chilly glass of beer on the table. "I'm sorry. I should have done something sooner. I'll talk to him and make it clear that I'm the elected leader of this group, and that we're only going on missions I have thoroughly vetted."

"The problem is—how can you thoroughly vet them when most of them need to be made quickly, before a child dies from exposure or is taken by the Others?" Samuel asked.

Isabelle shot him a bitter glance. "I *know* what the problem is, Samuel."

Davidov spoke from behind the bar. "I have an idea. Why not bring in a new leader?"

"That's brilliant. Why didn't we think of that?" Samuel could barely contain his impatience. "Who?"

From the shadows in the far corner, a man's deep, calm voice said, "I believe Davidov is talking about me."

# Chapter 41

————❖————

Knife in his fingers, Caleb swiveled toward John and held it at the ready.

Obviously, Caleb didn't like being surprised.

But Jacqueline knew John, remembered him from the past, and she laid her hand on Caleb's arm, restraining him. "It's all right. You know him. That's John Powell, the lost Chosen."

Caleb nodded. "I remember." He kept the knife in his hand.

"John Powell, the crazy Chosen?" Samuel Faa was equally angry at being fooled, and he didn't do restrained displeasure. That guy was open-ass pissed.

"That's me," John said easily, and with his hands raised, walked from the shadows into the light around the table.

"John." Jacqueline rose and walked toward him to kiss his cheek. "It's good to see you. Are you back in town to stay?" She was, like her mother, a lovely, gracious woman, good at defusing tense situations.

Good thing, because this one was guaranteed to be tense. "Maybe. I heard there was an opening on your team."

Glances were exchanged.

John waited.

Davidov stepped out from around the bar and strolled over to stand beside John. "I asked John here. Irving asked John here. We knew Isabelle reluctantly accepted the job of leader. We know Gary isn't the right man for the job. We thought John was a good choice to guide the team. A little background about John Powell . . ." And he talked about John's military experience, his experience with the Chosen Ones team, and the disaster that sent John fleeing. He told them everything.

John was grateful for that. He had told the truth to Genny. If he had to talk about it, he would talk to Genny.

But that wasn't possible, was it?

The silence, when Davidov had finished, was profound and thoughtful.

But the knife had disappeared up Caleb's sleeve.

John took that as a good sign.

"If we take you on, what guarantee would we have that you wouldn't abandon us in our hour of need?" Aaron asked.

"Yeah, us poor babies have abandonment issues." That guy Samuel never bothered to restrain his sarcasm.

"I didn't abandon my team in their hour of need,"

John said. "We were in a situation beyond my control. I lost my team, all except one, and that one was Gary. I brought my leader home and left after I knew he was settled. If I am allowed the position of leader to your group, I promise to do everything in my power not to place us, any of us, in situations that are inherently un-workable. With only one team of Chosen alive, we owe it to the children as well as to ourselves to take care."

Jacqueline testified for him. "John had a good repu-tation for being sensible about the missions and calm in the face of danger. It was Gary White that created the situation that caused John's failure. We've all wit-nessed near disasters under Gary's leadership." She looked around the table, pinning the Chosen with her gaze. "Davidov's suggestion is sound. I vote for John Powell to take over the leadership position"—she turned to Isabelle—"if that is acceptable to Isabelle."

Isabelle inclined her head. "If you know John, Jac-queline, and believe in him, I would be relieved to re-linquish the position."

Charisma nodded.

"Any objections?" Caleb asked.

John watched as Samuel, especially, struggled be-tween his desire to thwart any of Davidov's sugges-tions and granting Isabelle her wish. He shrugged halfheartedly.

The other men yielded more easily, although Alek-sandr examined John thoughtfully.

The boy was young, but his family had taught him caution.

"That's decided, then." Although Caleb's glance at John promised they would have a talk later.

That was fine with John. The guy looked like he'd been run through a meat grinder. He had his reasons for caution.

John moved to the table and accepted a place between Charisma and Rosamund. Placing his hands flat on the table before him, he said, "Now *I* have a question. Five years ago, when I signed my contract with the Chosen Ones, I was working for the Gypsy Travel Agency. When I arrived in New York yesterday, I at once went to their headquarters."

Charisma sadly sighed and played with her bracelets.

"There used to be a building there. Now there's nothing there but faded crime-scene tape . . . and an immense hole in the ground. Perhaps you all could enlighten me?" He raised politely curious eyebrows, but at the same time . . . he was furious.

Because what he wanted to say was—*What the hell happened?*

"You mean your friend Davidov didn't tell you?" Samuel snapped like a junkyard dog.

John wanted to snap back. What the hell was going on here in New York City? "No. He didn't."

Davidov brought another round of beers. "I figured it was up to the Chosen Ones to convince John to face the danger on your behalf."

John glared at the damned Viking. "You never tell anyone anything, Davidov. I swear, it's your worst trait—and that's saying something."

Across the table, Samuel relaxed.

Ah. He didn't like Davidov, either.

Davidov didn't care. "Ale?" he asked John.

"Please." John suspected he was going to need it.

The Chosen Ones glanced at each other up and down the table.

John was pleased to see the solid camaraderie between them, and at the same time, they shut him out. He would have to earn their trust, and that was as it should be.

But for now, they exchanged looks until, somehow, they settled on who should tell their story.

Charisma started. "Back at the beginning—it was about seven months ago—we were all called to the Gypsy Travel Agency building in SoHo to choose whether we would become one of the Chosen Ones. We signed our contracts, some willing, some less willing"—she shot a meaningful glance at Samuel, then at Jacqueline—"and we were called into the New York subway to meet with the seer for approval."

"Zusane, right?" John remembered the lady as a glamorous bombshell with a foreign accent and a way of making a man feel very, very special.

"My mother," Jacqueline said. "Or rather, my adopted mother."

Isabelle took up the tale. "She had been the seer for the Chosen Ones for years, and since she drew her strength from the earth, we had to go underground to meet her. Meanwhile, at the Gypsy Travel Agency, they prepared to celebrate the confirmation of a new team. You know what kind of party I'm talking about."

"I remember." Former Chosen always celebrate new Chosen with a huge cocktail hour and dinner, giving awards and making speeches. It was like Hogwarts, but with huge egos everywhere.

"A traitor slipped through security." Isabelle looked like a fragile young woman, and John knew from the information Davidov had given him that she was an American aristocrat. Yet she recited the facts matter-of-factly, without emotion or alarm. "He set up an explosion in the Gypsy Travel Agency that went off when everyone was in the building."

"Almost everyone," Aleksandr said. "We were safe."

"Zusane sensed the blast at once and went nuts. Caleb led us out of the subway. Irving Shea had been the CEO of the Agency . . ." Isabelle lifted her eyebrows, subtly inquiring as to whether he knew Irving.

John nodded. Oh, he knew Irving. In Russia, he had received letters from Irving.

"Of course, Irving was retired and had been for years. At the time, he was ninety-one . . . ?" Isabelle looked around, seeking confirmation.

She got nods all around.

She continued. "He still went into his office at the Gypsy Travel Agency every morning."

"Because he wouldn't let a little thing like retirement get in the way of his work." Charisma smiled, obviously delighted by the old man's feisty spirit.

"That afternoon McKenna drove him home for his nap," Isabelle said. "So he wasn't there for the explosion, but he came after us. If we hadn't had Irving, I don't know what we would have done. His home is a mansion and protected. We all stayed there and we were safe."

Everybody smiled, happy with her recitation.

Charisma twisted a strand of her platinum blond

hair around a finger. "The problem was that Jacqueline, who had replaced Zusane as our seer, had never experienced a vision."

John looked at Jacqueline.

She nodded ruefully. "And the person who had set the explosion at the Gypsy Travel Agency was one of the team. *Our* team."

John looked around the table.

"That's why there's a vacancy." Caleb flexed his fists. "Jacqueline figured out who the traitor was, and she and I took him out."

"What about the visions?" John would hate to think the team didn't have a functioning seer.

"I discovered my way to visions," Jacqueline assured him.

"She damned near got killed," Caleb said grimly, sliding his arm around her shoulders.

"Zusane *was* killed." Samuel turned pale.

"My God, you're kidding." When John remembered the vibrant woman, he couldn't imagine that she was gone. "What happened?"

Jacqueline looked down at her hands in her lap. "I failed her."

John realized he was treading on thin ice. "I'm sorry, Jacqueline, for your loss. I know you must miss your mother."

Jacqueline looked up, puckishly amused. "Oh, she visits every once in a while."

John didn't know what to say to that.

"The thing is"—the boy, Aleksandr, took up the story—"we've done okay. We don't have a damned bit of experience. All the research material at the Gypsy

Travel Agency got blown to hell and gone. We're totally faking it. But Isabelle has been using Irving's library to research past Chosen cases, and we've been going out there rescuing abandoned babies. And we were pretty proud of ourselves until . . . Gary showed up. At first he seemed okay, just getting his strength back while he observed us. Then he advised us. For sure he tells a good tale about past missions he's led."

"I was with him for three years," John said. "He's brilliant."

"And erratic!" Charisma snapped.

"Yeah. That, too," John acknowledged.

"The guy is crackers—all about treasure and glory; and even when he does lead us out to protect the children, he's looking for the flashiest way to do it." Aleksandr took a breath. "Don't get me wrong, I'm the least of the team and I know it. Mostly I'm just supposed to go to college and be there for computer aid. But I can see when there's a problem, and that problem is Gary."

"I don't like to sound like I'm campaigning for the position, but I can handle Gary, and I will keep you safe." John accepted a pint from Davidov.

"Why?" Isabelle asked.

Caleb nodded. "Good question."

Samuel gave her a glance full of pride, then hid his approval in his glass.

"Why what?" John asked.

"Why have you come back? Why now? And why help us when we're poised on the brink of disaster?" Isabelle hammered home her questions. "You've got an ulterior motive. What is it?"

John knew the answer all too well. "Not too long ago, someone told me that if I hold myself responsible for the deaths of my team members—and I do—then I should use my special gifts to destroy the bad guys and make life better for the Abandoned Ones." The picture of Genny rose in his head. He saw her as she had been that day, standing over him, naked, wet, and glorious, lecturing him, telling him her truths. "She was right. So I've come here. I have the skills to help you. I hope you'll let me."

The glances went around the table again.

Aaron Eagle spoke first. "We'd like that."

An understated acceptance, but John was satisfied.

Rosamund spoke up without a hint of self-consciousness. "The most difficult part of the whole situation is that there's a prophecy hanging out there that applies to this situation, but we know only part of it."

"A prophecy?" John hated ephemeral stuff like prophecies.

But Rosamund's eyes shone. Clearly, she loved her prophecy. "When each Chosen finds his or her true love, that is a brick in the wall that defends us against the Others."

Caleb took Jacqueline's hand and kissed it. "I always knew it was Jacqueline for me, but after she joined the Chosen and we declared ourselves, I swear, man"—Caleb grinned at John, happier than John could have ever imagined him—"there was this happiness bolt that went through the whole group—"

Charisma gave him a thumbs-up. "It was major cool."

John didn't like the way this was heading, but they

were so excited, talking over the top of each other, he didn't want to interrupt their joy-fest.

Aaron was smiling at Rosamund the way a man in love smiles at his woman. "We got the same thrill when I brought Rosamund back to the mansion and we made our commitment to each other. That's the important part—commitment. Then we *know*."

"They're not just talking about the fact that when the Chosen find their true loves, their marks are expanded." Rosamund sounded prosaic, but she blushed under Aaron's steadfast regard. "Aaron's mark grew and expanded. Jacqueline had an eye on her palm; now she has one on each palm. For Aaron and Jacqueline, their powers have stabilized and grown."

"That's important," Aaron said, "because until I met and loved Rosamund, my powers were erratic, and even fading."

"Yet still we have a problem. It looks like everybody *has* to find their true love." Samuel sounded doleful, a lawyer who didn't believe in true love and didn't believe he would find it, anyway.

"Looks like?" John questioned.

"Okay." Samuel leaned forward and stared John right in the eyes. "Here's the bad news—we don't know the whole prophecy."

John thought about that. "But you know part of the prophecy."

"We think we do." Rosamund's eyes sparkled with pleasure. "Prophecies being what they are, translated from who knows how many languages and vague to start with, it could turn out that what we think we know is contradicted in the second part. I've searched every likely source in Irving's library and mine. I've read stone tablets. I've studied hieroglyphics."

"I've searched for it, too," Jacqueline said. "I've looked into crystal balls, shaken dice. . . . I'd gaze into the entrails of chickens if I thought that would help."

"We don't know what's brought on these disasters, and we don't know how to cure them," Aleksandr said.

John pondered the situation. "So everyone here is looking for their true love?"

"That's right," Caleb said. "That's the one part of the prophecy we know—well, we're pretty darn sure—is the truth."

Bleak and cold with despair, John said, "Then, perhaps, you should think twice about taking me as your leader."

All heads swiveled toward him.

"Genesis Valente was my one true love, but I was a coward." She had called him a coward, and she was right. "I was afraid to trust her. I refused to make a commitment. Now it's too late." He put his hand to his shoulder where the lynx had ripped him apart. "My love died seven months ago in a snowstorm in Kazakhstan."

John stood outside the door of a nondescript brownstone in the Bronx.

The meeting with the Chosen Ones had gone well. He had told them the truth about meeting Genny, their visit to the *rasputye*, how he had destroyed their chance for happiness, and her fatal decision to leave when she did. It made sense that they should know the truth and the fact he had whacked their chances of ever having everyone on the team find their true love.

They'd taken him on, anyway. They had been *that* desperate to shuffle Gary aside.

So John had been elected, and he looked forward to starting. Because Genny was right. He needed to use his special gifts to destroy the bad guys and make life better for the Abandoned Ones.

But first—

He rang the doorbell.

First he had to break the news to Kevin Valente that Genny was dead.

# Chapter 42

———✦———

*Two Years Later*

John stuck his head into Irving's study. "Have you got a minute?"

Irving looked up from the huge leather-bound medieval-monk-inscribed book he was studying. "John. Of course. Come in."

Irving had grown old in the last year. The man thrived on work, had met head-on every challenge created by the loss of the Gypsy Travel Agency. But finally age had caught up with him, and now he divided his time between his bed and his study, searching compulsively through heavy tomes and ancient scrolls for the prophecy, which they all knew was there somewhere.

Irving removed the reading glasses off his face, not realizing another pair remained on the top of his head. He hefted himself out of his chair and wedged his walker in place. "I'll fix us some tea. Sugar in yours, right?"

"That's right." John could have made tea in half the time. But taking over the task would have made Irving feel twitchy, old, and useless, so John seated himself across at the long library table and waited patiently as Irving made his painstaking way to the cupboard and removed a teapot and two fragile china cups and saucers.

"Where is everybody?" Irving asked. "On a mission?"

"Caleb's taken Isabelle and Samuel out to handle a problem near the orphanage. Minor stuff."

"You keep flinging those two together, don't you?" Irving smirked.

"Samuel and Isabelle? Yes, but it never takes. They desperately want each other. But Isabelle doesn't trust Samuel. Samuel doesn't trust Isabelle." John sighed. "I want to shake them both."

"Yes. Time is not so unlimited as they like to think."

"Speaking of star-crossed lovers, that woman who watches the mansion is still out there on the street corner," John reported. "She looks cold this morning."

"Fascinating! I wonder who she is." Irving pulled the pair of glasses off the top of his head and examined his selection of loose teas.

Like John believed that. "I don't know, but she keeps your window in sight."

Irving began the long, laborious process of measuring leaves into the pot. "I've met so many people in my life, and I'm afraid my memory is failing . . ."

*Conveniently failing.* "She's about sixty-five or seventy, looks like a Gypsy fortune-teller, and someone split her nose right down the middle. Ring any bells?"

Irving pretended to stop and think. "Not right

offhand. Does she have any other distinguishing marks?"

"At least once a day, when one of the Chosen sets foot out of your mansion, she sends a message to you via us. *Give Irving my regards.*" John waited.

Irving pretended to be blithely oblivious.

"Having someone deliver a message into our brains is disconcerting, to say the least."

"She sounds like a powerful mind-speaker to me. Maybe she's wiped my memory?"

John snorted. Irving knew who she was, all right. He just didn't want to tell anyone. "We could bring her in. You two could meet."

Irving shot John a glance that was the exact opposite of his feeble-old-man act. "Not a good idea."

"Probably not." Because something was going on between those two, and it wasn't a love-fest. "But I do know her name is Dina."

"Why do you know that?"

"Because the other day, when it was raining, Charisma went out to give her an umbrella and she asked her."

"Charisma is a foolish girl."

"Charisma has good instincts." John let the matter rest there.

Irving's study was a cavernous room . . . a remarkable room. His massive bed occupied the far end; and while it was carved from some precious wood, and gargoyles hung from each tall post, it was the larger study area that made the unwary retreat into the hall.

When questioned, Irving always said the study was simply a room dedicated to learning, with the library table, his easy chair and ottoman, an illuminated world globe on a tall maple stand, and enough seating for all of the Chosen around the table. But his brown eyes twinkled when he said it, for on the floor-to-ceiling bookshelves, precious texts and fragile scrolls competed with empty-eyed human skulls. Glass cases displaying antique jewelry and glassworks from the Renaissance jostled for room with a jar of yellowed teeth and half a dozen African masks. And John didn't even want to know what those odd-shaped human hair toupees had been created to cover.

A small leather pouch tied with a red string sat on the table beside Irving's open book.

"I haven't seen that before," John said. Although it did look familiar.

Irving poured hot water from the electric kettle into the china pot, peered inside, then with shaky fingers placed the lid on top of the pot. "You don't recall this?"

"No." But some kind of memory was nagging at John.

Irving prompted him. "That sack came from the Andes, rescued from a collapsing cave in a glacier . . ."

"My God, I'd forgotten!" John leaned across the table and picked it up. "Is that the one we risked our lives for? It doesn't look like much."

"In terms of actual value, it's worth nothing. But Jacqueline said she dreamed about it, so I got it out. She opened it and tried to find out why it was calling her."

"No luck?"

"She said she could make a connection, but it wouldn't go through." Irving got a bag of cookies out of the cupboard and filled a plate. "Don't tell McKenna I've got these. He says they're bad for me. But if I eat them, what am I going to do, die young?"

John grinned at Irving's tart observation. "So does Jacqueline think she'll be able to make this thing"—he jiggled the leather sack—"connect?"

"For all that I've been around this soothsaying stuff for so long, I don't really know how it works. She tried to explain by saying it was like a network signal that isn't strong enough to pick up a cell call, like on one of those obnoxious TV commercials."

John stared at the bag, trying to recall where he had seen something else similar. *A leather purse tied with a blue string* . . . "What's in there?"

"Bones."

Now he remembered. The pool. The falls. Making love to Genny . . . twice.

As the memory washed over him, he closed his eyes in pain. Then opened them again, and gazed at the twin of the leather sack she'd brought up from the bottom of the pond. "Human bones? Finger bones?"

Irving stopped his puttering and turned to John, his brown eyes intent. "I had no idea *you* included prophecy among your talents."

"Genny found something like this in the *rasputye*."

"Well, well. How interesting that you should be in on both finds." Irving contemplated the pouch in John's hand. "What happened to your sack?"

"It wasn't *my* sack. Since Genny found it, I believed it was meant for her, and she took it when she left. I'm afraid it's gone forever, probably burned along with her body in the cremation ritual." John wondered when he would stop speculating, suffering, imagining Genny struggling against snow and wind, and slowly succumbing to an awful ice-covered shroud of death.

Sometimes when he woke at night, the memory of her was so vital, so close, he felt he could touch her. Then he went to the computer and looked through records in countries around the world, seeking her, thinking that if he stumbled on the right combination of circumstances, he would find her. But she was a ghost, always out of reach, and guilt racked him for allowing Brandon to ambush and distract him. She hadn't deserved to die because he had let his guard down.

"Artifacts of power are never gone forever. They have a will of their own—and if they're meant to be united, someday, somehow, it will happen." Irving turned back to his tea. "There are twenty-seven bones in the human hand. That sack contains eight. I wonder how many the other one contains."

"I don't know."

"A good bet would be nineteen."

"If there are only two sacks."

"Ah. Very astute. You do think like a military strategist. That's why you've been so successful at leading the team." Irving got down a lacquered Korean serving tray. "You came to visit at a good time. I was wondering if you'd like my collection of power tools."

"Power tools?" John's eyes widened.

"That's what I call them." Irving cackled with an old man's wicked mirth. "They have powers."

"Got it." John relaxed, knowing he was going to hear about some cool, eccentric stuff.

"I've got a mariner's telescope that's reputed to ex-

tend your vision beyond the horizon. I've got a chunk
of amber that supposedly gives the wearer the strength
of the early Cretaceous ant trapped inside. That's no
small thing, you know. Ants can carry ten to fifty times
their body weight." Irving carefully placed the teapot,
cups, sugar, and spoons on the tray. "If only I could get
it to work, maybe I could carry this tray to the table."

"Would you like some help?" John rose.

"Please. I find I can't maneuver the walker and carry
the tray at the same time—and McKenna shouts at me
when he catches me motoring around on my own."

"I'm with McKenna. Last time you fell, you broke
your glasses and almost your nose." He fetched the
tray and laid it at Irving's place at the table, then sat
and waited while Irving made his slow progress back
to his chair.

"I do hate being this wobbly." Irving went through
the ritual of seating himself—using his walker and the
arms of the chair to lower himself into the seat, placing the walker within arm's reach, pushing the chair
under the table. When he was situated to his satisfaction, he poured tea and continued his conversation as
if life's interruption had never occurred. "I've got more
power tools, too, and I suspect in the right hands, some
of them might work. A wind machine, reputed to be
strong and directional, fits in a coat pocket. Oh! And a
crystal phial that is a light in dark places when all other
lights go out."

"How very Tolkien."

"You don't think he made all that stuff up, do you?"

"I hadn't . . . thought . . ." John blinked and decided
not to pursue the idea. "I would love to have your

power tools. But why don't you keep them for me until you're done with them?"

"Ah, dear boy. I've let McKenna know who gets what, but McKenna's no spring chicken, and he might bite it before I do. So I've been marking things for when I pass."

Since Irving's butler was approaching fifty and in fine shape, John was unworried. Accepting the cup, he plunked in three sugar cubes, stirred vigorously, and didn't make a face as he sipped.

He hated tea.

But Irving loved it, so John gritted his teeth and swallowed the hot, flowery brew as fast as he could, trying not to taste it.

"Now, what can I do for you?" Irving asked.

John put down his cup into his saucer a little too emphatically, and the delicate china clinked together. He winced—he hated to think what McKenna would say if he chipped an eighteenth-century piece of porcelain— and said, "I'm afraid I may need to test your power tools soon. I'm losing my power."

# Chapter 43

⫘

Irving's eyebrows shot up. "Losing your power, John? Really? Why?"

"I don't know why. That's why I came to you. I lift a garage door, and halfway up it slams down again. I try to use a stick on a thief's skull, and I trip him instead. And did you hear about the junkyard guard dog that chased me up a tree?"

Irving nodded and tried to hide his grin in his cup. "Indeed, I did."

"I thought I had him under control. Suddenly I didn't, and he charged. Luckily he charged *me* rather than Charisma and the infant, and I was able to keep his attention until she got over the fence." John winced and rubbed his posterior. "Bit me right in the ass."

Irving chortled.

"My mark, the one given to me by the lynx . . . it is fading." John put his hand to his shoulder. "If the prophecy is right—if I need my true love to maintain my powers—then I suppose it's a miracle I've kept it for this long."

Irving put his cup down and got serious. "You've lost all power? Big power? Little power?"

"I've only ever possessed big power."

Irving said, "Hmm."

The old guy might be failing physically, but John had to admit he was still sharp as a tack. "All right, I've been trying to cultivate subtle powers, too. Genny told me . . ." He cleared his throat. "Genny told me I should work on performing the little things. For instance, tying my shoes. Or pouring tea."

Irving put an alarmed hand over his teapot. "This is my favorite!"

"I won't try it right now. I've been working on the fine, er, motor skills ever since I left the *rasputye*, but with little success." John looked down at himself, every bit of him clad at the Big and Tall Shop. "I'm not a delicate kind of guy."

"So your substantial powers are waning and your subtle powers aren't trained."

"The team is handling the problem with its usual spirit—they're working around it as needed, and laughing at me every chance they get."

Irving smiled at him. "You've built a good team, John Powell."

"I inherited a good team, Irving Shea. I only wish there were more of them. The Others seem to be spreading like oil on wet asphalt."

"We can have only seven Chosen." Irving was firm about that.

"The Others aren't playing by that rule anymore."

"We *have* to play by the rules. I've broken the rules and we're paying for it now." Irving's voice got old-man wobbly.

"What do you mean?"

"I don't know. It's just a suspicion. But I know the truth is here"—Irving rapped the open book with his knuckles—"if only I could find it."

"The prophecy is in that book?" John leaned forward.

"This book"—Irving waved a hand around—"or one of these."

John collapsed back into his chair. "Or one of the thousands of books in Rosamund's library."

"There, too." Irving caressed the page, and his eyes lingered on the words. "I was reading about sacrifice. It's fallen out of fashion in the modern world, but sacrifice in the truest sense is an effective gadget."

John straightened in his seat. "What kind of sacrifice?"

"Traditionally, the sacrifice of one's life is the most valuable. To offer your body and soul to be extinguished for a good cause, or to save another's life, not knowing for sure what awaits you beyond this plane? It erases many faults, expunges many sins." When Irving looked up, his eyes were sharp and intent. "I mean, obviously if you're a mass murderer, one moment of sacrifice isn't going to cut it. But if you've made a mistake, a big mistake, I think perhaps that sacrifice might suffice to correct it. Of course, there's the obvious problem of the possible accompanying pain and torment involved in the passage from one world to the other, not to mention what will occur on the other side. But that's my problem, isn't it?"

John tensed. "Planning to sacrifice yourself, Irving?"

"I would if I thought it would do any good." Irving snorted. "But I'm so old, in the big scheme of things, my life isn't worth much. Now, about the loss of your powers—is this like that last time you had problems?"

*The last time he had problems?* John almost wanted to laugh at Irving's euphemism . . . but it wasn't funny. "You mean when five people died? No. When that happened, I didn't dare examine the circumstances for fear of what I would see. Then I talked to Genny about it, and she said . . . well, she said some scathing things."

"About Gary, I presume."

"And me. Since hearing her, I've met Gary again— she gave me the courage to look back, and I think . . ."

"You think what happened wasn't your fault?"

"I'm not trying to shift blame," John said hastily, "but we shouldn't have been there in the first place."

"Gary liked facing impossible odds and succeeding, as he did when his team entered the glacier and he brought back a leather bag full of bones."

John sat quietly, remembering his struggle against the weight and the force of the melting ice. "I was so close to dying that day. I was lucky." Or he had thought he was, for he lived, saved everyone's lives, and had become engaged to Sun Hee. "But without luck, I'm not the equal of a force of nature."

"Fair enough." Irving nodded, accepting John's explanation with seeming ease. "Do you think Gary is behind your problem? Your loss of power?"

John felt off balance. He was trying to explain why he no longer felt at fault in the five deaths which had sent him into exile—and Irving offered no resistance. "You've taken my explanation for my failure as if you never doubted it. If you believed in me after we lost five lives on the volcano, why didn't you make it known when I returned to the Gypsy Travel Agency headquarters?"

"As you know, I'm one of the few people who has never liked Gary. I always saw the tragic flaw in him, that grandiose desire to be the top, the best, the most acclaimed. Not because he valued the best, but because he valued the acclaim."

"Yes. We all see that fault now."

Irving continued. "But, John, when the incident happened, I didn't know you well, and circumstances looked bad."

"Because everyone knew I had just discovered Sun Hee was sleeping with Gary." The old grief welled up in John. "I hated the humiliation. Of course I did. And I myself wondered if I'd allowed my team to be killed for some madness of revenge. But then—if I was trying to kill them, why would I carry Gary to safety? Sun Hee was weak, but when Gary seduced her, he knew exactly what he was doing. He's the one I would have killed."

"Gary is a troublemaker here, and I'm afraid that his miraculous recovery was not as miraculous as it seemed."

John had heard Irving's theory before, that Gary had somehow escaped the coma that held him trapped for so long by making a deal with the devil. "It's hard to sign in blood on that dotted line when you've got no brain waves."

"Yet he regained consciousness." Irving sighed.

"You should have thrown him into the fire. It would have saved us a lot of trouble now."

The two men sat in concurrence, quietly sipping their tea.

Irving roused himself. "But the truth is, killing a person to save yourself trouble down the line is foolish. Sometimes that person has an important part to play, and we mere mortals can't judge the impact one man makes on the world."

"Genny told me that even if I was guilty, I was sacrificing my life for no good reason when I should be working to make up for whatever horrible things I had done. That's why I returned."

"She was a wise woman, your Genny."

"Yes. I was the one who was stupid." John confessed, "When I found out she lied to me . . . I should have known she couldn't be all real. I thought she was interested only in the lynx. And me. It is my destiny to fall for women with ulterior motives." He hated feeling sour about that, but nothing in the past two and a half years had changed those facts.

"What was her ulterior motive?"

"Don't be disingenuous, Irving," John snapped.

Irving looked startled. "I didn't know I was."

"She was there because you had sent her to recruit me. She seduced me for your sake, Irving, and the sake of the Gypsy Travel Agency."

"I didn't send her," Irving said flatly.

"Sure."

"I didn't send her," Irving repeated. "The Gypsy Travel Agency didn't send her. If she wickedly seduced you, it wasn't for us."

"But if it wasn't you . . . ?"

"Then it was for someone else who knew the extent of your powers and believed they could recruit you."

"The Others? No!"—John slammed his fist on the table—"I don't believe that of Genny. She wouldn't do that."

"Not knowingly, perhaps."

John stood. He sat. "Her father was a real asshole. Used to work for the Gypsy Travel Agency."

"I remember Kevin Valente all too well."

"She told me he was the one who pushed her into the commitment to talk to me. Do you think he would have manipulated her to work, all unknowing, for the Others?" John stood again, and paced around the room, trying to put it all together.

"Kevin Valente was the businessman version of Gary White. He sold out the Gypsy Travel Agency, and for his chance to succeed, I believe he'd sell his own grandmother."

"Or his own daughter." John felt sick.

Irving poured himself another cup of tea. "You know, John, if you've got a fatal flaw, it's that you *expect* betrayal. You say she had an ulterior motive for seeking you out. People always have ulterior motives—but most of us just call them *motives*."

"She could have told me the truth."

"Is it possible she made the same observation about you that I have? That you expect betrayal and respond accordingly?"

John stopped pacing.

"Genny didn't tell you all the facts about herself for fear you would reject her. As it turned out, she was justified. I think she simply did whatever she could to stay close to you." Irving sounded meditative. "Myself, I would have been flattered to know a woman wanted me so much."

Since John had entered the room, he'd been pole-axed with one truth after another. "I can't do anything about this. She's dead."

"Maybe. But for the past two years, despite the prophecy that the Chosen Ones' gifts are tied to their connection to their true loves, your powers have been stable. Reliable. Doesn't that mean she's alive?"

"She can't be alive. She came out of the *rasputye* into a blizzard. I spoke to the couple who found her. They said she was dead. Or rather"—John remembered all too clearly—"the wife said Genny was dead, that they cremated her. Why would this woman lie?"

Irving raised his eyebrows.

John answered his own question. "Because Genny asked her to. Because Genny didn't want me to find her. Because I didn't believe in her."

"Women are funny about stuff like that." Irving rubbed his chest. "Believe me. I know."

"Even after they said that, I searched for her. For months, I scoured the area looking for any sign of her."

"Perhaps she was hiding. Perhaps she moved quickly. Perhaps . . . the Others captured her and wreaked their vengeance on her for her failure to re-cruit you."

John leaned across the table. "For the love of God, Irving, don't even imagine that." Yet now, the idea took hold in John's head and his fear grew in leaps and bounds. The scratches the lynx had given him ached; he pressed his shoulder and realized they had opened.

Pulling his hand away, he stared in amazement.

Blood and gore stained his palm. "I have to go look for her." John could scarcely breathe. "If she's alive, I have to find her at last. And when I do . . . I will dedicate my life to her."

# Chapter 44

With a real affection, Irving watched John leave. The lad had such good manners, not spewing the tea across the table no matter how flowery a brew Irving chose. Irving supposed he shouldn't torment John in such a way. But this sudden descent into old age had left him with little he could do for entertainment. So the smallest, most petty distraction amused him—not to mention that watching a behemoth like John handle delicate two-hundred-year-old china made him want to chuckle. So he did, and leaned back in his chair thinking it felt good to laugh.

He hadn't laughed for a long time.

He spread his hand over the book open before him.

What he'd said to John—it wasn't true.

A sacrifice was a sacrifice.

A life was a life.

No matter how old you were, on the scales of eternity, each life weighed the same as the next. Because, of course, part of what he'd said to John was true: *To offer your body and soul to be extinguished for a good cause, or to save another's life, not knowing for sure what awaits you beyond this plane? It erases many faults, expunges many sins.*

Irving loved his life. He loved his study; he loved McKenna and the clever foods he concocted to tempt Irving's flagging appetite. He loved Martha and the way they could discuss their shared experiences at the Gypsy Travel Agency. Irving loved the present more than anything. He loved Jacqueline and Charisma and Isabelle and Samuel and Aaron and Aleksandr and John. He loved Caleb and Rosamund.

Most of all, he loved his work. He hadn't retired at sixty-five. No, he'd gone ahead and worked at the Gypsy Travel Agency part-time, and he wasn't just a figurehead. He gave them important input.

Then the Gypsy Travel Agency had blown up, and he became, not the aging former CEO, but the expert to whom everyone applied, the center of knowledge and of strategy, the wise old man. He believed that he was justified in saying that without him, the new Chosen would have been hunted down and killed, and the Others would have spread their chaos and their evil throughout the world.

Age was slowing him down. He knew it, and he hated everything about it: the indigestion, the walker, the incontinence. God, what a mess *that* was.

But in the big scheme of things, his pains were minor, and he hadn't lost an ounce of his intelligence . . . although he almost wished he had.

Because he had come to the conclusion that it was his

sin, and no other, that had brought on this catastrophe—
the explosion of the Gypsy Travel Agency building, the
loss of so many Chosen and support people, the destruction of the library and all the artifacts, culled from
the best of the archaeology sites around the world . . .

His fault. His fault. But he never intended to do anything but save the Agency.

He had been the one who took over the Gypsy Travel
Agency when it was failing. He had been a young
black CEO in a time when no black CEOs existed in
the white business world.

So he had done what needed to be done—*whatever
needed to be done*—to save the flailing concern and to
prove to the waiting world that men should be judged
not by the color of their skin, but by their intelligence,
dedication, and performance. Under his guidance, the
Gypsy Travel Agency had infiltrated rival travel agen-
cies to "study" their itineraries and clients. The gifted
had used their gifts to convince native peoples to re-
veal hidden, holy sites; and once that was done, the
people of the corporation, businessmen like Kevin Valente, had "acquired" the most valuable artifacts and
sold them to collectors. The Agency always made sure
to secure exclusive tour rights; then they'd whipped
up excitement in the press and led eager tourists on
expeditions.

Irving had even instructed the Chosen Ones to subtly use their powers with the wealthy to be named as
beneficiaries in wills—and obtained this mansion.

For everything he had done, he had told himself he
was justified. The Gypsy Travel Agency was the cover
and the financial aid for the Chosen Ones, and the

Chosen Ones did great good in the world. He had supported that good.

And then there was Dina. He regretted many things in his life, but what he'd done to her had been unforgiveable.

He knew it when he'd done it.

He knew it now.

Wearily he hefted himself out of the chair, got his walker, and made his way to the window.

There she was, standing on the street corner, smoking one of her interminable cigarettes.

She must be sixty-five now. No, seventy. But even with her ruined nose, she was still one fine-looking woman, slender and vital—and when he'd seen her for the first time, he had known she was the woman he was destined to love.

He'd thrown her away for the golden ring of success. Worse, he'd destroyed her when he did it.

Of course, she knew he was watching her.

Turning her head, she smiled coldly and blew a stream of smoke in his direction.

Her voice echoed in his head. *Hello, Irving.*

She was the most talented mind-speaker he had ever met.

But he had no gift. He couldn't answer her back. He couldn't tell her of his regrets, of the long nights he spent alone, of how he had worried about her and dreamed of a different outcome to their story.

If he could have told her those things, she would have been justified in spitting in his face.

But he could send a message: placing his hand over his aching heart, he bowed in her direction.

She straightened, stared at him, trying to see his thought.

*Yes, my dear, you can't read my mind, but you recognize regret when you see it, and love, and you wonder why I should feel this way . . . because you don't give your allegiance to the Others, no matter what they think.*

He had such a good life.

But now he believed—no, he knew—that the deeds he had authorized in the name of a healthy bottom line had ultimately broken the organization at its very foundation. The Gypsy Travel Agency and the Chosen Ones were meant to do good. No exceptions. Ever. That was *the* eternal law.

Now, no matter how hard Irving had tried, no matter how hard he had driven the Chosen and their mates, it hadn't been possible to discover a prophecy to reverse this free fall into evil. So the truth had taken root in his mind and was growing.

A sacrifice was necessary. And who better to sacrifice than himself—the man responsible for this disaster?

He heard a familiar step in the corridor.

*Ah. A sign.* A man like him believed in signs.

He smiled at Dina, a farewell smile.

She shook her head, started walking rapidly toward the mansion.

But Irving ignored her. He turned toward the door, and as Gary walked past he called, "Gary!"

Gary came back, stuck his head in. "Do you need something, Irving?" He looked so normal, so composed, not at all like a man who had made a deal with the devil.

"I was wondering"—Irving left his walker behind,

tottered toward the door—"if you could help me down the stairs."

John stood in the basement of the Arthur W. Nelson Fine Arts Library antiquities department, speaking to Rosamund about the possible routes a lone woman might take to cross Asia, when his cell phone rang. He glanced at the caller, answered, and listened to the frantic voice on the other side.

As the blood drained from his face, Rosamund asked urgently, "What is it?"

John shut the phone. "It's Irving. He fell down the stairs. He's not expected to live."

# Chapter 45

The guard let Gary into the building, then walked him to the elevator and used his key to call it. When Gary stepped inside, the guard pushed the button for the forty-fifth floor, then stepped out as the door shut.

Gary shot right up, no stops, then walked out and took a corner to the next elevator. Another guard, another key, another forty-five floors, no stops. Another floor. Another corner.

No guard this time. No one else on this floor.

He stepped inside the waiting elevator, straightened his tie, and pressed the lone, unmarked button.

He didn't know how high he climbed. He only knew his heart was thumping, his hands were sweating, and his usual bold confidence plunged as the elevator rose.

How had he, Gary White, famed team leader for the Chosen Ones, arrived at this moment?

Oh. That's right. John Powell had put him into a living death. *The bastard.*

And Osgood had rescued him from his coma. Revived him, given him mobility, speech, escape from the nursing home, from the smell of antiseptic, from the eternal, measured drip of the IV. For that, Gary owed Osgood everything: loyalty, service, success . . . and that success had eluded him. In two and a half years, he'd done nothing to impress Osgood.

The elevator opened. He walked through the empty foyer to the tall, wide door. Knocked.

His knuckles barely made a sound against the solid wood.

Nothing happened. He heard nothing, saw nothing.

He put his hand on the doorknob, took a breath, turned it, swung it open.

"Come in, Gary." Osgood's quiet, Southern-tinged voice grated Gary's nerves into fine shreds.

Gary strode into the office.

It was large. The walls were gray. The carpet was thick. The room was empty except for a vast, almost clean, gray metal desk. A puddle of light shone on its surface, right in front of the shadowy figure in the chair—and Gary found himself transfixed by the man's soft, veined, aged hands, so busily using a fountain pen and sorting papers. Hands that looked as if they belonged to a polite, pampered older gentleman.

Gary knew better.

"Shut the door behind you," Osgood said.

Gary shut the door.

The silence that followed was broken only by the scratch of the pen.

Osgood was a shadow behind the light: not tall, not handsome, with no distinguishing characteristics at all. The casual onlooker on the street wouldn't even notice him. That was Osgood's strength. That, and the fact that before he had invited the devil into his soul, he had been a ruthless, immoral, uncaring businessman.

That kind of possession made for a precise and evil melding of man and demon.

In New York State and all up and down the East Coast, Osgood controlled the gambling, the prostitution, the liquor, the drugs, the clubs. If corruption existed, he had a hand in it.

Now Osgood put down his pen and folded his hands on top of the papers. "Gary White. What have you done for me lately?"

Gary felt the exultation rise in him. At last, he had something substantial to report. "I pushed Irving Shea down the stairs."

Osgood didn't stir a muscle. He simply stared at Gary. Maybe he hadn't heard. Maybe he was incredulous.

Gary didn't blame him. What an unexpected boon!

So Gary repeated, "I pushed the old bastard down the stairs," and this time he allowed himself a charming smile and a voice full of pride.

"I heard you." Osgood's voice was curiously neutral. "How did this fortuitous event come about?"

"He asked me to help him down the stairs." Gary laughed at the memory. "He's so old, it was nothing to get him to the top and give him a push. He tumbled right down."

Another pause. "Did he yell?"

"Nope. Just went over and over and over. But when

he was at the bottom, I yelled enough for the both of us." Osgood's lack of response was starting to bug Gary. "He's got a broken hip for sure, a concussion, maybe a broken back."

"When you got down to him— I assume you ran down to him?"

"Yes! In case anybody had seen it, and I babbled all the necessary horror and concern."

Osgood disregarded Gary's acting skills. "When you went down to him, was he conscious?"

"Yes, and in so much pain." It did Gary's heart good to remember.

"Did he say anything?"

"No, I'm safe. He couldn't speak."

"Did he look at you? Did he smile?"

Gary froze. How had Osgood known that? "Yeah, he smiled. Brain damage, I figure."

"You *fool*." Osgood rose from behind his desk.

Gary had always thought Osgood's constant eerie calm was the most frightening thing he'd ever seen.

He was wrong.

Because he'd never seen him in a rage before.

Osgood paced toward him, and his eyes glowed— actually *glowed*—blue and virulent. "The old man suckered you."

Gary backed up. "No, he didn't! What do you mean?"

"The one thing, *the one thing* that would hand the Chosen Ones an advantage in this battle is the willing sacrifice of a life."

"Come on. A willing sacrifice wouldn't make that much diff—" Gary realized the foolishness of telling the devil himself how eternal laws worked. "Besides, Irving didn't know what I was going to do."

"He didn't? Really? Didn't he always dislike you? Hasn't he suspected you since your resurrection? And he asked you to *help him down the stairs*?" Osgood's face came nearer. He was merely a bald, middle-aged man of slight build. Innocuous. Except for the blue flames burning in the depths of his eyes. "What does that say to you, Gary?"

Gary had never heard his name spoken in quite that tone. "He's senile."

"He set you up. He made of himself a willing sacrifice." Osgood took Gary's chin in his hand.

His touch set off a sound in Gary's brain.

*Drip.*

Then another sound.

*Drip.*

And another.

*Drip.*

Gary knew that sound. He had lived with that sound for four long years.

It was the endless, measured splash of an IV.

"No!" he shrieked and writhed, trying to get away.

"Why not?" Osgood controlled him effortlessly. "We made a deal. I would perform a miracle. You would rise from your coma and walk and talk and be my creature for the rest of my life. You would serve me with all your heart and soul."

"I have! I am!"

"Yet although you live in the same house as the Chosen Ones, you don't lead them, because you clumsily tried to get them killed once too often. You don't bring me information, because they don't trust you. Now you tell me you pushed Irving Shea down the stairs, *exactly as he set you up to do.*" Osgood squeezed Gary's face so hard Gary felt veins explode under his skin. "Give me one good reason why I shouldn't put you back in a coma right now."

In a rush, Gary said, "John Powell—I'm blocking his power."

The office grew quiet.

Osgood's eyes narrowed. The blue flames flickered.

Gary prayed to a deity he no longer served.

Then—

"Better." Osgood caressed Gary's chin, and lightly slapped his cheek.

The dripping stopped.

Gary almost collapsed in relief.

Osgood walked back to his desk. He seated himself again, leaned back. In his calm, emotionless voice, with eyes empty of necromancy, he asked, "How are you blocking John Powell?"

Gary settled on the most straightforward story he could tell. "When the Gypsy Travel Agency tested me, they decided I was a powerful mind reader. But I always knew there was more to me. Before John Powell tried to kill me, I was practicing with throwing thoughts. I put a couple of people into comas myself."

"And aren't we proud of ourselves," Osgood mocked.

Gary wanted to snap at him. Instead, he took a long breath and reminded himself that he had trickles of sweat easing down his ribs from his fear of this man—this *creature*. "When John took my leadership position in the team, I wondered how best to hurt him—and serve you, of course. I thought if I could gain control of his powers, he'd be afraid to lead them into danger for fear he'd kill them like he killed his wife and his friends."

Osgood nodded thoughtfully. "Good. Undermine his confidence in himself and their confidence in him."

"Exactly."

"How's it working?"

"Like a dream. He tries to send out one of those big power waves—hold up a falling tree— and I block him. Or I don't. The Chosen don't trust his power to be there when it's needed. He doesn't trust it, either." Gary loved what he was doing to John. "The team still praises his strategies, but they know they can't depend on him."

"Good work. You can walk the city streets for another day." Osgood picked up his pen and started to write again.

"Why don't you just let me kill him?"

The pen paused. "The rules of the game don't allow that."

"We . . . that is, you blew up the Gypsy Travel Agency and killed them all."

"Not quite all, although at the time I had great hopes . . ." That imperturbable voice showed signs of stress. "But that was apparently not so much a victory for me, as I had dared to imagine, but part of some eternal plan to show the Chosen Ones they had wandered off course."

"I thought we *were* destroying them once and for

all." Then Gary cowered, thinking he had overstepped the bounds.

"If we handle this correctly, we are." Osgood's calm was back in place. The pen proceeded to its task.

Gary lingered for a moment, terrified to leave, terrified to stay. At last, he decided he had been dismissed, and sidled toward the door.

With cool disinterest, Osgood said, "Don't make me angry again. I would hate to have to return you to that slow, helpless, humiliating descent into hell."

Gary nodded, a single dip of the head. He reached for the doorknob.

Osgood spoke, freezing Gary in place. "Do you remember that leather pouch you brought back from the glacier in Chile?"

In a panic, Gary cast his mind back. *Glacier. Chile.* Which team had that been?

*Amina hanging on him in adoration. Sun Hee preferring John to him. The glacier melting around them, taking out the cave that contained only a leather sack* . . . Gary had been so disappointed. "The sack with the bones inside?" He couldn't keep his disdain from his voice.

"That's the one. It has become an object of interest." Osgood wrote with meticulous care. "Bring it to me."

"It's a relic. What if it blew up in the explosion of the Gypsy Travel Agency?"

Osgood looked up. "There is more than one sack. Any of them will do."

"B-but I don't know how many or where to start . . . ?"

Osgood stared, heavy lidded.

Gary felt a shock go down his spine. "I'll find it. Or them. I'll get them."

"You'll know you have all the sacks when the contents can be used to construct a whole skeletal hand."

"Right. I'll find it." Gary corrected himself again. *"Them."*

"Soon."

"Very soon." Gary wrenched the door open and fled toward the elevator.

Behind him, the door closed with a soft, controlled click.

# Chapter 46

———◆———

Genesis Valente stood on the street at the bottom of the long flight of stairs looking up at Irving Shea's mansion and the massive door that led inside.

She didn't want to do this, didn't want to take the chance of seeing John Powell.

But she had no choice. She owed the Gypsy Travel Agency, had no other way to pay them back, so she hefted her backpack onto her shoulder, climbed the stairs, and rang the doorbell.

At once, the tall door swung open.

A young woman stood there, dyed black hair cut short on one side, long on the other, pale skin and red lips.

She smelled like the earth; her aura glittered like diamonds.

She drew her talent from the earth, from the stones.

Genny tried not to draw in her scent, not to see her gift. But that was impossible. Ever since her sojourn in the *rasputye*, she had seen, smelled, felt the truth of the people she met. It was almost as if she had been given a gift . . . a gift she didn't want.

The young woman's black, kohl-lined eyes were red rimmed; she had been crying. "What do you know?" she asked. No, not asked . . . *demanded.*

"I know I'm looking for Irving Shea," Genny said cautiously.

Those vulnerable eyes filled with tears, and they freely ran down the girl's cheeks. "He's not here."

"Maybe I should come back at a better time . . ." Genny started to back away.

The girl wiped at her face, smearing her makeup. "He's in the hospital."

Genny halted. "Oh, no. What happened?"

"He fell down the stairs. His hip is broken and maybe his back. He's in surgery now, but . . ." The girl bit her lips to contain their trembling.

Genny was not the same woman who had gone to Russia over two years before. The time she had spent in Asia, the Philippines, Australia and the Pacific Islands had changed her. She had survived a blinding snowstorm, learned to fight in a revolution, used her business skills to start a wildlife rescue organization. She had looked back on her life in New York and Russia, at the relationships she had formed, and resolved never to be taken in again.

But this woman made her heart melt. Genny stepped inside the great entry hall, dropped her backpack, and put her arm around her. "I'm so sorry. I've met Irving Shea, and this is a grievous blow."

"He's always been there for us, you know? Lately he's been sort of shaky, but sharp as a tack. We never thought he'd take a tumble." Charisma pulled half a dozen tissues out of her pocket and noisily blew her nose.

"I'll get out of your way as soon as I can, then." Genny unzipped her backpack and fumbled inside. "I'm Geneva Bianchi, and I came to—"

The girl stopped crying and stared. "You're . . . Geneva? You're Genesis? You're *Genny*?"

Genny *knew* she had introduced herself with her new name, Geneva Bianchi, the name on her passport, the name she'd paid for in Hong Kong.

Yet this person had immediately leaped to the right conclusions.

The girl flung her arms around Genny's neck. "Of course you are! Why didn't I realize it at once?" Her bracelets jingled in Genny's ears, and it seemed they spoke a language.

"I'm sorry. Do we *know* each other?" Nothing about this girl was familiar, but then, business school was two and a half years ago, and since then, Genny had done almost nothing to remind herself of that time.

"No. No! I'm Charisma Fangorn. I'm one of the Chosen." Charisma jingled her bracelets in Genny's face. "I listen to the stones. I hear the earth sing."

"Yeah. I know." Genny hated knowing that the girl was gifted, and how.

She wanted to return the inner sense that the *rasputye* had given her . . . but it seemed customer service was closed. "What does that have to do with me?"

"I know you." Charisma jumped up and down, her short pleated skirt jumping, her strappy sandals doing a jig. "I know you! You're John's true love!"

A middle-aged butler hurried toward them and shut the door. "Miss Charisma, this isn't appropriate. Please take your guest into the library."

Genny reached into her backpack again. "No. Wait. Really, I can't stay. I simply wanted to give you—"

"McKenna, do you know who this is?" Miss Charisma kept one arm tightly around Genny's shoulders. "This is Genesis Valente!"

"Ah. Mr. John's young lady." A smile broke across McKenna's austere face.

*Mr. John's young lady?* Genny was not that. She had never been that.

McKenna continued. "A most propitious arrival, Miss Genesis. Welcome, indeed. May I take your coat and backpack?" He placed a hand on her collar.

She shrugged him off. "No, I'm not staying. I just dropped by to give you something."

"To Mr. John, no doubt. But I fear he's not here right now." McKenna's voice grew scratchy, as if he fought unwanted emotion.

*John's not here.* The tension in Genny's shoulders relaxed.

"He's at the hospital awaiting word of the surgery." McKenna glanced at the old-fashioned dial phone on the entry table as if willing it to ring.

"McKenna got to Irving's side first." Charisma patted his chest.

"What Mr. Irving was doing moving around without his walker, I do not know. When he recovers, I shall give him a stern talking-to." McKenna's dour appearance was belied by the moisture in his eyes. But he recovered immediately. "You two will want to make your introductions in the library. Make yourselves comfortable. I'll let the other Chosen know. Well, there's only Miss Jacqueline. Mr. Caleb, Miss Isabelle, and Mr. Samuel are away on a mission; and of course, young Aleksandr is in class. Nevertheless, Miss Genny, you'll meet them all soon enough."

"No," Genny said, "after I give you this artifact, I've got to be on my way."

The same deafness that afflicted Charisma also apparently afflicted McKenna. "Martha will bring refreshments."

"Good," Charisma said. "Genny's probably hungry. Aren't you, Genny?"

Genny surrendered. "All right. I can stay a little while." Especially since she didn't want to wrestle herself free from Charisma's hold on her arm.

Charisma dragged her toward the big open arch off the entry. "McKenna hates when we have a scene in the foyer. It offends his sense of propriety." She grinned at McKenna.

He did not grin back.

Charisma's face and voice softened. "McKenna, would you ask Jacqueline to come down? Genny needs to talk to her."

"Of course, Miss Charisma." He walked toward the wide, smooth sweep of steps that led upstairs, and nothing about his proper demeanor changed.

But Genny thought he might be hurrying.

This place was odd. Off kilter. A lunacy seemed to be alive in the air.

Genny tugged Charisma to a halt just inside the library, a gracious room of immense proportions. "Who is Jacqueline? Why do you say I need to talk to her?"

"Jacqueline is our seer. And my stones said that what you have is for her. Lately, they've been speaking to me very loudly." Charisma cocked her head and studied Genny. "I think maybe you're the reason. John's been having so many problems lately and we're worried—"

"John . . . is sick?" Genny didn't want to be concerned. But she was.

"Yes. Well, no. He's the head of our team."

In a way, Genny was glad to hear that. She was glad to know he'd come back to the real world and was doing what he was born to do. At the same time, she didn't care how mature she'd become in the last two and a half years. She didn't want to see him—which didn't keep her from asking about him. "What kind of problems is he having?"

"Problems with his powers." Charisma pushed Genny into a chair in front of the fireplace.

Books filled the shelves, oriental carpets covered the hardwood floors, and if Genny wasn't in a hurry, she would have wanted to sink down on the couch and take a nap.

Kicking off her shoes, Charisma paced in her stocking feet. "His powers aren't working right. We were pretty worried about him, thinking it was all about the fact his true love was dead and he was going to lose it—you know, *it*—altogether. We didn't know how to handle it because we're used to having someone who can, you know, knock a bullet aside if we need it."

"Very useful," Genny agreed.

"But now you're here, so he's going to be okay."

Genny had no idea what Charisma was talking about, and told herself she didn't care. She only cared about one thing. Handing over what she owed and getting out of here. "If you would take this off my hands—"

"I can't take it. It's for Jacqueline," Charisma said with absolute assurance, then twirled like a ballerina toward the door. "It's Martha with the tea cart!"

A dour woman in her seventies pushed the cart to the sidebar. "I brought drinks and snacks. Baked brie encased in pastry with cranberry jelly. Cherry tomatoes stuffed with yogurt and rice. Green tomato spread and sourdough bread." Every word she spoke sounded as if it had been chipped from ice.

But for Genny, she sang a siren's song. Genny rose, drawn to the cart, and gazed in awe at the delicacies. "I could stay for tea, I suppose."

Charisma seemed to know exactly what Genny felt. "Yeah, we eat like this all . . . the . . . time. Martha is the best."

"McKenna would have you believe he's the best." Martha handed Genny an icy can of Coke.

"We let him think that because he's a man." Charisma popped one of the tomatoes in her mouth.

As Genny filled her plate, she became aware of Martha's scrutiny. She scrutinized in return.

Martha's gray hair was braided and wrapped around her head like an Austrian yodeler, and dark eyes shone in her brown, wrinkled face. She was Romany, the kind of strong woman who frightened the hell out of men everywhere. Genny could see no gift in her soul, yet splashes of others' gifts clung to her as if she'd been exposed to the mystic for a very long time. One gift in particular had been imprinted on her being—a dark gift, one Martha resented . . .

"Thank you, Martha, for this feast," Genny said. "Never will you have a more grateful recipient."

Martha nodded, still watching Genny as if something about Genny puzzled her. "You are Kevin Valente's daughter?"

"You know my father?"

"I used to work at the Gypsy Travel Agency. You aren't like him." Martha nodded. "Good. You may have John." Turning on her heel, she left the room.

Genny stared after her. "I don't want John."

Charisma paid no attention to the exchange. "Have I smeared my mascara?" Going to the gold-framed mirror, she took one look at herself and burst into tears again.

"Are you okay, Charisma?" A tall, Nordic blond female stepped into the doorway.

Genny could see an eye in the middle of Jacqueline's forehead. It wasn't freaky. Nothing big and bulging. The eye didn't look around or anything; it was nothing but a dark outline.

And it seemed no one else could see it.

But Genny could. Genny knew. This was Jacqueline, the clairvoyant.

"No." Charisma's voice wobbled and she used another round of tissues. "I won't be until we hear from the hospital. But I do have good news." She gestured at Genny. "Guess who this is."

As Genny rose to her feet, Jacqueline examined her. "Someone who made you cry?"

"No!" Charisma said indignantly. "Some seer you are! This is Genesis Valente."

Somehow, Genny didn't think Jacqueline was nearly as surprised as she pretended to be.

Jacqueline also looked as if she'd been crying, but she was more restrained in her welcome. "John will be pleased to discover you're alive—and very surprised. It's been . . . what? More than two years since you disappeared?"

"Jacqueline!" Charisma was shocked. "She just got here. We'll yell at her when we get to know her better!"

"Actually, I can't stay. I came by because I believe I have something that belongs to the Gypsy Travel Agency." Genny dug to the bottom of her backpack and brought up a small crushed cardboard box. "I think it's valuable, or at least it's . . . influential." She unwrapped the leather purse she had found at the bottom of the pond in the *rasputye* and held it out.

Jacqueline gave a pleased sigh. "Ohh."

"What is it?" Charisma peered between the two women.

"It's what I need to find the prophecy. May I?" Jacqueline asked.

"Of course." Genny placed it in her cupped hands.

Jacqueline held it. Just held it, eyes half closed, and seemed to be listening to music no one else could hear.

Charisma put her hand on Genny's arm.

The two women exchanged glances.

Jacqueline shook herself, and with sudden enthusiasm, said, "Come on. Let's go to Irving's office." She led the way out of the library and up the stairs.

Genny followed.

Charisma brought up the tail.

Genny felt as if she were being corralled.

"Why do you say it belongs to the Gypsy Travel Agency?" Jacqueline called back.

"Because I owe them for the price of my education, and it's the only thing I've gathered in my travels that I believe would be of interest to them." Genny suspected the matching bag at her father's house would also be of interest to the Chosen Ones. In fact, she suspected it had come from the Gypsy Travel Agency, one of the relics he had stolen and not returned because everyone thought it without value.

But she didn't have possession of it, and couldn't take possession unless she went to her father's house. And that was a visit she did not desire to make.

Yet it had to be done; she knew it did. For two and a half years, her father had believed her dead. She'd seen his lament on the online networks, knew the bitterness of the truth—he cared so little for her, he had used his grief and loneliness to attract women.

When he realized she was alive, would he once again try to force her into the business world? Or would he recognize the changes in her?

She was betting he would once again try to use her. She suspected it would be a very unpleasant visit.

Now Jacqueline opened the door to a large room.

Genny walked in and stopped.

Behind her, Charisma laughed in a wavering way. "Weird, huh? It's Irving's study, and the stuff he has in here is positively spooky."

"But *this* is what we're interested in." Jacqueline

walked to the table, to an open medieval manuscript, where a leather sack identical to Genny's, except for the color of the string, sat waiting. "Early this morning, I woke and I knew there was something about this purse. I had Irving find it for me, because I believed I should be able to use it for a vision, an important vision. But no matter what I did, I couldn't get beyond the first stage. Now, this afternoon, you bring me this? Coincidence? I don't think so."

"Whoa. Cue the *Twilight Zone* music," Charisma said.

Genny nodded at the sack with the red string. "What's inside that one?"

Jacqueline smiled and carefully untied the blue string on Genny's purse. "Bones." She poured the bones out of Genny's sack, then the bones out of the sack on the table.

Eighteen finger bones rested on the table. Eighteen finger bones, yellowed with age, the same lengths and widths . . . the same hand.

"More spooky," Charisma said.

The three women sank into chairs around the table.

Jacqueline sorted the bones, carefully keeping them in separate piles. She picked them up, a sack's full worth in each hand, and shook them like dice. "Hm," she said.

"How did you find that, Genny?" Charisma was asking questions, but her gaze was fixed on Jacqueline, waiting . . .

Genny watched, too, fascinated and on edge, waiting for something profound to happen, and at the same time chatting as if nothing mattered. "When I first received the bag, I thought it was simply an odd old relic. Then as I traveled, it seemed to help me out. Guided me to shelter when I thought I was going to die. Helped me when I was attacked. Once, I even lost it, and it found its way back to me."

"Yes, there's something very powerful here." Jacqueline pushed the two piles of bones into mounds, then placed her hands over them. "I can't quite figure out how to . . ." She stiffened. Her head fell back against the chair.

In China, Genny had seen women and men who claimed to be oracles. When a vision possessed them, they frothed and fell, shouted and writhed.

Jacqueline was calm, coherent . . . here. She opened her mouth to speak.

Genny waited on the edge of her seat.

Jacqueline's eyes closed all the way. She relaxed and sighed. Opening her eyes, she looked at Genny and Charisma and shook her head. "The prophecy is there, just beyond my reach, but it won't quite coalesce. It's like this is a puzzle with a piece missing."

*Didn't that just figure?* Genny wanted to bonk her own head on the table.

Instead, she pushed back her chair and stood. "I know what's missing. Give me a couple of hours. I'm sure I can get it for you."

# Chapter 47

———◆◇◆———

Genny had traveled from New York to Russia to Kazakhstan, and around the world. She'd been gone two and a half years, and now she discovered the extra key to the lock of her father's house was still hidden behind the chunk of loose mortar at knee level to the left of the door. She stood on the stoop, looked at the brass key in the palm of her hand, and didn't know whether to use it. She'd gone in and out a thousand times before, but now to do so almost felt like breaking and entering.

Wherever else she went, she felt like a person rich with experiences, good and bad—she could make conversation with a senator, milk a goat, hold her own in a street fight, or drive a cab through the streets of Hong Kong. She knew she could do all those things . . . because she had.

What she couldn't do was become the woman her father had envisioned.

How would he react to her return? Would he even know her?

Because here on this street, people looked, but no one recognized her. She was a ghost.

The truth was, she would rather fight her way once more through that snow in Kazakhstan to the shelter of that yurt and try to communicate with people who spoke almost no English or Russian than to try to speak to her father.

With a sigh, she put the key back in its hiding place and rang the doorbell.

Avni opened the door.

Genny stared, slack-jawed. "Avni? What . . . ? How . . . ?"

Avni looked as she had in Rasputye: tall, thin, eastern Indian, smiling. Yet Genny saw differences . . . "Genny. I was hoping you'd come home today."

"Come home today? How would you know I was even here?"

"It's your father."

"What about my father?" Genny couldn't make sense of this turn of events. "Is he sick?"

Avni grabbed her wrist. "Come on!" She gave Genny a tug, pulling her across the threshold and into the dim entry hall.

The furniture hadn't changed since her grandparents' deaths. It looked like a nineteen-sixties sitcom in here, and for a second, she stood frozen in the memory of her youth.

The door shut behind her.

She whirled around.

Brandon stood there, his back pressed against the

door. He was thin to the point of gauntness. His white T-shirt was torn; his jeans sagged around his hips. He looked at her with sorrow, eyes full of tears. "Why did you come back? Why didn't you just stay away?"

Then something hard slammed into the back of Genny's head. She fell to her knees. Looked up. And saw Avni lifting the bookend once more.

John was making his hundredth circuit of the waiting room, his gaze on the clock, when his cell phone vibrated. He stopped pacing, glanced at the caller.

*Isabelle.*

"How is he?" As always, her voice was quiet, restrained, but he could hear the anxiety behind it.

"No one has come out for two hours. He's been in surgery for over five."

"What are they doing in there?"

"Orthopedic surgeon is replacing his hip and his shoulder joint. General surgeon is fixing anything else. How did the mission go?"

"Pretty standard. We followed the Others. Had a fight. We won." She paused. "I wish you'd let us know about Irving." She was angry.

He didn't blame her, but he'd had his reasons. "I didn't know if you were going to have to fight today, but there's always a chance and I didn't want you to be distracted. I didn't want to be pacing the floor for you, too."

"We're on our way down. Caleb, Samuel, and I."

"See you in a few." John hung up.

He couldn't believe he'd been talking to Irving just that morning. They hadn't really settled the issue of

John's powers. Irving seemed remarkably unconcerned by the problem, while John . . . Carefully, he targeted a chair across the waiting room. Slowly, with great control, he lifted it a few inches off the floor. Everything was working normally now. But for how long?

"Mr. Powell?" A weary-looking doctor stood beside him. "I'm Dr. Rodriguez. Mr. Shea is out of surgery and in recovery, if you'd like to follow me."

John stayed right on the doctor's heels. "What's the prognosis?"

"He's old. There was a lot of damage done—broken hip, broken shoulder, concussion. Dr. Allen replaced both joints. The good news is, Mr. Shea is still alive. Most men his age wouldn't have survived at all, much less live through five-plus hours of surgery. But add the internal injuries and the concussion . . ." The doctor looked troubled. "The next twenty-four hours are crucial. Even more crucial is whether he wants to live, and you know more about that than I do."

"He has a full and busy life with a lot of people who love him." But did Irving want to live? If this was the sacrifice he was contemplating, he would go before the sun set—very soon.

The doctor gestured toward a closed door. "Talk to him. Remind him of that full and busy life. I'll check in before I leave."

They shook hands.

John quickly sent a group text to the Chosen Ones and their support staff, repeating the doctor's comments. Then he entered the room where machines beeped and huffed.

A woman dressed in black was leaning over Irving,

speaking in a soft voice that sounded, to John, faintly familiar.

A curl of unease twisted through him. "Hello?"

She turned.

It was Dina. Dina from the street corner. Dina who smelled of cigarette smoke and who spoke so clearly in his mind. Her dark eyes met his—and she had been crying. "Hello, John."

"What are you doing here?" He strode to Irving's side, looked at the old man stretched out on the mattress.

Irving's face was gray and sunken, his eyes were closed and his nose was swollen. Tubes and tape covered him.

"You may have suspected—we have a history, Irving and I."

"Then you should leave."

She shook her head. "No. Right now I'm the only one he can hear, and trust me, he needs to hear my voice. Don't worry about leaving Irving with me. I will take care of him."

John couldn't believe Dina's nerve. "Why would I leave him with you?"

"Because your woman is in danger."

"My woman?" Dina was crazy. He rang the call bell. Got ready to forcibly evict her. "Charisma? Isabelle? Who . . . ?"

"They've got Genny at her father's house."

That stopped him cold. "Genny?"

"Isn't that her name? Brown hair, gold eyes, just arrived from Timbuktu?"

"She did not!" But the doubts of this morning returned to plague him. Was Genny alive? Was she here in New York City?

"She came to the mansion. Give your friends a call and check it out."

Striding forward, he grabbed Dina's arm and wrenched her around to face him. "How do you know this?"

Dina wasn't a bit intimidated by John's strength, by his fury. Coolly she asked, "Isn't it obvious? We've been watching her."

John released Dina's arm. "Why?"

"She's a person of interest."

"Genny is at her father's house?" John hadn't liked Kevin Valente when Genny spoke of him; he hadn't liked him when he had met him. And after Irving's revelation of this morning, that the Gypsy Travel Agency hadn't sent Genny to Russia . . . the idea of Genny at her father's house sent a chill up John's spine.

"Kevin Valente is a real prick." As if she heard a call, Dina glanced at Irving, leaned over him and smoothed his hair.

For a second, just a second, Irving's eyelids fluttered.

In a distracted voice, she said, "You'd better go. If you don't get there in a hurry, you'll lose your Genny . . . again. And this time, it will be forever."

# Chapter 48

The recovery room nurse removed Dina and re-
stricted her access. Irving received a stern lecture
about not giving up, but did not respond. Caleb, Samuel and Isabelle were in the hospital elevator on their
way up.

John ran outside and caught a cab. "A hundred
bucks if you can get me to the Bronx in under an hour."
He tossed five twenties in the front seat and barely got
the door shut before they shot away from the curb and
into rush-hour traffic.

He fastened his seat belt, braced himself, and called
Jacqueline.

She picked up on the first ring. "John, thank God
you called. Ask me the right questions and I'll tell you
everything."

So he did. And she did.

Genny had been at the mansion. She had left to return to her father's house. She had refused to allow

anyone to accompany her, citing family issues. She extracted a promise from Jacqueline and Charisma that they wouldn't tell John she had been there. Then she swore to return that night.

But now both Jacqueline and Charisma struggled with a growing unease.

"A vision?" he asked Jacqueline.

"No, just a feeling."

Charisma got on the line. "This isn't a premonition. It was the way Genny acted, like she didn't trust her own father."

"The guy stole from the Gypsy Travel Agency, got caught, took down his accomplices, and has been a bastard to his only child. Yeah, I don't trust him, either." He took a breath to ease the constriction in his chest. "Listen, I want Caleb, Samuel, and Isabelle to stay at the hospital to protect Irving. Is Aaron still in Australia?"

"The job was a success. He's on his way back. But his plane doesn't land for another hour."

*"Damn."* John looked around. The cab was already crossing the Alexander Hamilton Bridge, which at this time of the day was a testament to the driver's greed. "Where's Aleksandr?"

"In class. Do you need backup?" Charisma sounded brisk.

"Yes." He told her about Dina's warning.

"It's a trap," Charisma said flatly.

"Yes."

"And you're going to walk in willingly."

"Yes."

Charisma didn't try to talk him out of it. She was

the most practical woman he knew. "Do you have any weapons on you?" she asked.

"The metal detector at the hospital makes that damned difficult."

"Do you have a plan?"

"Yes." He didn't like the plan, but in a worst-case scenario, he had one. "I wouldn't be adverse to some insurance."

"I'll grab McKenna and a couple of handguns and I'm on my way."

"Be careful." He grabbed the door as they jumped the curb. "Traffic is wicked."

"Right."

John hung up and watched grimly as the seconds ticked by. The sky was gray; the short winter day was fading. He didn't know how many enemies he would face, what kind of gifts the Others would have. He had weapons coming, but not soon enough. He flexed his fingers. His nails glowed blue, a good sign that his powers were revving up under the influence of his grim determination.

But would the energy fail him at the crucial moment?

He jumped from the cab as it pulled up to the Valente brownstone.

What was the point of attempting to sneak up on the Others? They knew he was coming, and besides, he didn't have time for guile. Genny had left Irving's mansion over two hours ago.

He ran up the stairs, and stared at the front door.

It was slightly open.

*Shit. Not a good sign.*

Pushing open the door, he walked in. He was cautious, of course; he would just as soon not get knocked out as soon as he set foot inside. But if they had wanted to kill him, they would have done so already. And he knew what they knew: as long as they had Genny, they had him. He would go in regardless.

The house was cold.

He shut the door behind him.

The entry hall was empty, dim and narrow. A flight of stairs went straight up to the second floor. A light at the back of the house beckoned. He walked toward it and thought how very much this reminded him of the frozen cave in the Andes, another trap into which he had willingly walked. But then he had walked with friends. Now . . . Now he walked alone.

Toward the right, another stairway went down to the basement.

A woman's long trench coat was flung over the banister.

Genny's coat, and a lure to pull him in.

To the right, the light showed him a sitting room decorated sparingly in leather and hardwood furniture. The sound of voices drew him.

He stepped into the doorway.

A short, drugged-up troll of a guy squatted on the floor by the sofa, crying and wiping his tears on the hem of his T-shirt.

*My God.* Was that Brandon?

John recognized the tall, young Indian woman, the one from Lubochka's team. What was her name? She looked the same, yet she was thinner, with a cruel twist to her mouth and a bruise on her cheek. No wonder

Brandon resembled a bag of bones. He was in thrall to her and whatever drug she was supplying him.

She stood by a bare wooden kitchen chair in the middle of the room.

There Genny sat, wrists tied behind, head hanging, her clothes tattered and smoking. Burn marks pocked the carpet around her.

For the first time since he'd left Russia, John felt the savage rise in him.

*What had they been doing to her?*

"Look who's here, Genny." Gary leaned against the back wall, pointing a Glock at John in ugly triumph. "I told you he would come."

She lifted her head. She was thinner, tanned, as if she spent her life outdoors. Her body was no longer softly rounded, but street-fight ready. Her golden eyes were tough, intelligent, but when she gazed at him, her expression softened. "Did you . . . ?" She coughed, then continued hoarsely. "Did you bring the cavalry?"

The residue of tears and black soot smeared her face.

She had been screaming, he could tell.

"I am the cavalry." He walked into the room.

The tall woman created a spark in her hand.

"No, Avni, don't!" Genny strained at her bonds.

Avni tossed it at his feet.

He stomped it out.

No wonder Genny's clothes were smoking. Avni was a fire-starter. And she had been torturing Genny.

The savage spoke in his head. *I'm going to kill them. I'm going to kill them all.*

But John carefully contained his ferocity. When wielded correctly, surprise was a weapon.

Showing them his empty hands, he said, "I can't take you all out, not with Genny in the way, and I can't use my power in so many different directions. Besides"— he looked right at Gary—"I think someone's learned how to curb me. Haven't you, Gary?"

Gary's cocky grin made John want to punch him in the face. "You're right. Avni, let him go to her." He held the pistol negligently, because at this range, hitting John was no problem at all.

Avni stepped back, her eyes a glassy, dark brown.

John knelt beside the chair. He put one hand on Genny's tightly bound hands, and used the other hand to pat out the last of the fires. She had marks on her face, her thighs, her chest: burn marks, as if someone had been extinguishing a cigarette on her skin.

"There's only me. Will I do?" Staring into her battered face, he sent a small, warm pulse of power through her body.

"You'll do very well." She smiled at him, and whispered, "Thank you. I feel stronger."

"Yes." Although if he didn't pull this out of the bag, they'd both be dead. "Where's your father?" he asked.

"I don't know."

*Good. One less problem.* He had feared Valente had betrayed his daughter and fled. Better for her peace of mind that he hadn't, and easier for John that he had no one else to rescue.

John stood. "What do you want, Gary?"

"I want the same thing you want—a bag of bones."

John carefully kept his face blank, his voice neutral.

"A bag like the one we rescued from the cave in Chile?" The match to the one in Irving's study?

"Exactly. I searched and found it listed as one of the items Valente stole from the Gypsy Travel Agency."

"How interesting. Why do you want it?"

"For the same reason you want it."

"I don't want it. All I want is Genny."

"You can have her . . . after she tells us where to find the bag."

Genny turned toward Gary, so exasperated she shouted, "I don't know. I haven't seen my father in over two years. I haven't lived here in more than eight! How would I know where he put the stuff he stole when I was fifteen?"

Avni lit a flame in her hand.

Genny froze.

The guy by the couch whimpered and twisted as if the fire was burning him.

"Shut up, Brandon." Avni met John's gaze, smiled, then tossed the flame toward Genny's lap.

John unleashed enough power to bat it aside.

Avni turned and snarled at Gary. "You said you could control him."

"He can," John said. "If you let her go, I'll give myself up and you can do what you want with me."

Gary's handsome face puckered as if the thought was too foreign for him to comprehend. "What?"

Genny shook her head. "No, John, don't."

"Let her go. Promise you'll let her leave, and I'll let you tie me to the chair. With my hands bound, you won't even have to worry about containing my power."

Just as John had hoped, Gary couldn't resist the chance to hurt him. He surged forward. "Untie her," he said to Avni.

"No," she said. "It's a lie. It's a trap."

"Don't you know? John Powell isn't like *us*. He's one of the Chosen Ones," Gary sneered. "He *can't* break his word."

"You're one of the Chosen Ones, too, Gary," John said.

Gary's laughter turned to a snarl. "Not since the day you burned my team to death. Not since the day you put me into a coma." To Avni, he said, "Untie her! Then sit down, John, and take the punishment that is your due."

"No!" Avni said. "What good will that do us? We need that leather sack!"

Gary blinked at her.

Suddenly she was on the ground, flopping like a beached fish, a drop of blood oozing from her nose.

"Oh, my God!" Brandon leaped toward her, then away, jumping and flinging his arms up, then down and slapping his hands on the floor. He seemed to want to touch her, but he approached and retreated, approached and retreated. Whatever they had done to him was horrible; this was like watching the regression of man into ape.

Avni sat up slowly, wiped her nose with the back of her hand and stared at the crimson drop. She looked up at Gary. "What did you do to me?"

Gary grinned nastily. "The same thing I'm going to do to you again if you don't untie Genny."

John remembered that time in the cave when he

thought Gary had flung a thought at him; what had Gary done with his gift? How had he twisted it to become a weapon?

Avni crawled to Genny's side. With shaking hands, she untied her and pushed her out of the chair.

Genny collapsed onto her knees.

John helped her up, gave her another pulse of power, murmured in her ear, "Run."

Avni used the support of the chair to get to her feet. "Stop fondling your girlfriend and *sit down*."

John removed his coat.

The scratches on his shoulder had bloodied his shirt. They throbbed and burned, and he was glad. The Chosen Ones' prophecy said that when they found their true love and dedicated themselves to that person, their marks expanded.

John hadn't been born with a mark. He had earned it when he threw himself in front of Genny. Now the pain and blood gave him hope . . . hope that he was doing the right thing.

"Sit!" Avni said.

He did, and hoped Irving was telling the truth. He hoped a willing sacrifice, even one that wasn't a life, counted for something on the eternal scales of weights and measures.

Because Avni used the ropes to tie his hands to the posts on the back, and did a good job. They bit into his wrists, cut off the circulation in his hands.

John couldn't budge them—at least not by any normal means.

Quietly, carefully, he started to use his mind on the knots.

# Chapter 49

No one was paying attention to Genny.

Everyone was focused on John. John, willingly taking her place in the chair where they had tortured her. John, bound and helpless . . . and the center of attention.

He might be vulnerable, but he was still making them nervous.

She eased toward the hallway.

She didn't know where her father was—but she did know where he kept his weapons.

Then Avni's shiny obsidian-glass eyes swung her direction. She snapped her fingers. "Brandon! Hang on to Genny."

Genny turned on her heel and dashed.

Brandon lunged, grabbed her, gripped her wrist, ripped the scab off one of her burns.

She screamed in pain, then in protest. "You promised John I could leave!"

"Don't." Brandon tried to pet her hair. "You'll hurt yourself."

"Don't touch me!" She slapped at him.

He ducked and sniveled.

"Damn you, Brandon. Control her!" Avni raised her hands—a spark glimmered.

He twisted Genny's arms behind her back. "Please," he said. "Stop fighting. She'll hurt us. I love you."

"I thought you only loved me, Brandon," Avni mocked.

"I do. I love you, Avni." The poor fool had become nothing but a tool in Avni's hands.

Avni laughed. "You see what his love is worth, Genny."

"I love *you*," he whispered in Genny's ear.

She had to try. "Then let . . . me . . . go."

"I can't." He reeked of sweat and urine and something sickly sweet.

She wanted to gag.

Instead, she forced herself to relax. She stood calmly, got her breath, ignored his stench and the agony of the burns Avni had so carefully placed across her skin.

No matter how emaciated he was, Brandon was still stronger. Yet deep inside his belly, she could see a flame burning. Whatever Avni had given him was consuming him, destroying him. His mind was a ruin, his attention span destroyed.

She had to wait for her moment.

"John, look at your girlfriend," Gary said. "You gave yourself up for her. She can't *wait* to leave you."

John flicked a glance at Genny, looked toward the entrance. "You promised she could leave."

*Yes, I'll run when I get the chance.* Although he didn't intend that she return.

She had other plans.

"Gary promised. I didn't." Avni laughed, a harsh sound that sounded as if it tore at her lungs.

In the last two and a half years, Genny had learned a few things about survival.

Conserve your strength.

Weigh your opponent.

If you can only strike once, strike to kill.

Most important—the person who stays alive the longest, wins.

Genny intended that she and John should win.

"I can't believe you," she said, pinning Avni with her accusing gaze. "You loved the lynx, the outdoors, the wildlife studies. You helped me find my feet in a strange land. Was it all acting? I thought you were my friend."

"I was never your friend. I wanted to study in India, and instead I was in that lousy village on a mission. I was supposed to keep an eye on him." Avni lifted her chin toward John. "I was supposed to recruit him. I couldn't even get close to him. Then you showed up. So I told you all about what an animal he was, how good he was in bed. I got you interested in him."

Genny writhed in embarrassment.

John gave off such an impression of ease, his grin looked genuine and amused. "Is that right, Genny?"

"No." The single word was all too obviously a lie.

"You can tell me about it later." His smile looked casual, but his blue eyes were light and icy.

Genny could have told the Others he was furious.

But maybe they knew, for Gary snapped, "There isn't going to be a later."

"You, Genny . . . you were such an innocent ass. Always were so easy to influence." Avni's dark eyes gleamed with remembered elation. "You fell in love with him. Then *he* fell in love with *you* and it was perfect. I thought he'd follow you like a puppy to New York; I would remind him how much he hated the Gypsy Travel Agency and we'd have him. But it didn't work that way. Somehow, when he thought you had died, that convinced him to return to lead the Chosen Ones."

"John Powell was always so freaking honorable." Deliberately, Gary placed the pistol on the table. "Of course, all that honor didn't stop him from trying to steal my team while he thought I wouldn't notice. He undermined me. Made fun of me."

Avni paid no attention to Gary. "I never had a chance of winning. But I don't dare fail again." With a grimace at Genny, she lifted her T-shirt in demonstration.

Genny flinched.

Avni's skin was shriveled and melted; it looked as if she'd turned her flame on herself. And maybe she had.

"The master doesn't accept failure." Avni dropped her shirt and turned to Gary. "I suggest you remember that, and who you work for."

"I won't fail," Gary said coolly. Bending his head, he narrowed his eyes at John. His lids fluttered.

Genny heard a hum, high pitched and menacing.

As if he suffered a seizure, John's eyes rolled back

in his head. He jerked, then went rigid, his face frozen into an agonized grimace.

"John!" Genny yanked at Brandon's grip, trying to run to John.

Brandon yanked back, twisting her wrists until she released a single sob.

John went limp, his head lolling on his neck.

"John. Can you hear me? *John*." Genny turned to Gary, alight with fury. "What did you do to him?"

"I'm not like the rest of the Abandoned Ones. I have more than one trick to my repertoire. Watch." Once again, Gary lowered his head and stared at John.

Genny heard that otherworldly hum.

Gary's lids fluttered.

At once John went rigid, his back arched and arms strained against the ropes. His face was a mask of suffering.

"Let him go!" Genny shouted.

Gary held the pose. The hum continued. Suddenly, as if he had exhausted his power, he relaxed.

Again John went limp, sagging against the restraints. Was he unconscious?

Genny scrutinized him, looking for any sign of life— a pulse at his neck, a twitch of his fingers.

*Nothing.*

Gary sighed. And smiled. "I can twist my mind reading into mind assault. It's not so different, really."

"You've killed him," Genny whispered.

"No, I haven't." Gary was slimy with charm. "Not yet. What would the fun of that be? He has a lot more suffering in him before he dies. Perhaps you want to tell me where that leather bag is, and spare him more pain?"

"You broke your vow to defend the Chosen Ones and the children they protect. You tie people to a chair to torture them. You're a coward." She viewed him through a flush of rage. "Why would I believe a word you say?"

Gary walked over to her and slapped her, open-handed, with the force of his arm behind him.

She sagged in Brandon's arms, saw stars that whirled and blinked.

"Wrong answer," Gary said.

Brandon helped her get her feet under her. He held her with both hands on her shoulders.

Slowly, John lifted his head. His eyes were bloodshot, his complexion pale, but something had shifted under his skin. Something about the way he viewed the Others reminded Genny of the day he'd discovered his photo in her backpack.

They didn't realize it, but they had unloosed the wild man.

Gary had just made a big mistake.

"When I was in Russia, I was always worried about the Gypsy Travel Agency sending agents after me." John's gaze shifted from Gary to Avni and back. "It looks like I was worried about the wrong group."

Gary was oblivious to the return of John's savage self. "Did you ever tell your girlfriend why you were in exile?" He didn't wait for an answer, but turned to Genny. "He had to run away after he screwed up my mission. Sun Hee was his wife . . . Did he tell you he had been married?"

"I knew that, yes."

"Sun Hee was bored with John's pedestrian love-making." Gary aimed all his charisma at Genny.

"Now, Gary"—Genny laughed softly, intent on keeping Gary's attention fixed on her—"you forget. I've slept with John. I know better."

Gary's smile and charm faded. "He won't be worth much to you when I've finished with him." For a moment, his attention shifted to John.

She thought he was going to blast John again. "Why was he in exile?" she asked.

For a moment, he wavered, but the temptation to smear John's character proved too tempting. "Your wonderful hero burned his friends to death to get even with me and his wife—"

Genny cut him off. "For cheating."

"He put me in a coma." Gary put his hands to his head. "I could hear the dripping, the IV dripping, so slowly. I could hear the nurses talking. I could hear the TV. I knew the smells of that ghastly place. But I couldn't move. I couldn't speak. And always that dripping, one drop at a time, so . . . slowly. I would wait for it, like Chinese water torture . . ." He stood like a statue.

John was still breathing as if trying to vanquish the pain.

Avni waited, smiling slightly as she watched Gary.

Brandon's hands no longer gripped Genny so tightly.

But Genny wanted to know . . . "What happened then?"

Gary shuddered, once, and stilled. But he didn't

take his hands away from his head. "I heard a voice in my mind."

A chill slid up Genny's spine. "Who was it?"

"You know who it was," Gary said dreamily.

*Yes.* She knew.

"He knew my thoughts," Gary said. "He talked about my friends, about how they never came to see me anymore. He talked to me about John and how he had betrayed me. He told me all I had to do was give him the security code to the Gypsy Travel Agency and I could walk again. Walk the streets, be a man again and not a helpless wreck."

"So you said yes," Genny said.

"No! I was strong. I said no. But he promised me I would be healthy and dynamic. That I would serve him in this world and the next." Gary's hands curled in his hair. "I swore I wouldn't. But no one from the Gypsy Travel Agency ever came to visit me. They left me alone in the dark listening to that damned *drip*. And then . . ."

He paused so long, Genny prompted him. "And then?"

"Then I heard the nurses. I didn't have much longer. I had barely lived, and I was dying. I was the brightest, the bravest, the best. And I was dying. So I called to him . . . and I gave him the code . . . and after the Gypsy Travel Agency exploded, blew into bits so small they were never recovered . . . I was healed."

Genny glanced at John.

His color had returned to normal, and he viewed Gary the way the lynx viewed prey.

Avni could see it, too. Genny could tell. But Avni made no move to warn Gary.

"You betrayed the Chosen Ones," Genny said.

Gary dropped his hands and stared at John. "They betrayed me first. Irving . . . Irving never liked me, and I made him pay." He laughed. "It was great. He looked like a rag doll falling down those stairs, and I could hear those old bones crunch on each step."

The sheer, brutal pleasure and malice made Genny want to vomit.

"John betrayed me." Gary was breathing hard, still concentrating on John. "I'm going to make him suffer and die!"

*Not now, you're not. Not while I can still wave a red flag at you.* "No one betrayed you. You were the commander of the mission. The failure was yours." Genny was relentless, pounding at Gary. "In your heart, you know it. That's why you're so ashamed. You broke your word. You joined with evil. What happened at the volcano was your fault!"

"It was not!" Gary swiveled toward her.

Brandon scampered away.

John straightened in his chair.

Gary dropped his head and stared at Genny, his eyelids fluttering.

She heard that hum streaking toward her.

Heat, pain, and energy flew like a knife through her brain. Every muscle in her body went into a spasm; her back arched as she fought to hold her own against the hell of pain and torment.

Brandon caught her, held her upright, shouting unintelligibly.

John stood. With his wrists still tied to the wooden chair, he strained to lift his arms.

Gold and red flashed like an inferno of power.

Wood splintered.

With first one of the shattered uprights, then the other, he slammed Gary in the back of the head.

Released from her hell, Genny shoved Brandon aside. "Run!" she told him.

But Brandon covered his head with his hands and crouched on the floor.

John's power rolled through the room in waves.

Gary pitched forward, almost fell, then bounced back as if on a spring—and he was off his feet, rising from the floor.

He screamed, "Let me down. Let me down!"

John held his arms up, then twirled them, the wooden staves clacking together.

Still in the air, still screaming, riding on a wave of power, Gary tumbled through the entrance and out into the narrow entry. He slammed into the wall above the narrow basement stairs.

John followed, his brow furrowed with concentration. He held Gary out over the steps.

"No. No!" Gary understood now what John intended. "John, no!"

"Will you look like a rag doll falling down those stairs?" John asked, so cool, so calm in his anger. "Will your bones crunch on each step?"

"John, remember our years together," Gary shouted. "We were friends."

Genny snorted. Now he dredged that up.

Someone tugged at Genny's arm. She used her elbow in a combative dig. "Leave me alone, Brandon."

The point of a knife dug into her throat. She stiffened, held her breath.

Avni whispered in her ear, "I'm *not* Brandon, and I *will* kill you if you don't tell me where your father keeps his treasures."

# Chapter 50

Cold rage swept Genny.

*Oh, no, you don't.*

She stomped Avni's bony foot, grabbed her skinny wrist and dragged it over her shoulder, twisting until Avni's grip loosened and the slim, curved knife fell to the ground.

Avni screeched, wrapped her freakishly long arm around Genny's throat, and squeezed.

Genny gagged, choked. She lifted both feet off the floor, using the weight of her body to throw Avni off-balance.

Avni staggered forward.

The two women slammed into the wall.

Avni's elbow hit so hard, she dented the wallpaper.

But Genny's forehead hit just as hard. She blacked out, then struggled back to consciousness.

John shouted something—he'd seen them.

Distantly, she heard Gary scream, heard a body tumbling down the stairs.

Twirling Genny around, Avni held her like a shield. "I'll kill her. I swear, John, I'll kill her!" she shouted, and tightened her elbow. Then, "Brandon, give me the knife."

Genny clawed at Avni's arm . . . seeing the scene—John's focused attention, Brandon's blubbering dismay—through the haze of her pain and distress.

"Brandon, give me the knife!" Avni commanded.

He leaned down, picked up the blade.

He lunged toward them.

Genny was going to die.

And suddenly, she was free.

She fell to her knees, gasping, holding her throat.

John seized her by the waist, swung her aside as Avni crashed to the floor, eyes shocked, blood rhythmically spurting from the side of her neck. She struggled for a moment, then went limp.

Brandon stood, splattered with red, knife in hand, gaping at Avni's body as if he couldn't comprehend how Avni had died, that he had stabbed her. "She told me to give it to her. She said to give her the knife. She was hurting Genny, so I did. I didn't have a choice. I had to do it." He was babbling, using his bloody hands for emphasis. "Because I love Genny."

Genny tried to speak. She could only wheeze.

Moving with watchful care, John set her on the floor.

She sank to her knees, clutching her aching head.

John stripped away the ropes around his wrists and

dropped the shattered pieces of chair. Calm, strong, gentle, he took a step forward. "Brandon, drop the knife."

Brandon looked at John as if he'd never seen him before. "But I love Avni."

"I know you do. Drop the knife, Brandon."

"Avni gives me what I need." He extended the knife. "Without Avni, I can't live." And he stabbed himself in the abdomen. He carved himself open, the upward thrust aimed at his heart.

Genny groaned and covered her eyes.

But he gasped her name. "Genny!"

She looked up.

He grinned, and for the first time looked like the old, obnoxious Brandon. "Take care of . . . the yeti."

Then the flame inside him went out.

He dropped like a stone.

Turning back to Genny, John knelt beside her. "I tried, but I never quite got the hang of subtle power movements," he told her. Gently, he pulled her into his arms.

She leaned against him. She touched the three bloody marks on his shirt, caught her breath, collected her thoughts, trembled with reaction. Then she sank into him, became one with him. Because like it or not, this was where she was meant to be.

Under her ear, she heard him take a deep breath. He embraced her as if he would never let her go, then stood with her in his arms and carried her out of that horrible room and into the entry.

"Forgive me," he said. "I was afraid to trust you, and it cost me everything. I've been in hell every day for more than two and a half years. Even though I thought—no, *knew*—you were dead, I never stopped searching for you."

"And no matter how far I traveled, I couldn't forget you." She pushed gently against him until he let her slide to her feet. "Believe me. I tried."

He looked achingly amused. "Good to know." His expression changed; he pulled his vibrating phone from the inner pocket of his jacket, glanced at the text. "It's from Isabelle. Irving is still alive." He glanced out the front window at the night. "And the sun has set. That's good. That's very good. Excuse me while I answer?"

"Of course." She scrutinized him while he texted. A drop of blood had dried beside his eye . . . Had Gary's attack done that? A long, deep scratch marred his arm; a piece of splintered chair had slashed him.

The shoulder of his shirt was stained with blood. He was thinner than she remembered, and where before his face had been rugged, it was now sculpted, the skin stretched thin across his high cheekbones.

But he looked good with his dark hair grown out to businessman's length. And his light blue eyes, when he finished and looked up at her, became a deep, glorious cornflower blue.

They couldn't talk now; she knew that. They had a mission. But she saw his determination—and the savage lurking inside. They *would* talk.

Genny gestured toward the living room and down the stairs. "My God, John. How did this happen?"

"The bad guys wanted something very important. You refused to give it to them."

"I don't know where it is."

"I'll bet you have an idea."

"Well . . . yes."

His expression made the subtle shift back to responsibility. "Where do we look?"

"The first place is the junk drawer in the kitchen." She led the way toward the back of the house. "Anything in my father's possession that the Gypsy Travel Agency deemed of real importance, they removed as soon as his arrest had been made. Other pieces were left in place to be photographed as evidence of his wrongdoing."

The kitchen hadn't changed except to grow a little shabbier. Knives had scratched the wood-grain Formica countertop. Linoleum squares, put down by her grandfather, had curled at the edges. A wooden desk and chair filled the small breakfast nook, and on the stovetop, warped aluminum drip pans held bubbles of burned-on grease.

"What was left to him was considered junk. He had it all appraised, of course, sold anything worth anything . . ." She yanked open the junk drawer beside the copper-colored refrigerator and rummaged through dried-out pens, old batteries, pads of paper pilfered from Lizzie's Plumbing. "Unless he threw it away, the purse is in the kitchen somewhere. I remember seeing it around."

"Irving said"—John swallowed—"artifacts of power are never gone forever."

"Probably true," she said gently.

John was worried about Irving. She was sorry for his grief, but at the same time, so glad to see the proof of his caring.

"For sure, Father never throws anything away if there's a chance he might ever make a profit from it. That purse is around here somewhere." She lifted her hair off her forehead and in her mind, she walked the house, looking for that small leather sack with the yellow tie.

But her burns felt like hot coals on her skin, and John watched her closely, as if he was about to take her to a doctor regardless of the importance of their find.

"I'm fine," she told him.

"You don't look fine."

"Regardless, we need to find that—"

A door slammed behind them.

They turned together, hands up, ready for a fight.

# *Chapter 51*

———◆———

**K**evin Valente stumbled out of the broom closet. "Are they gone?"

Genny dropped her hands, astonished and appalled. "Father! Were you in there all the time?"

"Yes. I hid as soon as they came in." He twisted at the waist, back and forth, loosening his back. "Do you know how cramped it is in that closet?"

Genny stared at him, at the father she hadn't seen for so long, at the father who thought she was dead . . . and his reaction was to twitch the seam of his starched khakis back into place and complain about the space where he hid while she was tortured and almost murdered. All the hurt started to rise in her . . . and then it subsided.

Because really, what was the point?

He was what he was, and she could never change that.

More important, she now knew a few things about

herself. That she could survive and thrive alone in this world.

And that she didn't have to, because she had John.

She took John's hand. "Father, John and I are getting married."

John released a sigh.

She didn't know if it was relief or unhappiness. She lifted her brows at him. "Aren't we?"

"The sooner the better." John sounded quite sure.

"Did you want to ask me before I announced it?"

"I intend to beg you . . . later."

"Beg me to marry you?"

"That, too." He was *not* smiling.

His expression made her remember the waves of power and how he could change them to create desire . . . as if she could ever forget.

Her face grew warm.

"We'll talk," he said.

"Hm." He seemed to be planning more than talk.

*It had been so long . . .*

Turning her attention back to her father, she asked, "Will you want to come to the wedding?"

"Of course! How would it look if I didn't?" Her father focused on John. "I remember you. You're the one who came and confirmed her death."

"A rash assumption on my part." John kissed her hand. "Now, instead, I'd like to ask for her hand in marriage."

*Oh, John!* She squeezed his fingers and glared at him.

He looked surprised.

"I don't know that I should give my permission."

Her father hitched up his belt. "John, will you be able to support my daughter in a decent fashion?"

"Dad! What do you think?" Genny could hardly contain her exasperation. "He's one of the Chosen. I mean, what do they pay them, minimum wage? And now that the Gypsy Travel Agency has exploded, the Chosen are probably fighting evil out of the goodness of their hearts. Give it a break." She got to the heart of her father's concern. "We can't support you."

"Ah." Father stroked his chin as if he were still considering John's request.

So she charged on. "Since I really doubt CFG is holding my position, *and* the job market sucks, *and* I have no experience, *and* you can't support me, either, I'd suggest you give your permission."

"All right, fine," he said irritably. "Permission granted."

"Thank you, sir." John had a twinkle in his eye she didn't understand.

They really needed the time to have that talk.

"In the meantime," Father said irritably, "what am I supposed to do with the mess you left in my house?"

"We have contacts in the police department," John said briefly. "The matter will be handled."

Father inclined his head as if he expected nothing else.

His handsome face was still unlined, his dark hair handsomely streaked with silver, and she wondered if he had a painting stored somewhere in the attic, one that, like Dorian Gray's, revealed the corruption of his soul.

"We came here to get that leather sack of bones that has been rattling around here for years."

His eyes narrowed.

She could see him contemplating a deal. So she said, "Father, give me the artifact . . . or else."

"Or else what?" He mocked her; he had no idea who she had become.

"Or else I'll let the Others know you were here and heard everything that occurred."

That got his attention. "I didn't hear anything!"

"I know how to lie, Father. I was taught by an expert." Right now, she was as cold and indifferent as he had ever been. "You lied to me when I signed that contract that paid for my college."

"I did not." He looked absolutely assured . . . but a drop of sweat trickled down the side of his face. "You assumed it was the Gypsy Travel Agency who was loaning you the money."

She looked at him. Just looked.

"Oh, all *right*." He walked to the desk in the breakfast nook, pulled out a drawer and rummaged around. "What's the big deal, anyway? That purse was banging around the Gypsy Travel Agency for a hundred years before I . . . before it was fobbed off on me." He pulled out a leather sack tied in yellow ribbon.

With a sigh of relief, Genny took it from him.

John disappeared, then reappeared with Genny's coat.

Father added, "I had that purse appraised and it, and its contents, is worth nothing."

She weighed it in her hand. "Are all the bones inside?"

"The same bones that were always there," Father said.

"All right. Thank you." She awkwardly kissed him on the cheek. "See you around."

"She's in bad shape, but don't bother to worry about her." John helped her into her coat, and his voice weighed heavy with sarcasm. "I'll take her to the hospital for her burns." Once more, he pulled out his phone and glanced at it. "You don't need to call us a cab. One is pulling up to the door right now."

# Chapter 52

<hr>

Gary woke.

Where was he?

The last thing he remembered was the surprise of seeing John get loose from his bonds. Gary remembered flying through the air, hitting the wall, rolling down the stairs. The fear, the agony of bones breaking, then . . . nothing.

Where was he?

He could hear voices nearby. But who? *The Chosen Ones? The Others?*

*Osgood?*

A chill formed on his skin.

*Not Osgood.* After this failure, anything was better than Osgood.

Gary remained perfectly still, eyes closed, straining to listen, but he couldn't make sense of the words.

"Back again . . ."

"Should have been a little nicer to us the first time . . ."

"I told you a miracle like that would never last . . ."

"It's a tragedy he had to end this way. If only he would have cooperated, what a contribution to medical science he could have made!"

Women's voices, all of them. Three were eerily familiar. The fourth was cool, clinical.

But women . . . Gary was relieved. He could charm them or, if they were venal, he could overcome them. It was time to make his move.

He tried to open his eyes.

He couldn't.

He tried to move his hands.

He couldn't.

He tried to speak.

They must be restraining him! He must be drugged!

Because no matter how he struggled and fought, the women just kept chatting over the top of him as if he had all the life of a wooden plank.

"Where's he been?"

"I don't know. It's not like he sent us a Christmas card."

He heard wheels on a floor. Something metal rattled near his ear.

"From the shape he's in, he's lucky he lived through this."

"Lucky?" A snort.

"All right. He's lucky he can't feel anything. Is that better?"

*I can feel things!*

Something cold touched his arm on the skin inside his elbow.

He recognized the smell. A sharp, stinging scent . . .

Something bit him there.

That cool, clinical voice again. "Please remember, it's been well documented that some coma patients can hear and understand conversations although they can't respond."

*Coma?*

"Yes, Doctor."

*Doctor?*

"Do you have any special orders about the IV, Doctor?"

*IV?*

A digging pain in his arm.

Then Gary heard it.

*Drip.*

An eternal, slow, agonizing pause.

*Drip.*

Another pause.

*Drip.*

Gary screamed . . . but he never made a sound.

# Chapter 53

As soon as Genny sat down in the cab between Charisma and John, all her aches and pains made themselves known: a blinding headache, agonizing burns, throat hoarse from screaming. Put that together with the holes burned in her clothes, and she was a mess.

"I'm sorry I didn't get there in time to help." Charisma took Genny's hand. "I sometimes think the Chosen Ones would most benefit from a gifted member who could part the traffic."

John nodded his head. "Um-hm." He was texting, not paying attention to the two women.

"At least now we're going against traffic." Taking off one of her bracelets, Charisma slid it over Genny's arm.

The pain in Genny's head began to ease.

John put away the phone. "Everyone's meeting us at the hospital. Jacqueline is bringing the other two leather bags."

"I hope that's all of them," Charisma said.

He glared at her.

"What?" Charisma spread her hands. "It's a legitimate concern!"

"That's all of them," Genny said.

"How do you know that?" Charisma wasn't challenging her; she seemed genuinely curious.

"It's developing a warmth and a glow. I think it knows that it's going to join the others." The silence in the cab grew profound as John and Charisma contemplated the leather sack Genny held in her hand.

Charisma bent forward and looked at John. "I thought you said she wasn't gifted?"

"The *rasputye* must have affected her more than I had realized." John took the sack and put it in Genny's coat pocket.

"What does Isabelle say about Irving?" Charisma turned to Genny and explained, "Isabelle's our empath. She can touch a person, take on their illness or hurt—if it's not too bad, anyway—and help them heal."

"I see." Idly, Genny wondered how Isabelle's gift would manifest in her own newfound sight. How would a healer look to her?

Tenderly, John wrapped his arm around Genny's shoulders and shifted her close to him.

At once, she felt a low-level buzz of warmth. "I think you and John are healing me, too."

"No, we can't do that. But the right stones can ease your pain and I think John can share energy." In the flash of the streetlights, Genny saw Charisma grin. "Think of us as really effective aspirin."

"I'll do that. Now—what about Irving?"

"Irving won't let Isabelle cure him," John said.

"He's unconscious!" Charisma paused. "Isn't he?"

"He is, but you know Irving has the strongest will of any man I know. He's blocking her." They passed over the bridge into Manhattan, and John said, "Not much longer now, Genny. Hold on."

"I'm fine." She was actually feeling a little floaty, as if she'd been given drugs; and she must have gone to sleep, because the next thing she knew, the lights at the hospital shone in her eyes.

John helped her out of the cab. Then John and Charisma put their arms under Genny's and navigated their way upstairs.

As soon as the elevator opened on the waiting room, a tall man in a dark business suit joined them, walked with them, and shot words like weapons. "Everyone's here. You're the last to arrive. The medical staff let us all go in Irving's room. Isabelle says he's dying. That creepy woman Dina is beside the bed and she won't let anyone take her place. Isabelle says Dina's the only thing that's kept him here so long. Isabelle thinks he's waiting until everyone arrives to pass on." He scowled at Genny. "*What's* wrong with her?"

"What does it look like, Samuel?" Charisma snapped. "She's been tortured."

"Oh, for the love of . . . can't we just have a quiet deathbed scene without even *more* drama?" Samuel strode on ahead.

"Mr. Sensitivity?" Genny asked.

John laughed gruffly. "Exactly."

"He's a lawyer," Charisma said, as if that explained everything.

They made their way past the nurses' station to the door, still swinging from Samuel's arrival.

"Is this all of you?" A woman in scrubs stood; she looked both annoyed and worried. "Listen, I am sorry for the loss you're facing, but there are a lot of really sick people on this floor. No matter what happens, keep it quiet."

Charisma stopped and rubbed her shoulder, read her name tag and said, "We will, Makayla. We promise. Thank you for letting us be with him now."

Under Charisma's ministrations, Makayla visibly relaxed. "So many old people die alone because there's no one left. . . . Well, go on." She waved them on with the chart in her hand. "Remember—quiet!"

John guided Genny into the hospital room stuffed with people—thirteen of them, now that John, Charisma, and Genny had arrived.

Jacqueline and her husband, Caleb, stood shoulder to shoulder.

Aaron and Rosamund held hands.

Aleksandr was sprawled in a chair, a hand loosely held over his face.

Isabelle stood on one side of the bed, Dina on the other.

Samuel leaned against the wall, as close to Isabelle as he could get.

Their support team, McKenna and Martha, sat in chairs at the foot of the bed.

The newcomers got nods and whispered greetings, but the focus, of course, was the bed.

Since John had left, Irving had lost ground. His eyes were sunken into his head, his skin looked paper thin, and his hands, resting on the sheets, clearly showed the bones, the veins, and the arthritis that plagued him.

Tears welled in Charisma's eyes, and she made her way to join Isabelle at the side of the bed.

Martha rose and came to John's side. In a low voice, she said, "John, *she* must be made to leave."

"Who?" he asked.

She gestured toward Dina. "Her, of course."

"Apparently, Irving wants her here."

Genny tugged at his arm.

"Are you insane? That's *Dina*. She is one of the Others, and she has spent her life seeking vengeance on Irving for what he did to her!" Martha said.

That got John's attention. "What did he do to her?"

Martha glared at him, folded her lips tightly over the secret. Then in a furious whisper, she burst out, "Dina's probably in his brain right now tormenting him as he dies!"

Genny tugged his arm again. "John? Listen . . ."

John patted her hand. "One minute." He had only a few minutes ago suffered an attack on his own brain, and he would not have Irving suffering the same fate. To Martha, he said, "Isabelle said Dina was the reason he was hanging on."

"Because he loves her?" Martha's disdain scorched the air.

"I don't know. Does he?" John asked.

"John?" Genny's grip on his arm slipped. "I'm sorry, but I've lost my oomph." She collapsed.

John whipped around and caught her as she fell.

Aleksandr vacated his chair.

John slid her into the seat.

Genny's eyes were closed, her complexion the color of parchment, and her head hung as if it was too heavy to lift.

Isabelle came at once to her side.

Samuel followed.

"Can you help her?" John asked.

Isabelle clasped Genny's hand, stroked her arm, knelt beside her and cupped her face. And staggered. "John, she has a concussion!"

"Avni slammed her forehead into the wall." If Avni wasn't already dead, he would kill her again.

"Somebody struck the back of her head, too." Isabelle closed her eyes. "Let me work on that first. Next I'll take care of the worst of the burns." Then, although nothing had been said, she ferociously turned on Samuel. "I'll be fine. It's what I do. Stop growling!"

If John had had a smile in him, he would have smiled at those two. Instead, he watched as Isabelle spoke softly to Genny, got her permission to heal her, then with a sure touch worked her magic.

When she was done, Genny straightened, her eyes clear and thoughtful as she met Isabelle's gaze. "Thank you. I am well."

"Get some rest tonight." Isabelle started to rise.

Samuel grabbed her arm and hauled her to her feet.

"I can stand up by myself," Isabelle snapped.

"You're tired after the mission today," he answered.

She took a patient breath. "We are all tired."

Taking her arm, he turned it until the pale evidence of a burn was clearly visible. "And you have just exhausted yourself to heal Genny."

"I didn't heal her. She healed herself. I simply

helped." She yanked herself free of his grip and strode back to the head of the bed.

"Whew, didn't see that coming," Genny whispered.

But John heard her. "We're all hoping they settle what's between them before they explode."

"And rip off each other's clothes." Genny stroked her arm where a pale scar matched the one on Isabelle's arm.

For the first time since he'd seen Genny tied to the chair, her color was good, her gaze steady—she looked strong and healthy.

She looked like the Genny who had loved him, fought him, left him behind. Like the woman he had mourned and missed for over two years.

Lust kicked him in the gut.

To hell with Samuel and Isabelle. If there were any clothes to be ripped, he wanted them to be Genny's.

# Chapter 54

Genny looked up at him, her eyes big, soft, and golden brown. "John? I know that right now this seems inappropriate."

*She wants me.*

"Especially with Irving in extremis—"

Appalled, John glanced at the bed where Irving still clung to life.

What had he been thinking? To lust after a woman while they were in such circumstances?

He'd been thinking he hadn't had sex in two and a half years, and now the woman he loved was within reach and healthy. He was thinking he was horny.

Irving would understand.

Irving would approve.

Genny caught his hand and tugged at it. "John, are you listening to me?"

"Yes." Which wasn't strictly true. He couldn't tear

his attention away from her, but he wasn't really *listening*.

She said, "We need to get out the bones and put them together. *Now*. The purse is getting heavy in my pocket."

He glanced up.

Jacqueline was beckoning them.

*Just figures.*

Dina called hoarsely, "Irving wants you all over here."

So somehow, she was listening to Irving's thoughts.

Genny stood, walked to the bed, and John trailed her, wishing their reunion could be some other place, some other time. *Irving, my friend . . . did you know this conclusion would come to us so soon after your sacrifice?*

No, of course he didn't. He had offered himself in an act of blind faith. He had had no guarantee it would work.

The Chosen Ones pulled into a tight circle around the bed.

Dina indicated the bones should be placed on the rolling bedside table.

John supposed some people would find this scene odd or even disrespectful: thirteen individuals of different ages, genders, and races around a dying man's hospital bed, opening ancient leather sacks tied with strings of yellow, red, and blue and pouring petrified bones into three small piles. But most people didn't know Irving. No one here doubted this was what he wanted; no one here would disregard his wishes.

"This is right." Jacqueline counted. "Twenty-seven bones. Exactly right. The prophecy is right here. Now all I need is . . ." She placed her hand over one pile, then the other, then stepped back, shaking her head in frustration.

"The bones need to be assembled," Genny said, "into the shape of the hand."

Every eye turned her way—some with interest, some with incredulity.

John put his hand on her shoulder. "She has a feel for these artifacts."

"She feels it in her bones?" Charisma grinned.

A ripple of edgy amusement swept the room.

Charisma covered her mouth with her hand and looked apologetically at Dina. "I'm sorry. I shouldn't have—"

Dina gestured wearily, and in that heavy voice they all recognized from the words she had put in their heads, said, "He would laugh, too. That was why I loved him. Because he made me laugh. And why I hated him. Because he made a fool of me."

"You deserved it," Martha said fiercely.

"Shut up, Martha," Dina answered just as fiercely.

The Chosen Ones looked from one to the other, uncertain how to respond to the sharp, unexpected hostility.

Genny stepped into the breach. "I haven't met everyone here. I know Martha, but you're . . . Dina?"

Dina dipped her head, a single nod.

"I'm Genny." She reached out.

Dina reluctantly gave her her hand.

Genny shook it. "I had heard your name, but I hadn't realized you were sisters."

All sound ceased. All motion stopped.

Genny didn't know what she'd said. She glanced at John.

He stood frozen, only his pale blue eyes in motion, touching first Martha, then Dina, then Martha again.

"I'm sorry." Somehow, Genny had put her foot in it. "You're not sisters?"

Charisma stirred, rattled her stone bracelets, said, "Of course they are. We simply hadn't realized it before."

Martha said, "We're sisters by blood only."

Dina lifted her chin. "We had the same parents, but that was an accident of fate."

As if she was quoting some great tome, Rosamund asked, "In the end, what matters except blood and kin?"

Genny thought Rosamund was right.

Hadn't Genny allowed her father to go about his merry way without bothering to set him straight about what a monster of a father he had turned out to be? Possibly she'd kept her mouth shut because he wouldn't understand. But possibly she'd said nothing because . . . he was her father. And if she'd been adamant enough, if she'd held the mirror to his face and insisted he see the truth . . . what good would it have done? He would still be a thief—immoral and weak. Not a better man, but one who saw himself for what he was and despised himself.

She might get satisfaction from such a revelation, but what would be accomplished?

Nothing. Everyone was allowed their self-delusions. She would allow her father his.

Family. Friends. In the end, that was all that mattered.

Charisma heard every word as if Genny spoke inside her mind. She said softly, so softly, "It's time."

John heard her, of course. "Time for what?"

Charisma was staring at the stones in her bracelets. Gradually, she lifted her head and looked at John. "It's time. Take my hand."

Genny wanted to back away. What did Charisma mean? Why did she look so determined, so intense?

John seemed to understand. He clasped her proffered hand, then Genny's. Aleksandr took Genny's other hand. All around the room, hands were clasped, held tightly.

This was some kind of ritual, Genny realized. Something involving the Chosen Ones and their mates . . .

Until Martha stopped them. "*She* is one of the Others." She pointed at Dina. "She cannot be part of this."

"I don't belong here." Dina lifted her chin.

The energy in the room paused, faded—

One of the machines beeped an alarm.

Still sunken, still broken, still unconscious, Irving reached out and grabbed Dina's hand.

Caleb laughed, briefly, harshly. "He's not dead yet."

Dina's eyes filled with tender tears.

Martha turned her gaze away as if the sight of Irving holding Dina burned her.

But Charisma grabbed McKenna's hand, and McKenna took Martha's hand, and it continued until the connection was complete.

Reaction was immediate. Heat, light, electricity flashed around the circle, uniting Genny with everyone in the room. She felt Irving's pain, Dina's uncertainty, Martha's resentment. For that one instant, she could hear the stones like Charisma, see the future like Jacqueline, search the library with knowledge and instinct like Rosamund. All the talents, the passions, the laughter and tears were hers.

Then . . . she was once again Genny, but no longer alone. A part of them was in her. A part of her was in them.

"What was *that*?" Dina snatched her hands away and held them in fists against her stomach.

"That's how we know that we're supposed to be together," Isabelle told her.

"Not me. That's wrong." Dina looked around wildly, then muttered, "I need a cigarette," and pushed her way toward the door.

"No!" The voice came from the bed.

Dina froze.

Isabelle and Martha gasped.

John stared.

Irving's eyes were open, alert, commanding. "No," he said again. "Come back." His eyes closed.

The door slapped against the wall. Makayla stood there like an avenging goddess.

Aleksandr pushed the rolling table covered with hand bones behind him.

"What is going on in here?" Makayla pushed her way to Irving's side. "What did you do to him?"

"What's wrong?" Isabelle managed to look both innocent and in command.

Makayla checked the monitors, counted Irving's pulse, listened to his lungs. "It's like he had a defibrillator to his chest. He's stabilized. Doing better. All of a sudden." She whipped around, glared at them menacingly.

Charisma pumped her arm.

Genny smiled. "What good news!"

"That's miraculous." Samuel leaned toward Makayla.

She glared at him as if she knew his gift was mind control. "Don't you try anything on me." Pointing her finger around at the group, she said, "I'll be keeping an eye on all of you." With a final glare, she left, muttering, "I'll get the doctor in here as soon as I can."

Dina stood by the door, twisted her hands together.

Martha gestured toward the bed. "Are you going to come back? Or are you going to run away again?"

Dina's whole demeanor caught fire. "I didn't run away last time. After I gave him what he wanted, he tossed me out like garbage." She pointed to her mutilated nose. "Don't tell me *I* betrayed *him*."

"Then leave," Martha said. "Just leave."

"Irving came out of his coma to call you back." Isabelle sounded cool and sensible. "Of course, he's not *healed*. I hate to think that he would die without you."

Dina looked around helplessly. Pulled her cigarettes out of her pocket, looked at them, then put them back and trudged to Irving's side.

Displaying a tact that seemed almost miraculous for such a young man, Aleksandr said, "Let me put the bones together."

He had the knack for puzzles. He studied the three

stacks of bones. Then, one by one, he placed them on the table, starting with the wrist and slowly re-creating the thumb and fingers all the way to the end joints.

The Chosen Ones crowded around to watch.

On the bed, Irving breathed in, then out, each rise of his chest a labor.

At last Aleksandr stepped back.

The group drew a single indrawn breath.

Dark marks were etched on four of the bones—the bones that formed the palm. When placed together, they formed a clearly recognizable outline . . .

Jacqueline held her hand out, palm up.

Genny stared first at the black lines that marked Jacqueline as a seer, then at the bones on the table. "The eye."

"It's the same," Isabelle said.

"Like the bad twin when the world was young." Aleksandr stepped back. "That is creepy."

"Do you think this is the bad twin's hand?" Rosamund bent down to study the bones from the side, then stood on her tiptoes, adjusted her glasses, and examined them again.

"Duh." Charisma rolled her eyes.

Earnestly, Rosamund said, "For a hand to have survived since some undefined past 'when the world was young'—and for it to be the hand of the evil twin—and then to have it be divided into three packages that miraculously reunite here and now . . . that would be unlikely." Her mouth twitched in a half smile. "It would also be helpful."

Another silence fell as they contemplated the hand.

"Man, I hope they waited until she was dead before they removed it," Samuel said.

"The bones show no signs of chopping or sawing. So, yes. I believe someone probably removed the bones from her skeleton." Caleb sounded like he knew his way around human mutilations. "Jacqueline, can you see anything with this?"

Genny looked around the room. An elderly man lay dying on the bed, apparently still commanding the twelve people who watched spellbound as Jacqueline placed her hand over the bones in the exact imitation of the shape and position. Nothing happened; no fireworks or frothing at the mouth. Instead, Jacqueline said, "She died a natural death, very quiet and serene, secure in the knowledge that she would live again."

Caleb took her shoulders in his hands. "Jacqueline, are you there?"

She laughed. "Yes. I can see all the way back to when the world was young, and all the way forward into the mists."

John said, "Tell us what you see."

# *Chapter 55*

John unlocked the door to his ninety-second-story penthouse, held it open and flipped on the lights.

Genny walked into the stark foyer, then into the massive living room. "This . . . is yours?"

He watched her wander across the dark bamboo floor, touch the tall cut-glass Tiffany vase full of fresh flowers, trail a finger across the back of the soft brown leather couch, and finally look through the floor-to-ceiling windows at the view of Central Park. "I bought it about five years ago. Before the . . . tragedy in Indonesia."

"I see." She sounded dangerously neutral.

"After what you told your father, I hope you don't mind, but actually, I'm—"

"Rich."

"Right."

She discarded her coat onto the arm of his recliner. "I'd like to shower."

*That wasn't any kind of answer.* But he didn't care. She had successfully derailed his carefully planned explanation. Because she was going to shower. In his bathroom. In his home.

*Naked.*

He had had dreams like this, but never had he thought they could come true.

She started toward the open door where his bed was clearly visible.

"Of course." He hurried and caught up, showed her his bathroom—the maid had been in that day, so thankfully his underwear was in the hamper and not on the floor—then shut the door and left her alone.

And let out a gasp of relief. Okay. Everything was going to be all right. She intended to stay here and he hadn't even had to grovel.

Yet.

He discarded his trench coat and suit coat. His tie was in a pocket somewhere. His shirt was a bloody mess; he stripped it off, wiped himself off with a damp washcloth . . . and smiled.

The scratches on his shoulder were no longer bleeding, but they were deep and clearly marked. For Genny, he had given up his fear of commitment, and he had earned his mark.

He donned a T-shirt. Put on some jazzy music.

And he paced.

He opened a bottle of chardonnay. Placed it on the breakfast bar. Set out bottles of water. Opened a zinfandel in case she hated chardonnay. Paced some more. Sliced salami and cheese, then a good, grainy whole wheat bread. He was holding the bowl of tapenade when she walked barefoot out of his bedroom wearing one of his white shirts.

She'd rolled up the sleeves, turned up the collar. The hem almost reached her knees in the front and exposed her thighs on the side. She had buttoned all the buttons except for the top two.

She was still damp.

He could see right through the material.

She wore nothing underneath.

His body voted for action first, talk later.

But she was still fussing with the sleeves. "You were going to tell me how you got rich."

Okay. She wanted to talk. He would explain everything as quickly and efficiently as possible because . . . she was here, she was wearing his shirt, and she was naked underneath. "I was an immigrant with no family. I was used to doing without. I had a knack for investment. Then . . . the tragedy on the volcano. I put all my investments into federal bonds—which was splendid timing: I missed the downturn—and when I came back, I had all that and a little more. So I was able to take the stake I had and with some careful investing . . . I can take care of you in the manner to which you should be able to quickly become accustomed."

"And in the two and a half years since? You've done well?"

"I haven't been dating or having sex. At all. With anyone." A fact that had frustrated his friends. "So . . . yes."

She looked up and observed him. "Me neither. About the dating or sex thing."

That cheered him immeasurably. "Good. We've both

been concentrating on our goals. I've been leading the Chosen Ones and acquiring wealth."

"I started my wildlife rescue. And have been learning to depend only on myself." She glanced at the tapenade he still held, then at the feast behind him.

Hastily he put down the bowl and picked up a bottle. "Wine?"

"Soon. I like this place." She walked to the window again. "The view is spectacular at night."

"It's better in the daytime. The furniture, of course, is minimalist"—he didn't even know exactly what that meant, but his exasperated decorator had told him it was—"and easily changed, or you could add pieces as you like."

He quickly added, "I have contacts in the financial world and funding for your wildlife rescue program should be easy to obtain."

Finally she turned, leaned against the window, hands behind her, and smiled. "Are you *bribing* me to stay with you?"

"Is it working?"

She appeared to give it some thought. "I'm not particularly moved by wealth."

He was afraid of that.

"My father spent so much time chasing money, believing it would make him happy, and nothing would have done that."

"Wildlife fund?" he reminded her.

"I have a business degree and my father insisted I take extra courses on influence and negotiations, so I've done very well raising money for the fund myself."

"One of the many things I admire about you is your

impeccable good sense." He prowled toward her as she stood silhouetted against the window. "So what does move you?"

She turned to face the city and spoke to his reflection. "I believe that earlier you said something about begging."

"For your hand in marriage." He leaned against her, pressed her against the cool glass. He recognized her scent, knew it like he knew his own. Bending his head, he nuzzled the back of her neck.

She arched her head away to give him access. "I've already said we were going to marry. So why would you beg?"

"You deserve a proposal worthy of the woman you are."

"Of the woman I have become."

"I liked who you were in Russia. You were a woman who wasn't afraid to be my friend at a time when everyone else feared me. You loved the lynx, you loved the wilderness, and you loved the freedom. In the ancient, stifling atmosphere of Rasputye, you were a breath of fresh air." He remembered how she had been, so innocent and alluring. "That's why I—"

"Reacted strongly to my perceived betrayal?"

"I was an idiot."

"Why were you an idiot?" She was leading him. She wanted to hear him say it.

"Why would I judge you based on the behavior of my foster mother and my wife? And yet I did." He slid his arms around her waist, pressed his palms against her belly.

She was so alive, so warm.

"I couldn't leave my mistrust behind. Keeping it like a shield before me was easier than keeping my faith in you." He held her, his arms trembling. "Then I came out of the *rasputye* and discovered you had died—"

"I'm feeling fine. I took shelter with the nomads, traveled with them, milked their yaks." He felt her shake with laughter. "It was exactly the healing time I needed, and a dose of reality, too. I learned about survival in a hostile world, and what's important when all else is stripped away."

"That's funny. That's exactly what I learned here, when I was alone and without you."

She twisted around to face him. "That's why we belong together. We've learned the same lessons. We know the same truths. We're fighting on the same side." She slipped her hands around his waist. "And—"

"And at the end of the day, I would rather be with you than with any other person on earth." Dipping his head, he kissed her, and merely the touch of her lips and scent of her breath made him happy. "I love you. Please marry me, Genesis, so I can spend my whole life being your companion."

She wound her arms around his neck. His shirt rose to precarious heights and somehow, he wasn't clear how, two more top buttons had come unfastened. "I love you, too, and I would like that—very much."

He waltzed her away from the window and toward the bedroom. "Tomorrow."

"What?" She leaned back in his embrace and smiled up at him. "We have to have blood tests and stuff."

"As soon as possible." He paused by the doorway and kissed her persuasively.

She kissed him back, taking and giving, and when he let her come up for air, she agreed breathlessly. "All right. As soon as possible. As soon as I can get a dress."

Grimly, he said, "I'll go with you to pick it out."

She grinned. "Why would you do that?"

"Because if I do it, we'll be done in a few hours. If you go with Charisma, Jacqueline, and Isabelle, it'll take *weeks*."

"Why?"

"I have no idea." He slid his hands under the hem of her shirt. Caressed her thighs, lifted her buttocks . . . Oh, God, he was right. She was naked under there.

She pressed herself against his palms. Breathlessly she asked, "Should we have that wine now? To celebrate?"

"Later." He danced her toward the bed. "Later."

Later . . . after the love, after the wine, after the food, after more love, they tangled together on the couch, watching the lights play across the city.

"What do you think of the prophecy?" she asked.

"I think we're in for a tough four and a half years."

# Chapter 56

"*The world is changing.*

"*The rules are changing.*

"*The gifted are changing.*

"*Some who are not gifted now will develop gifts.*

"*The Gypsy Travel Agency is sacrificed to one man's ambition and his unwillingness to trust in the ultimate triumph of good.*

"*Now the Chosen Ones pay the price.*

"*Yet the sacrifice he offers might save them . . .*

"*In that, the fledgling Chosen can find hope. Before their seven years is over, each of the seven must find a true love. They will know they have succeeded with the blossoming of their badges and their talents.*

"*And some must find that which is lost forever.*

"*For rising on the ashes of the Gypsy Travel Agency is a new power in a new building. Unless hope takes wing, this power and this building will grow to reach the stars, and cast its shadow over the whole earth, and evil will rule.*"

\*   \*   \*

Osgood had informed the police chief he wanted So-Ho's early-morning streets empty.

She had, of course, obeyed. She owed her position to Osgood, and he made sure she never forgot it.

The cast iron buildings had since been demolished; their structural integrity weakened by the blast that had taken out the Gypsy Travel Agency. A chain link construction fence enclosed the whole empty block, and concrete trucks were idling while the mixers rotated their loads.

Osgood used his key to open the lock on the gate. He walked across the narrow strip of barren ground to the hole that plunged straight down two stories . . . the site where the Gypsy Travel Agency had stood.

The explosion had taken the building, the research, the libraries, the artifacts . . . the prophecies.

For a brief and glorious hour, he had believed the explosion had swept every single group of Chosen from this earth.

Instead, a single band of Chosen remained, untested, untried, without advisors or financing.

Osgood had been furious.

Then, when a suitable number of minions had been punished and his anger appeased, he had drawn breath and realized—it was a challenge. Of course. In this world, nothing was easy. And nothing was forever.

Did they know yet, the valiant little Chosen, about the prophecy? Were they in despair? Did they know what challenges confronted them? Or did they face the future shoulder to shoulder, chins bravely lifted and optimistic smiles pinned to their lips?

A smile grew on his lips, too, but it was the kind of smile that made grown men and women quail and small children scream and run.

From the specially provided long inner pocket of his custom designer coat, he pulled a three-foot-long, twelve-inch-wide polished silver sword case. He weighed it in his hand. Unlocked the latch. Opened it with a flourish.

Inside, cradled on black velvet, was the most magnificent white feather ever to make its way to earth. It shone with the light of a million tiny diamonds. It glowed with a life of its own. Long and elegant, it was the feather from an angel's wing.

He had been an angel once, chafing under the divine dominion. He had led a rebellion, fallen into hell, and now he fought for the souls of every human on earth.

He was succeeding very well, thank you.

But he was greedy. He wanted more.

He had waited a long time for the proper moment to sacrifice this last remnant of his service, the only feather not incinerated during his long fall from heaven. Taking careful aim, he allowed the feather to flutter free.

It rose first, as if it longed to return home.

Then it fell, slowly and majestically into the hole, down to the ground to nestle among the steel reinforcement bars that formed the frame for the building—his headquarters—that would rise on this site.

When the feather settled into place, flat against the scorched New York soil where so many good Chosen Ones had lost their lives, he carelessly tossed the case in after it. It banged and clanged its way onto the rebar and perched precariously near the end of the building.

Lifting his hand, he said, "Start the pour."

The construction lights flipped on, blindingly bright.

The concrete trucks moved into place. The pumps started up. Cement blasted out of the chutes, filling the void.

Osgood stood at the edge, watching as the feather flattened, quivered, and drowned beneath tons of gravel, lime, and water. He stood another five minutes . . . until he knew the feather was gone forever.

Then he walked away.

Turn the page for a glimpse at
Christina Dodd's
next Chosen Ones novel

## *CHAINS OF FIRE*

Available from Signet Select
in September 2010

Chilled, sleepy and exhausted, Isabelle fastened her seat belt, huddled into her coat, closed her eyes and let herself drift.

The road was winding, swaying her back and forth as Samuel drove its length, taking her back to her mother's house. Although it was three in the morning, she knew her mother would be awake, ostensibly supervising the cleanup, while in reality, she'd be waiting . . . for Isabelle to return with Samuel.

Isabelle had had so much experience with this situation, she knew everything that would happen.

Patricia would look them over, her eyes sharp, silently demanding an explanation.

Isabelle would give her one. *Mother, we had a job to do.*

Patricia wouldn't like that. But once she had ascertained that they betrayed no undue fondness for each other, showed no signs of lovemaking, she would invite Samuel to stay the night.

Isabelle would insist he do so.

He would agree.

Patricia would assign him a room so far away from Isabelle's he might as well be in Italy.

Isabelle smiled painfully. As if that would matter to Samuel. If she gave him the slightest encouragement, he would swim Lake Geneva and scale the Matterhorn to reach her. To sleep with her. To shake her world.

She turned her head to gaze at his warrior's profile, his chin shadowy with stubble, his dark gaze fixed intently on the road.

God, how she loved him. Most of the time, she could dismiss the knowledge that for as long as they both lived, she would love only him. But when she was tired, when her guard was down . . .

But no. No matter how much her body yearned, she wasn't going to give in to him again. She wouldn't allow him to destroy her once more.

The tires skidded on the pavement. The vehicle slipped toward the edge of the road.

She straightened in her seat and looked around. Moonlight sprawled over the vast snowy expanse of meadow that stretched to the right, over the dark silhouette of the medieval castle turned ski lodge snuggled against the sleek groomed slopes of the mountain, over the lifts and trams, over the parking lot waiting for tomorrow's influx of skiers. The narrow ribbon of road before them was shiny-slick with ice. On their left, the land fell away and only a snowdrift stopped them from falling into the dark precipice.

They were moving too fast, taking too many chances in these conditions—and for all that Samuel loved speed, she had never felt endangered by his carelessness.

"Samuel? What's wrong?"

"*Sh.*" He didn't lift his gaze from the road, but something about the way he held himself made her look again across the meadow and above.

The mountains rose abruptly toward the deep black velvet sky, blocking the stars, challenging the moon. In the daytime, their beauty lifted Isabelle's heart. Right now she remembered how cruel they could be. . . .

"Samuel, *what's wrong*?"

He slammed on his brakes, skidding again.

Her breath caught in her throat.

Yet he corrected so expertly that the car slid around sideways, slowed. Then he accelerated around the next corner.

In the headlights, she saw evergreen branches spread across the road and a huge trunk in their midst. The wind had caught the ancient evergreen and blown it over.

Except . . . the stump was cut. The tree had been deliberately used to block the road.

Samuel eased the car to a halt.

Now she knew why he had acted so out of character. Somehow, he'd caught the scent of danger.

This was a trap.

With a low curse, he put the vehicle in reverse and flung his arm over her seat, and with his body arched and his gaze fixed behind them, he backed up as fast as he could. At the driveway leading to the ski lodge, he slammed on the brakes, skidded back, then forward, then accelerated into the parking lot. In a low, terse voice, he said, "Emergency kit is behind my seat. Get back there. Get it. Stay there and jump out as I stop." He put the car into a skid, and they skated sideways toward the lodge.

The mountains, their peaks softened by huge mounds of snow, loomed menacingly in the windshield.

With a swift economy of movement, she unsnapped her seat belt and climbed between the seats. She grabbed the black nylon bag, heavy with the gear the Chosen carried when they could—flashlight, flare, first-aid kit, matches—and as the vehicle slid up over the curb and eased toward the ski lodge, she unlocked her door. As soon as they settled to a stop, she was out.

He was out.

They ran toward the ski lodge.

Her heels sank into the snow, and snow sifted through into her strappy sandals.

High above, she heard a deep, menacing boom.

She jerked her head toward the mountain and saw the snow lift off the slope like a cashmere blanket being fluffed by a giant hand. She stopped and stood transfixed as it settled back, slid toward them, gathering speed as it moved. . . .

She prided herself on her cool good sense. She was known for her serenity. But she screamed now. "Samuel! Avalanche!"

He leaned over, slammed his shoulder into her gut, lifted her and ran.

She gasped, the air knocked out of her, draped over

him like a sandbag and bouncing until she was almost sick.

"Hang on to the bag," he shouted.

She'd never heard Samuel sound like that before, but she recognized desperation when she heard it.

She heard the rumbling, too, and as Samuel slammed against the building, she heard another one of those deep, menacing booms far above.

Someone was setting off dynamite charges, creating avalanches that catapulted in their direction at high speeds under the influence of steep slopes and the weight of the snow.

And Samuel had known this was coming. Somehow, Samuel had known.

Samuel set her on her feet.

The ground beneath her shook as the massive wall of snow thundered toward them.

The ancient castle's wall rose four stories above them. On the second and third floors, windows had been cut into the stone to give the skiers views of the Alps. But here on the ground floor, security reigned supreme. One narrow window. A single heavy metal door.

He tried the lever handle, then said, "Locked," and stepped back to allow her access.

She handed him the bag, and pulled a long, stiff platinum diamond pin out of her hair. Kneeling beside the door, she inserted it into the lock.

Her unflagging calm made her the best lock pick in the Chosen. Yet never had she worked under such conditions, with the lock, the pin and the whole world trembling as death roared toward them.

Samuel flipped on the flashlight and aimed it at the window. "Glass is reinforced with mesh," he said.

She continued to work the lock.

"Need the light?" he asked.

"Please. No." The moonlight provided clear, even illumination. The flashlight's narrow beam would simply distract her.

The roll of the avalanche grew to a bellow.

Samuel stood immobile beside her, ostensibly calm. Yet she could feel him straining, desperate to grab her and run.

She found the mechanism with the tip of her pin. Lifted. Manipulated. Heard the lock click.

She opened the door.

Samuel grabbed her around the waist, lifted her like a child, and dashed into the dim interior, which was lit by a pale night-light and the moonlight shining through the window. They stood on a metal landing with stairs going up to the main floor of the lodge and down to the basement.

Samuel vaulted down the first five steps.

She caught a glimpse of the lodge's locker room.

The avalanche hit like a nuclear explosion. The window shattered. Moonlight disappeared. The electricity went out. Snow blew in with the force of a tornado, ripping at Isabelle's skin.

The stairs shook like a bucking horse. Samuel struggled to stay on his feet.

Then the metal cracked. The steps disappeared out from under Samuel's feet. And they fell . . . into nothingness.

# AVAILABLE NOW

# STORM OF VISIONS
## The Chosen Ones

# Christina Dodd

Jacqueline Vargha has always run from her gift. Until
Caleb D'Angelo forces his way into her life and
insists she take her place as one of the Chosen. She
flees, he pursues, but she can no longer deny her
visions, or the dangerous man who is her downfall...
and her destiny.

**"Dodd writes with
power and passion."**
—#1 *New York Times* bestselling author
J. R. Ward

**And don't miss *Storm of Shadows*!**

Available wherever books are sold or at
penguin.com